A MOTHER'S HOPE

A MOTHER'S HOPE

Katie Flynn

WINDSOR
PARAGON

First published 2009
by Arrow Books
This Large Print edition published 2009
by BBC Audiobooks Ltd
by arrangement with
The Random House Group Ltd

Hardcover ISBN: 978 1 408 42929 7
Softcover   ISBN: 978 1 408 42930 3

British Library Cataloguing in Publication Data available

Printed and bound in Great Britain by
CPI Antony Rowe, Chippenham and Eastbourne

For the late Valerie Fleeman, whose enthusiasm and help was unforgettable.

Acknowledgements

First and foremost, my sincere thanks to the late Mrs Valerie Fleeman, who gave me invaluable information regarding her father's hairdressing business in Bold Street. She had a remarkable memory and filled in all the gaps in my knowledge of the area in the forties and fifties, including shops, cafés and hotels. Valerie's father, Mr Mann, could truly boast of being 'Hairdresser to the stars' and was a wonderful character to put in to the book, playing a major role, as you will see, if you read on!

I should also like to thank Mr Geoffrey C. Seys-Llewellyn, BSc., FBOA, for the very useful information regarding albinos—I had to rewrite a chunk of my story after consulting Mr Seys-Llewellyn, but it's always worth it to get it right.

Prologue

It was a calm night, though bitterly cold; the stars twinkled in the sky above and the moon's light only served to deepen the shadows. The city was deserted save for those whose business it was to patrol the wartime streets. Folk were in their homes or already down in the shelters. Only a solitary girl, weighed down by a heavy basket, was walking cautiously but with the air of one who knows her destination, remaining always where the shadows were deepest.

But now at every side street she began to hesitate, suddenly unsure of her way, for she had not reckoned with the stygian darkness of the blackout which hid the street names and made the familiar strange. She had provided herself with an elderly torch but knew that if she used it she might easily be seen, cross-questioned, maybe even sent to the nearest shelter. And then of course the contents of her basket would be her own particular secret no longer.

She was hesitating on the kerb when she heard the distant thrum of engines, and even as her mind screamed 'bombers' moon!' the siren began to wail. The girl broke into a clumsy run. She was wearing a long dark coat and boots too big for her and now, filled with panic, she tripped and fell, landing painfully on hands and knees, feeling the blood trickling from her palms and down her shins. Hastily she scrambled to her feet and checked the contents of the basket, but the tiny baby within seemed not to have noticed her tumble.

Even as she grabbed her burden, a figure

appeared further down the street, shouting at her to get to a shelter and be quick about it. The girl spun on her heel and began to run, the breath sobbing in her throat. Hunted and terrified, she plunged down the nearest alley, emerging from the other end of it into a street which in her panic-ridden state she thought vaguely familiar.

But above the city the drone of the planes grew louder, their menacing shapes blotting out the stars. The girl stopped in her flight, sweat trickling down the sides of her face, and she saw that these houses were large and imposing and had porches in which her basket would be a good deal safer than if she were to abandon it near a humbler dwelling. Quickly, she crossed the pavement, climbed a couple of steps, and pushed the basket as close to a front door as it would go.

For a moment she hesitated, her hand going out towards the small round head of the child which still slept soundly within. Then she snatched her hand away and turned and ran up the street. It no longer mattered if she were caught, or sent to a shelter; she had left her unbearable burden with rich people. She remembered the conscience note she had painfully written, which would be the first thing the householder noticed when he or she opened the front door next morning: *I'll cum bak for her*, it read.

By this time the girl was a good fifty yards away from the porch. She stopped for a moment, a hand going to her thumping heart. The planes were directly overhead now, but her fear of the bombs was nothing compared to the fear of discovery she had been feeling a few moments earlier. She began to walk more slowly, reminding herself that what

2

she had just done would be best for her little daughter in the long run. Besides, perhaps she really would go back and claim the child one day. She turned to give the porch—and the basket— one last valedictory glance. I hope she'll be all right, she thought. I hope someone will love her the way I would have done had things been different. But now, relieved of her responsibility, she resumed her unhurried walk along the pavement. She could go to the nearest shelter . . .

*   *   *

A bomb fell from one of the enemy aircraft above and there was a tremendous explosion. Two houses disintegrated, clouds of dust rose and a solitary cat streaked past the scene of destruction, fur on end, eyes wide with terror. The occupant of the basket began to wail, the sound so tiny that it sounded more like the mewing of a frightened kitten than a human voice.

Presently, the dust settled. Workers came running, cordoning off the area, calling to one another. There was no movement, no answer to their shouts, no girl in a long dark coat to cry for help, or answer their calls.

Chapter One

It was the devil of a day. The rain was coming almost horizontally, driven by a fierce and chilly wind, and the tarmac was puddled with miniature lakes so that the youth, the only thing moving on the road, was already soaked to the skin and just about as miserable as a human being can be.

He had set out that morning with such high hopes, too. True, he had only been able to afford a single ticket on the bus he had caught from Liverpool to Southport, but he had told himself that if he got the job he was after he might be able to suggest an advance on the wages he would be earning. If not, he had hitchhiked before and could do so again.

He had hoped that, because the job was in Southport, his would-be employer would not question the address he had made up, for everyone knew that if you had no address your chances of getting a job were small. He could have given the address of the YMCA, of course, but that could be checked and he had not lived there for the best part of a month. But when he had given both his name and the fictional address to the young woman in the bar and been led through to a small office at the back, the man had taken one look at him and said that the post had been filled. He knew it wasn't true, because in that case the girl would have told him as soon as he had mentioned he had come for the job, but bitter experience had taught him that arguing would be useless. If they disliked you as soon as they set eyes on you—

which the landlord of the Golden Bear had clearly done—then the best thing, in fact the only thing, to do was to leave with a conventional word of regret and a plea that you might be contacted should another vacancy occur. Even in his soaked and icy state this made him smile, since for one thing he knew the man would never consider him for even the most menial of posts, and for another, as he had made up the address, any communication between himself and the landlord was an impossibility.

When he had folded up his flock sleeping bag that morning and pushed it into its usual hiding place behind a stack of bricks in a nearby builder's yard, the weather had been chilly but dry. If he had known that it intended to pelt with rain as soon as he turned his face towards Liverpool once more, he might have hitched a ride to Southport and saved his bus fare for the return journey, but of course he did not have any such knowledge; his main thought was that it's the early bird who catches the worm, and he had put all his endeavours into cleaning himself up and getting to the bus stop in good time. And how useless it had been! He knew from his many attempts to find employment in Liverpool that most people thought him incapable of manual work, and those were the only jobs for which he applied. The superintendent of the home had reminded him that any sort of clerical work was out of the question because of his poor eyesight.

He knew he was tall, skinny and pale, his face plain and his body weak-looking. How could it be anything else? The boys' home in which he had been reared was not a good one. Unsupervised

6

meals had meant that the majority of the food went to the strong. They got stronger, and boys like himself existed on what bigger and bolder boys allowed them, which was little enough. When he was sixteen he had been moved on, with the other boys of his age, to Brackendale Hall. A job had been found for him as an office boy in a biscuit factory. He had been happy there, but after a year another boy had come from the home and they had told him, kindly but firmly, that he must move on.

For a short time he had been a porter at Central Station, but then he had overloaded a trolley, causing an old gentleman's suitcase to fall on to the platform. The old gentleman had not accepted his apologies and had seemed to show pleasure at getting a young man sacked without a reference; for the stationmaster had not wanted to take him on in the first place and had felt vindicated in his opinion when the suitcase had fallen to earth.

Glumly, the young man remembered his eighteenth birthday. Again they had explained that a boy's stay in Brackendale Hall could only be of two years' duration, since by the time a lad was eighteen he should have established himself in some sort of paying work. But they had got him a place in the YMCA—six beds crammed close in an attic room—and had told him the rules. Perhaps the powers-that-be had not even noticed the resentment and dislike which had speedily become his lot. The other five boys hated him. Stupid tricks had been played on him: money had disappeared from the pockets of his old duffel coat; a bun which he had saved for his supper had been trodden on by a muddy boot; his bed had been soaked in what he soon realised was urine.

In the end it had been easier, almost pleasanter, to pick up an old sleeping bag at a jumble sale, find a deep and convenient doorway, and sleep on the streets. Others did it, God knew, and it would not have been so bad if only he could have found work. He drew the dole, of course, but the money was not enough to pay for a rented room, and though he might have had a bed in one of the lodging houses down by the docks, too many seamen carried knives for his liking. No, the streets were a safer bet.

The young man sighed and glanced to his right, where high sand dunes hid the sea. Not for the first time in his life, he thought about ending it, simply ploughing his way between the dunes and across the wet and treacherous beach to the sea beyond. But he knew he would not do it, not really. Life was precious, even though it was not good. He was young, and not all his previous experience had entirely killed his hope that, one day, things would be better. One day, someone would look beyond his ugly face and weak and drooping body, and see that he was willing to work hard and help others.

But today he decided he had been a fool to choose the coast road as a means of returning to the city. Not one single vehicle had passed him and he must have covered at least a mile already. He should have taken the main road, but because of the rain he had turned aside and taken this one, thinking that he would stand a better chance of getting a lift since traffic could pull over and stop here without causing an accident. Still, he knew that in two or three miles the road veered to the left, joining the main road not far from the village

8

of Formby. Then there would be traffic and he would have something to look at beside sand dunes on his right, long wet grass on his left and, of course, the driving rain.

Thinking of shops, he remembered that he had gone into a bakery in Southport before setting out to hitchhike home and had recklessly spent every penny he possessed on two cheese baps, a large broken sausage roll, which the girl behind the counter had let him have cheap, and a round of soda bread. The thought of the food made him hungry and he dug a hand into his pocket, fumbling for one of the cheese baps. He sank his teeth into it, and after eating half of it he felt a good deal better. After all, there would have been problems ahead for him had he been offered the job. The wages were much better than the dole, but he had no idea what accommodation would cost in such a smart and beautiful seaside resort.

He finished the bap and decided that if he had not got a lift by the time he reached Formby he would try for work there. Once again, it was a smart place, but you never knew. Someone might need a delivery boy, or a gardener; he would do anything.

At this point in his musings, he heard a vehicle approaching along the road behind him. Quickly, he jerked up his thumb, glancing over his shoulder as he did so. He was disappointed to see that it was a bus, a very old-fashioned bus, because no doubt they would expect him to pay if they offered him a ride. In fact a bus was one of the few vehicles which could be relied upon to expect a reward for giving someone a lift. Hastily, he lowered his hand, sticking it into his wet pocket. As the bus drew level with him he saw that it had a notice in the window and guessed from the shape of the letters—for he could make out little more—that it read *Out of Service*. It was too late for him to attract the driver's attention as it trundled past, its bow wave as it plunged through a puddle soaking him to the knees. The driver did glance curiously at him, however, and when, about fifty yards further down the road, the vehicle drew into the side and stopped, his heart gave a leap of hope and he broke into a shambling run.

Too late! The conductor, a hefty figure in his dark uniform, was helping a passenger to alight, and before the youth had run more than a few yards the bus had moved on. Disappointed, but not particularly surprised, the youth slowed his pace to a walk once more, staring with some curiosity at the passenger, who had set off at a run in the same direction as the bus, waving and calling. The driver, however, continued to accelerate and the vehicle was soon a dot in the distance.

He wondered why on earth she had got off at this particular point. There wasn't a house for miles. Now that he came to think of it, he realised that the passenger had not been so much helped to alight as ejected. A misunderstanding, perhaps? Had she climbed aboard the bus believing it to be on a regular route, only discovering when she came to pay her fare that it was not the one she wanted? But if so, why had she chosen to alight at such a desolate spot? And why had she then pursued it, shouting as she did so? It all seemed very strange, but staring ahead and rubbing the rain from his eyes he could just make out that the drooping shoulders and the way the passenger—

10

ex-passenger—was hanging her head, gave credence to his theory that she had not wanted to leave the shelter of the vehicle.

Because his legs were long, he was already beginning to overhaul her, and presently, when she was no more than six yards ahead, he addressed her. 'Excuse me, are you awright, miss? It looked as though that feller threw you off the bus; wharra pig, in weather like this.'

The woman jumped six inches with fright, which must have been the cause of the tirade she promptly turned on him. 'What's it to you, nosy? Men! You're all the bleedin' same. All I asked for was a ride back to the city; I'd ha' paid cash, but he said . . . he said . . .' She gave an enormous gulping sob as he drew level with her. 'He said not to worry about money,' she went on miserably. 'I didn't know wharr'e meant by "payment in kind" or I'd never have agreed, but I thought it were a rare chance to save some money.' She sniffed. 'The conductor were bad enough, but the driver were no better. When I shouted to him that I'd got money and would pay me way all fair and square if he'd stop his mate interferin' wi' me he said the bus was out of service and . . . oh, what's the use of talkin'! How many miles is it to Liverpool, anyway? This bleedin' road seems to go on for ever. Oh, I wish I were dead!'

The youth looked at her, wondering just what it was the conductor had meant by 'payment in kind' but not liking to ask. Instead, he said: 'It's a fair way. I dunno exactly how far. I came to Southport by bus, after a job, and I only had the money for a single fare. I thought if I got the job I'd ask for an advance on me wages, and if I didn't gerrit, then

11

I'd hitchhike. But there's no traffic on this perishin' road, so small chance of a lift. When I see'd your bus comin' I thought it were me lucky day, but then when it stopped it weren't to pick up at all but to chuck you out.' And then, curiosity getting the better of him: 'Why did he chuck you out? You had money for your fare, so wharron earth were he doin' makin' you gerroff?'

The girl sighed and turned towards him. What with the rain and his poor sight, he only got an impression of a very young girl, probably no more than fourteen or fifteen, with a thin face and large eyes. A lock of red hair, darkened to auburn by the rain, fell across her forehead, and she was wearing a red pixie hood and a grey mackintosh; a garment so much too large for her that the skirts of it reached her ankles. He opened his mouth to repeat his question but she cut in before he could do so. 'Wharra you starin' at? If you think my clothes ain't up to much, you look like a perishin' monk in that black duffel coat. The hood's so big I reckon your head must rattle around in it like a dried pea in an empty can.'

The youth looked at her, knowing that her aggression was caused by the situation; that she was hitting out at him because the bus and its occupants were out of reach. He said patiently: 'Was I starin'? Sorry, I don't mean to offend. Why did he chuck you out?'

They had been walking together, the youth matching his long stride to her shorter step, but now she stopped suddenly, staring defiantly up at him. 'I were sittin' quiet as a mouse on the back seat an' the conductor were sittin' beside me. Then he leaned over and started to unbutton me mac.

12

He said somethin' about warmin' his hands...I told him to leave off and then I...oh, I said I were a married woman and me husband were a big feller what 'ud half kill 'im if he interfered wi' me. It were a lie, of course, and he knew it. Then I ran up the aisle, shoutin' to the driver that his mate were misbehavin'. He drew in to the side and the conductor chucked me off. But the worst thing was that my purse must have fallen out of me coat and I didn't notice, so when I started walkin' and stuck me fist in me pocket there were nothin' there, norra penny piece. And...well, I reckon that swine will tek the lot...and it must ha' been near on ten bob.'

'I see,' the youth said slowly. 'So that was why you started to run after the bus. Well, I reckon you can say goodbye to your ten bob; we'll never catch up with him now. Unless he stops when he realises he's got your purse and waits for you to catch up.'

The girl snorted. 'Some chance! Didn't you see? The conductor were waving it at me through the back window and grinning like a monkey as the bus accelerated away. That's why I started to run after it. He'll pocket it and think himself justified; I know the type.'

'Wharra swine,' the youth said sincerely. 'But I reckon you're right and you won't get your dosh back. Wish I'd thought to take the registration number, but of course I didn't know what were happenin'.' He looked doubtfully at his small companion. 'Well, it looks like we'll both be hitchhiking; unless you've got some other idea, that is.'

'I've never hitchhiked, but I'll have a go,' the girl said equably. 'I'm stronger than I look.'

13

The youth nodded. 'Right, an' I dare say two of us will gerra lift easier than one.' He hesitated, then spoke up. 'I expect you'll think I'm being nosy again, but them as don't ask don't get told. Why were you in Southport?' He looked down at her.

'I were after a job too,' she said. 'It were a nice job. A sort of nursemaid, you might say, to two little children. I reckon I got an interview because me application letter were a perishin' work of art . . . now, don't you laugh. I spent two whole days writin' it and I bet I'd have got the job, too, if it hadn't been that both the gals who were interviewed as well as me came from Southport and had real posh voices. It were a live-in job.' The girl looked up at him, her thin cheeks flushing. 'It were a lovely house and the room that horrible fat blonde girl will have overlooks the sea. It was all done up in pink and white; the lady had even put lovely pictures on the walls. Oh, I'd ha' worked there for nothin', but it didn't help.'

'That's a rare shame,' the youth said sympathetically. 'So we're both still lookin' for jobs, eh? Well, I'm sure you'll gerra good one. Mebbe it'll be in Liverpool itself, then you won't have to move away.'

The girl snorted. 'I *want* to move away,' she said crossly. 'I'd rather live at the North Pole than those flats in the 'Pool. Anyway, what makes you think I'll gerra job an' you won't?' She looked him up and down. 'You're tall enough, an' I expect you're strong: most boys are. Lor', this must be the longest perishin' road in the bleedin' world. If I don't get somethin' to eat soon . . . what's the next village? Are there shops?'

The youth laughed, then dug a hand into the

14

capacious pocket of his duffel coat. He produced the remaining cheese bap and handed it to his companion. 'I've gorra broken sausage roll and some soda bread,' he informed her. 'What say we share the lot? And though there are shops in the next village, they won't be much use to us since we're both skint.'

The girl bit into the cheese bap, then grinned up at him, one cheek bulging. 'Thanks ever so; you're real kind,' she said. 'And I've just remembered, I made a couple o' jam butties before I left this mornin'. We'll have them as a sort of puddin' when all your grub's gone.'

The two of them continued to walk. The youth was about to suggest that they should exchange names when he got an uneasy feeling that they were being followed. He glanced at his companion, still eating her cheese bap; she appeared to have noticed nothing, so he looked quickly behind and let out a startled yelp. Almost on their heels was a creature which for a moment he thought must be a donkey, until he realised that it was a very large, very skinny dog. It had a long pointed nose, small ears and a deep chest, and even in that one startled glance he guessed by the rough and staring coat, and the way its ribs stood out, that it was hunger and the sight of the cheese bap which had made it follow them.

At his yelp, the girl turned too. 'I say, wharra huge dog! Ain't you lucky? I've always wanted a dog,' she said. 'Poor critter, you must have a job to feed it as well as yourself. Crikey, it's near on as big as a donkey!'

'Hey, that's odd; I thought it were a donkey when I first realised we were being followed,' the youth

15

said. 'But it ain't my dog, an' I tek it it's not yours either. I bet it's a stray what's been turned out.' He looked hopefully at his companion. 'If you don't want the soda bread, I'll throw it back along the road and mebbe he'll leave us. It's not that I don't like dogs, only if a car or a van comes along and sees him an' thinks he's with us, then I reckon we'll lose our chance of a lift.'

The girl chuckled. 'You won't get rid of him that easy; don't you reckernise a greyhound when you see one? If you give him food, he'll follow you anywhere. If we was picked up and given a lift, he'd run behind all the way to Liverpool. So you'd best make up yer mind whether you mean to take him on or leave him here to starve.'

The youth stopped and looked more closely at the gaunt creature. Its liquid dark eyes were fixed not on the hand groping in his pocket, but on his face. He thought of the cold doorway in which he slept and the fear which gripped him whenever a scuffer or some other figure of authority approached his hideout. And the worst fear: that a tramp, or some other homeless person, might envy him his snug retreat and come at him with boots and fists, or perhaps even with a knife. Surely a dog would at least warn him of an approaching stranger. He broke the soda bread, almost defiantly, into two pieces and offered one piece to the dog. He expected it to snatch, meant to throw the food on the ground, but there was something gentle in the way the creature slowly extended his long neck that told him his fingers would be safe. And indeed, the dog proved him right by taking the food with the utmost delicacy. The youth saw the animal's throat ripple as it swallowed and

16

offered the next piece with more confidence, watching it disappear with as much pleasure as though he had known the dog all its life. He, who had always had to fight for a share of the available food when he was young, was now feeding someone else; giving instead of taking. It was a good feeling. He dug his hand into his pocket once more and drew out the sausage roll, already broken into several pieces, then looked cautiously at his companion. He had promised to share the food, but . . .

The girl must have divined what he was thinking for she grinned up at him. 'Aw, go on, give it to him,' she urged. 'I reckon neither of us would like to see the poor bugger starve. Tell you what, he can have me jam butties when he's finished off that sausage roll.'

Confident now that he would not be bitten, the youth held out a long, thin hand with the pieces of sausage roll balanced on the palm, and the dog took each piece cautiously and with immense care, then licked every last crumb from his hand. When it was all gone, the girl handed over her two jam sandwiches and smiled as the dog dispatched them, his manner as grateful yet workmanlike as it had been over the sausage roll.

They had stopped to feed the dog and now they began to walk once more, the three of them keeping pace with one another. The dog's confidence that they meant him no harm was evident in the fact that he no longer hung back. 'We'll have to give him a name,' the girl said suddenly. 'Tell you what. We both thought he were a donkey when we first see'd him, didn't we? Why don't we call him Don?'

The youth felt a flicker of delight run through him. She had said 'we', which surely must mean that perhaps this was the start of a proper friendship, the sort of friendship other people had but which had never come his way. But it would not do to say so, of course, he realised that. Instead, he agreed that Don was a nice name for such a gentle and friendly creature, but added: 'If he is a feller; for all I know he might be a—a girl.'

His companion gave him a mocking look. 'A girl dog is called a bitch,' she said instructively, bending down and scrutinising the dog's undercarriage. 'An' this 'un's definitely a boy, I mean a dog,' she concluded. 'So Don will suit him down to the ground. I tek it you've got somewhere for him to sleep?'

They were walking now perhaps a little faster than before, the dog loping between them. He was as wet as they, the youth saw, but his step seemed jauntier, as though he had understood that he was not to be abandoned and was glad. 'Yes, he can share my sleeping bag,' he said. 'We'll keep each other warm, eh, old feller?'

'That's good,' the girl said. 'But if you've got no money how will you feed him? And yourself, of course?'

'Tomorrer's dole day,' he informed her. 'And there's folk what throws out odds an' ends of food. We'll be all right, don't you fret. How about yourself?'

'I've got some jam an' half a loaf, a bit of margarine and a couple of eggs,' the girl said. 'How far did you say we've gorra walk?'

'Well, I reckon we've covered five miles already. Formby's just around the corner,' he said vaguely.

'It'll be another twenty, mebbe, to the city.' He grinned to himself. 'If we were kids we could skip a lecky, except that they don't come out this far, but our best bet is to hitch a lift once we reach Formby.'

The girl heaved a sigh. 'Didn't you say no one will give us a bleedin' lift with the dawg along?' she said. 'How long will it take us to walk twenty miles? I don't fancy doin' it in the dark, and the light goes early at this time o' year.'

'I remember someone telling me once that most folk walk a mile in twenty minutes,' he said. 'That means three miles an hour, which means we could probably make it in about seven hours. I reckon I walk that much some days, just looking for work.'

'Seven hours,' the girl repeated thoughtfully, counting on her fingers. 'Me interview was half past ten, so I should think it's probably gettin' on for noon by now. It'll be full dark long before we reach the city. But then the street lamps will all be lit, so it shouldn't be too bad.' She grinned suddenly, shooting him a look which was pure mischief. 'Only you and Don will have to come back with me to my place and drop me off, like. I live in one o' them new tower blocks; ever been in one? There's lifts what never work 'cos the kids vandalise them, miles and miles of hard concrete stairs with rude words and worse pictures painted on the walls, and gangs of young fellers, ripe for trouble, hangin' around outside or squattin' on the stairs so's they can chi-ike you as you try to pass. I hopes as how you don't mind climbin' Everest to see me to me door.'

'Course I don't. It'll be interesting to see where you live,' he said. 'I have been in them flats, but

19

never further than a front door.'

'Nor you won't today,' the girl said sharply. 'Come to think, I don't know nothin' about you. You might be a mad axe murderer for all I know; you look like one in that stupid coat.'

'You've gorra nerve! I shared me grub wi' you. And you've seen how Don trusts me,' he added after a moment's thought. 'Dogs is a real good test of character, so I've heard.'

The girl laughed. 'I reckon you're right. Mebbe I'll let you in and show you round, but you can't stay, of course. Still, I dare say we'll meet up again. What's your name? And come to think of it, I've not told you mine yet. Ladies first, they say. D'you want me given name or the name I'd like to be called?'

The youth frowned. 'But you can't choose your own name,' he pointed out. 'There's nicknames, of course . . . but they ain't the same. And they change, anyway. Go on, then. What's your real name?'

'Gertrude Pleavin, but the kids in the home called me Gertie, which I hate. I've always liked the name Rose, though, so you can call me that if you want.'

The youth stared at her. 'Course I'll call you Rose, if that's what you'd like, but blow me down, I were brought up in a home too! Ain't that the oddest thing, that we should meet up like this?'

'Yeah. If this were a story you'd think it were pretty unlikely,' the girl agreed. 'And of all the places to meet up, this here road must be the strangest! But what d'you think of me name?'

'I think Rose Pleavin's a grand name,' the youth said. 'I'm Albert Thompson. I hate the name

Albert but it were give me when I were found.' He hesitated for a moment, then plunged on. 'I'm what they call a foundling; I was left in a cardboard box on the steps of a police station. Sergeant Thompson found me there so they gave me his surname. I dunno who chose Albert but the other fellers in the home hardly ever used it. It were all nicknames there, some of 'em pretty hateful.'

'But you're not in the home now,' Rose pointed out. 'You could call yourself any name you perishin' well please, like what I've done. You could be John, or Richard, or Paul . . . oh, anything. Go on, choose a name an' I promise I'll forget all about Albert; he never existed.'

The youth stared at her from the shadow of his hood, then smiled. 'Martin,' he said slowly. 'I've always liked the name Martin; yes, I'll be Martin Thompson. Thanks, Rose.'

'It's a pleasure,' Rose said formally. 'Don't go forgettin' you've gorra new name, though. D'you go back to the home often? How old are you, anyhow?'

He heaved a sigh and began to smooth the dog's lean head. 'I'm eighteen now and don't have nothin' to do with the home no more, thank Gawd. How old are you?'

He was looking at her face as he spoke and thought her expression suddenly shifty, though she answered quickly enough. 'I'm around fifteen, but I weren't dumped like you were. My mam loved me and would've kept me, but I were born during the Blitz. My mam left a note saying she'd come back and fetch me when times weren't so hard, but the nuns at St Mary's Home for Girls took me in and they reckon me mam must have been killed

21

the very night she left me on their doorstep, 'cos she never did come back.'

'So you were found too,' Martin said. 'But wharra co . . . coincidence, ain't it? The pair of us bein' foundlings!'

'I suppose,' Rose agreed. 'But if you're eighteen, why ain't you doin' your National Service? I thought all fellers of eighteen had to go into the armed forces for two years.' She looked at him admiringly. 'Don't say you thought up a clever scheme to gerrout of it?'

Martin gave a grunt of amusement. 'I reckon I could make a fortune if I could teach other fellers how to avoid being called up,' he told her. 'No, I failed the medical on two counts. Me eyesight's pretty poor and when I were a kid I broke me ankle. It's all right now but they said it weren't good enough.'

'Lucky you,' Rose said approvingly. 'But as for your ankle, it seems to have borne up pretty well so far . . . is that Formby I can see coming up ahead?'

'I reckon it must be,' Martin said, peering ahead through the driving rain. Truth to tell, he could make out very little. He had barely been able to see Rose's features and had longed to look more closely, but knew that it would have been rude, an intrusion.

As they approached the outskirts of the village, Rose's pace quickened. 'Wish we had money for fish and chips,' she said. 'But then I dare say they've not got a chippy here.'

'You're probably right, but if someone were to give us a lift, we might be in the 'Pool in time to offer to peel spuds in return for a few chips. I've done that when I've been desperate.' He reached out and fondled Don's small ears. 'I bet you've spent time hoverin' outside chip shops, begging for scraps,' he said. 'But them days are over, old feller.'

'Yes, you ain't a stray no more,' Rose said. 'You've got me and Marty to give an eye to you now and see you're fed.'

Martin felt a big smile spreading across his face; once again she had intimated that the two of them were in some way bound together, if only in their ownership of the great, half-starved greyhound loping along between them. 'That's right, old feller; if we get chips, you'll have your share,' he said, feeling his heart give a little jump of pleasure. 'And there's folk around what likes dogs as much as we do. We'll gerra lift, all three of us. I feel it in me water.'

Chapter Two

By the time the oddly assorted trio reached Crosby, Rose was very tired indeed. Had it not been for the fact that the rain had never ceased, so that she was literally soaked to the skin, she would have suggested finding shelter of some description. However, as things stood, she realised this would be madness, for to curl up wet and cold as she was would be courting disaster. At first the two of them had chatted, but as the rain continued to pour and dusk deepened they fell silent, too exhausted for conversation of even the most casual kind.

Martin had just said, in a flat and weary voice,

23

that their luck seemed to be out when a lorry drew up beside them. There was the sound of a window being cranked down and then a man's voice spoke. 'Well, if I ever saw three such drowned rats! Headin' for the 'Pool, are you? There's room in me cab for all three of you, if the dog ain't too proud to lie on the floor. It's a bit mucky, but I dare say you won't mind that.'

Martin seemed to be struck dumb, but Rose spoke for all of them, struggling to get the door open and saying breathlessly as she did so, 'Thanks, mister, you *are* good! Me and me pal have walked all the way from Southport—so's our dog, of course—and we're just about done in. I'm afraid we're awful wet. I'd offer to take off me coat to save your seat, except that I'm just as wet under it, and so is Marty.'

She was in the cab by now and Martin was scrambling in after her, carrying Don, for the dog had hesitated, clearly unsure of his welcome. Martin slammed the door and expected the driver to engage first gear and drive on, but instead the man looked at them and whistled. 'Phew. I called you drowned rats, but if you've come all the way from Southport on foot you must be half dead with the cold and wet.' He leaned down and picked up what looked like an old potato sack from under the dashboard, ferreted around for a moment, and then produced a large flask and a packet wrapped in greaseproof paper. 'The missus allus puts up enough hot tea and butties to last me the whole day, but I stopped off at a pull-in earlier. Drivin' in rain like this is no picnic, so I went and got me a hot meal.' He handed the flask and the packet to Rose. 'You're welcome to what's left. There's at

24

least a couple o' Spam butties wrapped in the greaseproof; you two and the dawg can have the lot.'

Rose took the flask and poured a careful cup, thanking the driver sincerely as she did so, while Martin handed round the sandwiches—one each for himself and Rose and one for the dog. For a moment there was no sound but sipping and munching. Rose had the first drink of tea and it warmed her beautifully, so she hurried to pass the next capful to Martin, knowing that he must be as cold and wet as she. The driver waited until they had finished drinking, then started the engine and moved off. Presently Rose asked him what load he was carrying.

'Farm produce, I reckon you'd call it,' he said cheerfully. 'Mornings I'm up on the Fylde, collecting sacks o' spuds, cabbages, sprouts, swedes and so on. Each farm gives me a list tellin' me where I'm to deliver. I'm not sayin' it's a marvellous job—I dare say I could get more deliverin' for one o' the breweries—but I've always liked me independence. The lorry's me own and it's up to me what time I start and finish. I'll probably never make a fortune, but I'm me own boss.' He turned and grinned at them. 'I joined the army at the start of the war; I were a Desert Rat, if you know what that means. I got made up to sergeant, and it gave me a taste for givin' orders rather than taking 'em. So when I got back to Blighty I used me savings to buy an old lorry, and the rest you know. Warmin' up, are you?' He grinned again. 'There's enough steam comin' off your coats to make me wonder if you've a locomotive hid somewhere!'

Rose giggled. 'I'm much warmer, thanks,' she said. 'Wharrabout you, Marty?'

Martin heaved a deep contented sigh. 'Sorry. I were nearly asleep,' he admitted. 'I'm real grateful to you, mister; well, all three of us are. I reckon that tea and them butties just about saved our lives.'

'You're right there,' Rose agreed enthusiastically. 'Please thank your missus for us. And now can you tell us where you're heading, so's you can drop us off somewhere convenient?'

The driver chuckled. 'I wouldn't turn a dog out on a night like this,' he observed. He glanced at Martin. 'Is this young lady your daughter?'

Rose gave a squeak of amusement. 'He's tall, but he's only eighteen,' she explained, before Martin could speak. 'We're—we're pals, that's all. We travelled to Southport by bus, looking for work, only neither of us found any, so we decided to hitchhike back. But until you came along, no one stopped.' She turned to Martin. 'Where is the best place to be dropped off, Mart?'

Martin began to say that anywhere in the city centre would suit him, but the driver interrupted. 'I said I wouldn't turn a dog out on a night like this,' he reminded them. 'I'll tek you to your door, wherever that is. I live on the Wirral meself.'

'Oh, you are good, 'cos I don't think any of us could walk another step,' Rose said gratefully. 'We're in one of them tower blocks in Everton what were built a couple o' years ago; d'you know 'em?' The driver said he did and, as they reached the city and met more traffic, she pinched Martin's hand and sank her voice to a whisper. 'It's awful late; what say you kip down on me floor, just for tonight? I can spare a blanket off me bed but I can't afford to switch on the electric, so it won't be very warm.'

'Thanks, I'll do that,' Martin murmured. 'To tell you the truth, I could sleep on a clothes line I'm so tired. I wish I could do something to repay our pal here, but . . .'

'You're right. We should do something to say thanks,' Rose agreed, ashamed that she had not thought of it herself. She turned to the driver. 'You've been so good, mister! Will you give us your name and address so's we can write a proper thank you? We'd like to, honest.'

As she spoke the lorry turned into Everton Brow. The driver pulled his vehicle to a stop by the first tower block and then turned to his passengers. 'No, no, there's no need to do owt of the sort,' he said gruffly. 'You've thanked me enough; I were young—and penniless—once meself, so I were happy to give you a helpin' hand.' He jumped out on his side whilst Martin and Rose were easing their cramped limbs into motion, and came round to open their door for them. 'Now in wi' you before this perishin' rain soaks you all over again.'

Rose, Martin and Don rushed for the building, then stood in the doorway and waved until the lorry was out of sight. Rose crossed to the lift and pressed the button but did not bother to wait. 'If it's workin', it's either on the ground floor with the door open, or else you hear a clattering, whining sound,' she told her companion as they began to mount the stairs. 'Never mind, we're almost home.' She turned to address the dog, who was hopping from step to step, never stumbling even though the stairwell was extremely dark. 'Good old boy, Don,'

27

she said encouragingly. 'I got some dried milk from the clinic the last time I was there . . .' She glanced at Martin, realising she had given away more than she intended, but it was clear from his expression that he had not noticed her solecism, so she continued to talk to Don. 'I'll make you up a drink of it, though it'll have to be cold. If there's any money left in the meter I'll save it to boil the kettle tomorrow morning. I do like a cuppa first thing.'

She looked back at Martin, who was beginning to struggle. She realised that he simply was not used to stairs, or not ten flights of them anyway, so she slowed her own pace to let him keep up. When they reached her door, she fished the key out of the letter box and opened up, reminding herself that this was the first time she had voluntarily invited a stranger into her home. She crossed the small hall, very conscious suddenly of her role as hostess, and flung open the door to her right. 'Sittin' room,' she said briefly. 'Bedroom's that door, bathroom's there, kitchen's here.' She opened the last door and ushered Martin and Don into a small fitted kitchen. 'Take off your coat; I'll fetch my old dressing gown for you. I've got a towel an' all. Come to think, you'd best take off all your clothes and wrap the towel round you. I won't bring the blanket through until you're dry.'

The tall young man turned towards her and Rose realised, with a sense of shock, that she had never seen his face. Oh, she had seen a pointed nose, the glint of teeth and eyes, but that was all. She saw him hesitate, then he undid the toggles of his hooded duffel coat and snatched it off. She could not help gasping, though she suppressed the

28

scream which rose to her lips. His hair was as white as an old man's, his face cadaverous and as white as a sheet, and his eyes . . . oh, God, his eyes were a pinkish grey! She had never seen eyes like them. But he was looking at her with such hopeless appeal that she hid her dismay and tried to speak naturally. 'You all right, Mart? Then I'll go and fetch that towel.'

*   *   *

Left alone in the small kitchen, the young man and the dog stared at one another. Martin had recognised the surprise and horror in Rose's face when he had shed his duffel coat, because he had seen it so many times before. His very first memory was of overhearing a conversation between the matron and one of her helpers at the Arbuthnot Boys' Home. He had been no more than three or four at the time, but even so he had been sufficiently intelligent to realise that he was the object of the conversation. It was high summer and the helper had been asked by Matron to take a group of the younger children to Prince's Park. Martin had pricked up his ears; he loved the park, loved the broad green expanse where a child could run and run without fear of traffic, loved the ducks on the lake, the birds in the aviary . . . oh, everything about it. But then the helper had spoken and Martin had known he would not be amongst the lucky ones.

'I can manage half a dozen, and if Miss Bates comes with me we can take ten,' Miss Cavanagh had said. 'But I won't take that one, with his white hair and pink eyes; gives me the creeps he does.

29

I'm always afraid he'll have a fit or drop down dead or something. My dad's a porter at the hospital and he says they don't live long anyway, which is probably a mercy.' She had shot a malevolent look at the small Martin, sitting on the floor of the playroom and building a wobbly tower with a pile of wooden bricks. 'Imagine having a baby and discovering it was like one of those rabbits you see in the pet shop.'

Matron had said, rather stiffly, that if Miss Cavanagh felt so strongly she would see that Martin was not included in the treat, and had then briskly changed the subject, which he supposed, doubtfully now, had been good of her. On the other hand, why had she not told Miss Cavanagh that she was talking a lot of pernicious rubbish? Matron must have known that he had understood every word Miss Cavanagh had uttered, yet she had not come over to him, picked him up for a cuddle and told him that it was all nonsense, that there was nothing wrong with him that time would not erase.

He had tried very hard to forget the incident but it had stayed with him, reinforced by the fact that he was regarded with suspicion and dislike by the other boys, and even by the staff. The only real understanding he had ever received was from a teacher who had kept him behind the rest of the class one day to discuss an essay Martin had written. Mr Brownrigg had told him that the essay was the best piece of work he had seen from a boy not yet twelve. 'It's an intelligent and inventive piece of writing,' he had said. Then he had looked thoughtfully at his pupil. 'I never see you playing with any of the other lads, Thompson. Even in organised games you tend to be kept on the sidelines. D'you know why that is?'

'No sir,' Martin had replied. He had hesitated for a moment, then added: 'Unless it's because I'm—I'm an albino.'

The teacher had nodded. 'That's it. It could be worse—yes, your sight is poor, but unlike some albinos you write perfectly legibly and never walk into lamp posts or misjudge distances—but the fact remains that you're different, and some folk think that's a reason to give you the cold shoulder. Later in life you'll see that anyone different may be avoided by others, which is what we call mindless prejudice. In your case, the fact that you were born without the usual pigmentation means some people will take against you, but you have to remember that being different doesn't mean you're any way inferior.' He tapped the essay on the desk before him. 'In fact, this work shows that far from being inferior, you are a good deal brighter than most.'

Now, standing in Rose's kitchen, he remembered both conversations, one with an echo of the dismay the small Martin had felt, the other with considerable pleasure. It was a shame that Mr Brownrigg had left the school at the end of the summer term, to be replaced by a crusty old man who did not like boys—any boys. The new teacher had scornfully dismissed Martin's work as 'ridiculous flights of fancy', and had given him consistently low marks, but Mr Brownrigg's words had been treasured, had helped Martin to drag himself out of the slough of despond into which he sometimes fell.

He was still gazing thoughtfully at Don when he

31

registered a drip, drip, dripping sound and saw that water was running from the dog's lean form and plopping on to the brown linoleum. Hastily, he looked properly at the kitchen. There was a low stone sink, which boasted a wooden draining board on one side and two large chromium taps. Slung between the taps was a grey floor cloth. Martin picked it up, then realised that it was not only the dog who was shedding water; he was standing in a puddle himself. He was about to employ the floor cloth to clean up when it occurred to him that it would be more sensible to use it to give the dog a good rub down.

He was kneeling on the floor, working on Don's emaciated body, when the door opened and Rose came back into the room, carrying a thin towel over one arm. She nodded approvingly as he scrambled to his feet, but stared with some dismay at the small lake which now covered a considerable proportion of the linoleum. 'Well, Don looks a good deal better and me floor a good deal worse,' she observed. 'I'd best fetch the mop from the hall cupboard, otherwise you might drop the towel and that 'ud be the end of that.'

'I shan't drop it,' Martin said eagerly, taking the towel from her and placing it carefully upon the draining board. 'But if you'll give me the mop, I'll get rid of the water for you.' He hesitated, then continued: 'Do you mean me to sleep in here? If so, I reckon I'd better put me wet clothes out on the landing, 'cos I don't fancy sleeping on the floor with them drippin' into the sink. I'll do me best to wring 'em out, but me coat's real thick and heavy.'

Rose laughed. 'You can't possibly sleep in here. There's an old sofa in me sitting room. You can lie on that and Don can have the hearthrug.' She twinkled up at Martin, then put a hand on the dog's head. 'He's almost dry,' she said. 'Wait on, I'm gonna make him some bread and milk.' She turned to a small cupboard and began taking out a tin of dried milk and the half loaf of bread she had mentioned earlier. 'We'll have the eggs boiled tomorrow, for our breakfast,' she said chattily and turned to give him a beaming smile. 'Would that suit you, Mr Thompson?'

Martin, mopping the floor vigorously, thought that she looked almost pretty when she smiled. She had taken off her own coat and pixie hood and he saw with some surprise that she was not the skinny little creature he had thought her in her big flapping mackintosh. She was wearing a long, loose blue dress, old and faded and very full, and a pair of carpet slippers. He saw that in order to keep the slippers on her feet she had to shuffle, and he grinned at her. 'You've been shoppin' at jumble sales, same as me,' he said, laughing. 'Why, you could get two of you inside that dress.'

He had spoken jokingly and was surprised and even a little dismayed when the colour rushed into her face and she turned on him, her eyes sparkling angrily. 'Fancy you noticing!' she said, her voice rich with sarcasm. 'There are two of us inside this dress, and if you make one more crack like that you can bloody well go and sleep out in the rain. And if you catch your death, you horrible creature, it'll serve you right.'

Martin could only stare. What the devil did she mean? Two of them inside the dress? Instinctively, he looked down, half expecting to see a second pair of feet beside the carpet slippers; what *could*

33

she mean? 'I'm sorry, Rose. It were rude of me to criticise your dress,' he said humbly. 'I didn't mean no harm, but I don't understand. There aren't really two of you, so I suppose you were jokin', like I was, only you looked awful cross. Please don't turn me out.'

His apologetic tone put her anger to flight and she laughed again, reaching out to pat his long, bony hand. 'Oh, Mart, you don't know nothin'! I'm havin' a baby, you fool! I'm six months gone and I didn't think I showed much, but I reckon the lady in Southport must have guessed because she kept giving me funny looks, and when she came through and told us who had got the job she patted my shoulder and said she was sorry but it really wouldn't do and she hoped I'd understand.'

'A baby!' Martin breathed. 'A baby's even better than a dog! Though I suppose it's a big responsibility, being a mother. Will it sleep in your bedroom, or will the council let you move to a bigger place once it's born?'

Rose shrugged. 'I dunno. I was going to put it out for adoption, but I'm not sure what to do for the best.'

She patted her stomach tenderly, glancing down as she did so, and Martin saw the loving look on her face and thought suddenly that she would not part with her baby if she could help it; she would be a good mother for all she was scarcely more than a child herself. 'Oh, well, if they won't give you a bigger flat for a while, I guess you'll manage,' he said quickly. 'If there's anything I can do to help...but I dare say now you've seen me face you won't want me around, norreven as a pal, in case it—it affects your baby, me being an albino, like.'

Rose opened her eyes very wide, then gave a derisive snort. 'Don't be so daft. This baby were made six months ago. I've been attendin' classes at the Oxford Street Maternity Hospital, an' they tell you straight, honest to God they do, if they think there's owt wrong. What's more, there's a nurse what lectures us on how we mustn't believe old wives' tales ... you know, if a hare crosses your path the kid'll have a deformed lip, or if a cat hisses at you it'll come out arse-side up. So seein' a feller what's an alb ... alb ... oh, heck, a feller what has white hair an' that isn't goin' to make one mite of difference to me baby. It's already formed, from what they telled us—dark hair or light, blue eyes or brown, even good teeth or bad 'uns. See? D'you understand, Mart?'

'I think I do,' Martin said cautiously. 'By gum, I'm learnin' a lot today. Tell you what, though, if you did get a bigger flat and I manage to get a job, mebbe I could be a lodger, like. It 'ud be grand to help with the baby and you could have all me money, so long as you fed me and Don, of course.'

He knew it had been the wrong thing to say as soon as she turned to stand the bowl of bready milk down before the dog. She said nothing, but the set of her shoulders and her very silence spoke volumes. Knowing he had put his foot in it for a second time, he said hastily: 'Oh, Gawd, what an idiot I am! Of course you wouldn't want no lodger, and anyway, the council aren't likely to offer you a bigger flat just so you can rent a room. Forget I even said it, would you, Rose? It was just a joke.'

'Well, I'm glad of that,' Rose said rather distantly. She had been squatting down beside the

35

dog, but now she straightened and walked towards the kitchen door. 'I'll go and fetch a blanket off my bed while you undress and dry yourself off. The central heating is supposed to come on at eight o'clock in the morning—if it comes on at all, that is. When you're respectable, knock three times on the kitchen door and I'll come and give you the blanket. You can drape the towel over the back of me chair before you go through into the sittin' room. We've had a pretty hard day of it, so we'll probably sleep in tomorrow. Why don't you and Don stay in bed until I shout you that breakfast is ready?'

'Right. Thanks, Rose. I'll do just as you say,' Martin said. As soon as the kitchen door shut behind her, he tore off every stitch of clothing and attacked his long white body with the towel. When he was as dry as he could get, he banged on the kitchen door and presently, wrapped in a blanket, he went through into the sitting room, Don padding softly behind him. There was no sign of his hostess, and as he folded himself on to the small sofa he thought unhappily that she had still not entirely forgiven him for his thoughtless remark. He also thought how much he would have enjoyed Don's bowl of bread and milk, but he acknowledged that the dog's need was greater than his. After all, his dole money fed him adequately, if not well, whereas the greyhound had probably been starved for weeks.

He woke once during the night to find that Don was stretched out beside the sofa, his big body on the floor but his head actually resting on Martin's feet, and he guessed that the dog wanted to be sure that he would not be left behind should

Martin decide to move on. Immensely heartened by this sign of trust and affection, he told Don he was a good boy, the sort of dog any feller would be proud to own. Even when the light woke him and he discovered flea bites all over his legs, he told himself it was a small price to pay for such friendship.

The expected shout that breakfast was ready came shortly after ten—he had heard a church clock chime the hour—but Rose herself did not appear, though she handed him his dried clothing round the door. Martin glanced out of the window as he dressed, and gasped with pleasure. The view was incredible, like nothing he had ever seen before. Miles and miles of houses, St Anthony's church, the great estuary of the Mersey, beyond it the Wirral and beyond that the blue of what must surely be the Welsh hills.

But he had no time to linger, for through the thin wall which separated sitting room and kitchen he could hear Rose moving about, and did not want to rouse her annoyance a third time by being late for breakfast. He and Don entered the kitchen hastily, therefore, to find the table laid for two people. There was only one chair, a ladder-backed wooden one, but Rose must have brought another seat through from her bedroom since there was a box-like object with a pillow on top drawn up on the opposite side of the table. An egg, neatly decapitated, was set in each place and lying on the table were two rounds of bread and margarine, neatly cut into fingers. Between the two place settings were a barrel of Saxa salt, the half jar of jam she had mentioned, the remains of the loaf and two cups of gently steaming tea.

Martin's mouth watered; he hadn't had a boiled egg since he had left the home, but he did not immediately sit down. 'Which is mine?' he said as Rose turned from the sink.

'You'd best have me hope chest since you're taller'n me,' she said, indicating the box and pillow with a jerk of the head. 'Hurry up, Mart, or your egg will be cold and you won't be able to dip the bread into the yolk. I've saved the heel of the loaf and some of the milk mixture for the dog, so we won't have to eat with him sitting there envying us every mouthful.'

Martin complied. The egg was just as he liked it and he finished his much faster than Rose finished hers, for she had lingered to crumble a good half of what remained of the loaf into the milk mixture and put it down for Don who, with his usual cautious courtesy, would not touch it until bidden to do so, though saliva trickled from his mouth.

When she saw that Martin had finished, Rose, halfway through her own egg, paused to cut him a generous chunk of bread, smear it with margarine and add a good helping of jam. 'That'll fill in the chinks,' she said thickly. 'Go on, Mart, eat up. There's a lot more of you to fill than there is of me, though since I'm eating for two I'll have my share of the bread and jam. Fancy another cuppa?'

He did, but got up to pour it for himself, to save Rose moving, and seeing him lift the teapot she pushed her own mug towards him. 'The milkman won't climb all them stairs, nor he don't trust the lift,' she said, pushing her empty egg cup aside and starting to cut another slice from what remained of the loaf. 'He got stuck in it for three hours a few months back—I weren't here then but he told me

38

all about it—so now if we wants milk, we has to go down to the foyer when he shouts. That's why I always keep dried milk in. I like it better than the sterilised, and conny-onny's a bit sweet for my taste.'

'This tea tastes fine,' Martin said, returning to his seat and taking a gulp from his cup. 'Can I ask you why this box is called a hope chest, or will you get cross?'

'Course I shan't get cross,' Rose said, as though she had never been cross in her life. 'In fact, when you've finished your breakfast, I'll show you what's in it, then you can help me carry it back to me bedroom.'

Martin was so keen to discover what he had been sitting on that he finished his bread and jam in record time, but Rose did not open the lid of her hope chest until they had washed up their crocks and cutlery. She was clearly of a tidy disposition and Martin, a tidy person himself, thought this was praiseworthy. If I had a flat, even a tiny one, I'd keep it neat as a new pin, he thought wistfully. I'd save up every penny to buy paint and wallpaper and that. It might take time—well, it would—but I'd make it real nice. I'd start with the kitchen, and when that was all modern and shining I'd have a go at the sitting room. I'd do the bedroom last.

'Marty, I'll let you have a quick peep at my stuff and then I really think you ought to take Don downstairs for a piddle. I'm pretty sure he didn't lift his leg in me sittin' room, but he must be bustin' by now.'

Martin acknowledged the truth of this, though the dog showed no sign of a desire to leave the flat, and he watched with interest as Rose threw the pillow to one side and heaved up the lid of the box. Smiling with pride, she began to display the contents. 'A white shawl, 'cos it would look odd to wrap a girl in blue or a boy in pink, and two blankets to fit a cradle.' She rubbed them against her cheeks, her expression blissful. 'They're soft as thistledown and brand new, just like the shawl, though you'd be surprised at how 'spensive even baby things are. Then there's these nightgowns. I bought them because it don't make no difference whether it's a boy or a girl, babies still wear nightgowns in bed.' She flourished one under Martin's nose. 'I did the embroidery round the necks and round the waistbands. It's mostly lazy daisies and love knots, with satin stitch to fill in the petals, of course. It took me ages 'cos I ain't good with me needle, but I soldiered on.' She pointed to the last items in the box. 'Them's nappies, 'cos all babies need nappies. I couldn't afford many— they're real expensive—so I got six towelling and six muslin.' She laughed. 'It ain't much, but I've a pal what helps me out, and she's collectin' all sorts for me as well. I've not told her I'm doin' the same, so it'll be a nice surprise when I show her the stuff I've bought meself.'

'I think you've done a grand job,' Martin said sincerely. 'I especially like the little red dots; are those the love knots?'

Rose gave a crow of amusement and began to laugh helplessly, punching him playfully on the shoulder as she did so. He did not understand her reaction, but was delighted by it. It was the sort of gesture he had often seen amongst his schoolfellows, but had never shared. After a moment, he let his puzzlement show. 'What's so

40

funny?' he demanded. 'It were a compliment, weren't it?'

Rose wiped tears of amusement from her eyes. 'I said I weren't good wi' me needle. Them's blood spots from where I dug the perishin' thing into meself rather than the material,' she said between gasps. 'Oh, Mart, you do me a power o' good, honest you do!' As she spoke Rose began folding the shawl and blankets, carefully piling them back into the box, but she looked up when Martin cleared his throat.

'Rose . . . if you really are going to have the baby adopted, why are you spending your money on— on clothes and that?'

'Well, you can't go handing a kid to its new mother without a stitch to its back,' Rose said reasonably, then gave Martin a crooked little grin. 'To tell you the truth, though, Mart, I've already decided that I shan't part wi' me baby. I've not told anyone else because they'll say I'm too young, and it's selfish to deprive the baby of parents—mum *and* dad—who have lots o' cash and that. But this baby . . . oh, it's hard to explain, but I'm pretty sure now that I'll keep it meself.'

Martin beamed at her. 'I'll help, if you'll let me,' he said eagerly. 'Even after feedin' Don I'll be able to spare a bit of me dole money. I see you ain't got no woolly ball to hang on the front of the pram, nor no rattle, nor a soft toy. Couldn't I buy the little 'un something to play with? I like babies, and Don and me would like to feel we'd helped, even in a small way. What d'you say?'

Rose gave him an awkward glance. 'Well, I'll think about it,' she said grudgingly. And then, clearly thinking an explanation was due, she

41

added: 'I don't know if you can understand, Marty, but I've never had nothin' which was really an' truly me own. They were dead keen at the home that we should learn to share. Our toys belonged to everyone; we were never allowed to say a particular doll or teddy was ours. You might take a doll to bed with you for a week and then one of the staff would notice—or someone would tell on you, more likely—and the doll would be passed to someone else. But this 'un . . .' she stroked her stomach, her expression one of loving tenderness once more, 'this 'un's all me own, and I want to keep it that way.'

Martin was so dismayed that he broke into speech before he had thought. 'But you said your pal was helpin' you out,' he said. 'Why can't I buy a few things as well?'

He watched Rose's cheeks flush pink and stepped back, waiting for the explosion of wrath which he felt sure was to come. But she just shook her head slowly and continued to pile her possessions back into their box. 'I can't explain,' she said in a small, tired voice. 'You're ever so kind, Mart, and I know you mean it for the best, but to tell you the truth, I wouldn't have let me pal give me one or two things except that I mean to pay her back. I'll get a job, a proper one—oh, I'll do something, though I don't know what yet—so she don't lose by what she's done for me. I've not mentioned it before, but she got me this flat and told lies for me; she said I were eighteen though she knows, none better, that I'm not even sixteen yet. She gives me money, too, 'cos there's no dole for someone my age, but I get all the free stuff from the clinic. Oh, it's too complicated to explain, but she's been not just a friend but a—a—I can't think of the word, but you know what I mean.'

'I think you mean benefactress, don't you?' Martin said. 'And now it's high time I took Don downstairs, else he'll be piddlin' on your nice clean floor.'

'Right,' Rose replied. 'Off you go then, the pair of you.'

Martin hesitated, looking round for his coat, which Rose had draped across the clothes horse that stood in front of the stove. Most of what Rose had said had not seemed to make sense, but he knew he had been listening with only half his attention because he had been dismayed at what he took to be a denial of friendship. He thought she was trying to tell him that any attempt on his part to help with the baby would be resented. But he was used to people elbowing him aside, misunderstanding what he said, making it clear that he was a nuisance, that they didn't want him around; and he thought that he really should learn to follow his own rules. Don't grumble or complain, just quietly leave. That way, if he and the other person met up again, there need be no ill feeling or awkwardness between them. He would accept his dismissal, and simply be grateful that until he had gone too far by suggesting that he might buy the baby a gift Rose had seemed friendly enough.

He picked up his coat. It was warm and dry and he shrugged himself into it, flicking the hood forward and doing up the toggles with fingers that were only slightly unsteady. He wrinkled his nose at his socks, which were old, holey and, alas, rather smelly, but pulled them on and reached for his

43

boots. The possession of the boots was a constant pleasure. He had bought them from a street trader who had let him have them cheap since he had intended to keep them for himself, only to discover that they were too narrow. He had looked doubtful when Martin had asked to try them on, but to Martin's delight the boots fitted and were extremely comfortable. They must have been made for someone with long slender feet just like his, and he thought now that he would never have managed the walk back from Southport in his old pair.

'Why are you starin' at them boots?' Rose said, suddenly impatient. 'Fancy puttin' on your coat an' doin' it up an' all and then standin' there in your socks.' She pulled a face. 'Phew! When did you last wash them perishin' things? They stink to high heaven.'

Martin felt the hot blood rise up his neck and flood into his face. He shoved his feet hastily into the boots, then bent and tied up the laces. He could not explain that washing clothes when you were homeless and sleeping rough was pretty well impossible. And if he said anything, she might take it as an attempt to get her sympathy. Instead he straightened, put his hand on the kitchen door, then turned towards her. 'Thanks for everything, Rose,' he said huskily. 'I'll wash me socks first chance I get.'

He opened the door, snapped his fingers for Don to follow him, and raised his hand in an uncertain half-wave before setting off down the long flights of stairs.

*   *   *

Left alone in the kitchen, Rose picked up the box of baby things and carried it through to her bedroom, placing it carefully at the foot of her bed. Every morning, when she awoke, she glanced immediately towards the box, and every morning the same sense of pleasure and accomplishment enveloped her. She had worked hard and had often gone without a meal in order to purchase items for her hope chest.

The thought made her pull a wry face. If only she had learned to knit! The handiwork teacher at the school which Rose and the other children from St Mary's had attended had taught everyone to knit except Rose, who was naturally left-handed and had never managed to master the art. Instead, she had spent her handiwork lessons inventing stories and telling them to the other girls in a whisper.

'Go on, don't stop there! What happens next?'

'Please, Gertie, don't kill off Sir Francis de Bourgh. I'm in love with him, so I am.'

'I'll kill you off an' all if you call me Gertie; you know I like to be called Rose,' Rose had hissed in a furious undertone, and because her stories had made handiwork lessons bearable her fellow pupils had agreed to use the name she preferred, though not of course in front of the teachers.

However, it was a different story when the handiwork teacher discovered the reason for Rose's sudden popularity, which had the girls gathering together round the one member of class who could be relied upon to ruin any handiwork she was given. Miss Wheatley thought she had devised the perfect punishment for the pupil she most disliked by sending her down to the kitchens,

45

saying that she might as well make herself useful there, peeling vegetables, washing up and doing any cleaning necessary. 'Working in kitchens is what you'll probably do when you leave this place, for you're fit for nothing else,' the teacher had said spitefully. 'I've told the cook to expect you on Monday and Wednesday afternoons.'

'Oh, but Miss Wheatley, we only do handiwork on a Monday; Wednesdays we do hockey in winter and rounders in summer,' Rose had protested. 'Or sometimes we're took for a nature walk in Prince's Park. Even outings in the charabanc is usually on a Wednesday afternoon; you can't mean me to miss them.'

Miss Wheatley's eyes had glinted and Rose knew that she would have done better to say nothing. But it was too late; she had burned her boats. 'Perhaps it will teach you a lesson to miss games and outings for a few weeks,' the teacher had said. 'I'll explain to the rest of the staff why you will be otherwise engaged on a Wednesday for a while.'

If Miss Wheatley had ever known how her plan had misfired she would have been furious, but since she never visited the kitchens and never remembered, either, that the punishment was only supposed to last for a few weeks, she remained ignorant of the fact that Rose actually came to look forward to Monday and Wednesday afternoons. Cook was a fat, comfortable woman, proud of her ability to produce good nourishing food for the staff and pupils of St Mary's without ever overspending her budget. She had greeted her new young helper somewhat doubtfully, but had soon realised that Rose was fascinated by everything to do with cooking. At first, Rose had

46

just peeled potatoes, chopped cabbages and sliced carrots whilst chattering to the kitchen staff and asking intelligent questions about the work in hand. Soon Cook had taught her to sauté the vegetables she had prepared so that they might become part of one of her delicious stews, and when she had discovered that Rose could be trusted to whip a batter or knead a bread mix she had actually suggested that she might like to make a couple of Victoria sponges for the staff's mid-morning break.

Very soon, Monday and Wednesday afternoons had become Rose's favourite times of day. She had learned to make scones, teacakes and buns. Cook had introduced her to the mysteries of gingerbread, which started life in a saucepan on the stove and ended up emerging from the oven as a delicious dark brown confection.

'Cooking's hot hard work, but I loves it,' Cook had said. 'And even if you never take up a post as cook, it'll stand you in good stead when you're married and have a home of your own.'

Rose could not imagine herself ever being married, but she had known that one day she would leave St Mary's and thought that even if she was only feeding herself, and not a hungry family, she would still be grateful for the knowledge Cook had instilled.

But now, having placed the box in its usual position, she turned her attention to the small, rather shabby little dressing table in front of the window. She pulled open the bottom drawer and produced an ancient tin which had once contained Lyons coffee, which she carried back to her bed before wrenching off the lid and pouring the

47

contents, mainly pennies, sixpences and shillings, on to the counterpane. The rain had stopped, and though the sky was overcast, and the wind gusty, she thought she might take some of her money and do a little shopping. She needed both bread and milk, and if she went all the way to St John's Market she could buy food a good deal more cheaply there than in the smaller shops on Heyworth Street.

Her friend had given her a book by a doctor who was a great believer in fresh fruit and vegetables. He advised his readers to make nourishing stews and broths from cheap cuts of meat and Rose had speedily realised that cooking for herself was the most practical way to survive. In addition, she had begun to make simple cakes and biscuits, which she sold to a nearby old people's home. The matron, Miss Haverstock, a huge woman with a flourishing moustache and twinkling black eyes, had told Rose that she herself loved home cooking but was too busy looking after her ladies and gents to spend time toiling over a hot stove, so was glad to pay small sums for Rose's cakes and buns.

At first, when a cake had refused to rise or Rose had left a tray of mince pies in the oven too long, she had not liked to take them to the old people's home, but the matron had told her not to be so daft. 'I pours custard over most of me puddin's and the old 'uns gobble them up,' she had said. 'Of course, I can't pay so much for what you might call damaged goods . . .' here, she had given Rose a very odd glance which Rose did not understand in the least, 'but I'll pay for all your ingredients. Would you think that was fair?'

Rose had said it was very fair. However, she

48

thought the old people in the home were far too nosy, far too interested in herself, though Matron had assured her that they meant no harm and that her occasional visits gave them something to think about and discuss amongst themselves. Some weeks before, one of the old ladies, sharper than the rest, had come hobbling up to Rose in the long, drab corridor leading to Matron's office. 'You're in the fambly way, ain't you?' she had said slyly, giving Rose a poke in the ribs. 'I can always tell; it's something in the way you walks. So when's it due, eh, or don't you know?'

Rose had drawn herself up to her full height, which was only five foot four, and had said frostily: 'If you are referrin' to me slight bulge, that's a horrible growth, that is, what'll probably kill me off before me time, and weren't you ever taught that it were bloody rude to make personal remarks?'

The old lady's look of sly mischief had changed to one of extreme malevolence. 'I were taught to tell a good girl from a bad one,' she had hissed. 'As for your bulge, time will tell, won't it?'

Furious at being outwitted by a toothless old woman, ninety if she were a day, Rose had searched her mind for a sharp reply, but had found none. Nose in the air, with her basket of goodies held protectively across her bump, she had sailed past the old woman, heading once more for Matron's office. But she could not help wondering if everyone knew, and at the last moment had turned impulsively back. 'Sorry, I shouldn't have told that stupid lie,' she had said grudgingly. 'You're right, I am expectin', though why that should make me a bad girl I don't know.'

The old woman had tottered wheezingly up to

49

her. 'Ah well, we was all young once,' she had said vaguely. 'Go along wi' you; when you're as old as me, you get to know a thing or two. An' whatever your faults, young woman, you're a dab hand at Bakewell puddin's.'

'I'm real glad you like me bakin',' Rose had said, knowing that she sounded humble, but not caring. 'But I'd be obliged if you wouldn't tell no one else about me—me condition.'

The old woman had chuckled. 'Half of 'em's daft and the other half's dotty,' she had said, 'but they'll be able to see for themselves soon enough, queen.'

At this point, the door of Matron's office had opened and that lady had beckoned Rose inside. 'Thought I heard voices. What's Little Red Riding Hood got for us today?' Her voice had been arch but her eyes had scanned the basket greedily, and since she made no mention of the conversation she had overheard Rose had assumed that she knew nothing.

Now, Rose was counting her money and deciding how to spend it. She needed ingredients if she were to bake, and she really should get some cheap meat and vegetables so that she could make a sustaining meal, because yesterday she and Martin had had almost nothing. She wondered whether it would be cheeky to ask Martin for a contribution when he came back to the flat, but decided that, knowing he had no money on him, she could scarcely do so. He could come shopping with her. Naturally, she would also go with him to collect his dole, and only then would she suggest that he might like to contribute a bob or two towards the stew she intended to cook.

Satisfied, she selected some money from her hoard and tucked it into the pocket of her thin jumper. Then she returned to the kitchen, poured herself another cup of tea, and waited. Glancing at the battered old alarm clock on the windowsill, she realised that Martin had been gone some time and thought approvingly that he must have decided to take Don for a proper walk, though after yesterday's marathon a walk would, she thought, have been the last thing the pair of them wanted. However, she might as well be doing something useful whilst she waited.

She went to a small cupboard over the sink and checked the contents, for it was here that she kept the ingredients for food which she hoped to sell. She had baking powder, flour, a large square of margarine . . .

Checking the cupboard meant making a list of things which were either not there or running short. She wrote the list, went to the window and peered out. He really was taking his time . . . but there was nothing wrong with that. It had felt very strange, on waking this morning, to realise that there was someone else in the flat, and not only a stranger but a man, albeit a young one.

Time passed. Eventually, alarmed, Rose left the flat, locked the door and clattered down the long flights. She wondered, with some concern, whether Martin had been confused by the fact that the tower blocks were all so similar, and had gone into the wrong one. Then she remembered Don; he would not let harm come to Martin, she was sure of that. But she did go into the nearest two blocks, only to come out again convinced that neither youth nor dog had made any such mistake. Martin

51

seemed to her to be bright enough. She went over in her mind his leaving of the kitchen and came to the conclusion that he had taken her remarks for dismissal, and had gone back to—to—oh, dammit, he had never given her his address!

Sighing deeply, she toiled back up the stairs and took her coat off the hook behind the door. She slipped into it, then picked up her marketing basket, telling herself impatiently that if Martin had chosen to go off without so much as a proper farewell there was nothing she could do about it, and she certainly could not hang around the flats waiting for him. She really must do some shopping. Quickly, she transferred the money from her pocket to her worn little black purse, which she then pushed into her coat's deep pocket. She picked up her list and pocketed that as well, then found an old envelope upon which she scrawled: *Martin—gone shopping for grub. Back soon. R.*

Leaving the flat, she attached the envelope to the door, carefully locked it, and set off down the stairs. She had not liked to put the time of her possible return on the envelope, because you never knew: someone might come all the way to the top floor, realise that she was out and would not be returning until five or six o'clock, and break in. God knew there was little enough to steal, but suppose they found her hope chest, or her money tin? Her blood turned to ice at the thought and for a moment she dithered. If Martin returned and found the door of the flat locked . . . but what did it matter, really? It was not as though he were an old friend; he was just a chance acquaintance, and she knew that if someone broke in she would never feel safe in the flat again. She did not always feel safe now, because there were four flats on the top floor and she knew almost nothing about any of the other occupants, save that at least two of the families indulged in drinking bouts which were followed by violent rows. Once, a man had hammered on her door, demanding admittance, clearly mistaking it for his own abode. When morning came and she had tried to open her door, a huge man had been lying across it, clearly having fallen asleep without managing to identify his own apartment.

She ran up the steps again and tore the envelope down, crumpling it into a ball and dropping it into her pocket. Martin knew she had no food in the house, would guess she had gone shopping and would either wait or come back later. Satisfied, Rose descended the stairs again and headed for the tram stop. She did her shopping, choosing what to buy with all her usual care, thinking how strange it was to be considering another person, wondering whether Martin preferred cabbage or sprouts, being extra specially nice to the butcher so that she might beg a bone for the dog and asking shyly whether he knew where she might buy cheap dog meat.

The butcher directed her to Billy, the dogs' meat man, who sold her what he described as 'lights': a glutinous mass of scarlet tissue which he assured her her dog would relish. 'But you've gotta cook it. Cover it wi' water and boil it up in a big old pan until it's a nice dark brahn,' he instructed her. He was a big hefty man, red-faced and jovial, with gingery hair and yellowish, broken teeth. 'What kind of dog is it? A big 'un . . . say an Alsatian . . . or a little terrier? I should have asked, 'cos that 'ud make six meals for a Yorkie and one for an Alsatian.'

'He's a greyhound,' Rose said. 'Someone must have turned him out, 'cos he was starving and soaked to the skin, but he's gentle as a lamb. Only I know with people, if they've been very hungry for a long time, you have to feed 'em gradual like. Is it the same for dogs?'

'Aye, you're right there. It's wicked the way they treats them greyhounds,' Billy said, twisting his big red face into an expression of disgust. 'They're pleased enough to rake in the money when the poor critters is a-chasin' that hare and winnin', but the moment they begin to flag it's out on the street and fend for yourselves. I like dogs better'n people; they don't cheat or steal or murder one another, like what some folk do.' He cocked his head on one side and grinned at his customer. 'I know what you're a-going to say. Dogs do steal sometimes, but they'll only do that when they're starvin', and it's people what starve them. D'you know that in the wild, when a wolf pack makes a kill, the puppies get first go at it? Then the others have a turn until everyone's fed. I read that in a book—I'm a great reader.'

Rose, dawdling home with her laden basket, thought that you could never tell about folk from appearances. Fancy a rough-looking fellow like Billy, the dogs' meat man, knowing so much and admitting to being a reader.

Back in the flat once more, she boiled up the disgusting-looking meat and had to open all the windows to get rid of the smell. Billy had told her that all his meat was marked so that anyone buying it could see that it was unfit for human

54

consumption, and sure enough the red mass had a stripe of green dye right the way across it, but Rose thought, wrinkling her nose, that it would be a desperate human indeed who was tempted to eat the horrible stuff.

She tipped Billy's offering into an ancient bucket and pushed it under the sink, thinking how delighted both Martin and Don would be to find that she had provided the dog with a good meal. Then she began to peel vegetables; when she had the stew simmering on the stove she would do some tray-baking for the matron. Miss Haverstock always paid promptly. Rose had found the old people's home by chance, and had realised at once that cooking for Matron was ideal. She told Rose what she required and Rose supplied it; the old people liked simple, easy to digest food, and were especially fond of cakes and pies.

Rose began to collect her ingredients, humming a little tune as she did so and realising, suddenly, that she had lied when she had told Martin she did not like living in the flats. In daylight, when most of the other tenants were out, she was content enough, particularly when she was cooking, her mind and hands occupied. She liked the small independence that selling her baking provided, too, and hugged the secret that she could earn money tightly to her own breast. She only hated the long cold flights of concrete stairs, the unreliability of the lift and the youths who congregated in the tower blocks, ripe for mischief. She feared the neighbours and their frequent drinking bouts and cowered in her bed when the men banged on her door and shouted lewd remarks in slurred voices. She guessed the remarks would get worse as her condition became more obvious.

In her heart she disliked her reliance upon her 'friend' because she was always aware that she had no real right to the place she called home. If Mrs Ellis chose, she could get Rose turned out tomorrow, and though Rose told herself constantly that the older woman would do no such thing, in the back of her mind there was always a tiny, niggling doubt. She reminded herself that the flat had been Mrs Ellis's idea and that she, Rose, had done Mrs Ellis an enormous favour. Casting her mind back, she remembered Mrs Ellis pleading with her, the tears running down her face, promising that she would do anything, anything at all, if only Rose would swear to her that she would never, ever . . .

Hastily, Rose pushed the recollection back to where it belonged. She was a very lucky girl to have such a friend and she told herself, as she had done many times before, that she would keep her promise; that wild horses would never drag the truth from her.

Carefully measuring the ingredients into her big yellow bowl, Rose began to count her blessings. There was heating in the flat during the winter months, though it was only turned on for a few hours, morning and evening; and she would have been the first to acknowledge that the views from her sitting room and bedroom were stunning. She had a tiny balcony across which she had strung a stout rope to dry her washing when the weather was clement.

One of her first purchases when she had moved into the flat had been the small Bakelite radio which plugged into the electric so she did not have the bother of buying batteries. To be sure, in order to hear her favourite programmes, she had to fill the electricity meter with shillings, but she thought it was a small price to pay for entertainment. *Pick of the Pops* was a great favourite, but so were *Mrs Dale's Diary, The Billy Cotton Band Show* and, best of all, *Paul Temple*. She only had to hear the music start to be transported to another world, where Paul and Steve reigned supreme, and evil was always vanquished.

She had the radio on now, playing what she thought of as background music because she had it turned very low. The kitchen was warm and comfortable with the sweet smell of baking, and she was just telling herself that she much preferred her own company to that of anyone else when she heard footsteps on the stairs outside. She thought it must be Martin and Don, and was surprised to realise that she was quite looking forward to feeding them both, though as a rule she was happier alone and considered other people an intrusion. Was Martin different? She remembered his strange face, his horrid pink eyes and the long, thin length of him, and decided that she had little interest in the youth but was keen to see Don again. She had always wanted a dog and all the previous day had enjoyed his friendship. Martin was just a boy, even though he was eighteen, and so peculiar-looking that now she was glad the inside of the lorry's cab had been dark, as it had meant that the friendly driver had seen them only as an ordinary couple of young people, rain-soaked and weary.

She was actually crossing the hall and heading

57

for the front door when the footsteps shambled past and she heard the sound of a key grating in a lock. Disappointed despite herself, she turned back to the kitchen and her work, feeding the meter with a couple of shillings so that the oven would not go off at a crucial moment in her cooking.

For the rest of the afternoon, she put Martin and Don out of her mind. They had undoubtedly gone to Martin's place but would, she was sure, turn up at the flat again quite soon. After all, Martin had offered financial help if she would be kind enough to feed himself and the dog. A fully grown greyhound was not easy to miss and not easy to feed, either. Martin would undoubtedly be round for scraps to satisfy Don's appetite. Rose turned the radio up a little louder and ignored the next set of footsteps on the stairs.

Chapter Three

Martin slouched along the street with Don so close on his heels that the dog's nose collided with his calves whenever he stopped to look in a shop window or to stand on the kerb, waiting to cross. He had been to collect his dole money for the third time since his visit to Southport, and was fighting a ridiculous urge to make his way to Everton Brow and the tower block in which Rose Pleavin lived. After all, he reminded himself, she had definitely taken to Don and had seemed to suggest that they might share responsibility for him. He knew of course that she could not seek him out, and chided himself for cowardice because he would not return to the flat for fear of a rebuff. He had promised Rose that he would wash his socks, which were more hole than wool, but instead he had gone straight from her flat to Paddy's Market and spent the last of his precious money on two pairs, not new but not full of holes either. Now he felt that she would think him lazy and a spendthrift should she see the new socks.

Then, of course, he had gone along to the Labour Exchange, who had given him his dole but had not been able to help him find a job. However, by haunting the builders' yards, he had actually got a couple of days' labouring for a bricklayer whose usual workman had taken to his bed with an attack of flu. It was hard and heavy work but the extra money was welcome, though Martin knew better than to tell the Labour Exchange he had found a temporary job. He had done that once and had had no money at all for six terrible weeks, apart from his small earnings, which had ceased after a fortnight anyway. This job had been similar in that the bricklayer had employed him for a couple of days which had turned into the best part of a couple of weeks, but after that the usual labourer had come back to work. The brickie had paid up the money owing to Martin but it had been done grudgingly, which Martin thought unkind. He had performed every task put upon him while Don waited patiently outside the building site, even though the dog's affection for Martin was such that he rarely wandered more than a couple of yards away from his master.

Of course, human nature being what it is, Martin had hoped that another labouring job on the site

59

might come up. He dreamed of a permanent wage which would enable him to rent a room for himself and Don, for despite the fact that it was now mid-February the weather showed no sign of spring. In fact, heavy snowfalls had taken the place of the rain, blocking major roads and causing chaos even in the city. Naturally enough, the severe weather brought all building work to a halt, so Martin was not the only one unable to find a job.

Martin's doorway was deep but he felt sorry for Don, who was too big to get into the sleeping bag and so curled up in the space between Martin and the door. He had proved his worth already, though, and Martin knew he had reason to be grateful to the big dog. A large man, probably a tramp, had tried to oust Martin from his sleeping place a couple of days after he and Don had got back to Liverpool, and as soon as the big dog realised that the man was trying to take Martin's place his gentleness had fled. He had shouldered his way to the front of the doorway, his lips curling back to reveal a set of workmanlike teeth. His ears had flattened and his head had gone forward, whilst a blood-curling growl had issued from his open mouth. At the same time, a ridge of hair all along his back had risen up and Martin, who had heard the term 'his hackles rose' without understanding it, now saw exactly what it meant. Don was saying: 'This is *our* place, and if you try to so much as put a foot over our threshold, I'll have you!'

The tramp had read the message correctly, had said Don was a dangerous wild beast and should be put down, but had backed off. Don had stood in the doorway, growling beneath his breath, until he must have concluded that the tramp was no longer a threat. Then he had returned almost sheepishly to Martin's side, licked his cheek and curled up. Martin had put his arms round the big dog's neck and given him a hug. 'Thanks, old feller,' he had whispered. 'I couldn't have found a better pal than you if I'd searched the whole world over.'

The dog had licked his cheek again and Martin had tried to dispel the memory of a small freckled face fringed with untidy red hair. She was just a girl, not even a particularly nice one, who had seemed to offer him friendship and then snatched it away again. But when I have a home of my own and a proper job, I believe I'll go back, he had told himself, snuggling down into the sleeping bag and pulling his feet up because the end of the bag was still damp from the previous night's snow. After all, she is going to have a baby; I remember reading once that a woman what's in the family way acts different from normal. Mebbe when the baby's born she'll realise that she needs a friend.

For the next couple of days he had got a job delivering newspapers—someone else, bless 'em, had gone down with the flu—but the job did not last. The rightful owner came back and Martin was once more wandering the cold streets and trying for any job that came up. Before meeting Don, Martin had had a vague idea that dogs lived on bones, but was soon disabused by a friendly butcher who had told him that he should buy dog biscuits and meat scraps. 'Else the poor old chap's teeth will fall out,' he had assured his customer. 'And you wouldn't want that, eh? Greyhounds is grand dogs, loyal and loving. Here, I've some scraps of meat in the back—gi' me a tanner and

61

they're yours.'

Martin had shelled out willingly but found himself wishing that he, too, could eat dog biscuits and scraps. The cold was beginning to tell on him; his feet never seemed to get warm and when he examined his toes by the light of his torch he was worried by the fact that the nails looked a very strange colour and his flesh did not respond when he tried to rub it into life. This was his first winter of sleeping rough and he thought, ruefully, that he could not have chosen a worse one. Several times he had found dead pigeons, their little frozen corpses pathetic signs of the extreme cold. He had taken one back to his doorway, plucked it and presented it to the dog. Don had given him a reproachful look, or so Martin had interpreted it, and had not eaten the offering.

Nights were bad, because Martin began to fear that the cold might take him in his sleep and he'd wake up dead, but days were almost worse. Before the dog had come into his life Martin, along with other unemployed men, had spent long hours in the Picton Library on William Brown Street, or in the museum next door, or the Walker Art Gallery. He had read books, newspapers and magazines, studied the museum exhibits and gazed with pleasure at the paintings. But now this was impossible, because no dogs were allowed inside any of the public buildings and Martin could not bear to leave his friend outside in the cold whilst he himself was warm.

It was much the same in cafés and restaurants. As a customer, he would have been welcome in most of the city's many eating places, but as a dog owner he had been told brusquely to 'leave the dog outside or find yourself somewhere else to eat'. Martin, the least aggressive of men, had almost had a stand-up fight with a café proprietor on Lime Street. He and Don had gone in and Martin had taken a seat in the darkest corner, pushing the dog under the table, if not out of sight at least out of everyone's way. The waitress had approached, and Martin had opened his mouth to ask for a pot of tea and a round of toast when there had been a slight scuffling from beneath the next table and a Yorkshire terrier had shot out and begun to yap furiously. Its owner, a plump woman in her forties, with stiffly permed and bleached hair, had dragged on the little dog's lead but had said, in a voice loud enough to almost drown out her dog's yapping: 'That's all right, Sparky, my love, don't you fret. Mr Huxtable will turn the horrid creature out, see if he don't.'

Hot on the heels of the remark, the proprietor had waddled over to her table. 'Everything all right, Mrs Ponsonby?'

Mrs Ponsonby had picked up her pet, trying to muffle its barks against her huge bosom, and pointed a trembling finger at Don, sitting quietly beneath Martin's table and not so much as glancing at Sparky. 'Oh, Mr Huxtable, my poor little man is terrified by that brute there,' she had said. 'Make that person take it away before it leaps on Sparky and crunches him up.'

Mr Huxtable had turned in a majestic fashion towards Martin, who had broken into speech at once in defence of his friend. 'This here's Don, and he's gentle as a lamb,' he had said. 'He won't hurt anyone, I promise you. But it's mortal cold out—'

63

Mr Huxtable had wagged his head reprovingly. 'We don't have dawgs in here,' he had announced firmly. 'Gerrout of it, the pair of you!'

'But you let the lady bring her dog in,' Martin had muttered. 'And it's her dog that's makin' all the fuss. Why don't you tell them to leave?'

Mrs Ponsonby and Mr Huxtable had both swelled with indignation and, upset though he was, Martin had had hard work not to smile. He thought they could both have modelled for Tweedledum and Tweedledee in the Alice stories, but had decided that his best move would be to order the pot of tea and the toast for which he had been longing. So he had smiled at the objectionable pair, smoothed his hand along the greyhound's silky neck and said to the waitress, 'A pot of tea for one and a round of buttered toast, please.'

Mr Huxtable had actually hesitated, looking uncertain, but Mrs Ponsonby had swung round on him, her bulging cheeks flaming beneath their layer of powder. 'If you serve that—that wastrel, I'll never come into this establishment again,' she had hissed. 'Take it or leave it.'

Mr Huxtable had turned to Martin. 'No one will serve you. Go on, gerrout of it! We don't want the likes of you in here, dog or no dog.'

For a moment Martin had fought an urgent desire to give the fat little proprietor a good shove in his pot belly and see him reduced to the figure of fun he had thought him. Then he had sighed, shrugged and put a hand on Don's head, rising to his feet as he did so. 'C'mon, old feller. I reckon it's one of them places where they toasts yesterday's bread and spits in the tea,' he had said loftily. 'I'll tell all me friends it's run by a feller who knows no better than to insult his customers before refusing to serve them.'

Mr Huxtable had begun to bluster, Mrs Ponsonby had used regrettable language and, as Martin and Don had stalked past, the Yorkshire terrier had leaned out of his mistress's arms and grabbed Don's ear. Martin, roused to fury by the uncalled-for attack, had seized the little dog by the bow on top of its head and had slapped it resoundingly, whereupon Sparky had released his grip on Don's ear, leaving half a dozen bleeding tooth marks, and tried to attack Martin.

'Why, you wicked young devil,' Mrs Ponsonby had screeched. 'How dare you hit my little dog, you great bully! I'm going straight round to the police station—me brother's a policeman—and you'll find yourself behind bars, or me name's not Ponsonby.'

The waitress, an interested observer, had snatched up a scone from the serving hatch and pressed it into Martin's hand. 'Don't take no notice of old Mrs P. You go along to Lily's Tea Rooms on London Road,' she had whispered. 'She's me auntie and she don't charge half of what old Huxtable does. Tell her as how Nellie sent you and she'll let the dog in an' all.' Aloud, she had said: 'Sorry about the fuss, mister, but Mrs Ponsonby is a regular, and what with the snow an' all . . .'

Martin had muttered that he quite understood and had left, but the nasty little incident had been a reminder of his vulnerability. If someone reported him to the police, then it could only be a matter of time before they discovered that he was

65

sleeping rough and took some action, perhaps forcing him to take a place in one of the lodging houses down by the docks. Worst of all, they would take Don away from him. He really must be more careful.

So now, because he could not visit such places as libraries and museums with Don, he walked miles, because at least walking was warmer work than merely hanging about outside the big stores to get what shelter he could from the wind and snow, and to enjoy, whenever the doors opened, a gust of warm air from within. He told himself constantly that March, when it came, would bring the first breath of spring. But this was hard to believe when the snow was piled up on the pavements in little-used side streets and the lake in Prince's Park was frozen solid.

He often pictured Rose, holed up in her warm little flat at the top of the tower block, but his image of her was becoming increasingly blurred. He sometimes thought, ruefully, that he had left it too long to go calling on her; she would wonder why he had not come before. He reminded himself that she had seemed to love Don as much as he did. By now she might be thinking he had deliberately avoided her in order to keep the dog to himself. The thought was a dismaying one and he decided, not for the first time, that as soon as he got a job . . .

That evening Martin was feeling almost cheerful, despite the fact that it had started snowing again. After collecting his dole money he had decided to splash out on some fish and chips. The proprietor's wife at the nearest chippy had taken a liking to Don and usually saved him what looked

66

to Martin like a disgusting mess of fish bits, which she doused generously in batter and fried up whenever she saw Martin and his dog in the queue. Martin thought her a lovely lady, though her sandy hair, little pale blue eyes and large turned-up nose gave her a close resemblance to a pig. The impression was not helped by the bright pink overall she always wore, or by the fact that she snorted rather than laughed when amused. But she was kind and must have guessed that he was sleeping rough, for whenever he bought fish and chips, which he did now at least twice a week, she always handed him, along with the food, a pile of newspapers. Newsprint was excellent insulation and Martin was grateful both for Don's scraps and for the tactfulness with which she handed over his bedding.

So now, mouths watering with anticipation, Martin and Don joined the queue and presently left the shop, Martin clutching the beautiful hot parcels to his chest beneath his duffel coat and Don raising worshipful eyes to his master's face. Martin made straight for the builder's yard, hauled out his sleeping bag from its hiding place behind the pile of bricks, and draped it round his neck. Then he and Don hurried to the doorway which had been home to them since leaving the tower block. Martin made his arrangements, piling up the new newspapers and fishing the old ones out from the bottom of his sleeping bag, where he put them when he removed every trace of his occupancy before daylight each morning. He was pretty sure that Mr Seddon, who owned the shop, knew that Martin was his uninvited guest each night, but turned a blind eye. Perhaps Mr Seddon had known hard times, understood Martin's desperation, but whatever the reason his doorway was a life-saver and he had become one of the people to whom Martin felt he owed a great debt.

Having spread out his newspapers, checked the direction of the wind—it was blowing away from the doorway—and inserting himself into the sleeping bag, Martin unwrapped Don's fish pieces and laid them out before him. 'Would you like 'em salt and vinegared, sir?' he said, in a squeaky falsetto. 'Ketchup is tuppence extra; d'you fancy ketchup?'

Don gave him an indulgent glance; it was clear that neither salt and vinegar nor ketchup appealed, but the big dog always waited for Martin to unwrap his own food before he himself started to eat. Very soon both were giving satisfied but regretful sighs and Martin was scrumpling up the outer wrappings and settling back. 'Weren't that just grand, old feller? And now I believe I could nod off, 'cos I'm full of good food and me sleepin' bag is only slightly damp on the outside.'

With some reluctance, he took off his trusty duffel coat and the thickest of his three ragged jerseys. Then he slid out of his spare pair of socks, which he wore during the daytime both for extra warmth and because that way he was unlikely to lose them. He pushed the clothing to the very end of the sleeping bag—extra insulation—and stood his precious boots against the shop door, where no thieves were likely to come upon them. Then he cuddled down, using Don as a pillow.

Sometimes Martin lay for ages, shivering with the cold and wondering what would become of him if the severe weather did not lift soon, but tonight he slept deeply and was almost startled out of his life when he became aware of a bright and dazzling light focused on his face and a booming voice, almost in his ear. He hitched himself on to one elbow and peered in the direction of the light, conscious that Don was beginning to bristle. He looped a restraining arm round the strong, grey neck. 'Whazza marrer?' he said thickly. 'We ain't doin' no one no harm, me and me dog.'

He had screwed up his eyes against the bright light but now he glared at the intruder and was astonished when the man uttered a startled oath, which was followed by a crash as he dropped his torch. 'Bloody 'ell!' the hoarse voice remarked. 'What the devil is you? You'd best come out of that . . . unless you're a two-headed monster or a vampire, of course, in which case you can stay where you are whiles I fetches a stake to drive through your heart.'

'I dunno what you mean,' Martin said; then, as he scrambled to his feet, he chuckled. 'Oh, I see. You saw me dog's eyes as well as mine, and of course mine must look rare strange by torchlight. Come to that,' he added truthfully, 'I reckon they're pretty odd by daylight, but we're neither of us doing any harm, honest to God we're not.'

'I dare say,' the man said. 'But you aren't doing yourself much good either, lad. Why aren't you in a hostel, or in your own home, come to that? It's only just stopped snowing and from the look of the clouds it'll start again any minute. Now come along with me and I'll get you a bed for the rest of the night, even if it's only an empty cell at the station.'

The man bent and picked up his torch and pointed it at himself. It illumined his helmet and a

69

round and rosy face, confirming that he was a policeman. 'Thank the lord my torch isn't broken or I'd have had to pay for a replacement,' he said. 'Put your shoes on, lad, and pick up your belongings. Then we'll be on our way. I'll see you comfortably settled with a nice hot cup of tea and a couple of good thick blankets, and tomorrow morning we'll talk about your future. I guess you haven't got a job or you wouldn't be sleeping rough. How old are you, by the way? You can give me the rest of your details when we reach the nick.'

'I'm eighteen,' Martin muttered. 'And what'll happen to me dog? I can't see any scuffer letting him share me bed.'

'There's dog pounds and kennels and that; he'll be all right,' the policeman said vaguely. 'Hurry up with your boots; I'm beginning to feel cold even if you aren't.' He looked up at the sky and heaved a sigh. 'There, I told you, it's starting to snow again. *Will* you get a move on, young feller!'

He bent as he spoke, clearly intending to pull the sleeping bag out of the doorway, and Martin seized his chance. He shot past the man's bulky figure, knocking him as he passed and sending him sprawling, and began to run down the street. His feet skidded and slipped on the frozen pavement, but he scarcely noticed, though it did occur to him that he had not had time to lace his boots and he must not spoil everything by coming a cropper. As soon as they reached a side street, Martin and Don swerved into it, and after dodging into every little alley they saw Martin slowed and looked behind him. There was no sign of the policeman, who must have guessed that he was unlikely to catch

70

the two fugitives, but Martin realised that he was now in a desperate situation indeed. His sleeping bag and his collection of newspapers had been left behind, along with his coat, thick jersey and spare socks. What was even worse was that the doorway was lost to him, for he could not possibly go back. He had no doubt that it would be watched, and though the scuffer had seemed a kindly man and would probably take his sleeping bag back to the police station, he would leave the newspapers where they were. Mr Seddon would not be pleased to find them there, especially since he would also find the greasy chip wrappings which Martin would normally have disposed of in the dustbin at the back of the builder's yard.

He had no idea of the time and even less idea of where he was, for so constantly had he changed direction that he was now completely lost. His situation was not helped by the fact that it was beginning to snow quite heavily. For a moment, tears pricked in the corners of his eyes and he actually considered giving himself up to the law and taking whatever punishment would await him for sending the scuffer flying as he and Don had made their escape. He had not meant to do it, but who would believe him? Then he looked down at Don and knew that he could not hand himself in. He was determined that he and the big dog should not be parted, yet unless he found shelter he knew they would not survive for long. He supposed that he might be able to persuade the lady in the chip shop to look after the dog for a few days, but that would mean returning to the area he had just left.

He was beginning to shiver and looked round desperately for some sort of shelter. There were

71

plenty of houses around, but none of them had so much as a porch in which he and the dog could take refuge. Telling himself to stop panicking, he examined his surroundings carefully. He had somehow managed to take only turnings which led uphill and suddenly he thought of the tower blocks up on Everton Brow. He was pretty sure that if he kept on climbing he would see the blocks and could make for them, and though he could not possibly expect Rose to answer the door to him in the middle of the night, at least he could lie down somewhere in the foyer of her building until daylight. It would not be warm but at least he would be out of the snow, which was already beginning to penetrate his thin clothing. And when it was daylight, he would explain his situation to Rose and ask her to take care of Don whilst he returned to the police station and faced the music.

Immensely cheered, he began to climb.

*   *   *

Rose woke. She had cramp in one foot and a desperate need to pee, but even as she sighed to herself and began to shrug off the covers she thought that it was not just the cramp or the urge for the lavvy that had woken her. There had been a sound—not a particularly loud or aggressive one—that was unusual enough to bring her back to consciousness. So she sat up on one elbow and listened hard . . . and there it was again, a sort of skittering, scratching noise.

Rats! Rose gave a shudder, then scolded herself. So far as she knew there had been no talk of rats in the block; she herself had never even seen a

72

mouse. Besides, she had personally left the door to the foyer a little open when she had come in from a shopping expedition that evening because she knew that the feral cats which lived on the scraps she and some of the other tenants put out would be glad of the shelter. Those cats would not allow mice—or rats—to take up residence in a block where they were fed.

Comforted, she swung her feet out of bed and reached for her torch, thinking smugly how fortunate she was to have her own bathroom and lavatory. Of course the home had had such things, but she knew that many private houses did not. She had visited friends from school who had to use a chamber pot by night or a privy in their back yard by day.

She never closed her bedroom door now because when she needed to go she wanted to do so immediately. She left the bathroom door open too, which gave her a clear run. She had told Mrs Ellis rather shyly about this sudden change and the older woman had said that it was the result of the baby pressing against her bladder, so Rose had stopped worrying. She had just finished and was about to pull the chain when she heard a snuffling sort of sound, as though someone—or something—was breathing so close to her front door that it must have been that which had woken her.

Under normal circumstances Rose was far too afraid of her neighbours to open the door at night; indeed, she hesitated to do so during the day without first demanding the credentials of whoever had knocked, but for some reason she went straight to the door and began to unbolt it. Then she opened it a crack and peered through. There was someone lying directly outside her door, but before she could wonder who it was she heard a shrill whine and there was Don, grinning at her and wagging his tail.

Rose's heart bounded; they had come back! She flung the door wide, then bent down and shook Martin's shoulder. He was shivering violently, his clothing wet, and to her dismay she saw that he was not wearing a coat or any other outer garment. 'Martin, come inside at once! You must be mad to come out in this weather without so much as a coat,' she said. 'What's happened? Had a row with your landlord? I thought you might be at the YMCA, but they said not. But never mind that, you can tell me presently. Come on in and I'll light the stove.'

Martin muttered something and tried to get to his feet. Rose attempted to help him but he was too heavy for her and in the end he crawled across her little hall before collapsing in the kitchen. Rose was frightened but lit the oven, leaving the door open to warm the room. Then she half filled the kettle and set it on the stove, telling Martin brusquely that he must get out of his wet clothes as quickly as possible. She hurried into the bathroom, grabbed a towel and then hesitated. Turning back, she put the plug in the bath and turned the hot tap on full. She remembered reading somewhere that the best way to treat an ice-cold body was to immerse it in warm water, so instead of taking the towel to Martin she hung it on the rail and then returned to her uninvited guest. He had stripped down to his trousers and was looking a little better, though still white as a ghost—but when was he

74

not?—and exhausted.

'I've run you a bath. You best gerrin it and warm up, and when you're feelin' more like yourself the kettle will have boiled and you can tell me what's been happening over a nice cuppa,' she said. 'Honest to God, I seem to spend half me time rescuin' you and old Don here from the weather! Remember last time?'

He grinned and said hoarsely: 'As if I could forget. But I didn't like to impose . . .'

Rose shook her head at him. 'Bath first, talk after,' she said, pushing him towards the door. 'I'll cook up some porridge; that'll line both our stomachs, 'cos wakin' in the middle of the night has made me hungry as a wolf.'

Martin shambled across the hall and disappeared into the bathroom and Rose turned back into the kitchen and began to make porridge. Don had laid himself down in front of the open oven door, but when she fetched an old blanket from her bedroom he curled up on it without complaint and she realised that he was in much better condition than he had been the last time she had seen him. So Martin's been feeding him and probably half starving himself, she thought and felt a stab of guilt because she had not guessed that Martin had needed help even more than Don. Then she scolded herself for stupidity; he had walked out on her, not the other way around. He had gone without a proper farewell, taking the dog, which she had thought they would share, with him.

She had meant to search the city centre, to ask folk in shops whether they had seen a tall, skinny, rather odd-looking boy accompanied by a large greyhound, but apart from a visit to the nearest

75

YMCA she had always been too busy. As the weeks passed, of course, she had become so involved with the intricacies of childbirth, getting books out of the library, comparing notes with other mothers-to-be or young women who had already given birth and were eager to talk babies with anyone who would listen, that she had pushed Martin and Don to the back of her mind. She had told herself that they would turn up one day and had never dreamed for one moment that they needed her. If they did, why on earth had they not come calling before?

The porridge was steaming in the bowls and Don was licking out the saucepan when Martin shuffled into the kitchen. She saw with approval that he had wrapped himself in the blanket which she had hung on the outside of the bathroom door and put her old carpet slippers upon his feet, and was relieved when he grinned at her. 'Sorry to barge in on you, Rosie,' he said. She could tell he was trying to sound humble, though it didn't quite come off. 'But we was desperate, me and the old feller here.' He glanced around the room, then pointed. 'You've gorra second chair!'

'That's right,' Rose said. 'Me friend, the one I told you about, got fed up wi' standin' or using my hope chest so she give me an old chair which she was goin' to throw out. But don't change the subject. What happened to you after you left here that morning?'

'It's not a very nice story,' Martin said apologetically. 'I've had a couple o' temporary jobs, takin' the place of fellers what were off wi' this here flu, but apart from them things have been pretty bleak for me and Don . . .'

The story did not take long to tell but it appalled Rose. 'You're a fool, Mart,' she said roundly. 'If only I'd knowed what were happenin' to you . . . well, you could be sure I'd have done something to help. But you haven't said why you went off like that, nor why you didn't come back.'

'I thought you didn't want me around when you wouldn't let me buy a woolly ball for the baby,' Martin said, looking shamefaced. 'I'd made up me mind that I'd come back and see you just as soon as I had a proper job and somewhere to live. Part of the trouble has been old Don here. He's the best pal a feller could have but folk what let cheap lodgings won't take dogs, especially big ones. Even places like the Picton Library won't let a dog inside the doors. Though in fact Don saved my bacon more'n once when I were sleepin' in Mr Seddon's doorway. It's a grand, deep doorway, well out of the wind and snow, so if it hadn't been for Don seeing off tramps and that I'd soon have been turned out. But of course a scuffer is different. I don't deny old Don bristled up and muttered beneath his breath, but he never growled or showed his teeth like he done when tramps or other down-and-outs tried to take our place.' He looked at Rose from under his lashes. 'And it was me that knocked against him and sent him sprawling, though it was an accident,' he said. 'But once the scuffers know where you're kipping down, you can't ever go back. It don't matter who's on that particular beat, the scuffer on duty will check Mr Seddon's doorway every hour or so. In fact it's a perishin' miracle that I weren't picked up weeks ago.'

'I know there's been a lot of this flu you

mentioned amongst the police force, so scuffers have been pretty thin on the ground, and if the doorway was as deep as you say they simply mayn't have noticed you,' Rose observed. 'Particularly when you think that it's snowed heavily most nights for—oh, for ages. What's more, a lot of scuffers are happy enough to let a tramp lie warm and dry rather than having to find him a bed which the feller won't want anyway.' She grinned at him. 'So mebbe your luck was in. Only personally, if I were you, I'd rather sleep on me sitting room floor than the deepest doorway in Liverpool.'

Martin scraped his porridge bowl energetically, then went over to the sink and began to wash up. He picked up the porridge saucepan and ran water into it, commenting as he did so that Don had made such a good job of licking it out that washing up seemed unnecessary.

Rose laughed. She, who so liked her own company, realised with surprise that she was enjoying entertaining both Martin and the dog. Indeed, she knew that with the half of her mind not engaged in listening to Martin's story she had been planning a quick dash to the shops, where she would buy dog biscuits and any meat scraps a butcher would sell her cheap. 'Thanks for the suggestion, but I think I prefer to have it thoroughly rinsed out,' she said. 'Dog lick is awful sticky. And now we'd best make plans, Martin, 'cos I don't mean to let you out of this place until you swear on the Holy Bible that you won't run away again.'

Martin began to agree but his words were cut off by an enormous, jaw-cracking yawn and Rose realised that he was in no condition to think logically. 'Sorry, Mart. I'm pretty tired myself, but you must be absolutely shattered. The sitting room isn't as warm as the kitchen but I reckon the sofa's softer than the kitchen floor. I'll fetch an old cushion and you and Don will probably be asleep before I shut the door. I'll give you a shout in the morning—your clothes ought to be dry by then— and we'll talk about what to do next. Is that all right by you?'

Martin nodded and got to his feet. 'You are good, Rose,' he said gratefully. 'See you in the mornin'.'

Rose had thought that she would sleep as soon as her head touched the pillow, but this did not prove to be the case. As soon as she closed her eyes, a picture of Mrs Ellis appeared behind her eyelids, wagging a reproving finger. Then others joined her: teachers from school as well as Miss Haverstock and some of the old people, to say nothing of various neighbours in the tower block. They were all pointing at her and she could read disgust and disapproval in their narrowed eyes. She knew at once what they meant. Nice girls, decent girls, did not invite young men into their homes. Of course it was nobody's business but hers, really; she could say to neighbours and others that Martin was the father and they were going to marry, but Mrs Ellis at least would not be taken in.

If I let Martin stay in my flat, then Mrs Ellis will get me evicted, Rose told herself gloomily. She will say that we made a bargain and Mart was no part of it. The neighbours don't matter because I don't believe she knows any of them. But word gets around and the last thing on earth I want to do is marry Martin. He's nice all right, but . . . oh, weird!

79

Imagine waking up one morning to find a pair of strange reddish eyes glaring at you from the pillow next to your head. And there's more to marriage than glaring eyes; there's all that grabbing and prodding . . . I don't ever mean to go through *that* again. Not with anyone, least of all someone who ought to be in a perishin' circus!

However, she did not think she could bear to see Martin return to his life on the streets. If only she could find him a job! She knew, of course, and guessed that he knew also, that his appearance was against him. People in shops and offices thought his strangeness would affect their business, whilst other jobs needed more physical strength than employers thought he possessed. He looked weak, being so long and thin and pale, though in fact he was strong enough.

So if she could not invite Martin to stay, what could she do for him? She could offer to take Don off his hands, but that could only be during daylight hours. At night Martin needed the dog's protection, and anyway, she doubted that Don would willingly stay with her in the flat whilst Martin scoured the streets for work. If only Martin was not so weird-looking! She thought he had grown a good deal weirder since they had last met. His white hair was shaggy and unkempt, as well as far too long, and what clothing he had was almost in rags and sadly in need of a wash. His nails were grimy and broken off short and though he had told her that he had eaten at least one good meal a day she thought that he must have exaggerated, for he was horribly skinny, the bones of his elbows and shoulders far too prominent.

Desperately, Rose turned the problem over and

over in her mind. If he could only find work, then she could go with him to buy sensible warm clothing. She had her small savings but guessed he would not take her money, though if she could persuade him that decently clad he was far more employable he might at least borrow from her.

She was still trying to think of a solution when the sky outside the window turned from night to day and, abruptly, she fell asleep.

*   *   *

Martin awoke, feeling so strange that for a moment he thought himself a boy again, back in the sick bay at the Arbuthnot Boys' Home, for he was burning hot and aching all over. Then he glanced around him and knew at once that he was in Rose's sitting room, curled up on her sofa with Don's head resting across his ankles. The light outside showed that morning had come, for neither he nor Rose had thought to draw the curtains across.

He sat up on one elbow and listened: no sound. Gently, he disengaged his ankles from Don's weight and stood up. To his horror, the room whirled around him and the floor came up to meet him. He fell to his knees on the linoleum feeling weak and odd, telling himself that this was no time to come over all queer. He must pull himself together or . . . or . . .

He sat down on the sofa again. He had felt like this once before, long ago. He had not known it at the time but he had been sickening for measles and could still remember how dreadful he had felt for the first two or three days. His sight, never good, had become very much worse and Matron had ended up by taking him to someone she described as 'a special eye doctor', who had provided him with spectacles.

Sitting on the sofa, he pulled up the sleeve of his ragged shirt, his heart thumping hard. Could one get measles twice? He supposed it must be possible, but his arm was as pale as ever, with no sign of a spot. Well, if it wasn't measles, he was probably quite all right, and was just feeling hot because he was no longer used to indoor living. Very, very cautiously he stood up. Immediately, the giddy sensation attacked him once more, but this time he remained standing. He had intended to go through into the kitchen to make Rose a cup of tea and some toast, and now he told himself that since he appeared not to have measles, he might safely do this. He remembered that Matron had told him he must not infect other children, so he would not have dreamed of taking Rose so much as a drink of water had he found any sign of spots.

Standing, swaying a little, he began to shiver, which was absurd because he was burning hot. Hastily, he reached for his clothing but had to sit down on the sofa again before he could even begin to dress. Once clad, he pushed his bare feet into the old carpet slippers—he dared not bend to put on his socks for as soon as he tried to do so giddiness swept over him once again—and shuffled along to the bathroom to relieve himself. Remembering the hygiene rules instilled into him at the Arbuthnot, he washed his hands and dried them on the towel he had used the previous evening before setting off for the kitchen. He glanced towards Rose's bedroom as he crossed the hall and was surprised and rather gratified to see that the door had been left wide open. Clearly, she trusted him, and did not fear that he might spy on her whilst she slept.

Reaching the kitchen, he picked up the kettle and was surprised at how heavy it felt. He lifted the lid and saw it was half full, so he stood it on the stove and turned on the heat. Even that slight exertion set his heart banging once more, so he decided against trying to make toast and contented himself with pouring tea and milk into two mugs. He left his own on the kitchen table and set off to take Rose hers. Halfway across the hall, he realised that he was still shaking, which probably meant that he was also spilling. Sure enough, when he looked over his shoulder, he saw a trail of tea in his wake. He stopped, dismayed, then smiled as Don, following him, began to lick up the tea with great enthusiasm. Good old Don. Rose would never know how clumsy he had been.

Reaching her doorway, he tapped, and when he heard a sleepy mumble he entered the room. He went over to the bed, trying not to stare as she sat up groggily, and set the mug down on the bedside cabinet, saying: 'I made you some tea, Rosie. I meant to make toast but I couldn't see the loaf and it seemed a bit cheeky to go ferretin' through your cupboards.'

He swayed again, put out a hand to steady himself and heard Rose's startled exclamation as the wall disappeared beneath his fingers and he crashed to the floor, sending the mug of tea flying.

Chapter Four

Rose acted quickly, jumping out of bed and bending anxiously over Martin's inanimate form. Then, heaving and panting, she dragged him into a sitting position and began to tow him towards the bed. Fortunately he came round, for Rose did not think she could have lifted him herself, and somehow the two of them got him between the sheets. Martin was greatly distressed, mumbling that he was sorry, that Don would lick up the spilt tea, that he would be all right in a minute. But Rose thought he looked dreadfully ill, and when she touched his skin it was burning hot.

'Shut up, Martin,' she ordered, dragging his jumpers off and pushing him down the bed when he made a feeble effort to get up. 'This is *my* home and I'm the boss, and I'm telling you to stay right where you are. Don't so much as sit up or I'll give you a clack round the ear.' As she spoke she seized her clothes. 'I'll dress in the kitchen whilst I get you a drink.' At this point Don, clearly following a tasty trail, entered the room and continued to clean up. Despite herself, Rose laughed. 'Men!' she said. 'You're all alike.' About to leave the room, she wagged a reproving finger at her quivering guest. 'I'm going to fetch you the blanket off the sofa, as well as a cup of hot, sweet tea, so just you stay where you are or it will be the worse for you.'

In the kitchen, Rose dressed hurriedly and drank the mug of tea which Martin had abandoned whilst she wondered what on earth to do for the best.

Martin looked really ill; his normally pale skin was almost salmon pink and his eyes, red-rimmed, were watering so badly that he appeared to be weeping even though he was not. When she had bent over the bed, she had heard wheezing sounds coming from his chest. Yet he must be strong, she thought, otherwise he could not have survived so many nights of sleeping rough in such weather.

By the time she had made fresh tea and watched Martin drink two full mugs of it, she had come to the conclusion that he might well have nothing worse than a feverish cold, but she decided, nevertheless, that she must call a doctor. She dared not have a sick young man on her hands, maybe for weeks. If he was really ill a doctor might advise hospital, and in that case—though she would visit him, of course—he would no longer be her responsibility.

Having decided on her course of action, Rose felt a good deal better. She would lock him into the flat and go along to the clinic on Brougham Terrace and ask a doctor to call. Mrs Ellis had a job, so she never visited Rose until after five o'clock. And I'll be back well before then, Rose told herself, putting on her thick winter coat and wrapping a scarf round her neck. She added hat, gloves and boots, then went softly across the hall and into her bedroom. Martin appeared to be asleep, but he opened his eyes as she approached the bed and gave her a watery smile. 'I'm real sorry to go and get ill on you, Rosie,' he said. 'Where's you off to? I don't like to ask it, but . . .'

'You don't need to ask anything, Mart. I'm going to take Don for an airing so he can do his business,' Rose said tactfully. 'Will you promise me

85

you won't gerrout of bed, not even if someone knocks the door? Not that anyone will,' she added truthfully.

Martin promised and Rose was sure that he would keep his word. Why should he not? She guessed he must be feeling very poorly, and anyway, even if he could bring himself to walk away from her, she knew he would never abandon Don.

It was not a long walk to the clinic from Everton Brow, and once Don had done what he'd come out to do, Rose found herself enjoying the sharp crisp air and the pale sunshine, for the snow clouds had drifted away and the blue sky overhead seemed to promise that spring was on its way at last. Don had neither a collar nor a lead, but he paced alongside Rose, never moving far from her side and occasionally nuzzling her hand as though to remind her of his presence.

They sauntered down Everton Brow and along Village Street, turning into Everton Road and heading for Brougham Terrace. Once there, however, Rose was faced with the dilemma which Martin had described. She could scarcely take Don into the doctor's surgery, yet hesitated to leave him outside alone in case he was mistaken for a stray and taken off to a dog pound. Finally, and with some regret, she took off the little red tie from the neck of her maternity smock and knotted it loosely round the big dog's throat. Then she told him to sit and to stay, kissed the top of his smooth head, and went into the clinic.

An hour later she was ushering Dr Matthews into her flat. She knew the doctor from her own visits to the clinic and had told a number of inventive lies to the receptionist who wanted details of the new patient. 'He's me cousin, come to Liverpool from Ireland to look for work,' she had said glibly. 'He's been sleepin' rough in this terrible weather, not wantin' to put upon me in my condition. But finally it all got too much. He's real ill, so since I'm on Doc Matthews's panel I thought he might be kind enough to visit.'

Dr Matthews was elderly, almost due for retirement, but he and Rose had always got on well. Now he puffed out his cheeks eloquently. 'I deserve a medal for climbing those stairs but I'll settle for a cup of tea when I've seen my patient,' he said. 'If that feller's been sleeping out in this weather, he'll mebbe need more than an aspirin and a spoonful of Buttercup Syrup. Lead on, young lady.'

Accordingly, Rose led him into her bedroom. Martin had been asleep but he woke on their entry and Rose thought he had never looked worse. His whole face was still a bright, unnatural pink, his eyes seeming to have sunk deep into their sockets. They were still red-rimmed and watering, and when he breathed a cacophony of sound accompanied each inhalation.

The doctor stared for a moment and then said: 'Well, if it isn't young Albert! I've not seen you since you had the measles, but this is the first time I've heard of your Irish connections.'

Fortunately, Martin did not reply; Rose doubted if he even took it in, but she spoke quickly. 'Sorry, Dr Matthews. The truth is, Martin—I mean Albert—hasn't registered with a doctor 'cos he's never been ill. But sleepin' rough seems to have give him a feverish cold, like, and—and when he

87

came to me he collapsed, so I thought it best to get him some real doctoring. Someone once told me that my own doctor could treat a friend or relative who was visitin', so I said Albert was my cousin and came from Ireland, so's it 'ud be harder to check up than if I'd said, oh, that he came from Chester or somewhere.'

'Yes, all right, all right,' Dr Matthews said with a touch of impatience. He had been wearing a heavy coat and a thick, fudge-coloured scarf, but now he removed his scarf, stood his bag on the bedside cabinet and produced a stethoscope from its depths. 'I've no objection to treating young Albert here.' He jammed the stethoscope into his ears, pressed the business end to Martin's skinny chest and said: 'Not that I need a stethoscope to tell me that this young man's got bronchitis, or worse; I could hear an orchestra playing every time he took a breath.' He removed the stethoscope and returned it to his bag, looking thoughtfully at Martin. 'I think this calls for one of the new wonder drugs. Ever heard of penicillin?'

Martin shook his head but Rose said brightly: 'I have. Is it as good as they say, Dr Matthews?'

'It is good, especially for chest infections,' the doctor said. He ferreted around in his bag once more, produced a bottle of tablets and handed them to Rose. 'Give him one three times a day for a full week,' he instructed. 'I'm pretty sure that'll do the trick. I'll come in again, just to check, in two or three days . . . no, better not, those stairs are killers. You come to me, young lady, and tell me how he's progressing.'

'Thank you ever so much, Dr Matthews,' Rose said gratefully, ushering him out of the room. 'But do you mind not telling anyone, anyone at all, that he's staying with me? If folk found out, I might easily get evicted, because the lady who got me the flat wouldn't approve of Mart—I mean Albert—sharing my place.'

By now they were in the kitchen and Dr Matthews was reaching for his cup of tea. 'Is he the father?' he asked bluntly, jerking a thumb towards Rose's bump. 'Of course, you're too young to marry anyone yet, but I'd say Albert was a steady sort of fellow. And there's no harm in wearing a wedding ring and telling everyone you're married provided you turn the lie into truth as soon as you're sixteen.'

Rose, however, shook her head very decidedly. 'He's not the father and I wouldn't marry him even if I was sixteen,' she said firmly. 'To tell you the truth, Doc, we met by chance and palled up . . .'

The story of their abortive trips to Southport and the long trek home was soon told, and at the end of the recital Dr Matthews whistled softly beneath his breath. 'Well, I think that proves my point,' he said. 'He could have taken advantage of you and stayed in the flat, but he didn't, did he? He moved back to living on the streets, having decided not to visit you again until he had a proper job and a roof over his head. He only came back to Everton Brow when he had lost literally everything: sleeping bag, spare clothing and the use of that convenient doorway.' The doctor raised his thick white eyebrows until they almost disappeared beneath his shock of white hair. 'And what will happen when he's over this illness, eh? Last time he left the shelter of your home you didn't realise that he was sleeping rough, but you know now. Because of the terrible weather, I doubt there's so much as a single bed not filled in any of the hostels or lodging houses, and of course the dog will mean he can't even apply for a place at the YMCA.' He looked quizzically at Rose across the kitchen table. 'You could offer to keep the dog for him if he got a place, but it's not a solution, is it? Look, Miss Pleavin, if I procure a camp bed and a couple of blankets, would you let young Albert stay with you until he finds a job, and a place of his own? I might even help with a job, because there's folk who owe me a favour and once Albert's back on his feet I could use my influence on his behalf.'

Rose gnawed her lower lip. What would Mrs Ellis say? A bargain, was a bargain, but now that she thought about it she could see no real reason for her conviction that the older woman would not like the new arrangement. And why should she even know about it? Mrs Ellis had never shown the slightest interest in Rose's bedroom. Once or twice when visiting the flat she had used the bathroom, but mostly their short meetings took place either in the kitchen or in the sitting room. Whilst Martin was ill, Rose would shut him in the bedroom with Don, and see to it that Mrs Ellis never suspected the presence of anyone other than themselves in the flat. When Martin was well again, she must impress upon him that he could not remain indoors during daylight hours. Of course, she would go back to her own bed and he would have to make do with the sofa, for kind though it was of Dr Matthews to suggest the loan of a camp bed, any sign of it in the flat would immediately arouse suspicion.

She said as much to the doctor, who grinned,

then stood up and reached for his coat, hat and scarf, which he had hung on the back of the kitchen door. 'Oh well, I dare say you know your own business best,' he said. He looked round. 'Where's that damned great dog? You won't want him nipping out when I leave.'

'He's very obedient,' Rose said rather reproachfully. 'Didn't you notice that he hasn't got a collar? But when we take him out he sticks closer than glue to me or—or Albert, honest to God he does. And anyway, I've got to go shopping, so I might as well take Don at the same time.' She flicked her own coat off its peg as she spoke and began to put it on. 'I offered Albert porridge or toast, but he didn't seem to fancy either. Wharrabout soup, doctor?'

The doctor opened the kitchen door and stood in the small hall whilst Rose fetched Don, saying nothing to Martin since he appeared to be sleeping soundly. As the two of them descended the stairs, however, the doctor spoke. 'He won't want solids for a day or two; soup, Lucozade and hot drinks such as Oxo or Bovril will be quite sufficient. When he begins to feel more himself, he'll suggest food which he feels he can cope with. I take it you're all right for money? The boy won't be able to draw the dole until he's better. I suppose I could write a note explaining the situation . . .'

Rose, however, assured him that she could manage and the two parted outside the block, Rose promising to visit Brougham Terrace in a couple of days' time.

*   *   *

91

On the last day of the tablets, Martin tried to assure Rose that he was now completely well and could manage the journey to the Labour Exchange if she wouldn't mind looking after Don whilst he was away, but this caused Rose to get bossy once more. 'I know it's sunny and it hasn't snowed since you was took ill, but it's still perishin' cold,' she told him. 'What's more, Dr Matthews said you were to go down to Brougham Terrace when you finished his tablets so he could judge for himself whether you needed a second course, wharrever that may mean. So tomorrer, the two of us will toddle along there and get you signed off.'

Martin tutted. 'The two of us? You've made a point of keeping me hid away for a whole week and now you're talkin' as if it didn't matter if the whole world saw us trundlin' down the stairs. And wharrabout Don? You don't mean to leave him behind, I hope?'

Rose gave him a playful punch on the shoulder. 'You *are* better!' she said. 'Them tablets certainly did the trick. And it just goes to show that you really are strong, Mart, because the doctor was quite worried by that there orchestra he said were playin' inside your chest. And it's not done that for a full three days. Oh aye, I reckon you're strong as a bleedin' donkey.'

'Strong as Don,' Martin said gleefully, smoothing the big dog's head. 'As if we'd leave you behind, old feller.' He was sitting on the edge of the bed, fully dressed for the first time since his illness and feeling so full of energy that he thought he would scream if he was cooped up for another day. He said as much and saw Rose cock her head on one side in a considering sort of way.

'I know what you mean,' she said slowly. 'If it were to rain tomorrer I'd not want you to go round to Brougham Terrace and then on to the Labour Exchange. I've gorran umbrella but that would only keep the top half of you dry. And like you said, I'm not too keen on the neighbours seein' us both comin' out o' the flat at the same time and goin' off together. It 'ud cause talk.'

Martin sighed. He glanced towards the window and thought how good it would be to stretch his legs. At first, the sheer luxury of being in bed and being looked after had been enough, for Rose had taken good care of him, never trying to force him to eat what he did not fancy, helping him to the bathroom when he was at his weakest and bringing him hot drinks every hour or so. She had even come quietly into the bedroom three or four times a night, making sure that there was nothing he wanted. But now he glanced at her, seeing her indecision and hoping to be able to use it to his advantage. 'Rosie?' he said coaxingly. 'Rosie, suppose I do some shopping for you instead? Then I can take Don, because he could do with a walk, and I promise if I start to cough, or wheeze, or feel ill, I'll come straight home. How about that?'

'We-ell,' Rose said slowly. 'I don't know as I ought to let you, but it is a lovely day, even though it's chilly still.' She jerked her thumb at the coats on the kitchen door. 'Last time I were on the Scottie, I picked up an old duffel coat dead cheap. Go on, try if it fits.' It did, and Rose nodded approvingly. 'Right, you'll do. You can buy me half a pound of stewing steak, three nice onions and a couple of carrots. The doc said a sustaining stew would do you the world of good once you were eating solids . . . oh, and if you can carry them, we could do with some spuds.'

Martin got to his feet, knowing he was grinning like an idiot and not caring. He really must be better if Rose was agreeing to let him leave the flat. 'I'll come straight home like a good little feller,' he said gratefully. 'You're a queen, queen!'

*   *   *

Rose saw her two companions off and smiled to herself. She would have time to clean the flat thoroughly before they came back, because she guessed that Martin would not hurry. She had spoken no more than the truth when she said it was a fine day, for earlier she had taken a bag of rubbish down to the dustbins and had appreciated the freshness of the air, spiced still with frost but now showing definite signs of spring.

She had expected to feel a sense of freedom once Martin and Don had left, but instead she felt rather lonely. It had been her habit to leave the doors open and to shout through to Martin, telling him what she was doing and sometimes calling him through into the kitchen so that they could listen to a radio programme together.

Now, she took a quick look through her food cupboard and decided that she would nip down to the corner shop and buy the ingredients for three or four large Victoria sponges. Miss Haverstock must be wondering what had happened to 'her little helper' and though to the best of Rose's knowledge the matron and Mrs Ellis did not know one another, you could never tell how gossip would spread. She did not think Mrs Ellis knew

94

anything about her earnings from the old people's home, which allowed her at least some independence, but it might alert the older woman if someone said that the supply of baking for the home had suddenly dried up. As a governor of the orphanage, and a social worker, Mrs Ellis probably knew that Rose had loved her cookery classes; how awful if she put two and two together and first accused Rose of earning money on the side and then began to investigate the sudden cessation of Rose's little earner.

Rose finished making her shopping list and chided herself for her stupidity. What on earth did it matter if Mrs Ellis found out that she was earning money? Soon she would have a baby to keep, as well as herself, for though Mrs Ellis had been generous—was being generous—Rose realised that the older woman had never said that she would continue to support Rose once the child was born. I'll probably have to get a job, but it won't be easy because if I do I'll have to pay someone else to look after the baby, Rose told herself now. But I expect there are grants and things for mums who can't go out to work.

As she was leaving the flat, locking the door carefully behind her, another thought occurred. Suppose she asked Miss Haverstock if she could work at the old people's home? She could take the baby there, which would be a very real saving, and do all their cooking instead of just producing the odd cake or tray of buns. At present Mrs Poulson cooked for the residents, but she was old and wanted to retire and Mrs P and Matron had never got on. Yes, it was an idea; when she delivered today's baking, she might hint to Miss Haverstock that when the baby was born she would be looking for a full-time job. The older woman could only say no, after all.

She was just emerging from the tower block when, to her initial dismay, she saw Mrs Ellis approaching and heard herself hailed. 'Gertrude? I was just coming to visit you. Where are you off to, my dear? Can you spare me five minutes? Oh, is the lift working? I don't want to drag you up all those stairs again in your condition.'

Rose's mind did a rapid tour of the flat which she had just left. Yes, she had made her bed, changing the sheets since she intended to sleep there herself now that Martin was so much better. She had left the linen soaking in the sink. Fortunately, she had stripped the sofa, folded the blankets round the pillow and replaced the bedding in the small cupboard in the hall. The kitchen might be a slight giveaway because she had left her cooking utensils on the table, but what was wrong with that? Surely she was entitled to bake a cake or two without consulting Mrs Ellis.

'I'm not sure about the lift; sometimes it works and sometimes it doesn't, and I'm always afraid of getting stuck in it so I hardly ever use it even when it is working,' she admitted. 'But I don't mind the stairs; the nurse at the clinic says stairs are good exercise and I reckon they've done me no harm. Sometimes I go up and down six or eight times a day.'

Mrs Ellis laughed. 'Rather you than me,' she said gaily. 'Well, if you can spare the time, I've brought you a bag of sticky buns and a couple of oranges. I know you get orange juice when you visit the clinic, but Mr Ellis says fresh fruit is best so I bought the oranges, a couple of nice apples and a small bunch of bananas. You do like bananas, don't you?'

'Bananas are okay, I suppose,' Rose said grudgingly. She had been tempted to reply sharply, 'I'm not a bleedin' monkey', but had swallowed the remark unsaid. Mrs Ellis had been a true friend and could not possibly guess that Rose's one visit to a zoo had included watching a large gorilla deftly peeling a banana and then eating the peel and throwing down the fruit.

By now, they were halfway up the third flight, the lift having not appeared when Mrs Ellis had pressed the bell, and Rose remembered something she had forgotten before. Only two days ago she had seen, on a stall in Paddy's Market, a large stoneware bowl with *Dog* written upon it. She had bargained briskly with the stallholder, obtaining it for sixpence in the end, and she knew she had not put it away before leaving the flat, idiot that she was. It was full of water so that Don could have a drink whenever he wished, but if Mrs Ellis remarked on it, she would think of something.

Accordingly, when they reached the fifth landing she turned impulsively towards her companion. 'Oh, I am thoughtless, Mrs Ellis, dragging you up all these stairs! You're out of breath already and we ain't halfway yet. Tell you what, I'll take your bags and go ahead, and you can come up slow like. Or if you're only here to give me nice things, we can transfer them from your basket to mine and you needn't come any further.'

Mrs Ellis laughed breathlessly and Rose saw that her cheeks were very pink. She noticed that the mass of bright brown hair, which Mrs Ellis usually wore pulled severely away from her face and fashioned into a large bun on the nape of her neck, had been casually clipped back with a couple of tortoiseshell hair slides, and fell to her shoulders in a pageboy bob. For the first time she realised that Mrs Ellis was a pretty woman, and relatively young. Rose had always thought of her as quite old. She wore spectacles, but her eyes, large and light blue, seemed to sparkle today and to Rose's astonishment she had actually applied pale pink lipstick to her mouth. She wore, as she always did when she was working, a white blouse with a grey skirt and jacket, and her feet were shod in well-polished brogues, but there was something about her . . .

'No, no, I can manage the stairs, though I think it would be best if we both slowed down a bit,' Mrs Ellis said. But when they reached the seventh flight she was glad to hand her burden over to Rose and to admit that she meant to climb in her young friend's wake.

Rose took the bags and hurried ahead. She was actually in the kitchen and kicking Don's bowl out of sight beneath the table when Mrs Ellis entered the room. Hoping she had noticed nothing, Rose hastily put the kettle on the stove. 'Tea or coffee, Mrs Ellis?' she said cheerfully as the older woman sank on to a chair. 'I know you like coffee so I always keep some in, though I'm more for a nice cup o' char meself.'

'Oh, tea will be fine, dear,' Mrs Ellis said, and it occurred to Rose that her companion had never used the endearment to her before today. Clearly, something had happened to put Mrs Ellis in a very good mood indeed.

'I feel awful mean, offering you the food you've brought yourself,' Rose said, 'but I've not gorra lorra grub in right now, so . . . will you have a sticky bun with your drink?' Rose had used the expression 'grub' as a sort of test, because she knew it was one of which Mrs Ellis disapproved, but Mrs Ellis neither wagged a reproving finger nor frowned. Something was definitely up, Rose concluded.

Mrs Ellis accepted the cup of tea and the bun and then said rather shyly: 'I've not told anyone yet, not even Mr Ellis, but I've—well, I've had some rather good news. I went to see Dr Matthews, and—and he thinks . . . he thinks . . .'

Rose's heart, which had sunk to her boots on hearing the doctor's name, began to beat more normally. 'He thinks . . .' did not sound as though the doctor had spilt the beans to her mentor. 'What does he think, Mrs Ellis?' she asked encouragingly. 'I like Dr Matthews. He's ever so kind.'

'He thinks—he actually thinks that—that I may be having a little stranger of my own,' she said, the pink in her cheeks beginning to flame. 'It's something Mr Ellis and I have always wanted, but of course such things are in the hands of God.'

Rose, thoroughly mystified, stared at the older woman. 'Do you mean you're going to have a lodger living in your house?' she said. But a second glance at her companion's face made her abandon the idea. 'Oh, Mrs Ellis, are you trying to tell me you're going to have a baby?'

Mrs Ellis put a hand across her mouth and giggled, which made Rose stare even more incredulously. She had thought, many times, that

Mrs Ellis was a bit of a prig. If the woman meant she was expecting a baby, why on earth had she not said so? All this talk of little strangers was completely unnecessary, since having a baby was a natural process and nothing to be ashamed of. However, it would never do to say so. Instead, she said: 'That's wonderful, Mrs Ellis, I expect you and your husband are very excited. When is the baby due?'

'I'm not sure,' Mrs Ellis said, looking confused. 'I have to go to the clinic for tests; I expect they'll tell me then.'

'Yes, I suppose so,' Rose said. Another thought struck her, not a welcome one. 'Oh, Mrs Ellis, that'll mean you'll stop work. I'm going to look for a job as soon as my baby's born, of course, but what will happen until then? I can't expect you to go on paying my rent and that.'

'Don't worry, dear; I shall get various grants as an expectant mother myself and of course Mr Ellis's salary will support us both whilst I'm unable to earn. We shall continue to help you for as long as you need—we have an agreement, remember— so you mustn't worry that you'll be left high and dry. We are very much your friends. Now, tell me. When you first came to the flat you were so upset and angry over your—your condition that I never liked to question you as to your feelings. But lately you've seemed, oh, more mellow somehow, not so bitterly resentful. Have I read your feelings aright?'

Rose took her time to answer the question, because for some reason she realised that it was important. Finally she said: 'At the beginning I was sick every morning for weeks and weeks, and of

100

course I was worried, thinking I had some horrible disease and might die because food simply would not stay in my stomach. Then I went to the doctor and he told me I was expecting. Then I hated the baby; I think I felt I had been betrayed into giving shelter to someone I didn't even know. But now I suppose you could say I have come to terms with it. I was never a very patient person but I've learned that havin' a baby is one thing you can't hurry. So I cook and clean and shop . . . and wait. And when it's all over, I'll be me again.' She sighed deeply. 'Can you understand?'

Mrs Ellis nodded, as though well satisfied. 'Good, good,' she said vaguely.

Rose got up from the table. 'Would you like another cup of tea? The pot's still hot.'

Mrs Ellis thanked her but refused, getting to her feet. 'I have the day off work, which is why I've been able to come and see you this morning,' she said. 'I had intended to visit my mother's grave; she died when I was only a few months old and I was brought up by my grandparents. In fact it is their house that we live in now. But I really think I must go and see Mr Ellis and tell him my news before I go home to the Wirral.'

Rose stood up and slipped on her coat, then snatched up hat, scarf and shopping bag. 'I'll come down with you. Your news was so exciting that I almost forgot I was about to go shopping when we met earlier,' she said.

Secretly, she was hoping to avoid a confrontation between Mrs Ellis and Martin, to say nothing of Don. The trouble with Martin was that he was unforgettable, as Dr Matthews had proved. Mrs Ellis might have come in contact with Martin when he had been at the Arbuthnot, and if she saw him more than once at the flats and began asking questions, folk might begin to put two and two together and make five. If she walked with Mrs Ellis down to Everton Brow and Martin caught sight of them, she was sure he would have sufficient sense to steer clear. If it looked as though Martin and the dog had not noticed them she would chatter away to Mrs Ellis, focusing the older woman's attention upon herself.

These precautions, however, proved unnecessary. Mrs Ellis wanted to talk babies and was so clearly excited by the prospect that Rose wished she had not mentioned morning sickness. Not that it would necessarily attack her companion, for other expectant mothers had assured Rose that they had either escaped the bouts of sickness altogether, or suffered them for a relatively short time.

As they approached the tram stop, Rose realised what an enormous difference the other woman's condition must have made, for Mrs Ellis had never mentioned her mother before, nor the fact that she had been brought up by her grandparents. Emboldened by this, she said shyly: 'I didn't know you lived on the Wirral. Is it nice?'

'Yes, very nice,' Mrs Ellis said as they reached her little car and she slid into the driving seat. 'Thank you for accompanying me. And don't forget, I am still very much your friend.'

Rose stood and waved at the car until it was out of sight, then went thoughtfully down the road towards Heyworth Street, where she could purchase everything she needed for her baking. Thinking it over, she decided that Mrs Ellis's excitement, though strange at first, was perfectly understandable in the circumstances. The revelation that she had been brought up by her grandparents had come as a complete surprise, and Rose could not help wondering why the older woman had never mentioned them before. This seemed odd in itself; but then she had never pretended to understand Mrs Ellis.

Satisfied, Rose set off for the shops. Tomorrow, she reminded herself, Martin would go off to Brougham Terrace and perhaps Dr Matthews would have been able to persuade someone to give him a job. Mrs Ellis had said she would continue to support Rose for as long as necessary which meant, Rose supposed, until she herself was earning, so if Martin was able to make a contribution they ought to manage pretty comfortably.

Reassured by this thought, Rose fished her list out of her coat pocket and turned into the Maypole.

*   *   *

Don and Martin sauntered up the hill towards the tower block, feeling at peace with the world. The previous week he had gone, as arranged, to Brougham Terrace where Dr Matthews had pronounced him fit as a fiddle and added that he had spoken about him to a possible employer and arranged an interview for the following Monday.

Martin had been thrilled but apprehensive, and went along to Exchange Flags determined to do his very best to impress this Mr Cornwallis. He tied Don up to a lamp post with a length of rope and went into the Cygnet Insurance Company full of trepidation, mentioning Mr Cornwallis in a voice so faint that the girl on reception had to ask him to repeat the name. He knew, of course, that Dr Matthews had spoken for him, but the doctor had said that everything hung on the interview, so upon entering Mr Cornwallis's office he pulled himself together and shook hands firmly, looking his would-be employer straight in the eye, and doing his best to exude confidence.

Mr Cornwallis, an elderly man, grey-haired and stout, put Martin immediately at ease by saying that Dr Matthews regarded him as hard-working and trustworthy. Then he asked Martin whether he had previous experience of office work. Martin was able to tell him that he had worked in the office at the boys' home, where they had taught him a certain amount about bookkeeping and how to use their ancient Remington typewriter, and Mr Cornwallis nodded. 'The doctor explained that your appearance had sometimes worked against you, particularly the fact that your spectacles were broken and not replaced because of the cost,' he said kindly. 'Normally, we would ask for references, but the one which Dr Matthews has already given you is quite sufficient.' He glanced across his big desk at Martin's earnest face. 'I understand that your sight was badly affected by measles . . . as was my own.' He tapped his steel-rimmed spectacles with a plump forefinger. 'I would be lost without these. How were yours broken? And how have you managed without them?'

'Oh, there was a rough and tumble in the dormitory when I was at Brackendale Hall and they got broken . . . well, shattered, really,' Martin explained with a wry smile. 'I should have gone along to the warden's office and asked him to see about getting me another pair, but somehow I never got round to it. And besides, I didn't see much point because they were the third ones the boys in my dorm had bust. As for managing without them, I see everything as fuzzy but I get along all right. To tell you the truth, I've got a big old greyhound, a lovely feller. He walks close beside me, so when there's a pothole in the road, or a paving stone missing, he avoids it so so do I.'

Mr Cornwallis's thick grey eyebrows shot up. 'I understand, but you will need spectacles when you start work here. You will be delivering letters and parcels, fetching and carrying, taking correspondence to the post office and adding up your expenditure on stationery and stamps at the end of each day. You must go along to Dollond & Aitchison's on Lord Street and get yourself some spectacles as soon as you leave here.'

Martin stared at him, round-eyed. 'Does—does that mean I've got the job?' he said, unable to keep the incredulity out of his voice. 'Oh, Mr Cornwallis, I'll work ever so hard, honest to God I will. And I'll go straight along to Lord Street . . . only, what'll I have to pay? I've got my dole money, but I doubt if it'll cover the cost.'

Mr Cornwallis was scribbling on a sheet of paper. When he'd finished, he blotted it, folded it and handed it to Martin. 'I don't think they'll charge you for your spectacles since you are still on the dole,' he said. 'But if I'm wrong, I've told them to send the bill to me.' He grinned, suddenly and disarmingly. 'You can pay me back at sixpence a week, out of your wages!' He rose to his feet and held out a white, well-manicured hand. 'Good day, Mr Thompson. We'll see you next Monday; prompt at nine o'clock, mind. And get that hair cut!'

Martin had treated himself to a Bounty bar as a celebration and now, crossing Thomas Street and avoiding a bus by inches, he unwrapped the paper, took a bite of the chocolate within, and broke off a piece for the dog. Sweets had only come off ration a few years before and then they had been in short supply for some time, so chocolate was still a luxury to them all. 'Do you like that?' Martin asked, as the dog took the piece delicately from his fingers, eyes shining, and swallowed it more or less whole. 'You're a good feller, so you are.' Martin, who had bought Rose a Bounty bar as well, knowing how she loved the creamy coconut filling, told the dog that Rosie would probably go halves too. 'So you win out all round, old Don.'

Martin was forcing himself to walk slowly, despite an urge to break into a gallop because of his good news. He would be earning a steady salary, though he knew that if he had had to pay rent, electricity and such things as rates he would be hard pressed to provide himself with enough to eat. However, for the time being at least, Rose had assured him that such things were being paid for by Mrs Ellis. Rose had always been somewhat secretive about her friend, but Martin had finally persuaded her to explain how she managed to pay the rent from the small sum she drew, he assumed, from the state.

'Mrs Ellis wanted to help me because she said I were only a child meself,' Rose had said. 'She felt that it were partly her fault that I got meself in trouble because she were the captain of the Girl Guides from St Mary's when we were took on a hiking holiday in Snowdonia. I thought what happened to me there were just horrible; I were stupid in them days and didn't know about con . . . consequences. Mrs Ellis did, though. And when we both knew I were preggy, we made a bargain. She would get me a flat and see I got everything I was entitled to, provided I never let on I'd been interfered with. She said she might lose her job if anyone found out what had happened. You do understand, Mart, that I've gorra keep in with Mrs Ellis, no matter what.'

When Martin had returned with the shopping the previous week, Rose had told him of Mrs Ellis's visit and revealed that the older woman, too, was expecting a baby. 'I didn't even know she wanted one,' Rose had said, 'but I'm awful glad for her because she was tickled pink, I could tell. And she said she'll continue paying the rent and so on until I start earning myself.'

'Well, isn't that just grand,' Martin had said heartily. Rose had told him Mrs Ellis was a busy and successful woman. She was a magistrate, a member of the board of governors for at least two children's homes and possibly more, and worked in the Welfare Department. Her husband had his own business making cabling for the communications industry. Rose had explained that Mrs Ellis had no need to work since she did not need the money, but continued to do so because she was deeply interested in children and education.

Rose was lucky to have such a friend, Martin had

concluded, even though the situation still puzzled him somewhat. Rose took it for granted, but Martin could not help thinking that in his experience folk did not hand out money so freely without thought of return. Perhaps Mrs Ellis wanted something which Rose would be able to give once the baby was born, such as help in what he imagined to be a large country house. Martin knew that domestic service in private houses had practically ceased to exist, because girls wanted more freedom than such jobs allowed, and he guessed that a large house in a remote area would be difficult, if not impossible, to staff. If Rose went to work for Mrs Ellis it would pay the woman back in some degree for the kindness she had shown to Rose.

It did occur to him that the job Mrs Ellis might offer could easily be live-in, which would mean that he would lose his accommodation, but he would simply have to find himself somewhere else to live. He could go back to the YMCA, he supposed, except that he knew they would not have Don. He was sure that Rose would never abandon the greyhound any more than he would, but somehow he doubted that Mrs Ellis would welcome his four-footed friend into her house.

By now he had reached the tower block and was ascending the stairs, determined to tell Rose that he had probably only got the job partly at least as a result of her help and advice. She had frowned over the fact that he had no really smart interview clothes, and then gone off on some mysterious errand of her own, returning a considerable while later with a pair of grey trousers, a white shirt and a tweed jacket. 'I borrowed 'em off one of the stallholders in Paddy's Market,' she had explained. 'She's a good old gal and she's holdin' me best winter coat as a guarantee that she'll get her stuff back, so don't you go spillin' your dinner down none of this clobber or I'll have your bleedin' guts for garters.' The trousers were a bit short in the leg, as was the jacket in the sleeves, but with the addition of his own blue tie Martin had been quite impressed with his appearance and had thanked Rose from the heart. He had listened intently to every word of her subsequent lecture and wanted her to know that, between them, she and Dr Matthews had pretty well got him the job.

He slowed as he reached the top floor. Suppose Mrs Ellis had come visiting? He had best knock at the door and not simply burst in, though he knew Rose seldom locked it during daylight hours. When he and Don reached the tenth floor and he tapped on the wooden panel, the door opened so quickly that he guessed Rose must have heard their footsteps on the stairs. Before he thought, he gave her an exuberant hug, trying not to notice that she winced away as he did so. She stepped back, however, to allow him to enter, so he hoped the wincing had been in his imagination.

'I gorrit, Rosie! I got the job,' he said triumphantly.

'I knew you would,' Rose said complacently. 'You look grand in them clothes, and if the doc recommended you only a fool would turn you down.'

'You got the clothes, Rosie, so it's you I've got to thank,' Martin said. 'And the money goes up if I give satisfaction. I've gorra go to Dollond & Aitchison's on Lord Street to get meself some new specs, 'cos I'll be doin' close work . . . accounts and that. Mr Cornwallis—he's the boss—said I were to go straight there and they'll see me right. Only I couldn't wait to tell you that I'd got the job, an' I start work Monday morning, at nine.' He peered at her hopefully. 'Want to come to the opticians with me? I could tell you all about the job as we walk . . . or we could catch a tram 'cos I've still got some of me dole money left.' He dug into his pocket and produced the Bounty bar, pressing it into her hand. 'For you, Rosie, to celebrate. And now I'd best change 'cos you'll want to return these clothes and get your coat back.' Another thought struck him. 'But wharrabout next Monday? Will they expect me to be smart then as well?'

'Oh, blimey, I never thought of that,' Rose said, with some dismay. 'But we'll take this lot back and look for a decent jumper and some kecks what'll cover your ankles. That should do for now. I've got a little bit of money put by from me bakin'. You can borrow that and pay me back some time!' She turned to him, cuffing his shoulder lightly. 'And we must deal with your hair; you look like a perishin' dandelion clock!'

'Yes, Mr Cornwallis did mention it,' Martin said ruefully, smoothing back his bush of snow-white hair. 'It always looks better when it's short but I'm no hand with the scissors. I reckon I'd best go to a proper barber; there's several in Bold Street.'

'We'll get your hair cut as soon as we've ordered your spectacles,' Rose decided. 'Oh, Mart, I'm that happy for you! And of course me and Don will come with you, and afterwards we'll go along to Paddy's Market to hand in your interview clothes

110

and see what else we can find.'

Chapter Five

Despite Martin's secret fears, the optician assured him, having read Mr Cornwallis's note, that the spectacles would be free and ready for collection before he started his new job. Furthermore, whilst he was having his eyes tested, Rose wandered around the room, examining everything, and made a discovery. She turned to the optician, who was busy writing the results of Martin's eye test, and said, 'Excuse me, mister, but there's a pair of specs here wharr'ave got glass what looks almost blue. Could Martin have specs like that?'

'I was about to suggest it,' the man said frostily. 'When there is no pigmentation in the iris, strong light can cause pain. Tinted glass lessens the brilliance of the light.'

So when Rose and Martin joined Don on the pavement in Lord Street, Martin felt that a new life was opening up for him. He had tried on a pair of tinted glasses and could see for himself what an astonishing difference they made to his appearance whilst Rose, apparently awestruck, had said: 'Oh, Mart, why on earth didn't someone suggest tinted specs for you before? Your eyes look wonderful; dark purple instead of pink.'

So it was with a light heart, though he still had to keep a hand on the greyhound's head for the time being, that Martin set off with Rose to find a hairdresser. They walked along Church Street, crossed Ranelagh and entered Bold Street. Martin,

111

growing apprehensive, for Bold Street was a very smart area indeed, suggested that they might try somewhere less imposing. But Rose, who had very definite ideas of her own, shook her head at him. 'Your hair's been neglected pretty well all your life and needs expert attention,' she told him. 'I dare say it'll cost a bob or two, but a really good haircut will make a world of difference, I promise you.' She put a detaining hand on his arm, bringing him to a stop. 'Look, Mart, I had a word with one of the old people the other day and she told me that her daughter, who is on the stage and a very smart person, comes all the way back from London to have her hair cut and styled by a hairdresser whose premises are opposite the Newington. His salon is on the first floor, up a flight of stairs, and she says he's first class, so if we can find him . . .'

Martin, who had never had his hair professionally cut, for the staff at the Arbuthnot had done the job themselves, was overawed by Rose's suggestion. 'It sounds awful expensive to me,' he said. 'Oh, please, Rosie, it'll be too posh. I'll feel uncomfortable, honest to God I will.'

'Nonsense,' Rose said firmly. 'I've brought my baking money with me, so even if they charge a bit extra because your hair's such a mess we'll have plenty to cover the cost. Ah, see that board? J. G. Mann, Hairdresser to the Stars—that's the one for us! And don't you go trying to escape, because our money's as good as anyone else's.' She gave him an encouraging grin. 'Pluck up, old feller! Look, I'll go up first whilst you and Don wait here, then I'll come down and tell you the score.'

'But if this chap's as good as you say, he'll never agree to clip my mop,' Martin almost wailed. 'Oh,

112

please, Rose . . .'

Rose sighed. 'Look, Mart, people are a lot nicer than you might credit. I've found that if you explain things, folk are sometimes quite glad to be able to help. Take my cooking, for instance. It were the only thing I could do to make meself a bit of money on the side, so to speak, and Miss Haverstock didn't just turn me away or say that her cook could manage without help. I told her I were hard pressed to keep up wi' payments and were tryin' to furnish me flat, and she bought a couple of Victoria sponges for the old people's tea. So don't you worry about your haircut; Mr Mann's ever so nice, the lady said, and all we can do is ask. But you stay outside with Don while I talk to the boss . . . I shan't be above five minutes.'

'Oh, but suppose . . .' Martin began. He had just remembered that he had no idea whether he would be paid weekly or monthly. Still, a loan was a loan and he knew Rose well enough to realise that she would not pressure him to get her money back, since she understood his circumstances as well as he did himself.

Rose was as good as her word; scarcely five minutes had passed before she came clattering down the stairs and beckoned to him. 'Mr Mann is going to cut your hair himself,' she announced dramatically. 'Don and I will amuse ourselves while you're being done. And I hope you realise how lucky you are, because I explained about the dole and the new job, and he's goin' to do it for nothing—imagine that, from a feller what does the hair of just about every famous person in Liverpool!'

Martin thought briefly about rebelling, then

113

glanced at Rose's pink cheeks and shining eyes and knew he could do no such thing. So he straightened his shoulders, took a deep breath, and began to climb the stairs. The boys at the Arbuthnot had occasionally been taken to the pictures, and when he reached the salon and saw the numerous framed photographs of faces he knew from the advertising posters outside every cinema in Liverpool, his courage nearly failed him.

However, before he could turn and run, a man came towards him. He was of medium height and extremely good-looking, with light brown wavy hair and a strong, deeply cleft chin. He looked as though he were accustomed to command, but his smile was friendly and Martin began to relax. 'Mr Thompson? Your young lady has spoken to me and explained your situation. Well, as I told her, I like a challenge!' He gestured at the large room around him. 'As you can see, my clients today are mostly ladies, so I think you will be more comfortable if I take you into the cubicle at the far end of the room.'

Martin, horribly conscious of his ragged jersey and ancient trousers, wished that he was still wearing his interview clothes. Consequently, he was downright grateful when Mr Mann ushered him into the small room and sat him down on a black leather chair before a large mirror. The hairdresser ran his hands thoughtfully through Martin's hair, which Martin realised now must be at least eight or nine inches long. Mr Mann reached for a small spray gun and aimed it at Martin's head. 'This is only water,' he said reassuringly. 'But your hair is very fine and has to be cut when it is wet. My goodness, whoever cut your hair last appears to have used garden shears!'

Martin, who had been horrified by the sight of himself in the big mirror, gave a little laugh. He thought he looked a real sissy in the floral coverall the hairdresser had draped around his shoulders, but decided not to say so. Instead of remarking on his appearance, therefore, Martin admitted that he had been brought up at the Arbuthnot, where haircutting was done by the staff in a very hit and miss fashion. At Brackendale Hall, the warden had offered to do it, but since leaving there he had not had a haircut, needing his dole money for such things as food and the occasional tram fare. Mr Mann, combing Martin's now wet locks, nodded understandingly, produced his scissors and began to cut.

Twenty minutes later, Martin stood up and looked with awe at the quantity of white thistledown that now surrounded the chair. Then he examined his new look in the mirror. 'Gosh! I feel a different person,' he said, turning to the hairdresser and removing the floral coverall. 'I never knew a good haircut could make such a difference. Oh, Mr Mann, thank you so much. But what do I owe you?'

The hairdresser went over to a small cupboard and took out a dustpan and brush, with which he began to sweep up the piles of hair on the floor. He lowered his voice so that he could not be heard outside the cubicle, and said, 'Your young lady explained the circumstances and she's going to come back tomorrow with a cake, which will be quite sufficient. I don't normally cut men's hair, but leave that to the barbers. However, during the war, though I was officially a runner in the army, I was frequently asked to cut the men's hair when we were far from civilisation, so you see I'm not without experience.'

Martin thanked him again, and left the salon. His head felt most peculiar, light and airy. Mr Mann had used a touch of Brylcreem, but had warned Martin not to overdo it. 'You hair is so fine that if you use too much your scalp will begin to show through,' he had said tactfully. 'Good luck with your new job. You'll need a trim in five or six weeks, so if you would like to return, you can come in your lunch hour, or after work. We're quiet between five and six mid-week; I could fit you in then.'

On the tram to the market, Rose turned to her companion. 'I say, Martin, your hair looks great, honest to God it does,' she said. 'I never knew your head was such a nice shape. I told you it was always best to go to an expert, so next time don't argue with me, 'cos I always knows best, so I does. And now let's hope we can find you something halfway decent to wear. Mrs Thrower, the one who lent us your interview clothes, is probably our best bet.'

They reached the portals of Paddy's Market and Martin suggested, hopefully, that he and Don might wait for Rose outside, for the bustle within and the raucous shouts of the stallholders, to say nothing of the noise coming from the bargaining sailors and other customers, made him nervous. Rose, however, speedily scotched his hopes. 'You've got to come because I can't guess at sizes and you'll need something you're comfortable in,' she told him. 'Mrs Thrower's ever so nice; she'll let you try on if you take the clothes to the lavvies,

116

and no one's going to notice Don in this crowd. C'mon, Mart, don't be a wimp.'

Stung, Martin marched boldly into the market, stopping by the first stall but being dragged on by his companion. 'Not this one, you idiot,' she hissed. 'Mrs Thrower is three further along. While you were havin' your hair cut I nipped along to Fuller's and bought her a couple of doughnuts as a thank you for the loan; I just hope they've not oozed jam all over your nice interview clothes.'

'I hope so too,' Martin said fervently as they reached the stall in question. It was all right, however. Rose handed over the clothes, unmarked, and the bag of doughnuts, for which she was enthusiastically thanked. Mrs Thrower checked the garments carefully, then hung them at the back of the stall where her better clothing was out of reach of both dirty fingers and would-be thieves. Then she reached under the counter and produced Rose's winter coat, which she handed back to its owner with a smile. 'Anything else I can do for you?' she enquired. She looked quizzically at Martin, her bright little eyes taking him in from the top of his head to the tips of his scuffed and dusty shoes. 'Did you get the job, young feller?' she asked. 'If you did, I reckon you've me good clothes to thank.' And, when Martin nodded, she added: 'But what'll they say when you turn up for work in that lot, eh?' She jerked a thumb at his ragged apparel. 'I reckon you're going to tell me some hard-luck story and expect me to extend the loan of me decent stuff, but I can't do it. I've a customer coming in later who'll pay me fair and square for the jacket and the shirt, so I'd be obliged if you'd not even ask.'

Martin opened his mouth to reply indignantly, but Rose elbowed him in the ribs and cut in before he said a word. 'It were real good of you to loan us the stuff, Mrs Thrower, but what we're after now is a plain old shirt, a cheap jacket and trousers, and some sort of headgear . . . a flat cap, I reckon. You're dead right; them interview clothes gorr'im the job just about, so what 'ud you recommend as the right gear for an office junior?'

Clever Rose, Martin thought, as the woman's slightly aggressive expression turned to one of helpful interest. 'Ah, now let me think . . .' she said. She riffled through a pile of shirts, then pulled out a blue one which she laid on top of the pile. 'If you was takin' messages an' that, there'd likely be a uniform,' she announced rather regretfully. 'But office juniors is different. I'd say a blue or a grey shirt, what won't show the dirt, navy or grey trousers for the same reason, and either a V-necked pullover or a cotton jacket.' Mrs Thrower cocked an eye at them. 'Both, if you've got the dosh to spare.'

They left the market after half an hour's trawling through what was within their means, Rose's shopping bag fairly bulging. The only thing they had been unable to purchase were shoes, because there were none to fit Martin's long thin feet, but Rose had insisted that they purchase two pairs of thick socks. 'Your boots just ain't suitable,' she had said bluntly. 'But they'll have to do until you've earned enough money to gerra new pair. Tell you what, Mart, next time there's a jumble sale at the church hall on Everton Road we might just get lucky, because Father Shannon has got long thin feet and knobbly toes just like yours. If he's

118

chuckin' out a pair, then we'll grab 'em.'

'How do you know about Father Shannon's feet?' Martin asked suspiciously. 'I can't imagine the old boy conductin' services with no shoes on and I don't see how else you'd know.'

Rose gave a snort of amusement. 'We used to have an annual outin', from the home, and once Father Shannon stood in for a helper what didn't turn up in time to catch the cherrybang. He were good fun and I reckon he enjoyed it near on as much as we did. We went to Rhyl and he hooked up his cassock, took off his shoes and socks, and paddled wi' the rest of us. He rolled up his trousers too, of course, but one trouser leg fell down, so he were wet to the knee. I saw his feet then, and on that first day, when you came paddin' into the kitchen an' I saw your feet, I thought of Father Shannon at once.'

'Thank you very much!' Martin said. 'So me feet are thin and knobbly, are they? Still, I get your point, and I'll come to the next jumble sale with you; as you say, we might get lucky, 'cos new shoes is expensive. Oh, let's buy some chips, Rosie. It'll save you havin' to make grub when we get back.'

*   *   *

Martin had not expected to like his new job, but after a week of working at the Cygnet Insurance office he found that he was truly happy. It was a big and thriving establishment, and though at first he had worried that he would not be up to the work, he soon discovered that if he listened to instructions and followed them closely he could do everything required of him.

119

He was not supposed to start work until nine, but Thomas, the messenger boy, started at half past eight and made it clear he would be glad of a bit of company. Thomas was only fifteen, a shock-headed youth who rode his red bicycle all over the city and even down to the docks, where he was well known to most of the people who exchanged messages with the Cygnet office. Lucky Thomas was not only provided with the bicycle, but also given a smart navy uniform. He was a short, stocky lad, with ginger hair, freckles and a broad gap-toothed grin, and he took in his stride all the teasing which came his way. It was often said that his flaming red hair would ignite the navy pillbox hat that he wore, but whereas Martin would have felt criticised if such a remark were made to him, Thomas had a fund of rude replies and simply shrugged off any criticism.

Although Martin was three years older, the two got on well and Martin realised that for the first time in his life he had a friend. He acknowledged of course that Rose was also his friend, but their relationship was different. He and Rose looked after each other, but Martin knew that they had been thrown together by circumstance and not choice; he and Thomas had chosen to become friendly. He often thought that Rose was only waiting for him to become self-supporting before announcing a parting of the ways. Rose and her baby would follow one path and he another. He knew he would miss her horribly, but doubted if she would miss him. It was the difference, he supposed vaguely, between the friendship of two boys and that of a boy and a girl. Although Rose was so much younger than himself, she had matured even in the short period of time he had known her. He thought that some of this at least might be due to her condition, but remembered the doctor saying that young women grew up more quickly than young men.

Now that he was doing a job of work, he began to cast off his conviction that he would never amount to anything. Exchange Flags was a good place to work. The buildings—mostly insurance offices— were built round a paved area which had a pool and a fountain in the centre, surrounded by a convenient wall just the right height to make a comfortable seat.

It was a pity that Martin could not take Don to work with him but that was plainly impossible, so the big dog stayed in the tower block until Rose had done her housework and cooking. Then she would take him shopping with her, and when Martin had been in his job a week she actually took Don to Exchange Flags at a time when she knew Martin would be sitting outside. The day had been fine and Don, as always, on his best behaviour. Martin had taken him from group to group, introducing him to everyone he knew; as proud of his charge as any new father would have been of his offspring.

*   *   *

A week after her visit to Exchange Flags, Rose and Don headed for Brougham Terrace. Rose carried a large shoulder bag into which she intended to put the free dried milk, orange juice and cod liver oil that would be handed out once the doctor had examined her. Rose, who hated the cod liver oil, always accepted it with a grateful smile but, when she got home, poured it into a saucer for the feral cats, who thought it a rare treat. However, now that the birth was getting closer, she usually saved half for herself and, shuddering, would swallow a brimming spoonful each morning, following it up—oh, bliss—with a glass of orange juice.

Reaching the clinic, she tied Don up to the nearest lamp post as she always did, and took her place in the queue to see the doctor. To her pleasure it was Dr Matthews, not always the case since one never knew who would be taking the clinic, though the nurses rarely changed. Sister Simpson was chatting and taking details today, then bustling the women into the surgery. It always made Rose laugh, though inwardly, when Sister Simpson, fifty if she was a day, referred to girls of twenty or so as 'mother', but by now she had grown used to the strange ways of the medical staff and went happily into the surgery when her turn came. She had looked round carefully when she had entered the clinic, wondering whether Mrs Ellis might be present, but had seen no sign of her and remembered that weekly attendance was not thought necessary until the seventh month of pregnancy.

'Good afternoon, Miss Pleavin,' the doctor said as she entered and closed the door behind her. 'Hop up on the couch, my dear, whilst I check that all is well, though you look pretty fit to me. How are you feeling?'

Rose replied that she felt fine, thank you, and when the examination was over and she was seated in a chair opposite the doctor she asked him when he thought her baby would be born.

Dr Matthews smiled. 'Babies take their time, but there are certain signs by which we can judge when birth is imminent,' he said. 'I would say you have a little while to go yet, but of course I could be wrong. He beamed at her. 'So all I can do is advise patience, my dear.'

Rose smiled back. 'I am patient,' she assured him. 'Though sometimes it feels more like seven years than seven months. I was looking round for Mrs Ellis earlier, because she told me a few weeks ago that she was in the family way herself, and I wondered if she might be here. But perhaps it's a bit soon for her.'

Dr Matthews frowned, looking puzzled. 'You don't know?' he said. 'You can't have seen her recently or of course she would have told you. I'm afraid—I'm afraid it was a false alarm. It does happen sometimes that a woman becomes so desperate for a child that she actually decides to adopt, stops worrying about conceiving and so becomes pregnant. I thought that must have happened with Mrs Ellis. However . . .'

*　　　*　　　*

The day had been grey and cool and clouds continued to scud across the sky. Martin, on his way home, sighed and put up the hood of his trusty duffel coat. If he caught a tram he could get home more or less dry, but he was still terribly money conscious, worrying constantly that he and Rose might find it difficult to manage once the baby was born. Rose had assured him that they should be able to cope, but Martin imagined that babies needed all sorts of strange and exotic food and worried that they might not be able to provide such luxuries.

But tram fares were cheap, and as the rain grew heavier he decided he was being a fool. When a No. 13 passed him, slowing to pick up passengers at a nearby stop, he joined the tail of the queue and jumped aboard. By the time they reached the tower blocks he was glad he had done so, for the rain had now begun to fall in earnest and his duffel coat was already growing distinctly damp. Having lived rough for so long, Martin was indifferent to what the weather might fling at him, but he knew that getting a heavy coat dry again could be a problem.

He jumped off the tram and scooted for the flats, taking off his duffel coat at the foot of the stairs and giving it a good shake before beginning to run quietly up the flights. He always ran if he possibly could, first because it was good for him, he reckoned, and second because being an unofficial tenant, so to speak, he wanted to be seen by as few people as possible.

They had taken to hanging the key on a long piece of string inside the letterbox and now he pulled it out, let himself in and locked the door behind him. He kicked off his boots and padded across to the kitchen intending to put the kettle on, but as he entered the room Don ran across the floor to him, tail wagging in greeting, and Martin saw that the kettle was already hissing gently on the stove. So Rose was home, then. 'Hello, old boy,' Martin said, stroking the dog's silky ears. 'Where's your missus, then? Where's our Rose?'

Martin was about to put his head round the sitting room door when he saw Don heading for

Rose's bedroom. The door was open, so he followed him in after a brief knock on the wooden panel.

Rose was kneeling on the floor surrounded by a sea of assorted garments, and Don was vigorously licking her face and uttering little whining noises. Directly in front of Rose were two very old and very shabby Gladstone bags and at Martin's knock she turned towards him, revealing a face so tear-streaked and swollen with crying that for a moment he scarcely recognised her.

Martin crossed the room in a couple of strides and fell to his knees beside her. 'Rosie! Wharrever is the matter?' he asked urgently.

As he spoke, he tried to put his arm round her, but she shrank away, beginning to ferret amongst the clothing as though searching for something in particular. 'Oh, it's you, Martin,' she muttered in a hoarse little voice. 'I thought it was her . . . or maybe him. I meant to take the key off the door but I was in such a state . . . Martin, I've got to get away from here. One of the bags is for the baby's stuff and the other for me. Only—only I don't seem able to choose. I ought to take summer stuff . . . only it's still cold out and . . .'

Martin sighed, stood up and put his hands beneath Rose's armpits to heave her, not without difficulty, to her feet. 'The kettle's boiling and I'm going to make us a cup of tea whilst you come into the kitchen and sit by the stove and tell me what's wrong,' he said. He spoke as placidly as he could, though inwardly he was deeply perturbed by her seemingly irrational behaviour. 'Come along now, Rosie. I'll go and take the key off the door so if anyone comes they can't get in. We'll pretend

125

we're out if anyone knocks.'

He half feared that Rose would ignore him and drop to her knees once more, but she did no such thing. She tucked her hand into Don's collar and the pair followed Martin meekly into the kitchen, where Rose collapsed on to a chair and Don sat down beside her, his head in her lap and his anxious eyes fixed on her face. Martin brewed the tea, poured two cups, opened the biscuit barrel and set out four ginger nuts on a plate. 'You can tell me what's wrong when you've finished your first cup of tea,' he said firmly.

Rose nodded weakly and handed one of the biscuits to Don, who crunched it up without moving his head from her lap. Martin drank his own cup of tea, sipping cautiously, for it was hot, and watched Rose as she followed suit. He remembered that it was clinic day and began to imagine frightening things, but at least her bump was very much in evidence and, now that he thought back, he remembered her saying that the second Gladstone bag—or was it the first?—was intended for her baby clothes, so the worst had not happened.

Rose pushed her empty mug towards him and Martin poured them both a second cup, then looked questioningly at his companion. 'Well, Rosie? Are you going to tell me what's wrong?' he asked gently. 'Because I'm tellin' you straight, you aren't leaving this room until I've heard the whole story, and this time it had better be from the very beginning, and not just in bits and bobs.'

He half expected a brush-off, but Rose gave a tired sigh, patted the dog's smooth head, and began to speak. 'All right, though I don't see that much good can come of telling you from the very beginning, which was last August, at the guide camp in Snowdonia.'

'Look, since you're so upset that you seemed to be planning to run away, I think I've gorra know the whole story.' Martin said. 'How can I help you else?'

Rose sniffed and gave a watery chuckle. 'I'm not Else, I'm Rose,' she said. 'Oh, all right, Mart, I guess it had better be from the beginning. Only I— I promised I'd not say a word to anyone . . . but I didn't know, when I promised, what I know now.'

Martin, scarcely understanding a word of this, merely nodded and looked expectantly at the still swollen and tear-streaked face opposite. 'Carry on,' he invited.

Rose took a deep breath and began her story. 'Well, I was at Guide camp with a lot of other girls from St Mary's, and Captain—that's what we called Mrs Ellis—was in charge. It was grand fun. We went mountain-walking, canoeing, even swimming in Lake Something-or-other, and we all got along fine. Then someone caught one of these awful stomach bugs. I can't remember who was the first to go down, but I was real chuffed because I seemed to be immune or whatever the word is. Only then I got it, the very last person to do so, and I reckon I was even iller than the others. For three whole days I couldn't keep nothin' down and Captain was gettin' worried. Then on the fourth day I woke feeling weak, but much better. I had two cups of tea, a bowl of porridge and two rounds of dry toast with Marmite. The girls were going on an expedition up one of the easier peaks. They were taking butties for midday so wouldn't be back

127

till late afternoon. Captain asked me if I'd be all right alone, and of course I said I would because I knew I weren't strong enough to climb even a tiny mountain, and I planned to spend the day tidyin' the camp so Captain would be pleased with me when they got back. She'd been ever so kind while I was ill, you see.

'I saw the others off and began to tidy round the camp, but around midday I fancied a bit of a splash in the mountain stream which ran, oh, I dunno, ten or twenty feet from the camp perhaps. I stripped off my clothes because there was no one about, took a bar of soap and my towel, and found meself a deepish pool. I had a lovely wash. I even did me hair, and felt fresh as a daisy, honest I did.' She looked anxiously across at Martin. 'I didn't know . . . I never dreamed . . .'

'Of course you didn't,' Martin said soothingly. 'Do you want me to guess the rest? Someone came out of the trees and spotted you . . .'

'You aren't far wrong, but we'd better get it exactly right,' Rose said. 'I was padding back to the camp, wrapped in me towel, when a man appeared. I jumped a mile, I can tell you, but then I saw that it was Mr Ellis. I felt a bit of a fool but I gave him a little wave and a smile, because Captain had told us that her husband had booked himself into one of the hostels so that they could be together for a day or two. I'd only seen him once before, but I reckernised him. He called across to me, asking where Captain and the girls had gone, and I said on a climbing expedition. He pulled a face when I said they wouldn't be back till late and half turned away, and honest to God, Mart, I thought he was leavin'. I gave him another wave, shouted that I'd tell Captain he'd come callin', and went into the big tent, which was where I'd left my clothes. I was just givin' myself a final rub when I saw this great huge shadow appear on the tent wall, and then—and then . . .'

Her voice faltered to a halt and Martin spoke quickly. 'It's all right; you don't have to say nothin' else. So Mr Ellis is the father and Mrs Ellis is helping you—paying your rent and so on—because her husband is the guilty one. And of course if it came out there would be trouble for both of them because you're a minor. The folk at the home might prosecute Mr Ellis, for all I know, or Mrs Ellis, come to that. Am I right?'

'I dunno,' Rose said dully. 'You may be right, but it seems to me that rich important people can get away with all sorts. After all, no one else knew Mr Ellis had visited the camp that afternoon.'

'The wicked old sod; I wish I could get my hands on him,' Martin said between clenched teeth. 'I wish you could shout it from the rooftops, but you're right, of course: he'd simply deny it and say you were the sort of girl who'd go with anyone. Oh, Rose, you must hate the bugger.'

Rose put her head on one side and Martin saw with relief that her tears had ceased to flow, at least temporarily. 'I hated him at first all right,' she said thoughtfully. 'But then I remembered how he cried and called himself names, and said how sorry he was. He wanted me to swear I wouldn't tell, so I promised, because I didn't want anyone to know. I felt—I felt dirty and guilty, and as though it was my fault as much as his, though I knew in my heart that it wasn't, of course. I poured water into a basin and washed all over, and kept doing that

129

until Captain came back. I started to tell her that Mr Ellis had come to the camp hoping to see her, only in the middle I started crying and couldn't stop, and Mrs Ellis guessed. She went white as a sheet and then very red indeed. She made her hands into fists and took me along to her own tent. When we got there, she gave me a hug and said that if there were con . . . consequences, she would look after me.

'So when my monthlies didn't come, she explained that I was going to have a baby and got me the flat, told me about visiting the clinic and so on. We agreed that I wouldn't tell anyone what had happened. Mrs Ellis told St Mary's that she had got me a live-in job in her own village. I didn't know where that was then, but she's told me since it's on the Wirral.

'I did try to get away because at first it scared me that Mr Ellis must know that I lived in one of the tower blocks on Everton Brow. I was afraid he might come callin' . . .' she shuddered, 'because of course I felt I never wanted to see him again. That was why I tried for the job in Southport, but as you know I didn't gerrit and I suppose I was daft to try.'

'No, you weren't daft, but you still haven't explained why you were packing your stuff and planning to leave when I came in,' Martin pointed out. 'Go on with the story, Rose. Tell me the lot and let's gerrit over, and then we can talk about what's best to do.'

Rose sighed and wiped away a tear that was trickling down her cheek. 'This afternoon, I went to the clinic and saw Dr Matthews. We talked a bit about when my baby was due and then I

130

mentioned Mrs Ellis. I told you she'd said she was expecting a baby herself, so I asked how she was getting on. Dr Matthews told me it were a false alarm. He said it often happens when a woman decides to adopt and stops worrying about why she can't get pregnant. Then she relaxes and she does, see?'

Martin nodded, not really seeing at all but not wanting to interrupt the flow.

'I said how sorry I was and then Dr Matthews said not to worry because when my baby was born Mrs Ellis would love it as dearly as though it were her own and would bring it up beautifully, because she was such a good person. He said he hoped I knew how lucky I was to have someone ready and willing to take on my baby and give it the best of everything. Mart, I just stared at him whilst he rabbited on about my never even having to see the baby and how Mrs Ellis would find me a good job and continue to pay the rent on my flat.'

There was an appalled silence whilst Martin tried to take in what Rose was telling him. Finally, he spoke. 'But Rose, that would be stealing! It's your baby . . . didn't you tell Dr Matthews that you wanted to keep it? He's awful nice and I'm sure he'd tell Mrs Ellis for you if you didn't want to do it yourself.'

'I did try,' Rose said, and to Martin's dismay he saw the tears begin to well up in her eyes again. 'But he got up and came over and patted my shoulder and said that as far as he could see, my keeping the baby was impossible. He told me what the rent of the flat was—it's a huge sum, Mart—and began to list all the things I'd have to buy to keep myself and the baby. Oh, not just food, but heating, lighting and rates, whatever they may be. He said if I kept the baby I couldn't expect Mrs Ellis to go on supporting me. Then he asked me if there was any possibility of my marrying the father.' She gave a watery chuckle, wiping the tears from her cheeks with the heels of both hands. 'It was on the tip of me tongue to tell him that it were Mr Ellis, but I didn't because I could just imagine what would happen. After all, I had promised Mrs Ellis never to say who the father was, and from what Dr Matthews said she honestly believes that what she plans to do is what I want. You see, to begin with I really didn't want the baby and I reckon I said so practically every time we talked. Mrs Ellis said then that she would arrange to have it adopted and I was all for it. To tell you the truth, Mart, thinking back, I never really told her I'd changed my mind.'

'Well, *I* knew you wanted to keep the baby and I reckon, in her heart, Mrs Ellis knows too,' Martin said obstinately. 'If you didn't want it, why have you been collecting all them little clothes, and the nappies and all that?'

'She doesn't know about my hope chest because I was saving it as a surprise,' Rose reminded him. 'Of course, I still haven't got what they call at the clinic a complete layette, but I reckon I've got enough to be going on with.' She looked shyly at Martin, tears still trembling on her sandy eyelashes. 'To tell you the truth, Mart, I've always had an uneasy sort of feeling that she might try to interfere when the baby arrives. Oh, I don't mean adoption—I never thought of that. I thought she might try to tell me what to do . . . you know . . . oh, I can't explain, but I thought it would be better if I could manage without her help right from the start.'

'But wharrabout when it's older?' Martin asked.

Rose shrugged. 'It don't matter, because I shan't be here,' she said. 'If I stay, they'll take my baby, her and Mr Ellis. There won't be a thing I can do to stop them because they'll say I'm too young to look after it meself, or they might even say that Mr Ellis is the father and can do what he likes.' Martin began to protest, to say that he would support her, but Rose cut him short. 'It's no good, Mart,' she said miserably. 'He's a rich and powerful man and of course everyone who knows her admires Mrs Ellis. Anything they say will be believed. Any tale I tell would be dismissed as a tissue of lies. Even if they believed me, they'd still take the baby away and it's mine!' She glared across the table as though he had tried to contradict her words. 'So I'm going, Mart, going as far away as I can get, and I'm going now!'

'No, you aren't,' Martin said calmly, as Rose got to her feet and headed for the door. 'Just you sit down again, our Rosie, and begin to think with that bright little brain of yours! You say Mrs Ellis means to take your baby, and I believe you, so we won't lerrit happen. But she hasn't tried to take *you*, has she? And until the baby is born, anyone who wants to take it will have to take you as well. Gerrit? But if Dr Matthews lets on that you want to keep it, then I suppose it's possible that them wicked buggers might kidnap you, take you away to their castle and keep you under armed guard until after the birth. Is that what you're afraid of, princess?'

Rose, who had returned to her seat at the table,

133

gave a feeble giggle.

'The point is, queen, that if you run now, this minute, where do you mean to go?' Martin said. 'And what will we take with us? Then there's my job; I wouldn't like to let Mr Cornwallis down. If I could just give a week's notice, I'd get my money and there'd be no hard feelings. And we'd still be away in plenty of time.'

Rose reached across the table and clutched Martin's hands, squeezing them tightly. 'Mart, did you really mean it when you said "we"? Would you come with me? I were goin' to ask you if I could take Don because I remembered you sayin' he protected you when you were sleepin' rough, but I never thought to ask if you'd come as well.'

Martin shook his head reproachfully. 'As if I'd let you go without me!' he said. 'You've been rare good to me, Rosie, letting me share this flat, taking care of me when I were ill, findin' posh clothes for me interview so's I got the job, cookin' lovely meals . . .'

'Oh, shurrup,' Rose said with pretended wrath. 'You've no idea how much safer I've felt in this block since you and Don moved in. I'm not scared of the neighbours any more—well, not very—and it's been grand to have someone to go around with. Remember the picnic in Prince's Park, when we fed the ducks and went for a row on the lake? I know it were bleedin' cold but we had a grand day, didn't we?'

'We did,' Martin agreed. 'So are you going to leave in a week, instead of in a moment? Oh, Rosie, I know it's hard on you because you might have to see Mrs Ellis and pretend you don't know what she's planning, but honest to God, girl, I promise you it's for the best. We've got to get together all the money we can. We'll have to sell your furniture, or some of it at any rate, and any clothing which you don't actually need for the next few months. Money is a lot easier to carry than things, though we'll take some food of course when we go. I suppose we could leave it a little longer, but I reckon you'd feel a lot safer if we went in a week, like I said. Wherever we go, you'll need to put yourself on a doctor's panel and book a hospital bed for the actual birth. So I reckon . . . let me see, today's Friday, so we'll leave a week on Monday, after I've been paid. If we go first thing, we should be OK.'

Rose nodded. 'I suppose you're right and it would be madness to run away with nothing but a couple of bags and the clothes we stand up in,' she said. 'I just wonder how I shall keep my true feelings hidden if I meet Mrs Ellis!'

Chapter Six

'Is that everything?' Martin whispered, hefting the two bulging suitcases and trying to look as though they weighed almost nothing. He watched as Rose, in her turn, slung a knapsack over one shoulder and picked up her canvas marketing bag, which contained as much food as he had decided she could carry. Now, standing in the middle of the tiny hall, he looked around him, realising perhaps for the first time that they were about to leave the nearest thing to a real home he had ever known. They had shut the doors carefully so that anyone entering the premises might not see immediately that most of the furniture had gone. Only those items that Mrs Ellis had provided remained. They were still in the flat and could be reclaimed by her if she chose to do so, which eased Rose's conscience; at least she could not be accused of taking anything which was not her own.

Martin smiled to himself, remembering how Don had behaved when the men from the auction room had come to collect the stuff that was to be sold. The dog had rushed into the kitchen and lain down on his blanket as though to protect it from these marauders and Martin had shut him in, worried that he might not understand they had consented to—indeed encouraged—the removal of their belongings.

The thought made Martin remember how he had helped to carry the sofa down the stairs, and how a neighbour had popped out and addressed him, face alive with curiosity. 'Who's movin' out?' she had asked. 'I don't reckernise none of that furniture.'

'Top floor,' he had said gruffly, glad that he had been wearing his cap and coat, since she had obviously taken him for one of the removal men. 'Name of . . . oh, Evans, were it? But I dunno as they're moving out, just gerrin' a bob or two for the old stuff and replacin' it, I reckon.'

The old woman had sniffed. 'There's nowt wrong with that there sofy as I can see,' she had remarked enviously as the sofa passed her door. 'Goin' to Paddy's Market, is it? Or the auction rooms?'

'Auction,' Martin had mumbled over his shoulder, as he had begun to descend the next flight. 'On Tuesday next, if you want to purrin a bid.'

'Oh aye? When I win the bleedin' pools—' The rest of the sentence had been cut off by the slamming of the door. Martin had not known her, but when he recounted the incident to Rose later she had said that it must have been Mrs Templeton, the only person in the flats that she really knew. 'I take her in a bit of cake or an old magazine from time to time,' she had said. 'Poor old gal, she's rare lonely, shut away up here.'

Now, Martin raised an eyebrow at his friend. 'All right?' he enquired. 'Time to go?'

Rose nodded and slipped the rope into Don's collar. 'Might as well,' she said, with a little shake in her voice. 'Oh, Mart, I'll be that glad when it's over, and we're safe. If only they don't find out we've flitted until we've got away.'

'They won't; we've made our plans far too carefully,' Martin said. 'I'm going to Central Station and will make my way to Chester from there. You'll go down to the Pier Head and catch the ferry to Woodside. We'll meet up on Chester station and from there it should be safe for us to travel together. You've got further to go than me, so I'll give you ten minutes' start. Now are you clear what you have to do?'

'Of course I am,' Rose said rather crossly. 'When I get off the ferry, I catch the number one bus to Chester, then make my way to the station where you and Don will probably be waiting. From there we'll get on the train for Rhyl.'

'That's it, queen,' Martin said encouragingly. He hung on to Don's collar and gave Rose a little push. 'Off you go! See you later.'

137

It was past noon before Martin, Rose and Don climbed rather stiffly down from the carriage on to the platform at Rhyl station. 'Can we leave the suitcases in their left luggage?' Rose asked hopefully as, heavily laden, they staggered from the platform. 'We can always claim them back when we've found somewhere to stay.'

Martin, however, vetoed this idea. 'Folk may think we're runaways without no luggage,' he explained. 'Best if we take the lot with us.'

'Well, we are runaways,' Rose said rather peevishly, but Martin shook his head.

'We are nothing of the sort,' he said firmly. 'We don't owe rent because we've handed the flat back to Mrs Ellis and left the key on the string. We're neither of us school kids, nor we don't have parents to run away from, so you can rest easy on that score.' He had stood the suitcases down for a moment to argue, but now he picked them up and set off, turning to smile at her. 'Would Madam like a room facing the sea or would she prefer an inland view?'

Rose meant to reply gaily but she was too exhausted to make the effort. 'I don't care what the bleedin' place faces,' she said. 'I just want somewhere to lay me perishin' head, somewhere we can afford.'

'Right. We'll tell the landlady we just need a room for a couple of nights. We'll say we're on our way to somewhere further up the coast—that'll explain why we've got so much luggage—though of course if it's a nice place and we can afford it we might stay for longer. I mean to look for work first

138

thing tomorrow, and you never know your luck.'

*   *   *

Two hours later, sitting opposite one another at a small table in a café on Russell Road, Martin made a big decision. 'Look, queen, I can tell you're worn to the bone and I'm pretty tired meself. As for poor old Don, all this pavement work must have given him sore pads, to say the least. And d'you know why we've been turned away from every perishin' place we've tried?'

'Course I does,' Rose said at once. 'I'm clearly in the family way, and even if folk didn't notice first go off they'd turn us down 'cos of Don.'

'Wrong on both counts,' Martin told her. 'It's because you aren't wearing a wedding ring, you silly girl, and we're asking for two rooms. An unmarried couple, particularly when one of them's pregnant, could cause a landlady a lorra grief.'

'Oh, I *see*,' Rose said. 'But what are we to *do*, Mart? We can't possibly get married before tonight and I'm damned if I'll sleep on the beach. And anyway, I don't want to get married!'

'I'm not suggesting . . . look, you goose, when we walked down Regent Road to the front we passed a big Woollies. All we have to do is find a curtain ring what fits on your finger, pay over our penny or whatever, and tell the next landlady we try that we're Mr and Mrs Something looking for a room for a couple of nights.'

Rose chortled and leaned across to give Martin's hand a squeeze. 'That's a grand idea. I'm real sorry I don't want to marry you,' she said remorsefully. 'You're so good, Mart, and so kind, but I want to

139

marry someone tall, dark and handsome, what'll whisk me away to live a life of luxury. Only even me dream man needn't come around for ten or fifteen years, 'cos it'll take me that long to forget what horrible old Ellis did.'

'I'm not surprised. But for now, all I want to know is whether you'll go along with sharing a room and just pretend to be me wife,' Martin said.

'Don't mind sharin' a room, but I'm buggered if I'll be Mrs Something,' Rose said. 'Let's call ourselves Bunn, Mart, because I've got one in the oven, you know!'

After various ribald suggestions, which made them both laugh helplessly, Martin decided that they should use his real name—Thompson—since he thought that a change of his own surname would be not only superfluous but also unwise, just in case he had to claim the dole.

Immensely cheered by the sit-down, the cup of tea and the iced bun that had accompanied it, the three of them left the café and headed for Woolworth's. They had been pleased when the waitresses had taken it for granted that Don would enter the café with them, and were equally pleased when Woolworth's accepted the dog with complaisance. They found the haberdashery counter and bought a curtain ring, then went a little further along to where there was a display of costume jewellery, for Martin said that an engagement ring would give credence to their married status. He could see that Rose was really enjoying herself, for she chose a ring as though it had not been brass and glass but sapphires and diamonds, picking in the end a three-stone band of blue and white which twinkled as brightly, Martin was sure, as though it were the genuine article. He also noticed that afterwards Rose walked along with her hand held out in front of her, so that she could gaze at her new possession. He wondered whether to warn her not to make too much of it, but she was so plainly thrilled to possess even a little one-and-tenpenny ring that he decided not to be critical. If the next landlady they tried seemed suspicious, then he might have to mention it, but until then Rose should be allowed to enjoy her 'jewellery'.

Leaving the centre of the town, they approached another side street and marched, resolutely, up a short tiled path to the faded front door of a tall three-storey terraced house. It had a notice in its bay window reading *'Vacancies'*, so Martin knocked and after a few moments the door opened to reveal a small, mouse-like woman wearing an apron, with rollers in her hair. She peered at them for a moment without speaking, then fished in her apron pocket and produced a pair of spectacles, which she perched on her small snub nose. 'Yes?' she said, subjecting them—and their luggage—to a sharp scrutiny. 'Are you wantin' a room?'

Martin saw with apprehension that her mouth, which turned down at the corners, shut like a rat-trap when she was not speaking, and the eyes which scanned the small party were calculating rather than friendly. But he told himself that one should not judge by appearances and gave her the benefit of his brightest smile. 'Yes, that's right, we're looking for a room,' he said. He saw no point in explanations until they were asked for, so did not mention Don though, heaven knew, the woman could scarcely have missed the enormous

141

creature.

The landlady, however, now made it clear that she had indeed noticed Don. 'That's a greyhound,' she observed. 'Does he race?'

'No, no, he's retired, though he were a great winner in his day,' Martin said quickly. 'He's house-trained, of course, never barks and is very obedient. He's no trouble. My—my wife and meself . . .'

The woman stepped back and gestured them inside. 'Me hubby kept a couple o' greyhounds when we was first wed,' she remarked. 'Come in and we'll discuss things.'

Once in the hallway, the landlady introduced herself as Mrs Osborne and explained her terms. 'I'm well known for me winter lets,' she said smugly. 'Of course I don't go in for permanents— too many rules and regulations—so me winter lets has to leave before Whitsun. I used to say Easter, but times have changed and holidaymakers is comin' later for some reason. Mebbe it's the weather or mebbe it's 'cos the dates is so different; well, last year Easter Day was the tenth of April, as I recall, an' this year it's the first. I reckon, meself, folks is reluctant to come to the seaside so early and mebbe find they're in for days of rain and gales. Any road, you can stay here till the week before Whit, 'cos I need a week to clean the place through for the holidaymakers.'

'That's fair enough,' Martin said, before Rose could answer, 'if the room is satisfactory, that is. I don't have a job lined up yet but I shall start looking first thing tomorrow.' He smiled at the landlady. 'We're the Thompsons, by the way. May we see the room, please? Or is it rooms?'

142

'I've only one room left,' Mrs Osborne said sharply. 'It's on the top floor, which means a sloping ceiling but I dare say you won't mind that. I've an idea me best front may be comin' vacant in a week or so, but I charge more for that one, 'cos it's a grand big room. I'll give a knock to the door as we pass and if the Renaldos aren't in you can have a peep, but otherwise it's the back room on the top floor; take it or leave it.'

Neither Rose nor Martin spoke, so the landlady preceded them up a flight of carpeted stairs which ended on a sizeable landing from which three doors led off. She raised her hand to knock on one of the doors, but Martin said quickly: 'Please don't bother, Mrs Osborne. I'm sure the back room will suit us fine. If the better room becomes vacant and I'm in work, then perhaps we might think again, but for the moment . . .'

The landlady sniffed in a disparaging sort of way but flung open the middle door, revealing a bathroom and lavatory combined. The room was cramped and decidedly scruffy, with a large gas geyser over the bath, scuffed brown linoleum on the floor, and a hand basin with a glass shelf above it upon which were ranged a variety of different objects—toothbrushes, toothpaste and bars of soap jostled with safety razors, shaving foam, shampoo and hair cream. 'Geyser works on shillings; you can get a good deep bath for two bob,' Mrs Osborne informed them. 'You must work out for yourselves when it's your turn, though. Men shave in their rooms, save for the theatre folk, 'cos they has to look their best for Wednesday and Sat'day matinées and evening performances. I cleans the bathroom and keeps

143

the kitchen respectable 'cos it's what you might call mutual territory, but your room is your own concern an' I hopes as you'll keep it spotless. And when I say I cleans the kitchen, I mean the floor, the surfaces and the refrigerator. You'll do your own pots and pans, of course, and crockery and that, and wipe down anything else you've used.'

'Where is the kitchen?' Rose asked as the landlady led them up a flight of very much narrower uncarpeted stairs.

Mrs Osborne paused to answer. 'Ground floor,' she said briefly. 'Me and hubby and our fambly has the basement flat. I'll show you the kitchen on the way down.' At this point they reached a small and dusty landing and Mrs Osborne flung open one of the two brown-painted doors. 'This is the one,' she said, ushering them inside. 'I reckon it 'ud suit the three of you—and the babby, when it comes— though Mr Thompson will have to watch his head when he's gettin' into bed.' She gave an unexpected cackle of laughter. 'Me other third floor lodgers are Mr and Mrs Scott. Mr Scott is a big feller, though not as tall as you, and when he first moved in I told him if he kept knockin' plaster off me ceiling I'd add it to his rent.' She peered questioningly at Martin, who was still wearing his cap pulled well down across his brow. 'Well?'

Glancing round, Martin saw that it was a big attic room with plenty of space for Don's blanket, whilst he himself could kip down in a sleeping bag on the floor. There was a washstand with a jug and ewer on it, a small, rather rickety table, two kitchen chairs and a chest of drawers. It was clear why there was no wardrobe, because the sloping ceiling

144

came down to within four feet of the floor. In addition to the furniture there was a Primus stove and a very small electric fire, beside which was a coin meter.

Mrs Osborne began to extol the virtues of the room, urging them to come over to the window. 'You've gorra sea view,' she said proudly. 'It ain't many people as can offer a sea view this cheap. Well? Are you goin' to take it? I've not got all day, you know. Me hubby and me sons come in around six o'clock and expect a hot meal on the table.'

Martin smiled winningly at the landlady. 'We'll take it,' he said firmly. 'And we'll pay two weeks in advance. Is that satisfactory, Mrs Osborne?'

'Yes, that'll do, Mr Thompson,' Mrs Osborne said. 'Would you like to leave those cases up here? You'll want to get yourselves something to eat; if you go up to the prom there's plenty of cheap places where you can get a meal. I'll show you the kitchen on your way out.'

The three of them, and Don, hurried down the stairs and were shown into what must have been the original kitchen before the house was divided into bedsitters. It was a sizeable room with red quarry tiles on the floor, a large stone sink flanked by two wooden draining boards, a modern refrigerator and a gas cooker so old that Martin thought it must have been installed when the house was built.

Mrs Osborne led them in and waved a proprietorial hand at a row of dilapidated saucepans hanging on hooks above the cooker. 'Them's for use in the kitchen and not to be took to your own room,' she said. 'Likewise the kitchen utensils what's kept in the drawer beside the sink.

You can use the fridge for milk or butter, but not for things what smells strong, and don't you go takin' the tea towels—the ones on me airer, up by the ceiling—because they're for kitchen use only. I forgot to show you that there's a cupboard on the top landing with a carpet sweeper, dustpan and brush, cleanin' cloths and so on. You share 'em with Mr and Mrs Scott. Oh, and you've your own cookin' stuff—fryin' pan et cetera—in the bottom drawer of the chest by the window. The Primus stove is grand for boilin' the kettle and scramblin' a few eggs, or warmin' up a tin o' soup, but of course if you want a roast meal you'll have to use the kitchen.' She sounded regretful, as though too much use of the kitchen would spoil its far from perfect beauty. 'All right? You'd best come down into the basement so I can give you a copy of me rules book and your rent book, and you can give me your first fortnight's rent.'

'Rules book?' Rose hissed into Martin's ear as they descended the half-dozen stairs that led down to their landlady's flat. 'Wharrever next? Mustn't have a bath when you feel like it, only when you're allowed, only use the refrigerator for perishables . . .'

Martin dug a reproving elbow into Rose's well-covered ribs. 'Shurrup,' he hissed, as their landlady opened a green-painted door and ushered them into a large sitting room. Martin blinked. The carpet, patterned with flowers the like of which he had never seen in his life, was vividly coloured and the large sofa and four easy chairs were upholstered in a chintz so bright that he was grateful for his tinted spectacles. The walls were covered in dark red plush paper and a television,

146

set in a large cabinet, dominated the room. 'Gosh, a television!' Martin breathed. It was the first one he had ever seen, though they were widely advertised in newspapers and magazines. He would have liked to ask Mrs Osborne whether she ever allowed her lodgers to watch it, but did not do so for the landlady, he felt sure, was not the type to give favours.

Mrs Osborne crossed to a very fancy sideboard cum cocktail cabinet and pulled open a small drawer, extracting an exercise book and a sheet of printed instructions which she folded into four and handed to Martin. 'Them's me rules and this here's me winter-let rent book,' she said. 'Sit down a moment while I fill in your details.'

* * *

Presently, seated on either side of a small table in a fish and chip café, with hot food and cups of tea in front of them, they talked over the sheet of rules and wondered how easy it would be to find themselves paid employment. 'I don't suppose I'll get anything because no one's going to want to employ someone in my condition,' Rose said regretfully, between mouthfuls. 'But you will, Mart, I'm sure you will. And by the time the baby's born it'll be almost Whit, and I remember someone saying that there are always jobs in seaside towns once the weather begins to get better. They say old people come in droves in June, and of course the school holidays start in July, so parents bring their kids and the shops and cafés need all the assistants and waitresses they can get. Oh, we'll be all right so long as the Ellises don't come down to Rhyl to search for us.'

'I think we laid too good a false trail,' Martin observed. 'I daresay they might put out a proper search for you because even though you're having a baby you're still awful young to be on the loose. But remember, Mrs Ellis can't go to the scuffers without revealing that she has done some really bad things.'

'Hey, wharrabout Mr Ellis, then?' Rose asked indignantly. 'He were the one what did bad things, not Mrs Ellis. She's awright, she is . . . well, compared wi' him, at any rate.'

'Oh, Rosie, do *think*,' Martin implored. He took a long drink of his tea, then wiped his mouth with the back of his hand. He had taken off his cap and kept glancing around, but no one seemed to have noticed his dead white hair and pale skin. 'Mrs Ellis told the staff at the clinic that you were eighteen when she knew very well you weren't. And you said she'd told the staff at the children's home that she'd got you a live-in job somewhere on the Wirral. In fact she's made a liar of *you*, because she made you promise to stick to the story and not tell a soul the truth. And them's just the lies we know about; I bet she's told lots more, because once you start in lying, it's dead hard to stop. Oh, I know you think she were a good friend to you, but it were only so's she could steal your baby.'

'So does that mean she won't search for me?' Rose asked, brightening. 'At least it means we shan't have the scuffers on our heels. But I say, Mart, could *you* get into trouble for hidin' me away? If so, perhaps it ain't fair for me to expect your help.'

148

Martin pulled a face. 'I dunno, but I reckon if I say I thought you must be eighteen or nineteen to have your own flat, I'll be safe enough,' he said reassuringly. 'Besides, you said right at the beginning that people in the flats might think I were the baby's father. We might pretend, Rose, just to keep us both out of trouble, that it's true, 'cos you can't chuck a father in prison for taking care of his little baby and what-d'you-call-it wife.'

'Common law wife, I think it's called,' Rose said. They had left all their heavy luggage in their new home, but now Rose fished in her shabby little handbag and produced her clinic book, a variety of other documents, a large square ink rubber and a ballpoint pen, and began to work. Ten minutes later, she handed her clinic book to Martin. The name Gertrude Pleavin had been neatly erased and now read Rose Thompson.

Martin whistled and handed the book back. 'Who taught you forgery?' he said, grinning. 'That's a real neat job, Rosie; I don't reckon anyone will question it when you start going to the clinic here in Rhyl. Are you goin' to do the rest of your stuff as well?'

'Reckon I'd better,' Rose said, starting on the next piece of paper. 'I'm going to put me name down at the clinic as soon as I can, though I'm not looking forward to it. I'll ask Mrs Osborne where I should go; I reckon she'll probably know.'

*   *   *

Rosie awoke. For a moment she simply lay there, staring up at a ceiling which appeared to be only a matter of a couple of feet above her, and wondering where on earth she was. Then, turning her head slightly, she saw Martin's humped shape in the makeshift bed he had arranged for himself the night before, and recollection came flooding back. They had escaped! Everything had gone according to plan and they were now the official tenants of Room 6, Sunny Sands House, 27 Bath Street. Rose sat up on her elbow and Don, who had appeared to be soundly asleep curled up on his blanket, lifted his head and gave her the benefit of his most ingratiating grin. Rose grinned back, then snuggled down beneath the blankets again. There was no hurry today; Martin thought he stood a good chance of getting work, but even he would not want to start his job search so early in the morning.

Rose had actually closed her eyes when it occurred to her that what was coming through the thin curtains was sunshine, and this reminded her that she had no idea of the time. Hastily, she sat up and stared across at the tinny little alarm clock that Martin had bought when he had first moved into the tower block. She had remembered to wind it the night before but had not set the alarm and now saw, with considerable surprise, that it was ten to eight. If Martin was to have breakfast before he left, she had best wake him and put the kettle on to boil.

Rose jumped out of bed, then hesitated. It seemed awful mean to wake Martin, who had had an extremely tiring time of it the day before, but whilst she hesitated indecisively, Don made the decision for her. He stood up and pushed his long wet nose against Martin's neck, causing that young person to utter a muffled squawk before sitting up like a jack-in-the-box and exclaiming: 'Oh, my Gawd! I'll be late for work and they'll give me the sack . . . where the devil am I? What's goin' on?'

Rose, who had filled the kettle the night before, balanced it on the Primus stove and began to pump. Glancing over her shoulder as she lit the match, she said consolingly: 'It's all right, Mart, you haven't gone mad and you can't be late for work because you haven't found none yet. We're in Rhyl and we're goin' to make do with cereal and tea this mornin', so you can go to the Labour Exchange; the early bird catches the worm.'

'Well, how could I forget all that!' Martin marvelled, rubbing his eyes. He got out of bed, clad now in his shirt, socks and underpants, and walked across to the window to pull back the thin curtains. 'I say, look at that view! And the old girl were right: you can just about see the sea over the rooftops if you move your head around a bit.'

Rose joined him at the window. 'I'm not as tall as you, but even I can see a little bit of sea,' she said excitedly. 'Tell you what, Mart, I'll get dressed right now and bolt some of them cornflakes and a cuppa, and then the pair of us can walk Don on the beach. You won't want to start askin' for work until after nine o'clock.'

'That sounds fine, but wharrabout washin'?' Martin asked rather doubtfully. 'When we was in the tower block, I washed and dressed in the kitchen while you did the same in the bathroom, but here we've only the one room, and when a feller is lookin' for work he's got to be as clean as a new pin and as neat as he can afford.'

Rose sighed. This was one aspect of their sharing a room that she had not considered. She certainly

151

had no intention of washing and dressing in front of Martin, and guessed that he would feel the same. Then she was struck by a bright idea. 'I'll put me clothes on right away—shoes an' everything—and take Don round the block while you get ready,' she said. 'No one will think it odd because he's a big dog and needs all the exercise we can give him. After today, we can sort it out easily, I'm sure.'

Martin thought this was a good idea but suggested that instead of taking the dog at once, Rose should pop down to the kitchen and meet some of the other tenants whilst enquiring whether it would be possible for her to cook porridge on one of the gas rings. Rose agreed and hastily threw a voluminous maternity dress over the underwear in which she had slept, shoved her feet into her flat and comfortable shoes, and set off. She went down to the kitchen, but found it occupied by only one other person, a pretty, dark-haired girl who was peering anxiously into a small saucepan balanced on the stove. The girl turned as Rose and Don entered and uttered an exclamation, which was echoed by Rose. For a moment they simply stared at one another and then Rose began to giggle, for both of them were wearing identical maternity dresses, and both appeared to be in the same advanced stage of pregnancy.

'I'm awful sorry to laugh. You must think me dreadfully rude,' Rose said, smiling at the other girl. 'But wharra coincidence, ain't it? I mean you and me, both in the family way and both wearin' the very same dress.'

'You can say that again,' the dark-haired girl said. 'You must be in number six; my—my husband

152

said he heard someone moving round last night. Old Ozzie will be chuffed to bits to have let her very last room. She's always boastin' that her winter lets are the cheapest and best in Rhyl. Oh, by the way, I'm Millie Scott.' She held out a slender hand and Rose saw, enviously, that her beautiful filbert nails were enamelled pale pink and that she wore, on the third finger of her left hand, a broad gold band.

'How do you do, Millie,' Rose said, taking the hand and shaking it warmly. 'I'm Rose Thompson and my—er—my feller's Martin. I came down to ask if I could cook porridge on the stove. I don't want to do it this morning, but perhaps tomorrow . . . We only arrived in Rhyl yesterday, and I've got to take old Don here out for a widdle, so probably by the time I get back Martin will have eaten his cornflakes and be ready for the off.'

'You'll be all right to cook porridge because most of us make do with cereal or toast for breakfast, and over the weekend anyone who isn't working will want a lie-in,' Millie informed her. 'But I say, fancy her letting you keep a dog, especially up on the third floor. She's a real tartar; the words "you can't, you shouldn't, you mustn't" are her absolute favourites. But of course they say number six has been vacant all winter so I suppose she'd have grabbed almost anyone . . . sorry. I didn't mean that the way it sounds.'

'I think she only let us bring Don because her husband used to keep greyhounds when they were first married,' Rose explained. 'Oh, if you're cooking eggs, they've just boiled over.'

Millie squeaked and whipped around, grabbing the small pan off the flame so jerkily that the water

153

slopped over and half extinguished the ring. 'Oh God, and Scotty gets quite nasty if I hard-boil his breakfast egg,' she said. She hooked two eggs out of the water and plopped them into a couple of egg cups. 'But if I behead them now and stick a knob of butter into the yolk, he'll be in such a hurry to get it ate that he probably won't even notice. I did the bread and butter up in our room and Scotty's making the tea. You go off with your dog, and by the time you come back I'll have had my breakfast, Scotty will have gone to work and we can have a nice natter. We might trot along to the clinic so that you'll know where it is.'

'I promised Martin that Don and I would go with him to the Labour Exchange when we find out where it is,' Rose said regretfully. 'I suppose you couldn't wait until I get back?'

'Course I could,' Millie said promptly. 'I've got some ironing which wants doing so I won't be wasting my time. You give me a knock when you get back and we'll take a look round the town.'

'Oh, that would be grand,' Rose said gratefully, 'because we don't know anything about it. I came here once, on a school trip, but that were ages ago and they marched us in a crocodile down to the beach and back to a big café—the Seagull, I think it were called—and then it were a rush through the streets to reach the coach before it set off back to the 'Pool.'

'Well then, off you go,' Millie said, picking up a small tray with the boiled eggs in their neat little egg cups perched on it. 'I'll introduce you to the other tenants later, because most of them turn up in the kitchen at some time or other. And I'll wait for your knock.'

154

'Thanks ever so,' Rose called, as her new friend left the kitchen and began to climb the stairs. 'See you in about an hour.'

Returning to her own room presently, she told Martin all about the other tenant. 'I want to go down to the beach and have a paddle, but I guess we'll have to do that another day, since we've got to go the Labour Exchange, and then Millie and me's goin' to do the town!'

Rose, Martin and Don set off into the bright and sunny morning, chattering gaily of the fun that they would have once Martin was settled in work. 'Oh, Martin, I'm so happy that if it wasn't for my bump, I'd turn cartwheels all along the prom.'

Martin laughed. 'Then I'm glad you've got a bump because I dare say we'd be taken up and flung in prison if you went around showin' your knickers in such a brazen fashion,' he said. 'But I know what you mean. After having to be so careful that no one saw us together, and spending the last week planning our getaway, I feel free as air and happy as—as a sand boy. What is a sand boy, any road?'

'I dunno,' Rose said, rather breathlessly, slowing her pace. 'I say, that's the funfair, ain't it? Can we go up there later?'

'We've got no money to spend on rides and that,' Martin said rather dubiously. 'Still, it won't hurt to take a look.'

An hour later, Rose was knocking on Millie's door and announcing, in thrilling tones, that Martin had got a job, thanks to her.

'Well, isn't that wonderful,' Millie said with real enthusiasm. She took a thick scarlet coat from its hook and put it on, then added a bright red beret and scarlet mittens. Then she picked up a large straw shopping basket and adjusted the beret at a jaunty angle on her smooth black hair, turning to look anxiously at Rose as she did so. 'Is that all right?' she asked. She snatched up a curved clothes brush from a small hallstand and handed it to Rose. 'Just brush my shoulders, will you? I don't want specks of dandruff or loose hairs on this coat because God knows when we'll be able to afford another.'

'Why on earth would you want another?' Rose said, vigorously brushing, though there was not so much as a speck of anything on the beautiful red material. 'I bet you haven't had this coat long; it's got one of the new shawl collars.'

'True,' Millie said, as they left the room. She closed the door carefully, saying as she did so: 'Scotty's been talking about getting a lock for the door ever since we moved in, but it doesn't seem worth it. I expect we will remain until Whit, when hopefully we'll be able to rent not just a room but a little house, or a flat. You see, once the baby's born I mean to go back to work. My parents made me attend secretarial school for six months and then I got myself a job as secretary to the managing director of the factory where Scotty worked.'

The two of them clattered down the stairs, but on reaching the hall Millie stopped suddenly, tugging at Rose's arm. 'But what about your dog? I don't think they'll allow him in the shops . . . or has your feller taken him?'

Rose shook her head. 'No, he's not with Mart. We took him down to the beach earlier and let him belt along the sand until he was exhausted while

156

we walked up to the funfair; then we went back to our room and left him flat out. He'll be fine; either Mart or meself will take him out again before we go to bed.'

'That's all right then,' Millie said as they emerged on to the pavement. She gazed from left to right. 'You never told me about your feller's job; I'm so sorry, rambling on when you must be dying to explain. Let's walk along the prom and you can fill me in.'

'Right,' Rose said. 'Well, I suggested that we might visit the funfair—just to look, you understand—and it was closed, but there were one or two chaps painting and greasing . . . oh, you know, maintenance I suppose it's called. And Mart had a bit of a laugh wi' one feller and said he were lookin' for work, and he said to go to the office, because people were always movin' on . . . oh, look at that sparkling sea. How I wish we had time for a paddle!'

'Yes, yes, but go on,' Millie said impatiently. 'You're as bad as me for getting off the subject. 'So you went to the office, and . . . ?'

'And they wanted someone on the dodgem cars at weekends, to tek the money and see that folk didn't just sit tight wi'out payin' again, and they could also do wi' another hand on the gallopers because they need repainting,' Rose said quickly. 'Gallopers is what they call the roundabout. The pay isn't much, but the chap in the office said that if Mart was satisfactory it 'ud be steady work. Then someone said the Mad Mouse—that's what they call the scenic railway—needed overhauling, greasing and so on, which will be at least another month's work . . . and once the summer starts there will be all sorts of work available.'

'And can you manage on what he'll earn?' Millie asked, her voice rising to a squeak. 'I suppose since it's what you might call casual work he'll get the money in his hand and go on claiming the dole.'

'Oh no, we couldn't do that,' Rose said at once. 'You see, Mart had a good job in Liverpool so he didn't have to claim the dole, and if he starts claiming it now someone might get suspicious. We'll manage real well, honest to God we will. I've still got my Post Office book and so on, so we'll be okay. And I'll get some sort of job.'

'Well, good for you; and if you're earning, I suppose Ozzie's rent isn't too bad. I don't know exactly what Scotty earns but I know when I was a secretary my top take-home pay wasn't all that good. But I managed to have a lot of fun and buy fashionable clothes, and even go on holiday.'

'Yes, but I expect you were living at home and not having to pay rent,' Rose pointed out as they crossed the main road and headed for the prom. 'Oh, do let's go down on to the sand, even if it's only for a moment. I know I said I'd like to paddle but I wouldn't want your lovely coat to get all salty.'

'Well, all right, we'll walk along the beach for a bit,' Millie said. 'I shan't paddle, though, because I bet the water's freezing and if I catch a cold Scotty will say I did it on purpose. I don't know about your Martin, but I think Scotty's mother spoiled him something rotten. According to him, meals should be on the table so that he can come straight in from work, sit down and eat, and when things go wrong he has to look round for someone to blame.' She sighed. 'But I expect all men are the same.'

At this point, they lowered themselves on to the sand and slipped their shoes off. It felt deliciously warm to Rose's bare toes, and after a moment's hesitation she glanced at her companion. 'I don't think Mart's at all spoilt; quite the opposite. He spoils me because—because of my condition, and he spoils Don because he's always wanted a dog. In fact, he's the most unselfish person I've ever met.'

Millie considered this, her head on one side. 'Aren't you lucky?' she said. 'I expect it was a silly thing to say—that all men are the same—because I know very well everyone's different. Why, my own father is usually very easy-going, though I suppose you could say he's under my mother's thumb. At least, when I started going out with Scotty, it was my mother who said I'd live to regret it, and when she said that if Scotty and I married we need never darken their doors again, Father went along with it. So you see, although you could say my father paid the piper, it was my mother who called the tune.'

Rose was fascinated by this glimpse into family life. 'But why didn't they like Scotty?' she asked. 'I know I've never met him, never even seen him, but if you like him, I'm sure he must be very nice.'

'Oh, he is,' Millie said quickly. Too quickly, Rose wondered? 'He's most awfully handsome; all the girls in the factory are crazy about him. Oh, did I say he's trainee management? That means he'll be earning a lot of money one day. When he asked me out I was over the moon, and when he suggested we should marry, I simply thought that the two of us could talk my parents round. Only it

159

didn't work out like that. I took Scotty home, of course, and my mother was horrible. She kept looking him up and down and Scotty got cross— anyone would have—and when he gets cross he says things he doesn't really mean. So you see he rubbed my parents up the wrong way and they did the same to him. They absolutely forbade me to have anything more to do with him, which meant secret meetings, which were kind of exciting . . . can you understand?'

'I can understand that the way they treated you, and him, made you more determined than ever to get married,' Rose said after some thought. 'Couldn't they see that?'

Millie shook her head sadly. 'No, they couldn't. All they could see was that Scotty worked in a factory and wouldn't, they said, ever amount to anything because of his attitude. Even when I told them I was expecting Scotty's baby, they didn't relent. I thought they'd help us, release some of the money my grandfather left me, but they simply refused. They said I'd made my bed and must lie in it. So of course I got angry and went to see the family solicitor. I wouldn't let Scotty come too, in case he lost his temper, but it was no use. Grandpa's money is held in trust until I'm twenty-five, or until I marry a husband of whom my parents approve. Of course I had to tell Scotty and naturally he was furious. He wanted to confront my parents but I knew that would only make things worse.'

By now, the two girls had reached the tiny waves and Rose dipped her toe into the creaming surf. It was as cold as Millie had predicted, but Rose longed to hitch up her skirt and have a proper

160

paddle. However, Millie was turning back towards the prom so Rose, eager to hear the rest of the story, followed. 'So you and Scotty eloped, like in a Georgette Heyer book,' she said. 'Ain't that romantic, though? Go on with the story, Millie. What happened next?'

'There isn't much more to tell,' Millie said ruefully. 'We came to Rhyl because Scotty got the offer of promotion, with more money. We're much better off here because even the tiniest room in Liverpool costs a bomb and we both feel we're starting a new life. I've rung my parents a couple of times to suggest that we might visit them, but whoever answers the phone, even if it's my father, they just say "better not" and then put the phone down so quickly that I don't have a chance to argue.'

'Are you an only child?' Rose asked curiously. 'If so, your baby would be their first grandchild. I bet you anything you like they'll take you back just to get their hands on the baby. But of course, if you've brothers and sisters . . .'

By now the two were scrambling back on to the prom and Millie, pushing her feet into her shoes, turned to Rose and nodded vigorously. 'That's what Scotty says, because I am an only child, but I'm not sure myself whether the baby will work the magic.' She dusted sand off the skirts of her beautiful coat, picked up her straw bag and watched as Rose tried to get the sand off her wet feet. 'Still, you may be right. The only thing is, they might want to see the baby and even me, but if they won't let Scotty come too . . .' She sighed, then shook herself briskly. 'Are you ready? Let's get going then, and on the way you can tell me how you and Mart ended up in Ozzie's palatial apartments.' She grinned impishly at Rose. 'Your Martin must be well over six feet and he's a good deal older than you, isn't he? I was hiding behind my door when Ozzie brought you up to have a look at the room and I saw his white hair. There was just one lock sticking out from under his cap.' She giggled. 'I thought he was your father until I heard you calling him Mart.'

Rose laughed too. 'He's not quite nineteen and his hair is white because he's an albino,' she said frankly.

Millie's eyebrows shot up. They were beautiful eyebrows, thin and winged. Rose, examining her new friend's face, thought her not just pretty but beautiful. Her skin had a sort of translucence which goes with truly black hair and her eyes were very large, and such a dark blue that they could have been called navy. Looking at her properly for the first time, Rose realised that though Millie had seemed sophisticated, she was probably not much older than Rose herself. She was saying, 'An albino? I had an albino rabbit and a cousin of mine had an albino cat, but I didn't know a young man could be called that! Well, well, you learn something new every day. Oh, I'm sorry if I'm being rude, comparing your Martin to my rabbit, but I've honestly never heard of a person being all pink and white.' She clapped a hand to her mouth, then spoke through her fingers. 'Yes I have, though. Have you ever read *Jamaica Inn*? The clergyman who lured the ships to their doom with false lights was an albino.'

'Oh, but you've made him sound horrible, luring ships to their doom,' Rose said, dismayed. 'Mart

162

wouldn't hurt anyone, honest to God he wouldn't. It's just that his hair is white, yours is black and mine is red. It's—it's something we're born with.'

'Yes, I know that really,' Millie said quickly. 'I didn't mean anything by it. So he isn't even nineteen yet? Scotty's twenty-four and I shall be eighteen in a few weeks. How old are you?'

'Well, I'm almost sixteen,' Rose admitted.

By now they had reached the high street and Millie pointed ahead. 'See that big shop in front of us? It's Marks & Spencer, and on half-day closing they sell off their perishables cheap, so we want to go in there at around half past eleven every Thursday to pick up the best bargains. They do wonderful beef and onion pies; Scotty loves 'em.'

Chapter Seven

When Isobel Ellis was getting ready for work on Wednesday morning, it occurred to her that she had not seen her young friend for what must be ten days, and she felt a faint stirring of guilt. Normally, she tried to pop into the tower block a couple of times a week, just to check that all was well with her protégée, but her disappointment over the doctor's sad news that she was not pregnant had made her shy away from visiting the child. However, she told herself firmly that she was not the type of woman to give way to despair. After all, she had accustomed herself to the fact that at forty-three, and after ten years of marriage to her beloved Frank, she was unlikely to have a child of her own. Several years earlier, knowing how she longed for a family, Frank had suggested adoption but Isobel, after weeks of painful indecision, had decided against it.

The trouble was she had seen too much, coming into contact as she did with the seamier side of life in a big seaport. Though it would never do to admit it, she suspected that she and Frank would find it hard to love a backward or possibly mentally disturbed child, charming though it might have been as a little baby. It would be impossible to check the parentage, for most of the mothers who offered their babies for adoption either could not or would not give details of the man who had fathered their child.

When she had first realised that Gertrude Pleavin was expecting a baby and that her own dear Frank had fathered it, she had been appalled. She had a great admiration for Gertrude, whom she thought both lively and intelligent, and had berated Frank for the wicked thing he had done. But he had begged her to forgive him, explaining his actions as being as much a puzzle to him as they were to her, since there had been no affection on either side; indeed, he and the girl had scarcely known one another and he thought her an ugly little thing. He had put it down to temporary madness and had positively grovelled at Isobel's feet, begging her forgiveness and swearing never, never to do such a thing again.

When she had told him that Gertrude was pregnant, however, he had first promised financial support and then suggested that they might adopt the baby. Isobel had felt outraged that her husband should suggest her accepting his bastard, for that was what it amounted to. But Frank had persisted, reminding her how fond she was growing of the little Pleavin girl and how fond, he hoped, she was of himself. 'This way, you'll know more about the father even than you do about the mother,' he had pointed out. 'Darling Bella, this is probably our best possible chance of having the family we both longed for. You say Gertrude doesn't want the child—how could she, when she's scarcely more than a child herself?—so there would be no problem. Indeed, to have two people of excellent reputation and affluent means eager to take on the baby should seem to her like a dream come true.'

At first, Isobel had been unable to accept the idea, but gradually, as the weeks had passed, she realised that Frank was right. Gertrude would doubtless be delighted to know that her baby was going to a good home. When she had believed herself to be pregnant, she had decided to say nothing about adoption to Gertrude, but once she knew she was not expecting she had begun to look forward once more to the time when she could start her role as an adoptive mother.

The clock on the mantelpiece striking the hour brought Isobel abruptly back to the present. She had been sitting on a kitchen chair with her schedule for the day spread out before her, but now she got to her feet, chiding herself for daydreaming; if she did not get a move on, she would be late for her first appointment and she prided herself on always being on time.

She arrived at her office and was soon totally absorbed by her work, and only when she had finished her canteen lunch did she allow her thoughts to return to Gertrude. Several times

Frank had questioned her as to how she had broached the subject of the adoption with the girl and she had deliberately kept her replies vague, not wanting to tell him that she had never actually admitted her plans. Indeed, why should she, she had asked herself often enough. It would be a delightful surprise for Gertrude to know that her child was going to be brought up in a loving household where money was no object. But of course she really should say something now, because of her own dashed hopes. It was only fair that she should tell Gertrude there would be no Ellis baby, and after that it would be easy to reveal her plan that she herself was going to be the person who would adopt her young friend's child. She did not think Gertrude would be surprised— she must have guessed—but it would be nice to have such good news confirmed.

The canteen was at the top of the large office block in which Isobel worked; there was a lift but she preferred the stairs and hurried down them. She loved giving presents, especially to Gertrude, who was always so touchingly grateful for the smallest gift. She glanced at her wristwatch as she reached the ground floor, but hurried past her car and went straight to Blackledge's. She bought a bag of doughnuts, then went along to the nearest bookshop to buy a copy of *Pride and Prejudice*. She found one which had delightful illustrations, so she paid the sum required, popped it into her shopping bag and set off for the tower block.

Once there, she hurried up the long flights and felt pleased when she reached the tenth floor, scarcely out of breath at all. I do believe I have Gertrude to thank—or at any rate the tower block—for the fact that I'm in such good condition for my age, she thought rather complacently, approaching the door of the flat. She tapped briskly, waited a few moments, then hauled up the key on its length of string; she had queried this habit with Gertrude, suggesting that a stranger might let themselves in, but Gertrude had not seemed bothered.

Isobel let herself into the tiny hall and closed and locked the door behind her. Gertrude was clearly out, probably shopping or possibly visiting the clinic, so she headed straight for the kitchen. She would make a pot of tea and set the doughnuts out on a plate, so when Gertrude returned it would be to a warm welcome.

As soon as she entered the kitchen, however, Isobel knew there was something wrong. The room was icy cold and there was no smell of food, no sign of human occupation. Isobel's heart began to beat unevenly; had something awful happened to Gertrude? Wild thoughts jostled one another as she left the kitchen and headed for the bedroom. Dear God, would she find the girl lying on her bed, either in the last throes of labour or . . . oh, no, not dead? I've not been near for days and days . . . anything could have happened, Isobel told herself, her mouth dry with terror. Oh, please God, let her be all right, let me not have done awful harm when I meant only good!

She hurled the bedroom door open with such force that it crashed into the thin wall with a sound like a bomb exploding and immediately she saw that the room was empty, not only of Gertrude, but of furniture too. The bed had gone, and the dressing table and chest of drawers, though the rickety wardrobe leaned, drunkenly, against one wall. Isobel crossed the room and opened one of the wardrobe doors, though not without difficulty. As she had already guessed, it was empty. She stepped back and stood for a moment, letting her glance rove around the empty room, whilst her heart resumed its normal pace. What did this mean? Had thieves come when Gertrude was out and stripped the flat of everything saleable? The wardrobe was an old one that she herself had given the girl; not even thieves, she supposed, would have wanted that.

Hastily, Isobel checked the bathroom. No soap in the soap dish, no toothbrush, no flannel or towel. Had the child started the baby and been rushed into hospital? But she had been promised faithfully, by Dr Matthews himself, that she should be informed as soon as Gertrude went into labour.

Next, she checked the sitting room. Almost all the furniture had gone, and the rag rugs and the chipped ornaments which had once graced the mantelpiece. Gnawing her thumbnail, Isobel returned to the kitchen and immediately saw the envelope, which she had scarcely noticed before. She approached it cautiously, as though it might explode, and saw that it was addressed to her. Her hand shot out, hesitated, then picked it up. She tore it open; a plea for help? But if thieves had broken in why had Gertrude not contacted her? She had never given the child her home address, but the girl must have known full well that she could be found in the big block of offices, or even through the children's home. But doubtless the pages within the envelope would contain some sort of explanation.

Isobel sat down with a thump on one of the wooden kitchen chairs and read the words that Gertrude had written, feeling her wrath slowly increase.

Dear Mrs Ellis,

I have left you the key to the flat, so's you could get in, as well as the wardrobe from my room, the nest of tables in the sitting room, and the kitchen table and two chairs, because they are yours and not truly mine, though you did give them to me.

You have been very good, very jenerous, but the time has come for me to move on. Don't worry about me, I shall do very well. I have the promise of a job once the baby's born and thank you again for all you have done for me.

Yours sincerely,
Gertrude Pleavin

For a moment, Isobel was so angry that she could not think straight. How dare the nasty little creature simply walk away from her without so much as a goodbye? And she must have made the money for her escape by selling the furniture, though even in her fury Isobel had to admit that the girl had sold nothing save for those articles which she had bought herself. But where on earth would she have gone? In common with most other foundlings, Gertrude had no known relatives and precious few friends. In fact, since she had moved into the tower block she had lost touch with those friends she had had, because Isobel had insisted on it. She had told Gertrude that because of Mr Ellis's involvement she had informed the authorities that she had got Gertrude a live-in job in a grand house in her village, and she did not wish to be shown up as a liar if Gertrude invited old pals to visit the tower block.

For several minutes Isobel remained where she was, feverishly reading and rereading the letter and telling herself that the girl could not simply disappear. She would find her, would trace her through hospitals, or clinics, or the children's home . . . no, she could not do that because she herself had told the authorities she knew where Gertrude was.

Isobel made a decision. First she would enquire of all the neighbours in the block whether they knew where the young girl on the top floor had gone. Surely someone must have noticed! Then she would go to Frank's office and demand that he help her run Gertrude to earth.

She was about to leave the kitchen when she realised that she was trembling and in no state to be taken seriously. She saw that the cooking stove was still in its place and the small tin kettle was on the draining board, and decided that a cup of tea and a doughnut would calm her down and give her something to think about beside Gertrude's defection.

It was a disappointment to realise that there was neither tea nor dried milk in the cupboard, but she boiled the kettle anyway and was about to pour hot water into one of the two china mugs she had given her young friend when a better thought occurred to her. She would go to the flat next door on the excuse of borrowing a pinch of tea, and would ask the occupant if he or she knew when the girl in the neighbouring flat had left.

Isobel knocked on all the doors of the tenth-

170

floor flats, but no one answered, though she had the uneasy feeling that she was being scrutinised and guessed that they thought her, in her neat grey suit and black court shoes, to be authority of some description. However, she struck lucky on the first flat she tried on the next floor, though the occupant took so long to get to the door that Isobel had almost given up when it creaked open. A thin and much wrinkled face appeared and small, sharp eyes glinted questioningly at her from behind wire-framed spectacles. The owner of the spectacles was enveloped in a huge floral overall and as she took in her visitor's appearance, she opened the door a little wider, revealing matchstick-thin legs in wrinkled lisle stockings which ended in a pair of incredibly large tartan slippers.

'Yes?' the old woman said uncompromisingly. 'If it's about me complaint, then you'd best come in. Us don't want the neighbours a-flappin' their great lugs an' hearin' me business, though I dare say they've guessed it's me what wants 'em to shut their great faces after midnight, same as it says in me rent book.'

Utterly at a loss, Isobel nevertheless obeyed the woman's crooked finger and presently found herself in a sitting room the twin of Gertrude's on the floor above, except that it was so crammed with furniture that she had difficulty in following the old lady through the forest of elderly armchairs to where she now perched on a large sofa, patting the seat beside her invitingly.

'Now, missus, I've writ to the council, traipsed all the way to their offices and got one o' me sons to visit the housin' department, 'cos I'm stuck up here

171

since the lift don't never seem to be workin' an' I can't manage all them wicked stairs. If it weren't for me sons I could starve to death, 'cos I can't get out to do no shoppin' and there ain't many as'll deliver up here. D'you know, you're the first person to come an' see me about me complaints— and what's the use o' that, in the miggle of the afternoon when the noise starts at nine o'clock in the evenin' and goes on till three in the mornin' or later, very like?' she demanded. 'I know I'm old, but I've got ears like a bleedin' bat and I needs me sleep, same as everyone else, even if I don't work down at the docks, 'cos tellin' me I can lie in of a mornin' is the only comment me neighbour made when I shouted at 'im through the keyhole to stop the din or I'd call the scuffers.'

Isobel cut in hastily when the old lady paused for breath, realising that unless she stopped the flow she was unlikely to escape before midnight. 'I'm awfully sorry, Mrs—er . . .'

'Templeton's me name, *Mrs* Templeton,' the old lady said, emphasising the title. 'I'm a respectable woman, a widder these ten years gone, and mother of four sons. And me and Sam had been married fourteen month afore I had me first, not like some as I could mention. I'll be bound half the women in this block had the baby first and the weddin' next. Oh aye, things are very different from when I were a gal.'

She paused again and Isobel jumped in quickly. 'I'm so sorry, Mrs Templeton, but I'm nothing to do with the housing department,' she said apologetically. 'In fact I came to borrow a pinch of tea and to ask you if you knew anything about the young girl up on the next floor. She's a—a friend

172

of mine and I popped in just now, as I do from time to time, to have a chat and a cup of tea. Only the flat's empty and a good deal of furniture is missing, and to tell you the truth I'm rather worried. She—she's in the family way, and—'

'Oh, that one,' Mrs Templeton said. 'Can't say I know her exactly, but a-course I used to see her goin' up an' down. Her old father come and give her a hand when they came for her furniture. I thought at first he were from the auction rooms—I looked outa me window and saw Henderson's van outside—but then I remembered seein' him about, off and on, when I'd opened me door to watch the world go by.' She chuckled. 'I axed 'im where he were takin' the sofa—it were a real nice one—and he said to the auction room, so naturally I wanted to know where they was movin' to. He said they weren't, they were gettin' new furniture, but I knew that were a lie 'cos I see most things what come in an' out of here, an' no new stuff has passed me door.'

'Oh, I see; then I suppose my young friend has moved away and forgotten to leave me her new address,' Isobel said feebly. 'I saw her a couple of weeks ago; we had a cup of tea at Lyons in Church Street. Can you remember when the furniture went?'

'Oh, I dunno,' the old woman said vaguely. 'The days are all alike here. But I suspicion they left the place themselves more recent. I heard the three of them tiptoeing down the stairs . . .'

'The three of them?' Isobel said incredulously. 'Has she had the baby, then?'

Mrs Templeton gave a snort of laughter. 'Nah, course not,' she said scornfully. 'I meant that damn

173

great dog. But I don't reckon they'll have gone far 'cos she must ha' been quite near her time by the looks. I see her once or twice goin' out of here with a basket of stuff she'd been bakin'. If you asks me, I reckon she sold 'em to folk what either had no bake ovens or was too lazy to cook for their selves. But as I was sayin', missus . . .'

Isobel, however, had got to her feet. She did not wish to be impolite and she was sure the old woman did not mean to deceive her, but she knew very well that Gertrude had no father, and in fact knew no old man who could have assisted in her escape, if escape it was. As for the huge dog and the baskets of baking, Mrs Templeton must have got muddled. After all, she looked at least eighty, and it seemed unlikely that she managed to sort out one neighbour from another. It was perfectly possible that the old white-haired man really had been from the auction rooms, but the dog . . . well, it was clear that Mrs Templeton was confused, to say the least, though it would never do to remark on it.

'Well, thank you very much, Mrs Templeton, for your help and your time,' she said firmly, heading for the front door. 'One thing: I shall be popping up to the flat from time to time. If you hear anything at all concerning the whereabouts of my young friend, I should be most grateful if you could let me know. My name's Ellis and I work in the Social Services Department.'

She had opened the front door and was about to step on to the landing when Mrs Templeton came out of the sitting room and began to hobble towards the kitchen. 'No need to rush off, queen,' she protested. 'You came for a borry of tea; I can

174

make you a cup an' we can have a nice jangle over where your young friend has gone. Why, there's an old people's home . . .'

But Isobel, feigning deafness, was already halfway up the flight and had no intention of turning back. She guessed that Mrs Templeton was just eager for company. Isobel knew from her work that those who have outlived their generation are often lonely, and decided that she would alert the appropriate department to Mrs Templeton's plight.

On the upper floor once more she fished out the key, unlocked the door, and returned to the kitchen. She could try borrowing a pinch of tea from someone else but thought it would avail her little. One very young and pregnant girl, who kept herself to herself and took no part in communal activities, was unlikely to be remembered. Yet she did not wish to return to Frank and admit that she had not knocked at every door in the tower block. Once she had done so, she would go straight to his office and discuss what was best to be done.

Half-heartedly, she began to fill a mug with hot water. Her hand was actually reaching out towards the doughnuts, still in the paper bag in her basket, when she caught sight of the slim gold wristwatch clasped round her left wrist. It was a quarter to three and her next appointment was at three o'clock. Questioning neighbours would simply have to wait. Isobel buttoned her coat, hurried across the hall, locked the door and replaced the key, and set off down the long flight of concrete stairs.

*   *   *

175

When Isobel broke the news to Frank he simply stared at her, mouth agape. Then he said, in a tired voice: 'Well, that's that, I suppose. I just hope the poor kid hasn't done something desperate.'

'What do you mean?' Isobel asked. They were sitting in Frank's office, all thick carpet, low, luxuriously upholstered chairs and huge picture windows. 'Why should she do something desperate? I don't understand what you mean, Frank.'

Her husband took a deep breath. 'Dearest Bella, you must think me very stupid. You've talked about Gertrude and what she will do after her baby is born, but you have never once said that you've told her of our intentions and I can only assume that you didn't tell her because you were not at all sure how such news would be greeted. I know at first she talked of not wanting the child, but lately you've said yourself that she seemed resigned. If she had known that you meant to adopt the baby, then I would have no worries for her safety, or that of the child, but we must be honest with one another, my love. First, you didn't tell her because it seemed too soon; then you didn't tell her because you thought you yourself were pregnant. And lastly, you didn't tell her because you had known the rush of maternal feeling which came when you thought you were about to bear a child.

'I should have insisted that we tell her together so that she knew I wanted the baby as much as you did. But every time I suggested it, you refused point-blank to consider such a thing. Now

Gertrude has taken things into her own hands and disappeared. I grant you that she may want to keep the baby herself, but it's likelier that she simply wants to get rid of it and be free from guilt and responsibility. After all, if she put it out for adoption and the wrong people took it on . . .'

Isobel jumped to her feet, feeling a hot flush creep up her neck. 'The baby in the bus shelter!' she said in a husky whisper. 'And the one wrapped in newspaper and left on a beach somewhere in Norfolk . . . I don't remember where. Oh, Frank, she couldn't do something so wicked! Why, the baby on the beach died of exposure and the one in the bus shelter got pneumonia and was ill for months and months; I remember reading the case notes. Oh my God, we simply must find her! And we have every right, Frank, because whatever she may think, the baby is not hers to dispose of at will. It's your baby too, and that means it's mine as well. I'll do anything, anything at all to make sure that the baby is safe!'

'We'll do whatever we can, but I think you'll find it's remarkably little,' Frank said. 'We have no legal rights, you see, although I suppose you could say we had a duty of care. Certainly we will search for her; we'll put an advertisement in the paper, begging her to come home . . . no, dammit, we can't do that because she doesn't know where we live, but there must be a way . . .'

Isobel nodded. 'I'll go back to the tower block tomorrow, wearing my oldest clothes, and I'll knock on every door and question every occupant,' she said wildly. 'Surely someone must know when she left and where she went.'

Frank also rose, came round his desk and took

177

his wife in his arms. 'The baby isn't due for several weeks, and first babies are almost always late,' he said calmly. 'I know I frightened you, making you remember the baby in the bus shelter and so on, and it was very wrong of me. I know nothing of Gertrude, save what you've told me, but you've given me the impression that she's a good, kind girl, not the sort who would abandon a lost kitten, let alone a tiny baby. So you must stop worrying, my love, and do as you have just suggested. Take the day off work tomorrow and I will word an advertisement that Gertrude will understand, though no one else will. Now, will you promise me to stop worrying? Tell yourself that Gertrude is well and happy and that we will find her before her baby is born.'

*   *   *

True to her word, Isobel took a day off work, dressed in a pair of slacks and a jumper which she usually wore for gardening, and visited every single flat in the tower block. This time she found that folk answered her knock when she persisted, but for all the information she gleaned she might as well not have bothered. Even the other occupants of the tenth floor scarcely seemed to have noticed the quiet young girl who came and went without bothering anyone, though one sharp-faced woman remarked nastily that if the girl had been complaining about noise then she, in her turn, would complain about the girl's encouraging animals to come into the flats.

'Are you referring to a big dog, a really huge one?' Isobel had asked eagerly. Perhaps she had wronged Mrs Templeton and Gertrude had indeed kept a big dog hidden away somewhere, though it seemed unlikely. Furthermore, she knew that her protégée was aware of the 'no pets' rule, so why would she jeopardise her tenancy by introducing an animal into the flat?'

But the woman was speaking. 'A dawg? Now is that likely?' she said scornfully. 'No, it's them bleedin' cats. When the weather were real bad and the snow were down for weeks at a time, she and some of the other tenants left food for them in the foyer. I even see the odd saucer o' milk left for 'em from time to time.'

'Yes, I remember Gertrude mentioning feral cats,' Isobel acknowledged. 'Well, I'm sorry to have bothered you, Mrs—er—er, and do let me assure you that no one has complained about noise, or anything else for that matter.'

'Oh aye?' the woman said in a disbelieving tone. 'I don't know why they haven't, 'cos the walls is thin as paper, the bloody lift never works, the woman what's supposed to clean the stairs don't bother . . .' But Isobel was already turning away.

She emerged into the open air feeling thoroughly dissatisfied and, with a sigh, gave up on the occupants of the flats and returned to her little car. It seemed that Gertrude had added invisibility to her other accomplishments. Isobel started the engine and headed for Henderson's.

They were very nice in the auction rooms, searching diligently through their records, but were unable to help at all. They had checked, naturally, to make sure the stuff was not stolen, but were hampered by the fact that they had no record of a transaction with a Miss Pleavin or a

Miss Ellis, for Isobel remembered that the flat was rented in her own name.

'If you could give us a definite date . . .' the office manager said. 'Our information is filed by name and date . . . the address is useful, but it might take weeks to trace without a name or a date.'

'Oh, well, never mind, it isn't that important,' Isobel said airily. 'I don't suppose a description of some of the furniture . . . ?'

The office manager shook his head sadly. 'Unless it were gold-plated, the fellers wouldn't notice,' he admitted. 'To them a chair's a chair and a sofa's a sofa; just another item to go under the hammer. I'm really sorry I can't help, Mrs Ellis. Are you going to try other auction rooms? If so, you've one helluva task ahead of you—excuse my French—because there are a lot of us in the trade.'

Sighing, Isobel said that it was scarcely worth it, since a neighbour had spotted the name Henderson on the van which had collected the furniture, but she thanked the man for his efforts and left, wondering what her next move should be. It seemed likely that Gertrude was not using her own name, which would make the task of tracking her down even more difficult.

Isobel returned to the flat. She had spoken to the housing department herself, explaining that the young cousin on whose behalf she had rented the flat had found herself a live-in job in another part of the country and would no longer be needing it.

'Is it empty? Has Miss Ellis actually left?' the official behind the big desk had said at once. 'If so, I can get a family to move in after the weekend. We're desperately short of accommodation, though rebuilding is going on apace.'

Isobel had opened her mouth to admit that there was a wardrobe, a kitchen table and a couple of chairs still in situ, and had then changed her mind. She wanted rid of the flat, wanted never again to have to climb the awful Everest of those concrete stairs, but before that happened she and Frank between them could easily carry everything downstairs, even that horrible old wardrobe. The official, pen poised over a large form, had been looking at her curiously, and Isobel had hastily burst into speech. 'Yes, yes, it's completely empty,' she had gabbled.

The man had nodded, seeming satisfied, but had held out a hand. 'Could I have the key, please?'

'Oh, I'm so sorry, I've not got it with me, but I can bring it in tomorrow, if that's all right,' Isobel had said.

The man had nodded and written something in the box on the form he had been filling in. 'That will do very well,' he had said. 'Good morning, Mrs Ellis.'

*　　　*　　　*

Dr Matthews sat at his desk in the surgery and watched the ample form of his latest patient making her way out. Through the open doorway he could see that only one other patient was waiting to be seen and was glad of it, for already it had been quite a day. Folk had limped and coughed their way into his surgery ever since nine o'clock, and he was desperate for a cup of coffee and a biscuit, almost as desperate to see a smiling face instead of a suffering one.

So when someone tapped and entered, and he

saw Mrs Ellis looking fit as a fiddle, he smiled with genuine pleasure. 'Good morning,' he said jovially. 'I do trust you are as well as you look! And how is our mutual friend? I've not seen her for several weeks. Sit yourself down now, and if you've no objection I'll ring through to my receptionist and we can both have a cup of coffee whilst you tell me what's amiss. I trust Miss Pleavin enjoys her usual excellent health?'

Mrs Ellis sat down in the chair and waited whilst he ordered two cups of coffee through the intercom. Then she leaned forward and he saw, with some dismay, that there was a crease between her brows and a worried look in her usually calm brown eyes. Oh dear, then all was not right with one of his patients. He wondered if it was her phantom pregnancy playing on her mind, but this was clearly not so, as he realised as soon as she spoke.

'Dr Matthews, do you know where Gertrude Pleavin is? Oh, I know all about patient confidentiality, but I have supported her financially throughout her pregnancy. I thought her grateful, but a few days ago, when I visited the tower block, I discovered that she had left without a word to anyone. Did she tell you—'

The door opening cut the sentence off short. The receptionist was an elderly lady who had for some years thought it her duty to stand between Dr Matthews and his patients. Now she handed Dr Matthews his coffee with a benevolent smile, then stood the second cup down on the desk, nicely placed to be just out of Isobel's reach.

He waited until the door had closed behind her, then turned back to his patient. 'Now calm down,

182

my dear, and begin at the beginning. When did you discover—if you did discover—that Miss Pleavin was no longer living in the flat?'

He saw Mrs Ellis take a deep breath and lace her fingers round her knees. She bent her head and remained quite still for a few moments, then began to speak. 'I hadn't visited Miss Pleavin for some while . . .'

When the story was told, Mrs Ellis handed the doctor the note that Gertrude had left for her. Dr Matthews steepled his fingers and stared down at the letter. He read it through twice, then gave his visitor a long and thoughtful look. He folded the note and handed it back across the desk before he spoke. 'My dear, there is one thing you have not mentioned. I have always assumed that Miss Pleavin knew of your intention to adopt her child, but it is clear to me from this note that you have never discussed the matter with her, otherwise why should she not mention it herself? In fact the only reason I can think of for Miss Pleavin's decision to move on has to be the baby. I know in the early days she resented the fact that she was pregnant and had no desire to become a mother, but young women in her condition frequently change their minds. They are not practical because they're thinking emotionally, not logically. They dread childbirth yet want to do right by the baby. When I last spoke to Miss Pleavin, I told her what a lucky girl she was to have you willing and eager to adopt the child.'

He heard Mrs Ellis give a smothered exclamation and begin to say angrily that he had no right, but he flapped a hand soothingly at her. 'Don't forget, Mrs Ellis, that I had no idea you'd not shared your intentions with the young mother herself. I take it I'm right: she didn't know until I inadvertently spilled the beans.'

There was a short pause, then Mrs Ellis nodded her head reluctantly. 'Yes, you're right; Frank has already chided me for not telling her. But oh, Dr Matthews, she's simply disappeared and I'm desperate to find her. I'm sure when she knows how we shall value her child and love it, she'll see sense. But first we have to run her to earth.'

After his patient had left, Dr Matthews collected the paperwork he would need for his home calls and set off in his baby Austin. He remembered visiting the girl's flat when the young man—Albert, wasn't it?—had been ill and during Mrs Ellis's visit he had wondered, fleetingly, whether she knew of the friendship. As the conversation had proceeded, however, he had realised that she did not suspect for one moment that Gertrude Pleavin had a friend with whom she might have left the city. Thinking it over now, he knew he would not say anything which would help the Ellises trace the girl; why should he? Mrs Ellis had not seen fit to tell Gertrude that she meant to adopt her child, and now that he came to consider it he began to wonder just why this particular baby meant so much to the older woman. He had talked to her about adoption before and knew she had never seriously considered it, so why in heaven's name had she suddenly changed her mind? There was of course one possibility which would explain everything . . .

Every time he returned to his little car after a home visit, Dr Matthews thought about Gertrude Pleavin and the Ellises, and he finally came to the conclusion that the matter was none of his business, nor that of Mr and Mrs Ellis. The decision to 'move on', as the girl had said in her letter, was final and should be accepted as such. But he still thought that Isobel Ellis would make an excellent adoptive mother and decided that he would talk to her about taking on someone else's baby as soon as the opportunity arose. He decided also that he would try to dissuade her from pursuing young Gertrude. Having resolved on the course of action he should take, he put the matter right out of his mind.

Chapter Eight

The day that Millie and Rose spent together was to be the first of many. For a start, they examined the town thoroughly, searched the many cafés and milk bars for the one offering the cheapest cup of coffee and bun, and went into Marks & Spencer. Having so little money at her disposal, Rose had never been particularly interested in clothes, but Millie had a keen fashion sense and insisted that they examine the racks of colourful skirts, slacks and tops before making their way to the end of the store where more practical items, such as beef and onion pies, were on sale.

After much careful consideration, Millie made her purchases, including a couple of individual meat and potato pies, two packets of biscuits and two small bottles of fizzy lemonade. 'We'll have a little picnic on the beach,' she said as they queued to pay. 'And then we'll go along to the clinic on

185

Marsh Road and explain that you intend to remain in Rhyl until after your baby's born. I'm going to have mine in the Stanley Hospital at St Asaph, so I expect you will as well because I don't think there's a maternity unit at the Alexandra.' She giggled. 'Wouldn't it be strange if we found ourselves giving birth on the same day? Gosh, I wish we could arrange it because I wouldn't be nearly so terrified if you were with me. When are you due?'

'Towards the end of next month, I think,' Rose said rather dubiously. 'To tell you the truth, no one seems quite sure. Every time I saw a new doctor at the clinic in Liverpool he would disagree with what the previous one had said, and the nurses were just as bad. Still, there was an elderly one I rather liked, and she said babies came in their own time and not to worry myself until I felt the first sign. She meant pain, of course, but that's a word they seem to avoid. When are you due, Millie?'

Millie was beginning to say that she, too, was due next month when they reached the top of the queue, and by the time she had paid for her purchases and they had left the store, emerging into bright sunlight, babies and birth seemed a long way away.

When they had settled on the beach and were beginning their picnic, Rose asked her new friend whether she had managed to get some sort of layette together. 'I've got nighties, nappies and a couple o' them little matinee coats,' she said proudly. 'Oh, and I got some of them rubber knickers 'cos they was goin' cheap in Bunney's, only afterwards someone told me that new babies need really tiny ones an' I never looked at the sizes until it were too late.' She spoke rather thickly through a mouthful of meat and potato pie. 'Go on, wharr'ave you got?'

Millie stared at her. 'I thought they'd give us stuff in hospital!' she said. 'Oh, lor', it's been bad enough buying smocks and trousers with expanding waistbands for myself. No one's asked me what I'd got for the baby!'

'But Millie, everyone knows that babies have to have clothing,' Rose said, truly shocked by her new friend's ignorance. 'Didn't they tell you that your husband—or your mother—must bring in nappies and clothes and that, the day before you and the baby are released? They told me. Don't you even have a shawl?'

'Oh, I've got a shawl and some of those little coats you mentioned, and I believe I've got some nappies. I've a very old aunt—she's a great-aunt really—and she sent me a parcel of stuff which her own daughter had used years ago, so I dare say I shall be all right.' She dug her companion playfully in the ribs. 'Good thing I bothered to bring them with me, else poor Scotty would have had to go out and buy nappies and things, and he wouldn't like that one bit!'

'I expect you'll be all right then,' Rose said comfortably, dusting pastry crumbs off the front of her shabby grey coat. Millie did not seem to be short of money, so she imagined that Scotty would be able to make good any shortfall in his wife's preparations. They had been sitting on the soft sand at the top of the beach and she turned to give Millie a hand as her friend struggled to stand up. 'What's next? Back in Liverpool, you were really supposed to go to the clinic on the same day each week. Is it like that here?'

187

'Oh, I go whenever it occurs to me,' Millie said cheerfully. 'They grumble and tell me my record is the untidiest they've ever seen. The clinic is a good way out of the town, so we'll catch a bus.'

They reached the clinic, a low, one-storey building within a stone's throw of the bus stop, and Millie led the way inside. There was a short queue at the desk, and they joined it. Rose's heart thumped uncomfortably as she waited, suddenly feeling as though the word 'runaway' had been tattooed across her forehead. She handed over her card to the pleasant-faced young woman behind the desk and had begun a stammered explanation when the woman cut across her words. 'Don't worry, love, you're in good company here,' she said. 'I hear the same story over and over . . . your husband's job didn't pay well, your lodgings were that expensive you scarce had a penny over for food, or you were living with your parents and they fell out with you or your husband. Someone told you that there was always seasonal work in Rhyl, starting at Easter, and that you could get a room here cheap, so you decided to make the move. Am I right?'

'That's right, and my husband's got a job already, doing maintenance in the funfair,' Rose said proudly, feeling her heart slow to its usual pace. 'And we've got a room too, though only till Whitsun. It's quite a nice room, in the same house as my friend here.'

'Well, isn't that grand! And you couldn't have a nicer neighbour than Mrs Scott,' the woman said, beaming at her. She wrote on Rose's card, then directed her to a row of chairs against the wall. 'You won't have long to wait; it's Dr Shaw today

188

and she's always quick. Then you go to that table over there for your cod liver oil and so on . . . but I'm sure Mrs Scott will take you under her wing, though she's only been here three or four weeks herself.' They were turning away from the desk when she added: 'One piece of advice I will give you, though. Try for accommodation well away from the front, and if possible before Whitsun. Once the season gets under way, every landlady in Rhyl will put her prices up.'

'Thank you very much,' Rose said. 'We'll take your advice, won't we, Millie?'

'Of course,' Millie said politely, and then added, lowering her voice: 'Everyone tells you the same thing, but if you ask me, old Ozzie will have a job to let our attic rooms. They're right at the top of the house, miles away from the kitchen, and personally Scotty and I wouldn't mind paying an extra half-crown, or even five bob, just until we've saved enough to get something a bit better.'

Despite Dr Shaw's reputation, the two girls did not leave the clinic until halfway through the afternoon, but both felt well satisfied, for Dr Shaw had said that she thought they would quite probably give birth within a few days of one another. 'Whoever pops first will let the other one know at once,' Millie said excitedly. 'They let your husband stay with you for a bit, but not for very long, I believe.' She squeezed Rose's arm. 'Speaking for myself, I'd rather have a girl with me than any man, no matter how much I like him. Will you come with me, Rose?'

Rose laughed and said that of course she would, though she didn't really believe that Millie would prefer her company to Scotty's when the time

189

came. 'I intend to faint myself if I possibly can,' she said. 'At my last clinic, they kept on saying that it didn't hurt a bit, and anyway they would give us gas and air, whatever that may be. But I did manage to ask one or two of the mothers who had already had a baby what it was like, and they said it was no picnic.'

'Don't tell me, don't tell me!' Millie squeaked. 'It'll only give me nightmares and put me off the whole idea. Ah, here comes the bus. Give him a wave and waddle as fast as you can, then we'll be back in town in time for tea and a sticky bun at the Russell. It's my favourite café and very convenient.'

*   *   *

Rose and Martin had finished their breakfast and taken Don for his usual gallop along the sands, and Martin had gone off to work. They had invested in an ancient camp bed and rigged up a curtain that could be pulled across to give each of them a degree of privacy. Rose had explained the camp bed to her friend by saying that her size and the increasingly warm weather made sleeping in the same bed uncomfortable for them both, and Millie had accepted it without comment.

By now, she and Millie had spent a good deal of time in each other's company, but she had still not admitted to her friend that she was neither married to Martin, nor using her real name. She had consulted Mart and he had agreed wholeheartedly that they should keep such information to themselves, as Millie could be quite scatty. Nevertheless, Rose sometimes found the

190

desire to confide almost irresistible.

Now, feeling more or less worry-free, she had settled down to the task of preparing for motherhood. She rejoiced in her friendship with Millie and had been pleased and flattered when Scotty himself had suggested that the four of them should go out for a drink one evening. As Rose had guessed, he was an extremely attractive man with dark wavy hair, brilliant blue eyes and a cleft chin. He wasn't as tall as Martin, but he was a good deal sturdier and only a couple of inches shorter, and the two men got on well. Rose suspected that this was because Martin always deferred to Scotty, but whatever the reason, both girls were glad that the young men had taken to one another.

'At home, Scotty seemed almost jealous if I mentioned girls I had been friendly with before I knew him,' Millie had admitted. 'I suppose it made him feel left out . . . anyway, he really seems to like your Martin, and he certainly approves of you and me spending a lot of time together.'

'So do I,' Rose had said with a grin. 'D'you know, Millie, I've never had a proper girlfriend before, and I didn't know what I was missing. I say, why shouldn't you be godmother to my baby when it comes? Can I be godmother to yours?'

Millie had agreed and Rose had been both pleased and flattered. After that the talk had switched to names and Millie had promised that they would go to the bookshop on Queen Street and see if they could find a copy of *The Complete Book of Baby Names* which had just been published and she wanted to buy.

Rose had thought this an excellent idea. Today

was the appointed day, and since the book contained not only names but also the meanings of names she was just wondering what she would discover about one or two of her favourites when there was a crash and a squawk from outside the door. Hastily scrambling to her feet, she jerked the door open to find Millie swaying on the landing, a hand clapped to her face. 'Oh, Millie, wharrever have you done?' she exclaimed. 'For one awful moment I thought you'd fallen down the stairs.'

'No, but I walked slap bang into the edge of the door,' Millie moaned. 'It got me right across the cheekbone; I hope I haven't broken anything. Take a look, would you, Rose?'

'Well, move your hand then,' Rose said, and gasped. There was a red weal across Millie's cheek and she had a rapidly blackening bruise around her eye. 'What you want is a cold compress, queen. I've got some water in my jug, so if you come into my room and sit on the bed for a moment I'll deal with it for you. However did you come to do it?'

'I was on the landing when I remembered I'd left my purse on the table. I turned to go back for it and, as I said, walked slap bang into the edge of the door. Oh, oh, it doesn't half hurt!'

'It'll hurt more in a moment,' Rose said apologetically, dipping her flannel into the water jug and then laying it gently across Millie's cheek and eye.

Millie hissed in her breath, then turned her head to look, lopsidedly, up at her friend. 'Oh, that actually feels better!' she said in an astonished tone. 'But I can't go round with a wet flannel clutched to my face, and I don't intend to spend the rest of my life shut up in my room. What'll I

192

do, Rose?'

Rose removed the flannel and examined her friend's wound. 'The skin isn't broken, but I could put a piece of lint and some plaster across it, and you could buy a pair of cheap sunglasses to hide your black eye,' she said rather doubtfully. 'I suppose there are such things as eye patches, if you don't mind looking like Long John Silver.' She chuckled suddenly. 'Wharrever will Scotty say when he comes home? He'll think you and I have had a real falling out!'

Millie chuckled too. 'He knows I'm a bit clumsy. Now where's that lint and Elastoplast?'

*　　　*　　　*

The two girls finished their shopping in plenty of time, including the book of babies' names, but when Rose suggested that they should go back to No. 27 for a sandwich and a cup of tea, Millie vetoed the suggestion. 'There's something I want to show you,' she said. 'It's a fair walk and it's somewhere we've not visited before, because . . . oh, but you'll see when we get there . . .'

As she had said, it was a fair walk for two women in the last stages of pregnancy, but they enlivened it with their constant chatter. It had come as a real surprise to Rose to learn that Millie's parents lived in Formby, which was not, after all, so very far from Liverpool. 'Well, my father works in Liverpool, but of course Formby is very posh,' Millie had explained. 'We've got a huge house and a lovely garden; I miss the garden. Father often says that before the war the owners had a full-time gardener and two full-time helpers, but now we

193

manage with a couple of men who come in for a few hours each week. Father loves gardening, so he doesn't mind the work, and of course I helped as much as I possibly could. Daddy—I mean Father—says I've got green fingers and that everything I plant or look after thrives. So you see, even if I wasn't a first-rate shorthand typist, I could get work as a gardener.'

As they walked, her friend pointed out the brilliant yellow of forsythia, the strawberry pink of flowering currants, and the beautiful blooms which looked to Rose like her namesake, but which Millie assured her were actually camellias.

Presently, they reached what looked like a compound of some description. There were a number of large, one-storey buildings, some with cars parked in front of them, surrounded by wire fencing. Millie gestured ahead. 'Industrial units,' she said. 'I came round here when we first moved to Rhyl, spying out the land so to speak. There's one firm who always seem to be advertising for staff, so I made some enquiries and apparently they make pyjamas for most of the big stores. I was afraid at first that the advertisements meant there was a constant turnover of staff, which usually indicates bad employers or discontented workers. But I got talking to a girl from there and she says they are overwhelmed with orders and are actually taking over the unit next door. What is even more to the point, however, is the last unit on this row. You'll never guess what it is!'

'Does it make cakes or doughnuts?' Rose said vaguely. 'No, I know, does it make prams? We're going to need one of them. I don't s'pose we'll run to a pram each, but we could share, turn and turn about.'

'You're not far off. It's a crèche,' Millie said triumphantly. 'And believe it or not, the pyjama factory is so desperate for workers that they pay the cost if you use it.'

'Gosh,' Rose said with well-simulated surprise. 'That seems very generous. They must be good employers, then.' She waited a moment, hoping Millie would expand on what she had said, then metaphorically threw in the towel. 'Millie, what's a crèche?'

This brought forth Millie's infectious, bubbling laugh. 'I *thought* you didn't know,' she said triumphantly. 'But how should you? I remember you saying that you'd only been to a council school and they don't do languages. Crèche, my dear little ignoramus, is French for nursery, and this particular crèche looks after your baby for you for the active working day. Comprends? Or do you understand, as us dull English say?'

'Gosh,' Rose said again, but with far more enthusiasm this time. 'Only don't you have to be good at needlework and so on to make pyjamas? I told you I weren't no good wi' me needle.'

'You don't have to be,' Millie said impatiently. 'Good Lord, girl, where were you brought up? No, don't answer that, I was being silly. The girls make the pyjamas on great big industrial sewing machines; anyone can do it, even me, and I'm a worse needlewoman than you could possibly be because I've never even tried my hand at sewing on a button. The pay's pretty good, better than I'd get as a secretary, believe it or not, so what do you think? Shall we apply as soon as we've popped?' She grinned at her friend. 'Shall we go in right now and apply? I can just see their faces if we did!'

'Millie Scott, you're awful!' Rose said, as they turned away. 'But it's a grand idea, so it is. I just hope the work isn't all taken by the time our babies arrive. Tell me, Millie, how soon will we be able to start work after the births? Mart an' me manage okay, but I won't deny the extra money would be useful.'

'We'll ask when we go to the clinic,' Millie said. 'I say, Rose, I'm most awfully glad you like the idea. And now, what about a sandwich and a cuppa? We can walk to the Botanical Gardens from here; they've got a café and the prices are really reasonable.'

'What are you going to give Scotty for his supper though?' Rose asked. 'Mart 'n' me's going to have fish 'n' chips.'

'Once the other tenants start coming in they do rather take over, and there's a limit to what one can cook on a Primus stove,' Millie agreed. 'But I bought some potatoes yesterday, so if I get a nice steak and kidney pie from Parry's on the corner, and some tinned peas, then Scotty shouldn't grumble.'

'That sounds nice,' Rose said approvingly. She knew that poor Millie could not cook for toffee nuts, but suspected that Scotty was not privy to his wife's lack of culinary skills. Millie, unblushingly, presented the pies she bought as all her own work, and this seemed to satisfy her husband. Rose had offered to give Millie simple cooking lessons, but they had not got round to it yet. As for Rose's own plans for their evening meal, she told herself that fish and chips was just a little white lie so that Millie should not realise how tight money was, particularly towards the end of the week. If she had said they intended to dine on *chips* and chips, Millie might have offered a loan, and Rose would have been embarrassed and would not have known how to refuse.

As they walked towards the Botanical Gardens and the café, Rose dug a hand into her coat pocket and tried to check that she could indeed have a sandwich and still buy chips, but when they entered the café Millie went straight to the counter, ordered two cheese sandwiches and two cups of tea, and said firmly that it was her treat. 'Left to yourself, you would have done your shopping and gone back to your room and made yourself a sandwich for almost nothing,' she pointed out. 'I will say this for Scotty: he's not mean with money. I bet he gives me twice what you get, and you've got Don to feed as well as Martin.'

'Martin gives me as much as he can possibly afford, honest to God he does,' Rose said at once. 'The trouble is, his money varies from week to week, so of course we have to be careful.'

They went over to a window table, settled themselves comfortably, and began to eat, whilst Millie shook a chiding finger at Rose. 'I wasn't meaning to say that Martin wasn't generous, because I know he is, and I know that both of you worry a bit when we have a day of rain, like we did last week, and the funfair lays workers off. But won't he be thrilled when he hears about the pyjama factory?'

'I don't think I ought to tell him until we actually get the jobs,' Rose said, after a short pause for thought. 'I say, I wonder what we should do about

Don? I don't like to think of him being left alone in our room all day. I know Mart will offer to take him to the funfair . . .'

'Or you could put him in the crèche,' Millie suggested, smirking. 'You could say he was your baby's big brother; I'm sure they'd see the likeness!'

'You cheeky mare!' Rose said wrathfully, trying to lean across the table to give her friend a clout, but missing due to her bulk. 'Still, I'm sure we'll manage something; we always do. Martin and I chew our problems over in the evenings, when there's nothing good on the wireless, and between us we find a solution to most things. Are you going to tell Scotty about the jobs?'

Millie took a sip of her tea, then shook her head. 'No, I can see that you're right. If it doesn't come off, he'll be . . . oh, I suppose he'll be disappointed, because though we're quite well off really, he's always made it plain that he expects me to work. Well, why not? It seems fair enough to me.'

'Yes, it is fair,' Rose agreed. She began to get rather wearily to her feet. 'We'd best get going now, though; you'll want to buy that steak and kidney pie before the shop closes and I want to be at the head of the queue for the chippy when it opens. So we're agreed? Not a word about the pyjama factory until we can say: "Tara! We've got jobs!"'

Millie nodded enthusiastically. 'Yes, we're agreed, because I'm sure you're right. No point in raising expectations and then having to admit it didn't work out.' She glanced at her wristwatch and gave a squeak. 'Heavens, look at the time! We'd better get a move on!'

198

Rose had been enchanted by the Botanical Gardens, and because the girls took it in turns to decide what they should do, they undertook the walk there several times.

On their next visit to the clinic, the nurse told them that they would probably be able to start work three or four weeks after their babies were born. 'We'd best get our act together,' Rose said, as they walked back to the lodging house. 'I'm going to teach you to do some simple cooking. We must do it before the babies come, because afterwards I bet our free time will be fairly limited.'

Accordingly, the cooking lessons began the very next day and to Rose's relief and pleasure, Millie loved them and proved an apt pupil.

One Sunday, the four of them had a picnic on the beach, and whilst Rose and Millie collected shells and paddled, the men skimmed stones across the waves and talked about buying a bat so that they could play beach cricket. By the time they were trailing home, pleasantly tired, Rose and Millie had warned the men that they would have to make do with a sandwich supper. To Rose's surprise, Scotty grumbled and said he needed a hot meal after such an energetic day. Millie said she would open a tin of tomato soup and he shrugged and said he supposed it would have to do. 'How about baked beans on toast then . . . as well as the soup, I mean?' he said suddenly.

Rose and Martin both laughed, thinking that he was joking, and Martin suggested that he might like to share Don's tripe and biscuits. But before Scotty could answer Millie cut in, saying that she had no baked beans but could rustle up a tin of Heinz spaghetti. By now they were entering the house and Rose, glancing at her friend, saw a look of apprehension on her face. 'I've got a tin of baked beans you can borrow,' she said. 'Or we'll do a swap if you'd rather; I'll take your spaghetti and you have the beans.'

'Thanks, Rose,' Millie said gratefully, and when they reached the top floor she accepted the beans and handed over the spaghetti, giving Rose a conspiratorial wink as she did so. 'Hope you enjoy the spaghetti. You couldn't lend me some bread, could you? I seem to have run out.'

Rose handed over half a loaf, but when she and Martin were back in their own room they exchanged thoughtful glances. Keeping his voice well down, Martin said: 'Scotty's awful selfish, ain't he, Rosie? He never give a thought to what Millie were goin' to eat . . . or d'you think they'll share the baked beans? Or she might have the soup, I suppose.'

'Millie says he's been spoiled and you can see what she means; I don't think it occurs to him to wonder what she'll have,' Rose admitted. 'But Millie's got a lot of determination; I'm sure she isn't going to starve. Now, what about us, Mart? I've still got half a loaf so we can have spaghetti on toast and then fill up the chinks with bread and jam.'

200

Chapter Nine

Because they had had such an energetic day, both Rose and Martin went early to bed and Rose, at any rate, slept deeply almost as soon as her head touched the pillow. She was awoken by muffled sounds which she could not at first identify. The sounds stopped, but she realised, with considerable reluctance, that she was going to have to use the large chamber pot which had done such yeoman service over the past month. Sighing, she swung her legs out of bed, smiling to herself as she realised that it must have been Millie's efforts to get in and out of bed for the same purpose that had woken her.

She was getting back into bed again when there was the sound of footsteps on the landing and someone knocked on their door. At first the sound was tentative but then, as she approached, her feet cringing from the cold linoleum, the knock was repeated, much more urgently, and someone began to turn the knob.

'I'm coming . . .' Rose was beginning, when an impatient hand switched the light on and Rose saw that her visitor was Scotty, pale-faced and distraught. His dark hair stood up as though he had had an electric shock and he was wearing a jacket over blue cotton pyjamas.

'Oh, Rose, I think she's bloody well started on the baby and I'm half out of my mind with worry,' Scotty gabbled. 'I want to go down to the telephone box on the corner so I can ring for an ambulance, but she won't let me. She says they told you at the clinic that you shouldn't ring for an ambulance until the contractions were coming every five minutes. And hers aren't, not yet. But suppose something goes wrong? I'd be no use, honest to God I wouldn't. When I said better safe than sorry, she grabbed my jacket and said I mustn't leave her here alone in case the baby just popped out. What'll I do, Rose?'

Rose patted his arm reassuringly. 'Don't get in such a state, Scotty,' she said as calmly as she could. 'I'll go and sit with Millie while you make the phone call to the hospital. They'll ask you questions and then either send for an ambulance or tell you to wait for a bit.' She turned to the camp bed where Martin was struggling into a sitting position. 'It's okay, Mart, you go back to sleep. I'm just nipping in next door to sit with Millie while Scotty rings the hospital; there's nothing you can do.'

Martin, however, continued to scramble out of bed. 'Off you go then,' he said thickly, and turned to Scotty, who was still hovering uncertainly in the doorway. 'Want me to go and make the call so you can stay with Millie?' he asked, and even as he spoke he was reaching for his trousers. 'I dare say Millie will feel more comfortable if you're with her.'

Scotty watched Martin push his feet into his worn boots and reach for the thick, paint-stained jersey which he wore for work, then glanced down at his own pyjamas and bedroom slippers with a look of such surprise that Rose, slipping on her own coat over her winceyette nightie, almost laughed aloud.

'Oh!' Scotty said. 'Tell you what, Mart, I'll nip

back and put some clothes on, then we can go down to the box together. If there's a problem, two heads are better than one, and—and I'd be grateful for your company.'

'Right,' Martin said briskly. He turned to Rose, now buttoning her coat. 'See you presently.'

Scotty and Rose made for Scotty's room, where they found Millie sitting on the edge of the bed, a blanket round her shoulders. She was looking white and scared but brightened at the sight of them, though it was only Rose whom she addressed. 'Thank goodness you're here, Rosie,' she said, her voice shaking slightly. 'I'm sure it is the baby, but the contractions are coming every fifteen minutes, and they did tell us not to bother them until they were coming every five.' She raised her head and directed a scornful glare at her trembling husband. 'And don't you be fooled, Robert Scott, because I call them contractions. They're bloody awful pains, much worse than I ever imagined, and since I don't want to start with a telling off you can just forget telephoning . . . oh, oh . . . no, it's all right, it's gone off.'

'You poor thing,' Rose said. She turned to Scotty. 'Grab your clothes and go and put them on in our room and ask Martin to make us all a nice cup of tea, and fill a hot water bottle.'

As Scotty left the room, his arms full of clothes, she turned back to her friend. 'They said at the clinic that a hot water bottle helped the con—'

'Helped the pain, you mean,' Millie snarled. 'Oh, oh, oh, here comes another!' She looked up at her friend, her eyes scared. 'I say, Rose, that wasn't fifteen minutes from the previous one, not even ten. D'you think Scotty's right? D'you think he ought to ring for an ambulance?'

'I dunno,' Rose said, frightened of giving wrong advice and downright horrified by the idea of the baby's being born here. 'Tell you what, if you have another couple of contractions—pains, I mean—ten minutes or less apart, then we'll tell the men to call for an ambulance. We won't wait until they're coming every five minutes, just in case the phone at the end of the road isn't working. Ah, here comes the tea.'

By this time, Rose had got Millie into bed and her friend's colour was beginning to creep back. Scotty came over with a cup of tea, his hand trembling so much that the cup was only three-quarters full by the time he gave it to his wife, or tried to give it to her, rather. Millie put out a hand towards it, then changed her mind. 'Even the smell of it makes me feel sick,' she said fretfully. 'Where's that hot water bottle? Scotty, you're to do just as Rose tells you. When she says you're to phone, then you're to do it at once, d'you understand? And for goodness' sake take Martin with you, because you're in such a tizzy that you'll probably give the hospital the wrong address, or forget my name or something.'

Rose bit back a laugh, but clearly Millie was finding the whole experience of childbirth so daunting that she did not care if Scotty took offence.

Martin appeared with the hot water bottle and Millie grabbed it, cuddling it gratefully; then she looked consideringly at the cup of tea that Rose was sipping. 'Perhaps I could have just a tiny drink,' she said. 'My mouth is awfully dry; d'you think it'll make me sick, Rose?' Rose handed over the cup of tea and Millie took a sip, then drank deeply and was promptly sick over the side of the bed. 'Oh, Rose, I'm so sorry,' she said, tears glistening on her long lashes. 'How far apart are they now—the pains, I mean? Oh, that tea was lovely, and the bottle is such a comfort. I'm sorry to be such a nuisance.' She pointed to the puddle of regurgitated tea by the bed. 'Would you mind awfully fetching the mop and bucket from the landing cupboard? I'm sorry to ask, but if you leave it it'll still be there when I get back from the hospital because Scotty'll say it's women's work and wait for someone else to clear it up.'

Rose hurried out and immediately the door of their room swung open and Martin appeared. 'Time to go?' he asked anxiously. 'Scotty's in a rare old state, but at least he's dressed now; I think the sooner we get Millie into hospital the better.'

Rose grabbed the mop and bucket and nodded vigorously. 'Yes, ring for the ambulance,' she said. 'I'll help Millie to dress and put some clothes on myself, though I suppose it'll be Scotty who goes with her in the ambulance.'

This, however, did not prove to be the case. Millie rejected any suggestion that Scotty might accompany her, saying that he was so frightened he would only make her worse. She reminded Rose of her promise to go with her and Rose, remembering, said doubtfully that she supposed it would be all right.

It was now three in the morning and the ambulance charged silently through the starlit countryside, but when they reached the maternity unit it was all bright lights and bustle. Millie clung to Rose's hand, insisting to the nursing staff that she must have her friend with her to give her moral support, and the staff agreed that until she went into the delivery room this would be in order. Once they had got their patient into an extremely ugly green gown and into bed, a comfortable middle-aged midwife handed Rose a timer, which she had thought at first glance to be an alarm clock, and told her to ring the bell which dangled beside the bed when the contractions were coming pretty steadily, a couple of minutes apart.

Millie sighed deeply and relaxed against her pillows. 'I'm so glad you're here, Rosie,' she said contentedly. 'Scotty's a—a dear, of course, but he's no use in a crisis, and he clearly thinks birth is just that. Will he come along presently, d'you think?'

'He and Mart meant to follow by taxi,' Rose assured her. 'When they arrive, do you want me to go into the waiting room so that Scotty can be with you? It might be best, I suppose.'

Millie, however, shook her head decidedly. 'No. He can come in when it's all over and see the baby, but not until then. Honestly, Rosie, he faints at the sight of blood. Promise me you won't let him come in until the baby's born. Well, he won't want to see anything unpleasant.'

So Rose promised, and when a nurse came in and told them that Mr Scott had arrived, she went out and repeated Millie's words and saw the look of relief which crossed Scotty's countenance. 'You're a real brick, Rose,' he said gratefully. 'Will it be long now?'

Rose said she hoped not, and Martin echoed this, since he did not want to miss work. He left the hospital at seven o'clock, telling Scotty that he must walk Don before heading for the funfair. He told Rose severely that she must not forget her own condition and do too much and went, assuring Scotty that he would return when work finished for the day, if Millie had still not had the baby by then.

There followed a lengthy wait whilst the contractions got closer. Millie started saying repeatedly, 'I wish I hadn't done it, I wish I hadn't done it,' making Rose stifle giggles. However, when the plaint changed to: 'If I'd known it was going to hurt this much I'd have tied a knot in Scotty's willy,' Rose grew embarrassed, not for her own sake but for the midwife, who popped in from time to time to see how things were going. She told Rose comfortingly, when Rose tried to apologise— in a hissing whisper—for her friend's frankness, that she had heard far worse, and having checked the baby's heartbeat and Millie's pulse she disappeared again.

'And do you know, they gave me a bloody enema?' Millie announced when they let Rose re-enter the small side ward from which she had been ejected. 'No one at the clinic told us that we'd have to have a bloody enema!'

Rose murmured soothingly that she had not known about the enema either but she was sure there must be a good reason . . . and then Millie plunged into another pain and the subject of enemas was dropped.

In fact it was not until well on in the afternoon that Millie was taken to the delivery room. A mere twenty minutes later the midwife came into the waiting room, asking for Mr Scott. 'I think he must have popped out for a moment,' Rose began, for there was no sign of Scotty, but even as she spoke he appeared in the doorway.

He was eating a huge bar of chocolate from one hand and holding a bottle of beer guiltily behind a rolled-up newspaper in the other. Clearly he must have been shopping in St Asaph, tired and hungry from the long wait. He stared at Rose, scattering beer and the remains of what looked like a Cornish pasty all over the waiting room floor. 'Is it born? Is she awright?' he asked thickly and Rose realised, with dismay, that the bottle of beer, now lying on its side on the floor, was not his first. Scotty had either started his celebrations early or decided that his worries would be more bearable seen through an alcoholic haze. The midwife tightened her lips but told him, reproachfully, that his wife had given birth to a fine son, weighing in at exactly seven pounds. Then she left.

Rose brushed crumbs off Scotty's tweed jacket and told him, severely, that he could be in big trouble for bringing alcohol into the waiting room. 'Because it's no good pretending that the bottle on the floor was your first drink of the day,' she said. 'It's pretty clear to me that you've been celebrating early, but now you must pull yourself together, Scotty, because you don't want the staff to think you're drunk.'

Scotty stared at her owlishly. 'Drunk?' he said. 'Wharrever makes you say shc—shc—scandalous thing, Rose Thomps—Thompson? I can hold—hold my liq—liq—liquor! Did she shay we've gorra boy?'

'That's right,' Rose said resignedly. She had seen enough drunkenness when she lived in the tower block to recognise the uselessness of reproaches. She guessed that Scotty believed himself to be as sober as a judge, but thought it best to accompany

208

him to the ward, warning him in a hissing whisper to say nothing and to keep his head turned away when near a member of staff.

'Why should I turn my head away? That'sh rude, that is,' Scotty said reproachfully. 'I don't wanna be rude to anyone, I'm a father and f—fathers aren't never rude to nobody.'

'If a nurse or a doctor smells your breath, they'll kick you out, chuck,' Rose said as gently as she could. 'You want to see your wife and your new son, don't you? Well then, don't go huffing into anyone's face.'

'I am not . . .' Scotty began, but at this point the nurse returned to the waiting room and led them down a long corridor and into the ward. Millie was sitting up in bed looking totally exhausted, but she was in her own nightgown and the smile which crossed her face when she saw her husband and friend was one of pure delight.

'Have you seen him?' she asked eagerly. 'He's in the nursery, the room just past this one. He's really beautiful, with lots of black hair and teeny little hands and feet. He's in the cot nearest the door and he's got a thing like a wristwatch round his arm, with *Baby Scott* written inside it. D'you want to go and have a look at him? I can't come with you but I'm sure if you pick him up and bring him back to me, we can all look at him together.'

'I don't think we ought to do that,' Rose said doubtfully. 'But we'll certainly go in and look at the little darling. C'mon, Scotty.'

In the nursery, Scotty and Rose bent over the cot. 'Isn't he tiny?' Rose whispered. 'He's a bit like you, Scotty.' She giggled. 'His hair sticks up just the way yours did when you appeared in the doorway to say that Millie had started. Oh look, he's going to say hello!'

Scotty laughed. 'The little feller's yawning; he doesn't know his daddy yet, but he soon will. D'you think I could pick him up, Rose, or would they tell me off?'

'No, don't pick him up,' Rose said quickly, still very aware that Scotty was not quite himself. 'But you might stroke his little cheek.'

Scotty did as he was bid and chuckled delightedly when he felt the soft silk of his son's skin. They stood for a moment examining the tiny newcomer and then returned to the ward, where Millie greeted them so sleepily that Rose told Scotty they should leave now and return at visiting time that evening. 'I don't see why,' he said, pointing to the empty bed next to his wife's. 'You run along, Rose; I've had a hard time of it. I'll make myself comfortable here.'

Rose was beginning to ask him what he meant when, to her absolute horror, he kicked off his shoes, took off his coat, and climbed into the empty bed. She glanced round wildly. Millie was sound asleep, but there were women in the other beds who were not, and they began to giggle and comment whilst poor Rose tore the covers off the recumbent Scotty and tried to drag him out of the bed. She succeeded only when two of the other mothers took pity on her, and between the three of them they got his coat and shoes on and then manhandled an extremely reluctant Scotty along to the end of the ward. He was beginning to object to this treatment when a nurse, pushing through the swing doors, took in the situation at a glance and fetched a couple of brawny porters, who seized

Scotty and ejected him from the hospital. The fresh air brought him abruptly out of his stupor and he began to apologise to Rose, saying that he did not know what had come over him but that he would now call for a taxi to take them back to Bath Street.

Rose, however, shook her head. 'I'll stay here for a bit,' she said. 'Tell Martin I'm still at the hospital. See you at visiting time, Scotty.' She watched as he walked over to where a taxi had just disgorged its passengers and climbed into it. Rose waited until the vehicle was out of sight, then turned back into the hospital and approached the nurse who had summoned the porters. 'I don't think there's much point in my going back home now,' she said timidly. 'Heaving my pal's husband out of that bed and getting him to the end of the ward seems to have done something to my innards. I—I think, nurse, that the baby's probably started.'

She had half expected the nurse to tell her it was just imagination, but the girl did no such thing. She cast a quick, shrewd glance across Rose's bulging figure, then spoke. 'Stay here whilst I fetch a wheelchair,' she said. 'How close are the pains?'

Gosh, she actually used the word pains, Rose thought, amused, but she told the nurse that they seemed pretty continuous and waited obediently just inside the doors. Presently she was whisked off in a wheelchair to an examination room, where a weary young doctor confirmed that in his opinion she was already in the second stage of labour and should be admitted immediately. She was not taken to the ward where Millie lay, but to a smaller side ward, where various unpleasant things happened to her, including the enema to which

211

Millie had objected so strongly. Then she was left alone and found herself longing desperately for Martin. She even began to mutter his name and found some comfort in talking to him as though he were really there; how she wished he was! The pains were strengthening and the need for Martin was growing more intense. Rose sat up on her elbow and sent a desperate message. 'Hurry, Martin, hurry! Oh, I wish you were here!'

*   *   *

Martin had returned to Bath Street upon leaving the hospital, and been greeted ecstatically by Don. The big dog was clearly impatient to be down on the beach, so Martin did not bother with breakfast, but simply grabbed a hunk of bread, spread it thinly with jam and left the room. It was early still, but Martin realised he would have to cut their walk short or be late for work, so he decided he would take Don with him to the funfair. He had done this once or twice before and no one had objected, for Don never wandered off or showed undue interest in passing dogs. Not even a cat in full flight had caused the greyhound to do more than follow its rapid passage with interested eyes, so Martin had no qualms about taking Don to work with him.

Once at the funfair, Martin went to the paint store and collected his equipment. He was repainting the gallopers, a task he greatly enjoyed even though it was slow and intricate work. The man who usually did the job had seized gratefully upon Martin's offer to take over, for the work needed a steady hand and Alf admitted that as he grew older it was becoming more difficult to apply the paint without blurring the outlines. Usually, Martin kept his mind on his work, but today his attention kept wandering back to the hospital. He thanked God that it was Millie in the process of giving birth and not Rose.

He dipped his smallest brush into the tin of scarlet enamel paint and outlined the wooden horse's flaring nostrils. Rose had borrowed books on having babies from the library and Martin had read them assiduously, so now he felt sincere sympathy for poor Millie, but had it been Rose his anxiety would have been overwhelming. She was the best friend he had ever had and the thought of what she still had to go through made his toes curl.

By now, all the chaps on the funfair knew that Martin and Rose were expecting a baby, though of course they had no idea that Martin was not the father. When he had first started work, he had always worn an old woollen hat and had never removed his spectacles, but now that the warmer days had come and his fellow workers accepted him, he took off his hat whenever they went into the offices in wet weather to eat their snap. Only one man had commented on his appearance and he was elderly, bad-tempered and sharp-tongued. Martin had removed his spectacles because he'd got a speck of paint on one of the lenses and old Norm had stared at him before calling the attention of the other men to him. 'Look, fellers, we've got a bloody freak workin' wi' us,' he had said. 'I reckon we ought to shove 'im in a tent and charge tuppence to go inside and see the human white rabbit.'

Martin had felt the hot colour creep up his neck

213

and invade his face and knew that everyone was staring at him, not understanding what Norm was getting at. Hastily, he had jumped up, replaced his spectacles and reached for his woolly hat, but before he could abandon his food and simply run away—which was what he felt like doing—the foreman had flapped a hand at him, indicating that he should sit down again, and had then turned to address Martin's persecutor. 'How an ugly old bastard like you can criticise Martin I can't imagine,' he had said calmly. 'You've a vicious tongue on you, Norm, and if you don't control it, you can start lookin' for another job. It won't be difficult to replace you; in fact, if you hadn't been with us for about a hundred years, we wouldn't have re-employed you last autumn.' He had glanced towards the window. 'Ah, the rain's stopped; it were only a shower. Back to work, fellers!'

Martin had expected that the other chaps would follow Norm's lead and perhaps start calling him the Freak, but it was soon clear that the nasty little episode had instead turned them against Norm. They had continued to treat Martin as they had always done; he was a fellow worker who pulled his weight and was never slow to offer help, and as such they accepted him as one of themselves.

'Hi, Mart. I see you've brung Don along. Does that mean your old lady is having the baby?'

Martin turned and grinned at the speaker. He was a dark-haired, skinny young man named Ted, a couple of years older than Martin himself, and the two had become firm friends. 'God, Ted, you nearly made me jump out of my skin,' he said, resting his brush on the small tin of paint. 'No,

214

Rose hasn't started yet, but her pal Millie has. Rose went with her in the ambulance and Scotty and meself followed in a taxi, but of course I had to get back so I could walk Don and come to work, so I don't know what's gone on and shan't know until visiting time tonight.'

Ted pulled a face. He was a married man himself, though he and his wife had no children as yet. He glanced at the heavy watch he wore on his wrist. 'Our tea break's in ten minutes,' he pointed out. 'Why don't you nip down to the box on the corner and give the hospital a ring?'

'I might phone later,' Martin said judiciously, 'but I think it's too early; from what I've read in Rose's books, first babies take their time. I were just thanking God that it weren't my Rosie up at the hospital giving birth, but when her time comes I'll be with her, I hope.'

'Ain't your lodgings on the phone?' Ted enquired, and, as Martin shook his head, added: 'Not many are, come to think, but if Millie's baby has arrived I reckon your Rose would come round here to let you know. So don't worry, old feller.'

With that, he left, and Martin began work once more, though when the time for their midday break arrived he took Ted's advice and rang the hospital, who told him that Mrs Scott was still in labour.

Doggedly, Martin continued to work, but at four o'clock he finished the gilding on one of the wooden horse's bridles, carefully packed up his equipment, and went across to the workroom, where he conscientiously cleaned his brushes and pressed the lids on the little tins of enamel paint firmly into place. Then he went over to the office.

Mr Foster, sitting behind the big desk, raised an enquiring eyebrow. 'Everything all right, Thompson?' he asked, glancing at the clock on the wall. 'You can't have finished all the gallopers already.'

Martin, too, glanced at the clock and saw that it was only a quarter past four, but he had known as soon as four o'clock had struck, that he must leave. He was suddenly and absolutely certain that something was happening to Rose, that she needed him, was thinking about him. He could scarcely explain this to Mr Foster, however, and merely said that he had been told to ring the hospital after four. Then, having promised the foreman that he would come in at least an hour early next day, he left the funfair with Don.

He stood for a moment on the prom, considering his options. He was suddenly certain that Rose was still at the hospital, so he went to the box on the corner and rang them. He always felt guilty when describing Rose as his wife, but on this occasion he said it boldly. The young woman on the other end of the telephone asked him to hold and presently returned, to tell him briskly that his wife was indeed in labour and would be taken to the delivery room shortly. Martin crashed the phone down and ran out of the box, his heart beating a wild tattoo in his breast. Don stood up, his big dark eyes anxious, but right now Martin's thoughts were all of Rose.

Martin and Don were running along the prom when there was a screech of brakes from the roadway and a black taxi came to a halt beside him. The passenger in the rear seat wound the window down and a head popped out ... good

216

God, it was Scotty! 'She's had it! We've got a little boy!' Scotty shouted, waving a beer bottle as he spoke. 'Clever, clever Scotty's a dad . . . and Millie hasn't done badly, 'cos she's a mum now, you know!'

Martin dived across and dragged the door open, causing Scotty to fall out on to the pavement, where he lay for a moment, grinning and giggling. Martin stepped over him and jumped into the taxi. Don would have followed him, but the taxi driver gave a shout of protest and Martin got out of the cab again and heaved Scotty to his feet. 'Take Don back to our room, would you?' he said breathlessly. 'I see you've been celebratin' already. How's Rose? They told me at the hospital when I rang just now that she were in labour, so I've gorra get up there pronto.' He looked accusingly at the other man. 'You're bleedin' well drunk. A fat lot of good you'll be to Millie in that condition. Did you see Rose before you left the hospital?'

'Course I did, course I did,' Scotty said quickly. 'Only I had to get some stuff in the village.' He grinned slyly. 'I bought a bottle of whisky to wet the baby's head. Uh-oh, I've left it in the cab; hang on a minute.'

He pushed past Martin, grabbed a paper carrier that clinked as he cradled it in his arms, and got out of the cab once more. The driver promptly abandoned his place and came round, holding out a hand.

Scotty began to fumble in his pocket for the fare and poor Martin remembered that he only had about a bob on him. He grabbed Scotty's arm. 'Will you promise me you'll take Don back to Bath Road before you sample any of the bottles in that

217

there carrier bag?' he demanded. 'And can you lend me some dosh, old feller? Only I never have much money on me when I'm going to work. I want to take this taxi back to the hospital and I'm in a desperate hurry!'

Slightly sobered by the urgency in Martin's tone, Scotty agreed to see to the dog and paid the driver, saying loftily as he did so that the extra tanner was a tip; he then gave Martin a ten bob note. 'I've not got anything smaller,' he explained. 'You can pay me back Friday.'

Martin jumped back into the cab, which promptly began to move, the driver grumbling as he did a U-turn that if there was one thing he hated it was daytime drunks. 'I picked him up at the hospital thinkin' I'd get back to Rhyl in time for a nice cup of tea at the taxi office, only he wanted to go into St Asaph first to find something he'd left there, which turned out to be booze,' he said discontentedly. 'Where d'you want to go? Back to the perishin' hospital, I suppose.'

'Oh aye, it's the hospital for me an' all,' Martin said, leaning back against the cracked leather seat. 'Scotty ain't a bad feller, really. His wife had her baby earlier today, and mine is about to have ours, which is why I'm in a hurry.'

The taxi driver chuckled. 'So you want to be in at the birth, eh? Well, I'm tellin' you, I've got five nippers an' I never seen none of 'em born, nor wanted to. I don't hold with these modern methods . . . what good will it do your wife to have you faintin'? I mean there's nothin' you can really do, is there?'

'Yes there is,' Martin said indignantly. 'I've read all the books. I can hold her hand, rub her back,

218

fetch her a drink if she wants one . . . I can even time the contractions if that's what she wants me to do. And of course I can talk to her, take her mind off the pain.'

The taxi driver sniffed. 'Oh, well, hang on to your hat then, and I'll put me foot down. You'll be there in two shakes of a lamb's tail.'

He was as good as his word and drew up in front of the hospital with a flourish. Martin ran round to his door, paid him, and hurried into the foyer where he asked at the reception desk for Rose Thompson. A nurse was called and Martin was rather touched when the taxi driver appeared in the foyer and handed him a two shilling piece. 'That's for your kid when it comes,' the driver said gruffly. 'Good luck, mate. Hope it ain't twins.'

This fearful thought had never occurred to Martin, but he thanked the driver and then followed the nurse through some swing doors and on to a long corridor. Presently he was ushered into a small cubicle where a little nurse told him in an awed voice that his wife was about to be taken to the delivery room as the baby's birth was imminent, but he could see her for a moment.

*   *   *

When the door opened and Martin came into the room, Rose could only sob out his name and grasp his hands. He stroked the hair off her wet forehead and told her she was his brave girl, but then the door opened again and Martin was bundled out of the room. 'Not long now, young lady,' a green-clad doctor told her. 'Your husband arrived just in time.'

'Where are we going?' Rose asked feebly as she was wheeled along.

'To the delivery room, of course,' someone said. 'Goodness, I hope we get you there before the baby puts in an appearance!'

*   *   *

Martin was hovering in the waiting room, desperately anxious to do the right thing, yet longing to simply demand to be allowed to see Rose, when he was called. On entering the corridor, he saw her being wheeled out of the delivery room. With an upsurge of joy, he saw that she was tenderly cradling a small, green-clad body against her breast. She saw Martin and gave him a smile so full of relief and delight that all his worries disappeared. She was all right, and so was the baby! He stepped forward, putting out a tentative hand, and felt tears wet on her cheek. The nurse pushing the trolley stopped obediently as Rose gestured. Martin reached out and gripped Rose's hand tightly, whilst he fought to control the uprush of emotion which the sight of her had engendered. 'Oh, Rose,' he muttered. 'Oh, Rosie-posie, aren't you a clever girl!'

He looked down at the baby and saw a small round head covered in soft black fluff above a pointy-chinned face still red from birth, with long swollen eyelids and a pink and puckered mouth. 'Oh, Mart, isn't he the most beautiful thing?' Rose whispered. 'It's a boy. But you've not said how pretty he is.'

'He's the prettiest baby I've ever seen,' Martin said. 'Look at his little nails; I didn't know

220

anything could be so tiny and yet so perfect. What are you going to call him?'

The nurse, who had been pushing the trolley, cleared her throat. 'I'm sorry, Mr Thompson, but I have to get your wife on to the ward; corridors are draughty places,' she said apologetically. 'She'll be in the same ward as her friend, so if you'd like to go to the waiting room whilst we get her into her own nightie and dress the baby properly, I'll come along and fetch you and you can discuss names then.'

Martin immediately stepped back, watched until the nurse, the trolley and its occupants had disappeared, and then made for the waiting room once more. He realised that he felt as proud and pleased as though he really was the father of that tiny scrap. It would be wonderful to have a son of his own, but he must be content with the next best thing, and he knew his Rose. She was always generous and would share her baby as soon as she realised how much the little boy meant to him.

The waiting room was crowded and Martin realised that this must be because visiting time was approaching. However, there was still one vacant chair, so he sat down, smiled shyly at the man next to him and reached for a copy of *Homes and Gardens* which lay on the low table nearest him. He had barely turned the first page, however, before the door opened and the trolley-pushing nurse beckoned to him. 'Mr Thompson? Come with me, please. We've put Mrs Thompson in a side ward for now, since visiting time is so near, so you and she can have a chat,' she said, and Martin followed her eagerly. He was longing to hear any detail which Rose felt she could pass on, but even more than that he was longing to see the baby again.

The nurse showed him into the side ward, which was just a small room with a bed, a chair and a locker . . . and Rose, looking clean and neat in her own winceyette nightie, holding the baby, now shawl-wrapped, in the crook of her arm. She beamed at Martin and turned her head to kiss the child's soft cheek. Then she spoke, obviously aware of the nurse's presence.

'What'll we call our little boy, Mart? I know we talked about names, but we didn't decide for definite, did we? Millie's going to call hers Alexander.'

Martin was about to reply when the soft closing of the door told him that he and Rose were alone, so he said: 'The choice is yours, Rose, you know that. I'd never interfere . . .'

'Look, Mart, so far as the rest of the world is concerned, you and I are married, and you are the baby's father. He has to be *our* baby when we're talking about him—and not just in front of other people either, because if we do that we're bound to slip up.' She looked anxiously across at him. 'You don't mind, do you, Mart? I can tell from the look on your face that you're already really fond of him.'

'Well, in that case, I thought you'd—we'd—pretty well settled on Richard, only you said we'd call him Ricky. I can't remember exactly why, but it was something to do with a song you'd heard when you were a nipper.' He smiled lovingly at her. 'As for liking the little 'un, I reckon he's me favourite person, next to yourself.'

'Right you are, Richard Paul Thompson he is,'

222

Rose said. 'Would you like to hold him for a minute? I think you two should get to know one another as soon as possible.' Martin took the baby from her eagerly, then sat down on the chair by the bed, cradling Richard Paul in his arms. He was astonished by the heat that emanated from the small, solid body and saw that Rose was looking at him with considerable surprise. 'Well I never!' she said softly. 'Most men are scared of babies; they think they'll drop 'em or that the baby will piddle on 'em, but you're holdin' young Richard as though you'd been handlin' babies all your life.'

'I've never held one before, but I like it,' Martin said. 'I thought he'd be, oh, frail and cool, but he's solid and hot.' He glanced at the girl in the bed. 'Rosie, I think I'm in love.' Instantly, Rose's face, which had been happy and open, closed like a steel trap and her eyes refused to meet his. Dismayed, Martin realised at once that she had misunderstood him. He gave a rather artificial laugh. 'Not with you, goose, with young Ricky here. A feller doesn't fall in love with his pal, even if she does happen to be a girl. Now tell me about this little chap.'

As soon as Martin had cleared up the misunderstanding, he saw Rose's expression change to one of doting fondness. 'He weighed in at six pounds eight ounces, and he's twenty-two inches long,' she said, glancing proudly at the child. 'When I asked the doctor who delivered him why Ricky's hair was black, as I suppose you and I could both be described as fair, he said that most babies lose their birth hair when they are a few weeks old, so I might still end up with a red-headed one.' She gave a dramatic shudder. 'Yuk, I

223

hope not! I've spent me life being called Carrots or Sandy or Ginger and I wouldn't wish that on the poor chap.'

'Better red than white,' Martin muttered, but he said it too low for Rose to catch. 'Here, I'd better give you back to your mum, young Ricky, because visitors are coming along the corridor and Scotty may pop in. I expect he'll visit this evening. Have you seen Millie's baby, by the way? Scotty said it were a boy. What's it like? I don't believe he can be as pretty as Ricky.'

Rose smiled. 'Yes, I've seen him. She's called him Alexander—I told you, didn't I? Actually, they're rather alike. When I'm on the main ward, you'll be able to see for yourself because the babies all sleep in the nursery, which is a room further down the corridor. Each one is labelled round its little wrist, of course, so you can tell one from t'other.'

Martin had given the baby back to Rose and now he noticed how pale and tired she looked, and felt a stab of guilt. He stood up, then reached out a cautious hand and stroked her cheek. 'You poor kid, here am I chattering away, completely forgetting what you've been through. I'll be off now so's you can get some kip, but I'll see you tomorrer. When d'you reckon they'll let you come home?'

'I think it's about a week,' Rose said drowsily. She had already slid down the bed, but was still cuddling the baby closely. 'They'll move me into the main ward as soon as visiting is over, though, so don't come here tomorrow because this little room will probably have another woman in it.'

'Right,' Martin said briskly, opening the door.

'Have a good night, sweetie.' He was actually in the corridor when something else occurred to him and he poked his head round the door of the small room. 'Don sends his congratulations and tells me he's bought you a big box of chocolates. I'll bring them with me when I come tomorrow.'

He closed the door gently on Rose's chuckle and walked rapidly towards the foyer. The visitors had all disappeared, save for one figure coming unsteadily towards him. Scotty! For a moment Martin had to fight an urge to ignore the other man, but then he conquered it. Instead, he stopped. 'Hello, Scotty. D'you know which ward Millie's on? It's the second door on the left. Sorry I can't stop, but I expect Don will be crossing his legs by the time I get back to Bath Street.'

'Oh, he'll be all right. I took him out like I promised,' Scotty said vaguely. 'If you wait for me, we can share a taxi back to Rhyl; share the cost as well. Has your Rosie popped yet?'

'Yes, we've gorra boy. If I hurry I'll mebbe get the bus,' Martin said. Although Scotty had himself well in hand, his breath smelt strongly of whisky and Martin had no desire to hang about the hospital for another hour. 'See you later, Scotty.'

*   *   *

When visiting time was over, Rose found herself tucked up next to Millie in the very bed from which she had so recently dragged the indignant Scotty. They talked a little, but very soon the ward was quiet and the lights dimmed and Rose was filled with a vast sense of relief. The ordeal was over and the reward lay in the nursery, his small

225

mouth pursing and unpursing, his eyes occasionally opening, only to close again almost at once. And dear Martin had come when she needed him, but had made no claims. In fact she had had to insist that he both spoke and thought of little Ricky as though he were the baby's father. It was a piece of real luck, meeting Mart that awful day, she told herself now, snuggling down the bed. Yes, although she had not realised it at the time, it had been her lucky day.

She turned to whisper a goodnight to Millie and smiled when she realised her friend was fast asleep; soon, she slept herself.

Chapter Ten

Isobel climbed wearily out of her little car and saw that Frank was already home, which was no surprise really. She had spent a great deal of time searching the city for some sign of Gertrude but in future, she told herself firmly now, she was going to go along with Frank's wishes. He wanted her to admit defeat and begin to live a more normal, less frantic life.

Only the previous day, he had reminded her that by now the girl would have given birth. Both he and Isobel were sure that Gertrude would have gone to a hospital as soon as she had realised she was going into labour, so Isobel had kept tabs on every maternity unit within a ten-mile radius of the city centre. She had telephoned round almost daily and at one stage had actually driven out to a small hospital in the suburbs, where a girl named

Gertrude had booked herself in and had produced a baby girl. Isobel had rushed to the ward only to find a dark-haired, dark-eyed gypsy woman gazing dispassionately at her across the baby's head. Isobel had returned home, disappointed but still convinced that she would find the right Gertrude if she continued to enquire regularly.

Today, however, she had decided that wherever Gertrude was, it was not in the area. It was almost the end of May, and she was pretty sure that the girl would have had her baby by now. Isobel crossed the gravel drive, mounted the three steps and pushed open the front door. A comfortable-looking woman, crossing the hall, stopped as Isobel entered and smiled a welcome. 'Dinner in ten minutes; Mr Frank's already in the dining room,' she said cheerfully.

Isobel gave a small laugh. 'What's for dinner, Alice?'

Alice Widdowes was fifty-seven and had worked for the family ever since Isobel's birth, when she had joined the staff as a kitchen maid at the age of fourteen. Other servants had come and gone, but Alice had remained and now acted as housekeeper and general factotum to Frank and Isobel. She had known all about the adoption plan, of course, and had been almost as eager as Isobel to have a baby to fuss over and spoil.

'A roast: a leg of young Welsh lamb with the new mint from the garden, roast potatoes, carrots and some spring greens what were only cut this morning,' she said. 'And I hope as you'll concentrate on your dinner and not say one word about that Gertrude Pleavin, 'cos I'm tellin' you, she's long gone, and wouldn't thank you if she

227

knew you were on her tail.'

This time, Isobel's laugh held genuine amusement. 'You're right there; I'm sure she doesn't want to see me because she must know she's treated me abominably,' she said. 'I gave her everything, Alice, and wanted to go on helping her, but she threw my kindness back in my face and I do find it difficult to forgive her.' She shook herself, then smiled reassuringly into the older woman's worried face. 'It's all right; I'm really going to put both Gertrude and her baby right out of my mind. Dinner in ten minutes, you said? Good, because I'm hungry as a hunter.'

She went through to the dining room to find Frank, who must have heard her approach, throwing down his copy of the *Echo* and rising to his feet. He held out his arms and enfolded her in a warm embrace. 'My darling girl, I heard you talking to Alice and I'm so glad you've decided to come back to me. Ever since I did that terrible thing I've felt as though I had built a wall between us; felt that you were adding to it, brick by brick, making it higher. But now all that is over and our lives can get back on course. I know you think it is too soon, but I want us to reapply to become adoptive parents. What do you say?'

'I'll think about it,' Isobel said cautiously. 'I told Mr Reynolds today that I wanted to take a couple of steps down occasionally, so that I could actually work with children, and he suggested that I be put down as a helper on day trips. So let me get used to being with children again before we do anything more about adoption. Do you agree?'

Frank was beginning to say that she was, as usual, being both sensible and practical when the

228

door opened and Alice, pushing a trolley laden with covered silver dishes, entered the room. 'Ah, here comes our dinner!' he said. 'Goodness, Alice, that smells delicious!'

* * *

When the knock came on the door, Rose, with Ricky clamped to her breast, knew it would be Millie, even as it opened and her friend's head appeared around it. 'Don't say I'm ready first,' Millie said, her voice laden with sarcasm. 'I can't make out why it takes you such ages to breast-feed that little monster when Alex here gobbles his portion in ten minutes! However, when you've changed his nappy and given him yet another cuddle, I thought we might do our shopping and then go to the pyjama factory. I know the crèche doesn't accept babies under six weeks old, but if we apply today the boys will be the right age by the time we're interviewed.'

Rose nodded agreement. She and Millie had bought a big old-fashioned pram from a young woman who lived on the large council estate just off Marsh Road and it was a real boon, but just now Rose had other things than crèches and prams on her mind. She whisked the baby off her breast and laid him across her shoulder to bring up his wind, reaching for a clean nappy as she did so. 'Guess what happened just now?' she enquired. 'I mean guess what our Ricky just did!'

'A poo in his nappy,' Millie said promptly. She wrinkled her nose. 'Oh yes he did, I can tell from here. But wait until I tell you what Alex did when I'd finished feeding him earlier . . .'

229

'No, you listen, Millie Scott. Ricky *smiled* at me! No, don't you scoff, honest to God, Millie, he smiled right into me eyes as though he'd been doin' it all his life.'

Millie's eyes rounded and she turned the baby in her arms to face Rose. 'He did? Well, that's just what I was going to tell you! Alex smiled at *me* just moments ago! He did, he did; I'm not just fooling around. A big, beaming smile! Just wait until I tell Scotty, he'll be over the moon.'

'So will Mart,' Rose admitted. 'Isn't it odd, Millie, how the two of 'em do things together? Fancy them both smiling for the first time on the very same day!'

Millie turned Alex in her arms again and kissed the top of his downy head. 'I expect they'll do everything more or less at the same time,' she said. 'Walking, talking, taking out their first girl, getting married . . .'

Rose finished dressing Ricky, added a woollen helmet and laid him on the bed whilst she slipped into her own jacket. The June day was brilliant; sun streamed down on the town and she knew that by the time they had done their shopping and reached the factory both her jacket and Millie's would be dumped on the foot of the pram.

'Ready?' Millie's tone was impatient. Rose knew that her friend and Scotty loved Alex just as much as she and Martin loved Ricky, but perhaps because they had fewer financial worries they took parenthood far more lightly. Rose sometimes wondered if reading every book available on child rearing had been a good idea. When Ricky and Alex developed nappy rash, Millie bought a tube of Drapolene and applied it vigorously to Alex's

230

small bottom and then, it seemed, took it for granted that the rash would clear up. Rose agonised over every spot, bought different unguents which she could ill afford, and lay awake at night wondering if this was the start of measles, or something worse. If Millie thought Alex was too hot, she would airily rip off shawls and headgear. Rose, who had read that more heat escapes through the top of the baby's head than in any other way, was terrified to remove a stitch of his clothing, though when Millie had pointed out the other day that Ricky's little face was uncomfortably flushed she had taken her friend's advice and stripped off his thick coat—and had then waited for a chill to develop.

'Rose Thompson, are you ready, you wretched girl?' Millie asked again, as Rose clicked her fingers to Don and took one last, lingering glance around the room. She always left the place immaculate because she was pretty certain that Mrs Osborne had a good snoop round as soon as her tenants left the building, though so far Rose had not missed anything. The other tenants assured the two young mothers that Ozzie would nick anything left in the bathroom, kitchen or fridge, but did not think she would take from their rooms.

When Whitsun had arrived, Mrs Osborne had been true to her word and put their rent up, but she had not turned them out. She had also told them, nastily, that whilst she had holidaymakers in the house they might only use the kitchen when the guests had finished their own meal preparations. Rose, somewhat ruefully surveying the devastation which invariably accompanied

Millie's culinary excursions, could not entirely blame the landlady, for Millie and Scotty spread indescribable chaos wherever they went. Scotty had rigged up a line for small articles, such as the baby's bootees, which Millie washed down in the bathroom, but the nappies which she brought back from the brand new launderette five hundred yards from the lodging house, still damp of course but at least clean, she hung on the line in Ozzie's back garden. The landlady objected loudly; indeed, when she had washing of her own to dry, she would take Rose's and Millie's clean stuff and sling it down on the tiny patch of grass, pegging out her own articles whilst grumbling that she would be glad when they moved out, since they were more trouble than a hundred holidaymakers. When this happened, Millie gave the nappies a good shake and used them without any fuss, but Rose spent hours removing tiny blades of grass and bits of earth and felt guilty for not washing them again.

Now, Millie heaved an exaggerated sigh and headed down the stairs. 'I'm going without you,' she called over her shoulder. 'I nipped into the launderette earlier, so my nappies are up to date, if you know what I mean.'

The pram was kept in a cupboard at the foot of the stairs, and Millie yanked it out and thumped it through the front door, through the gate and on to the pavement whilst Rose, with the baby in her arms and Don at her heels, was still descending the stairs. When she joined Millie, her friend was just cuddling Alex down in the blankets, so Rose did the same with Ricky, hung her shopping bag on the hook at the end of the pram, and smiled at her friend. 'I put my nappies out at the crack of dawn,' she admitted. 'You and Scotty weren't even stirring. I just hope Ozzie doesn't chuck them on the grass before they've had a chance to get dry. Mart gave me a hand to hang them out because Ricky was still sound asleep after the six o'clock feed . . . oh, Millie, won't it be heaven when they give up the two a.m. one? Poor old Mart works like a dog on that funfair and though I try to get to Ricky before he wails and wakes Mart up, I'm afraid it doesn't often happen.'

'Alex is showing signs of giving it up,' Millie said happily, tucking the blankets round the two small bodies. 'As for waking up, Scotty never does. Not even for the six o'clock feed, though the alarm going off at seven has him grumbling loudly enough to wake both me and the baby.' She turned a conspiratorial grin on her friend as she wheeled the pram towards the prom. 'I haven't had a chance to tell you before, but Ozzie and Scotty had a right humdinger of a row yesterday over the nappies. He told her that if he caught her chucking our clean linen on the grass once more he would take her sheets and towels and throw them on to the beach, and then he'd report her to the public health people for good measure and see her prosecuted for every penny we'd spent at the launderette. First she went red as a turkey cock, then white as a ghost; she was furious, but she was frightened, too—and with reason. Scotty would do it, you know, if pressed.'

'Gosh,' Rose said inadequately. 'Millie, once or twice I've wondered . . .'

But Millie was bending over the pram and seized Rose's arm. 'Look at them!' she said urgently. 'Oh,

233

Rosie, they're smiling at one another!'

After this proof that their sons were indeed the most intelligent babies in the whole world, the two girls did their shopping. It was a Thursday, so Rose at least was short of cash, since Mart got paid on a Saturday. But both girls always saved a bit of money so that they might take advantage of Marks & Spencer's reductions.

Once they had finished their shopping, they set off to walk to the pyjama factory, Rose feeling a little apprehensive. Suppose they employed Millie and not herself? Millie was beautiful, clever and posh, whilst she herself was small and plain. Still, there was no point in meeting trouble halfway.

However, when they arrived at the factory gates, a nasty shock awaited them. The advertisement for staff had disappeared, and though Millie said stoutly that it must have fallen off in a recent gale, or been taken away by evil little boys, she was obviously worried. She looked at Rose, saw the colour drain from her cheeks, and grabbed her by the sleeve. 'Don't look like that. I'm sure it's just— just a silly mistake, but I'm going to make certain. Come along!'

It was Rose's turn to push the pram and she followed her friend in through the factory gates, saying repeatedly that she was sure it was not a mistake and wouldn't it be better to simply accept the fact that the jobs were gone and set about looking elsewhere?

Millie, however, paid no attention. She took the pram from Rose and pulled it into the shade, telling Don to sit and guard. Don, who had never been told to do such a thing before, looked somewhat bewildered, but obediently squatted beside the pram, looking not at Millie but at Rose, as though he suspected that the former had gone mad, but still trusted his mistress absolutely.

Rose had to laugh. The big dog was still somewhat in awe of the little bundles which appeared to have taken command of their lives, and even as she and Millie moved towards the doors he uttered a plaintive little whine as though he were asking them just what he was supposed to do should one of the babies cry. So she turned back, gave Don's narrow head an approving stroke, and then bent down and whispered: 'Stay, old feller, until us come back.' The anxiety faded from the big liquid eyes and Don settled himself more comfortably, his back actually resting on one of the pram wheels.

'Rosie, stop fussing that bloody dog and come on,' Millie said. Millie never swore and the fact that she had just done so was proof of her inner anxiety, no matter how boldly she might behave. 'After all, it's no sin to ask if there are jobs still going!'

They pushed through the big glass doors into a reception area. There was polished brown lino on the floor and two pale grey upholstered couches stood against the cream-washed walls. A receptionist sat behind a desk with a telephone and looked up enquiringly as they approached. 'Yes? Can I help you?'

Rose stared dumbly at the smart young woman in her pale grey suit and blue blouse, but Millie smiled winningly and leaned forward, both hands on the desktop. 'You can indeed. My friend and I have been coming past here now for several weeks and we've seen your advertisement for staff . . .'

Millie told their story crisply and well, explaining that both she and her friend had recently given birth to babies, but were very keen to make pyjamas, particularly because of the crèche facilities available, just as soon as jobs were advertised once more. So could the young woman please tell her when that would be?

The receptionist, who had been listening with amused attention to Millie's outpourings, suddenly began to look hunted. She said she wasn't sure; no one had told her . . . she knew the advertisement outside the factory had come down . . . did Millie know that the firm was building an extension because the big stores were so pleased with their product? Whilst the extension was under construction there was a good deal of mess . . . she rather thought the directors had decided to wait until the new building was complete before . . .

'But that might be months . . . years, even,' Millie said, dismayed. 'Rose and myself—this is Rose, by the way, Rose Thompson—are good workers; we shan't let you down by losing time or sewing crooked seams. Surely, if we . . .'

Millie continued to put her case, not noticing that they were no longer alone in the foyer. A tall, dark-haired man had come in behind them and was standing listening and watching the two girls so that Rose, aware of his presence, was unable to warn Millie that she was being overheard. Scarlet with embarrassment, Rose waited for the man to tell them to leave, to stop hassling the receptionist, but instead he leaned forward and addressed Millie in a deep, amused voice.

'So you and your friend are the owners of that big dog guarding the even bigger pram which is standing just outside the doors? And you want jobs in the factory? And you are not put off by the information Miss Cruickshank has given you—that we have suspended recruitment until the extension is built? Well, well, you certainly aren't easily turned aside from your purpose, young lady!'

Millie, who had had her back to the man, now jumped and turned to confront her questioner. Rose, watching events with a mixture of fear and amusement, saw the stranger's expression change at the sight of Millie's beautiful little face. She was used to Millie's looks, but now she realised what an effect those looks could have when Millie, blushing, suddenly rewarded the man with her most inviting and attractive smile. 'Oh!' she said. 'I didn't know . . . I thought it was just Rose behind me . . . but perhaps you can help us. I was just explaining to the young lady . . .'

'Yes, I heard,' the man said. 'I'm Peter McDonald, one of the directors. I spend a good deal of time here, though I work mainly in the mid-Wales factory; and you are . . .'

'I'm Millicent Scott, Mr McDonald, only most people call me Millie,' she said demurely. 'And this is my friend Rose Thompson. As you obviously heard, we're looking for jobs, and because of your crèche facilities we were hopeful . . .'

The man smiled and Rose, feeling very much a bystander, took in the crisp white shirt, dark tie and immaculate pinstriped suit. This was someone important, though she doubted whether he could invent jobs for them after what the receptionist had just said. But he had started to speak again. 'We shall be recruiting more staff once the extension is finished, so if you will fill in an

237

application form, I'll see you are both called for interview when the time comes.'

He smiled suddenly and Rose, who had found his air of easy competence rather intimidating, realised that in fact he was quite attractive and probably not more than thirty-five or six. When he turned towards her, it was to enquire which one of them was the young mother, and Rose found herself answering with a smile, she hoped, as warm as Millie's. 'It's the both of us,' she said ungrammatically. 'I mean there's two babies in that there pram; one's my Ricky and the other . . .' she jerked a thumb in her friend's direction, 'is Millie's Alex. So we'd both like our babies to go into the crèche whilst we're working, please, Mr McDonald.'

Mr McDonald frowned. 'Oh, Lord, now that may be a problem. You see, there's a limit to the number of very young babies that the staff of the crèche can take on. However, it will be some weeks before we begin recruiting again, so if you go along to the crèche when you leave here, take a look round and explain to the nurse in charge that you have applied for work with us, perhaps you may be lucky.'

'We'll go as soon as we've filled in the forms,' Millie said eagerly. 'We meant to do so anyway, didn't we, Rosie? Thank you so much, Mr McDon—'

But at this point the telephone on the reception desk rang. Miss Cruickshank picked it up, listened for a moment, and then turned to Mr McDonald. 'It's for you, sir. Shall I transfer it to your office?'

'Is it the shipping people?' he enquired. 'It should be. I phoned them this morning, but the

238

man I wanted was out, so I asked them to get him to ring me back. Yes, put it through to my office, Miss Cruickshank; I'm sure you can deal with these young ladies without any help from me.' He raised a hand in a gesture of farewell. 'Good luck,' he said, and was gone, leaving Miss Cruickshank to produce a couple of printed forms, which she handed to Millie and Rose.

'Which will you do first, visit the crèche, or fill in the application forms?' the receptionist enquired. 'My, but weren't you lucky? Mr McDonald has nothing to do with the staff as a rule, but since he's the managing director I suppose he can do pretty much as he likes. He's ever so nice, never too proud to speak to you. But of course, we don't see all that much of him because he spends a good deal of time at our factory in mid-Wales, and goes off on buying trips all over the world. So, you see, you really *were* lucky.'

The girls took the forms over to a table which Miss Cruickshank had pointed out to them. It was equipped with a tin mug full of biros, and it took the girls barely ten minutes to complete the paperwork. Then they returned to the receptionist. She was on the telephone, talking animatedly and making notes as she did so, but she took the forms, ran her eyes briefly over the contents and after a few moments replaced the receiver and turned to her visitors. 'These look fine,' she said. 'You've not given us a telephone number, but I see you're in digs, so I guess you haven't got one. Never mind, a letter is probably safer anyhow, because I'm sure you'll be called for interview.' The telephone at her elbow rang again and she pulled a face. 'The wretched things never stop,' she commented ruefully. 'I'll be seeing you!'

Half an hour later the girls were wheeling the pram back along the pavement, heading for Bath Street. Millie smiled at the babies, now sleeping soundly, then turned to Rose. 'It's a really nice place; I'd have no qualms about leaving Alex there,' she announced. 'What did you think, Rosie?'

Rose gave an ecstatic sigh. 'It was lovely,' she said. 'Oh, won't I have a lot to tell Mart when he gets back from work this evening!'

'Yes, same here,' Millie agreed. 'And we'd best make the most of our freedom because if you ask me, in a couple of months we'll be in full-time employment and not able to stroll around the Botanical Gardens or spend time on the beach.'

'We'll have weekends,' Rose pointed out. 'And evenings, of course.'

'We'll be cleaning, shopping and cooking at weekends,' Millie said gloomily. 'I've enjoyed being a lady of leisure; I'm not at all sure how I'll take to working all day.'

'I know what you mean, but the money will be nice,' Rose said. 'Poor Don will have to go to the funfair every day, though. Oh, well, I'm sure we'll work something out.'

*   *   *

Since the girls were not yet working, they managed to present their men with a hot meal each evening, unless the holidaymakers were very disobliging and refused to fit in with the more permanent members of the household. Scotty always grumbled on such occasions, of course, but Millie

240

had retaliated by stating that she was doing her best and that he was always saying they should move to more congenial lodgings. 'But you've done nothing about it; when I told you there was a bungalow for rent in Rhuddlan you wouldn't even go and look at it,' she had reminded him sharply. 'You can't have it both ways, Robert Scott!'

That had been on a Saturday afternoon when the four of them, complete with babies and dog, had caught a bus to Llandudno. They had climbed the Great Orme—Rose and Martin had been awed and delighted by the wonderful views—and then descended to the prom where they sat in a row on a bench, eating chips and chatting. Rose had laughed to herself when Millie had given Scotty the telling-off, because she had noticed that her friend only ever called him by his full name when he was in her bad books.

Scotty had sighed, then grinned as he caught Rose's eye. He had leaned over to grasp her hand and shake it in mock contrition. 'I'm always in trouble with cruel old Millie,' he had said mournfully. 'She doesn't love me when I'm too tired to go house hunting, but *you'll* forgive me, won't you, Rosie? You'll be my little friend?'

This had made Rose giggle, but she had noticed that Martin's face wore a wistful look so she had answered, bracingly, that she would be friends with anyone who would finish off her chips for her. Since Don had come eagerly forward at that point everyone had dissolved into laughter, and the Rhuddlan bungalow had been forgotten.

Now it was August, and Rose and Millie were preparing for a day on the beach. They had learned from bitter experience, now that the

241

school holidays had started, that the beautiful golden sands speedily became very crowded indeed. However, if they set out immediately after breakfast, they usually managed to get some space to themselves, particularly if they pushed the pram towards Splash Point, which was the less popular end of the beach. At what was known as the Voryd end there was the funfair and a number of stalls selling such things as cockles and winkles, doughnuts and ice creams; things which were altogether lacking at Splash Point.

On this particular day, it was already so hot by eight o'clock that even Rose did not wrap Ricky in shawls or warm woollens. He was wearing a nappy and rubber knickers and an ancient romper suit which she had bought from a second-hand shop in Market Street, whilst she herself wore a cotton dress and sandals. She had packed a pile of jam sandwiches and two bottles of lemonade, and as soon as she had tidied round the room had set off to join Millie. As was her custom, she rapped sharply on her friend's door, then flung it open. Millie was sitting in front of the dressing table mirror, a powder puff in one hand and a box of powder before her, and she jumped guiltily as the door opened. 'What on earth . . . ?' she began, then turned to smile at her friend. 'You're early today, and you're usually late,' she said accusingly. 'And if you've come in to remind me to bring a big bottle of water for Don, you needn't bother because it's already in my straw bag. And I'm almost ready, but thought I'd do my face for once.'

'For a day on the beach?' Rose asked incredulously. 'Wharrever for, queen? We shan't meet nobody, norrif we go up to Splash Point.'

'No-o, but it does me good to put my face on once in a while ...' Millie was beginning when Rose came right into the room and stared at her friend's mirrored reflection.

'Millie Scott, you tell big lies,' she said accusingly. 'How did *that* happen, may I ask?' She leaned forward and ran a finger down a dark bruise that marred the smoothness of her friend's cheek.

Millie sighed. 'Trust you to notice!' she said. 'I walked into the kitchen door when I was taking our porridge back upstairs. It didn't half hurt, and though Scotty went down and got a piece of ice out of the fridge and I held it against my cheek all through breakfast, it's still come out in this great dark bruise, so I'm doing my best to cover it up with powder.'

'Oh, Millie, as if powder could do it!' Rose exclaimed. 'You know what you are? You're what they call accident prone. Sometimes I think you only have to look at two or three stairs to tumble down them, or even up them. It's just been luck that you've not fallen when you're carrying your Alex. You really must be more careful.'

'I know, I know. Scotty's always nagging me to look before I leap. He says if I wasn't always in a rush, these accidents wouldn't happen, but I suppose I'll slow down as I get older,' Millie said. She pushed the puff into the box and closed the lid, dusted her hands fastidiously, and stood up. 'I've got the big black umbrella to shade the babies; have you got the smaller one for us?'

Having reassured themselves on this point, the girls checked that they had everything else they would need, and set off. As they had hoped, the

243

tide was on its way out and the far end of the beach deserted, so they spread out their rugs, positioned the old umbrellas and changed into their bathing suits. Alex and Ricky lay contentedly in the shade and presently Rose turned to Millie, who was leaning back, eyes closed. 'It's pretty warm, but it's going to get even hotter later on,' she observed. 'I think we ought to get off the beach and go up to the Botanical Gardens, or in fact go anywhere where we can find some shade. It says in the baby books . . .'

'I know, I know,' Millie said soothingly. 'Hot sunshine isn't good for small babies and it's not ideal for their mothers, either. C'mon then, let's have our swim, because I'm sure you're right. The heat's downright tropical this morning.'

The girls changed back into their cotton frocks and put on the ugly straw hats Millie had insisted they buy, because they were so cheap and would protect them from the glare. 'They're coolie hats, the sort of thing Chinese peasants wear in the fields,' Rose grumbled, for she had parted reluctantly with her sixpence. 'Ain't life unfair though, Millie? You make that hat look high fashion and I make mine look like a bad joke.'

Millie giggled but said: 'Rubbish, you look very nice. And now help me hump the pram back on to the prom and we'll walk along to the funfair and buy ices. I could just do with a cornet, and Scotty gave me five bob before he left today because I said we were going to the beach. I expect he meant me to bring fish and chips in this evening, but he didn't say, so I'll buy us each a threepenny cornet.'

Dreamily, Rose helped with the pram and then strolled along, barefoot, with her coolie hat shading her face and her body relaxed after its swim. Ahead of her, she saw a line of coaches with people descending from them and wondered if they came from Liverpool; wouldn't it be a coincidence if they were actually from the children's home where she had spent so many years of her life!

They reached the foremost coach and Rose smiled to herself as the children descending from it began to form into a crocodile, chattering brightly as they did so. 'Ooh, look at all that sand!' 'Ain't the sea blue?' 'I allus thought it were green.' 'There's shells; lickle pink ones, like the ones on the shell box on me mam's dressin' table.' 'See that big café there? Last year I 'member we had us dinners there.'

Rose turned to smile at the children as she passed them, and then felt her heart begin to beat a rapid tattoo. A woman was descending from the coach, a tall, slim woman with curly light brown hair. She was wearing a navy blue summer dress, with a white Peter Pan collar and cuffs, and as her feet met the paving stones of the promenade she raised her head and looked straight at Millie, whose turn it was to push the pram. Rose shrank back, taking hold of Don's collar and bending over as though to address him. She waited for the awful moment when Mrs Ellis, for she had recognised the other woman immediately, would transfer her gaze from the pram to herself, but instead the woman stepped forward, smiling rather shyly at Millie and peeping into the pram.

'Twins!' she exclaimed. 'What pretty little fellows. I assume they're boys, as they're both wearing blue?'

'That's right,' Millie said.

Even from the back, Rose could tell that her friend was about to spill the beans, to say that they were not twins, that the mother of one of them was coming along behind her, but before Millie could speak another adult descended the steps of the coach and addressed the woman bending over the pram. 'Will you go to the front of the crocodile, please, Mrs Ellis, whilst I take up the rear? It's going to be very hot later on so I think we'd best make camp under the pier. It's about the only place on the beach where we'll find shade and I don't mean to take children home suffering from sunstroke.'

Mrs Ellis straightened up, but cast one last, longing look at the babies in the pram. 'Yes, of course, Miss Quentin. I'm so sorry, but the sight of these beautiful twin boys took my mind off my work,' she said apologetically. She took a couple of steps away from the pram, and then turned back. 'What are they called, if you don't mind my asking?'

'Richard's the one on the left and Alexander's on the right,' Millie said promptly. 'And actually, they aren't . . .'

But the woman was turning away, hurrying to the front of the crocodile. Rose released her pent-up breath and grasped Millie's arm. 'Let's go over to that ice cream parlour on the other side of the prom and have a bit of a sit-down as well as a cornet,' she muttered. 'Millie, I know that woman you were talking to and if she comes back, or you see her again, please don't tell her the boys aren't twins. I'll explain once we're sitting down.'

And presently, explain she did. Oh, not

everything, not by a long chalk. But she did say that Mrs Ellis had worked in the children's home in which she had been brought up. 'She's got no kids of her own, you see, so I reckon she thought workin' with children was the next best thing,' she said. 'Then, when I got pregnant, she just sort of assumed I didn't want me baby and said she'd put it up for adoption. I were only fifteen and had no money, nor did poor Martin, so I reckon she thought she were doin' the right thing.'

'But why didn't you tell her you wanted to keep the baby?' Millie asked, giving her cone a quick lick. 'When you told her you and Martin were going to get married, surely she must have realised you would!'

'At first, I honestly did think I wouldn't be able to cope,' Rose admitted. 'The trouble was that I didn't know *Mrs Ellis* meant to adopt my baby. She was really good to me, gave me an allowance, paid the rent of the place where I lived, even lied about my age to get me a flat. I thought she was the best and nicest person, only then I discovered she meant to take my baby . . . our baby, Mart's and mine, I mean . . . so we ran away.'

'I see,' Millie said slowly. She ran a thoughtful tongue round the ice cream, which was rapidly beginning to melt. 'Or rather I don't see. You aren't afraid that she will steal little Ricky away from his rightful parents, are you? Because if she did, that would be kidnapping.'

Rose hesitated. Should she tell Millie that the Ellises did have a claim on Ricky, that he was in fact Mr Ellis's son? But she had promised Martin that she would not tell anyone the true story, and much though she loved Millie she did not want her

247

to know that Martin was not Ricky's father. So she said, as brightly as she could: 'I don't think I've told it very well, but the fact is the Ellises are rich and important people. Mrs Ellis told my doctor that I had agreed to the adoption—it was Dr Matthews who accidentally let it out that the Ellises were going to take my baby. Well, Martin and I got away, but if she found us I'm afraid it would be her word against mine. When she first got me my flat I had to sign all sorts of papers, and thinking back one could have been an agreement to let the Ellises adopt my child. So you see . . .'

'Yes, I do see, but I think you're worrying about nothing,' Millie said. She finished off her ice cream, wiped her mouth and began to get to her feet. 'Ah, I see Don has come in for your ice cream cornet. I wonder why Mrs Ellis didn't recognise you, though?'

Rose got to her feet and leaned over the pram where the two little boys both slept, dark lashes on cheeks which were flushed from the heat. 'She was too fascinated by the babies,' she said. 'I can tell you I thanked my lucky stars it wasn't my turn to push the pram, or I reckon I'd have been a goner.'

'And are you going to be scared of meeting your Mrs Ellis every time a school trip arrives in Rhyl?' Millie asked, rather derisively. 'Because if so, life is going to become somewhat complicated for the next five or six weeks. Honestly, Rose, I'm sure you're worrying over nothing. She can't snatch Ricky out of the pram and run off with him in broad daylight; why, she might even take Alex by mistake and then she'd be in real trouble. She can't follow you home because she's come here in charge of children and won't simply abandon them. No, I'm sure you've no reason to worry.'

'I expect you're right,' Rose said as they turned down Water Street. 'I'll try not to, because apart from anything else, I do know that Mrs Ellis is a good sort of person. She goes to church, has a very responsible job and does good works—if you know what that means. I'm not sure that I do. But if we do meet up with her, she'll want explanations and—and I'd simply rather not have to explain. Can you understand that, Millie? To admit to someone who has been good and kind to you, even if it was for the wrong reasons, that you ran away rather than tell her to her face that you meant to keep your baby . . .'

Millie shuddered. 'All right, all right, I *do* understand,' she said. 'I still remember how dreadful it was telling my parents that Scotty and I were going to have a baby. My mother went white as a sheet and started to keel over, and my father shouted and roared . . . it was dreadful. Daddy said I was killing Mummy, that I was wicked and selfish, and when my mother recovered enough to speak she told me that unless I agreed to come home and forget that Scotty and I had ever met, I need never darken their doors again. I never thought I'd ever hear that phrase used in real life, but she actually said it, honest to God she did, and meant it too.' She leaned over and squeezed her friend's hand. 'Dearest Rose, I *do* understand why you're afraid of meeting Mrs Ellis, because if I thought my parents might suddenly appear before me on the prom, I'd either run like a hare or die of fright.' She laughed, but there was no amusement

249

in the sound. 'Poor old us! So if you see Mummy and Daddy approaching, get prepared to run, and if either of us sees Mrs Ellis, we'll both do the same.'

'That sounds fine, except that I've never met your parents,' Rose said. She smiled for the first time since they had watched the children descending from the coach. 'You are daft, Millie!'

'I know I am,' Millie said sunnily. She looked affectionately at her friend. 'At least it made you smile, and when we get back to Bath Street I'll show you a photograph of my parents. I keep it hidden away from Scotty because I'm sure if he knew I had it, he'd tear it up. But I'm still hopeful that one day they will acknowledge that—that I did the right thing, especially now I've got young Alex here to plead my cause. He's awfully like his father, don't you think?'

Rose peered dubiously at Alex's small, sleeping face. 'Well, I suppose he is, so far as any baby resembles a grown-up,' she said judiciously. 'But whenever anyone mentions likenesses, I think of what Winston Churchill said: "I look like all babies and all babies look like me."'

'How true that is,' Millie said, nodding her agreement. 'I do love the things old Winnie says. There was the one where a politician named Gatepost called him a dirty dog, and Winnie said: "You know what dogs do on gateposts?" My father dined out on that for weeks.'

But Rose's mind was still on an earlier part of the conversation. 'I suppose I can see a slight resemblance between Ricky and his father,' she said thoughtfully. 'Oh, not his features so much, but the way his hair grows in a peak—' She

250

stopped short, suddenly aware of what she was saying and of the way Millie was staring at her. 'And his ears are a bit like Martin's, too,' she ended, rather feebly.

Millie frowned. The quizzical look on her face faded. 'If you say so,' she said. 'Don't think I'm insulting your beloved Martin, Rosie, but if I were you I'd just be thankful that Ricky isn't an albino. From what I've gathered, being different has caused your husband real difficulties, so I expect he was pleased as well when he realised he'd not passed his colouring on to his son.'

'Yes, he was very relieved,' Rose said, glad to have had her slip accepted without further comment. 'And now let's get weaving, so we can eat our snap as soon as we reach the gardens.'

'Our sandwiches, you mean, you little heathen!' Millie said, as she had said many times before. 'Not sarnies, not snap, not butties. If you're going to rise up in the world, you'll have to get rid of your Scouse accent. When I move into the secretarial side of the pyjama business, I want you with me.'

'I'm not sure that I'd feel comfortable in an office,' Rose said dubiously. 'But first catch your hare; we're not even factory workers yet!'

Chapter Eleven

Isobel Ellis had enjoyed the trip to Rhyl. Being with the children, helping them to make sandcastles, collect shells and paddle in the pools, had brought her own childhood back to her. She had known for years that she had been privileged, had wanted to give children of her own such a childhood. But that had been denied her and now she must look seriously at adoption, because she had agreed with Frank that they were unlikely to trace Gertrude Pleavin after so long.

Now, in a coach accompanying another group of children—ten to twelve-year-olds this time—she was letting her mind return to that last trip. Something had happened, something of importance, but she had missed the significance of it at the time and it still eluded her. Carefully, she relived that gloriously sunny day, starting with the moment when the children had filed into the coaches and she had sat down next to Miss Quentin, liking the older woman, knowing that the children liked her too, and anticipating a busy but delightful day.

The coach had roared down the tunnel and out into the sunshine of the Wirral. The children had been thrilled with everything; the great sandy estuary of the River Dee and the cattle and sheep grazing on the lush green grass. On reaching Rhyl, of course, the excitement had been almost more than the children could bear and Isobel had shared their pleasure. When the coach had drawn up on the promenade, Isobel and Miss Quentin had checked that each child had a hat and a jacket and had then ushered them down from the coach, checking that all the seats were empty, and following as the children began to form into a crocodile.

I was sent to the front of the crocodile, to guide the children down the steps and across the sand to the shade of the pier, Isobel reminded herself, then stopped short. No! Whatever it was that niggled at her mind had not happened on the beach, or under the pier. Ah, she remembered now. There had been a young woman pushing a pram with two babies tucked up in it; a very pretty young woman, wearing a straw coolie hat. The girl had twins, two beautiful baby boys, both clad in similar blue romper suits, and when Isobel had asked, the young mother had given their names, though for the life of her Isobel could not recall what those names had been. Why should she? She had been surrounded by thirty children, which meant thirty different names . . . no, twenty-eight different names, because there were two Johns and two Lizzies. So what was it that she had failed to notice about those babies?

She had tried to obey Frank's injunction not to even think about Gertrude and her child, and by and large she had kept her promise. Every now and then, however, she could not help wondering. Was the baby a boy or a girl? How was Gertrude coping with no Ellises to help her? Had she had the baby adopted?

Isobel's mind niggled at that first trip to Rhyl and the pretty young mother, with her twin boys. Suppose Gertrude had had twins? But it seemed unlikely. Isobel wound the scene on a little further, saw herself going to the head of the crocodile, saw her leading the children across the prom, even saw herself glancing back, seeing that the girl with the twins now had a hand on the collar of a large dog . . .

A dog! Someone had said that young Gertrude had kept a dog in her tenth-floor flat but she, Isobel, had known better. She had visited the flat a hundred times—more—and had never seen any sign of a dog, small or large. Who had told her about a dog? Was it the inquisitive neighbour on the floor below? Yes, she had mentioned a big dog, but at the time Isobel had not believed her.

'Miss, Miss, what's that there house? Is we nearly there? Oh, Miss, did you say you'd give a penny to the first one to spot the sea?'

Isobel came back to the present with a start as the coach entered Rhyl and the buzz of anticipation grew louder. She handed over a round brown penny, assuring the children that since it was indeed the sea ahead of them, they must be very near their destination at last. Previous experience told her that she should walk down to stand near the driver as soon as the coach stopped, so that she could prevent the children from simply leaping out of the vehicle and heading for that shining sand. This group was older, so she must be careful not to lose control. Daydreaming in the coach was all very well, but to do such a thing once the ebullient band alighted really would not do.

The coach drew up; Isobel shouted to the children to stop behaving like savages and line up, and wait for the command before they moved so much as a muscle. When the coach was empty, she and the other helper marshalled their charges and

254

set off for the beach. Isobel banished all thoughts of large dogs and ungrateful young women from her mind, determined to make the day a success. But she did want to find Gertrude so desperately, wanted to tell her . . .

'Miss, Miss! I left me swimsuit under me seat; can I run back and fetch it?'

Isobel sighed and wrenched her mind resolutely back to the present. She called the crocodile to a halt, returned to the coach, fished out the bathing suit and went back to the head of the line. She really must keep her mind on her work, she decided, and gave the order to move forward once more.

*   *   *

Rose finished buttoning Ricky into his coat and glanced around the room, checking that all was in order. She and Millie had started work at the pyjama factory a couple of weeks earlier and had speedily fallen into a comfortable routine, made easier by the fact that as soon as September arrived holidaymakers disappeared as though at a secret signal. Shops, cafés and even pavements became less crowded and though the sun still shone, it was a cooler, paler sun now. The girls walked to work, taking it in turns to push the pram, but Millie had remarked only the previous day that such walks would not be so pleasant when winter came.

'I can see we'll have to take to the buses when it gets cold,' she had said rather gloomily. 'Still, never meet troubles halfway, that's my motto . . . and I do enjoy the factory work, though I didn't

255

think I would at first.'

Rose had laughed, but now she went over to the window, with Ricky on her hip, and peered out. It was raining, the sort of steady, relentless rain which would probably continue all day, so she thought they ought to set out at once if Millie was ready. The staff at the crèche were very good and helpful, but if they were presented with wet children they might well expect some help in changing them into dry clothing.

Rose picked up the big bag that contained their sandwiches—the factory provided them with hot tea three times a day—and slung it over her shoulder. She let herself out of the room, thinking as she did every day that they really ought to fit a lock. Then she tapped on Millie's door. A muffled shriek from inside informed her that, as usual, Millie was not ready, but she went in anyway to find her friend changing Alex's nappy. 'I thought we ought to leave as soon as we could today, because of the rain...' Rose began, only to be interrupted by another squeak.

'Raining? It can't be. It hasn't rained once since we've been working. Oh, great heaven! And I've not made up the bottles yet. How come I didn't notice it was raining? Why didn't you come and tell me? Rose Thompson, you're a bad girl, and if we're late for work and get sacked, I shall jolly well know who's to blame!'

Rose sighed and moved across the room to where the kettle steamed on the Primus stove and two bottles, already containing milk powder, stood nearby. 'There's nothing wrong with your eyesight, is there, Millie?' she said reprovingly, laying Ricky down on the large double bed. 'Surely you must

256

have noticed the rain? Even if you didn't look out of the window, you could have heard it pattering on the slates overhead. In fact it's been raining most of the night.' She glanced across to the door and the hooks, from one of which hung Millie's waterproof. 'I see Scotty took his mac, so he obviously knew it was raining. Didn't he mention it?' As she spoke, she was pouring boiling water into the two bottles, shaking them well and putting them into Millie's bag.

Millie sat Alex up, reached for his coat and began to put it on him, giving Rose a guilty glance as she did so. 'He might have,' she admitted. 'Only that was hours ago, so naturally I thought the rain would have stopped by now. However, we're almost ready, aren't we, honey?' She grabbed Alex's white woollen helmet and buttoned it beneath his chin, kissing one round pink cheek as she did so. 'Oh, how I love you, Alexander Scott!'

Rose unhooked Millie's waterproof and handed it to her friend, then went and picked Ricky up and headed for the door. Downstairs, they squeezed both babies into the pram, erected the hood, clipped on the apron and set off into the downpour. They walked with heads bent, splashing through puddles and scarcely exchanging a word in their eagerness to get themselves and their children under cover. At one stage, a coach rushed passed them, sending a wave of water over both them and the pram. 'That was an executive travel coach, wasn't it?' Rose asked. 'I suppose the conference season must have started. Your Scotty said it goes on until Christmas, with all sorts of firms having conferences down here. Millie, what have you done *now*? You're bleedin' well limpin'!'

'Don't blame me this time, it was you,' Millie said accusingly. 'You spun round to give the driver of the coach a dirty look and I was holding on to the pram handle, even though it was your turn to push, and the wheel went right over my foot. So if I'm maimed for life . . .'

'. . . you'll know who to blame,' Rose finished for her. 'Well, I can only say it serves you right. You're wearing your old court shoes! Why on earth . . . ?'

Millie looked curiously down at her feet, her expression so comical that Rose laughed aloud. 'Am I? Well, so I am. I stood my wellies out, too, but in the rush of leaving early I suppose I simply forgot to put them on. Look out, here comes the service bus!'

Despite Rose's fears, the girls reached the crèche in good time and were actually clocking in ten minutes early. They were on piecework, so they started up their machines at once and were very soon absorbed, though they continued to chat to their friends as they worked. They had a ten-minute break for a cup of tea at half past ten, then stopped to eat their sandwiches two hours later. Management were planning yet another extension which, when it was completed, would be a canteen, but for now the girls ate their sandwiches in the rest room. When the weather was fine, which it had been until today, Rose and Millie usually went through to the crèche, though they did not enter the nursery but merely peeped at their offspring through the big glass doors. Both girls thought it would unsettle the babies if their mothers suddenly appeared, so they kept their visits brief and themselves out of sight.

Today, when they entered the rest room, Rose

saw that Millie was still limping and demanded to see what damage the pram wheel had inflicted. Millie, however, refused to remove her shoe. 'It's only just got dry, and it's practically welded to my foot,' she said. 'Besides, it hardly hurts at all now. I'll show you when we get home tonight—if there's anything to see, that is.'

Rose sighed but agreed to this, and during the afternoon forgot all about it. When work finished they went to the crèche, picked up babies and pram and began the walk home, not able to chatter freely as they usually did since the rain, if anything, had increased. They slogged along, heads down, shoulders hunched, shouting the odd remark but having to repeat most of what they said. 'I'm going to get some chips,' Millie shouted as they neared Bath Street. 'I've got some pork chops and a cabbage but no spuds, so chips will be easier than slogging round trying to find a greengrocer who hasn't yet shut up shop. What about you?'

'I'll get chips as well. Fourpenn'orth should do us,' Rose decided. 'The chippy on the prom opens at five thirty, so we can get them there. We can warm them up in the oven if the fellers are going to be late, though it's my bet that Mr Foster probably sent Mart home hours ago. He was supposed to be working on the swing boats today, and you can't paint in the rain. Oh no, not again!'

The last remark was prompted by a huge cream-coloured coach which drew up alongside a big hotel, sending out a bow wave which would have soaked the two girls if it had been possible for them to become any wetter. A number of dark-suited men, who had congregated in the entrance hall, began a dash across the pavement as the

259

coach door opened. So eager were they to get out of the rain that Rose was almost knocked over in the rush. She turned to glare at the man who had jostled her, then turned away quickly, addressing Millie in a trembling voice. 'Let's get to the chip shop before we're drowned,' she said, trying to move away from the crowd still pressing to get aboard the coach, but the man followed her, putting a hand on her shoulder.

'Gertrude? You are Gertrude Pleavin, aren't you? Well, well, fancy meeting up like this. I dare say you don't realise it, young lady, but you've made my wife very unhappy. In fact, I must ask you for your address so that—'

At this point, Millie interrupted. 'I don't know who you are or what you're accusing my sister of, but for a start she isn't Gertrude Pleavin and I doubt whether she's ever met your wife in her life.' She reached across and pushed the man's hand from her friend's shoulder. 'You're a bully, that's what you are, but you've picked the wrong person this time.'

Mr Ellis—for it was he—backed away from them, his eyes suddenly uncertain. 'Not Gertrude Pleavin?' he stammered. 'But I could have sworn . . . if I've made a mistake . . .'

Rose gathered all her courage together and stared defiantly across at him. 'You have made a mistake,' she said coldly, imitating Millie's posh accent. 'And if you persist, my sister and I will call the police.' She turned to Millie. 'I think this gentleman is a little the worse for wear,' she said loftily. 'Let's go.'

Before they could do so, however, the man had broken into an abject apology. He was still

260

muttering that it was all a horrible mistake when the coach driver put his head out of his vehicle and told him that if he did not get aboard the coach at once, he would be left behind.

Aware of having made a fool of himself, Rose's accuser scuttled aboard the coach and the two girls continued their walk along the promenade. Rose found that she was trembling, and as soon as the coach was out of sight she took Millie's hand in hers and gave it a squeeze. 'Millie, you're the best pal any girl could possibly have,' she said fervently. 'That was Mr Ellis, in case you haven't guessed. Do you think he believed you—that we're sisters, I mean? If so, it's a bit of luck because he won't say anything to anyone, especially not to his wife. Important men like him don't like to appear foolish and he did, didn't he? I bet all the other men on the coach are laughing at him behind his back! Oh, but whatever would I have done if you'd not been with me?'

'I expect you'd have managed,' Millie said. 'The cheek of him, though! If you've made his wife unhappy that's nothing to the unhappiness they caused you and Martin! But let's forget it, flower. Conferences can't happen more than once a year, I shouldn't think, so you're unlikely to bump into him again. But why did he call you Gertrude Pleavin, for God's sake?'

'Oh, it was what they called me at the home,' Rose said. 'Only I hated the name Gertrude so as soon as I left I called myself Rose. And since Martin is Thompson . . .'

'I see,' Millie said, seeming content with the explanation, but all through the walk up to the chip shop, the buying of the chips and the walk

261

home to Bath Street Rose worried over the incident and what the consequences might be. When she reached her room and found Martin brewing a pot of tea she could scarcely wait to tell him what had happened, and was reassured by his delight in both Millie's quick-wittedness and her own calm acceptance of the fib that Millie had told with such conviction.

He laughed when she repeated the remarks she had made, using Millie's posh voice, and said he was proud of her. 'You and Millie act like sisters; you're even beginnin' to look a bit alike,' he told her. 'Now you're not to go a-frettin' and worritin' over a chance meetin', queen. You love Rhyl, you know you do, and you love your job in the factory as well. You're earnin' good money and you're earnin' it regular; in fact, you're the main earner out of the two of us.'

'Oh, Mart, your money's pretty regular; it's only when the weather's real bad that they lay the chaps off,' Rose said, dismayed to hear him putting himself down. 'In fact, during the holiday season, you brought home more than I did.'

This made Martin laugh and give her an affectionate cuff. 'Oh, Rosie, winter's comin' on, and apart from Christmas there'll be very little work on the funfair. But I've got more confidence now. I'll apply for other jobs and I'll get one, see if I don't. But what I was trying to say was that I hoped you wouldn't let what happened today make you want to leave Rhyl. I reckon running this far will keep us all safe. After all, as Millie says, the Ellises have no claim on you or Ricky, and if they try to take the boy that's kidnapping, what's a criminal offence. So smile, queen, and let's gerron

262

with gettin' our supper 'cos I'm starving, so I am.'

Rose gave Martin an impulsive hug. 'You're right, of course you are,' she said. 'But I wish it hadn't happened. Seeing Mrs Ellis with that party of kids was bad enough, but at least we never looked one another in the eye. If we had, I'd have been sunk, because she knows me very well, you see. But Mr Ellis . . . well, we only met a couple of times and I were just a kid then. Now I've had a baby of me own it must make a difference, wouldn't you think?'

'I would,' Martin assured her. 'You were a wispy little thing when you and meself first met up. Now you're . . . oh, more solid, somehow.'

'Thank you very much! You think I'm fat,' Rose said with pretended indignation. 'Oh, Martin Thompson, you know how to flatter a girl!'

Laughing and teasing one another was a good way to forget what had happened that day, but when she got into bed that night Rose was frightened of falling asleep. She was sure she would have horrible nightmares, and when at last she grew so tired that she could no longer stay awake, she did indeed dream.

She was back in the tower block, baking a very large cake and worrying that it would not fit into her oven. When this proved to be the case she tried to cook it over the Primus stove, only Don came running in and knocked it over, and a fire started. Rose grabbed his collar and began to scream at the other residents to 'gerrout while the goin's good', but the only person who appeared to hear her was Miss Haverstock. She did not run down the stairs but came heavily up on to Rose's floor and barged straight into the kitchen, looking

263

hot and flustered.

'And wasn't I mistaken in you, young lady?' she demanded. She had a huge mop in one hand and a bucket in the other and proceeded to start clearing up the raw cake mixture, which was liberally scattered across Rose's kitchen floor. 'I thought you were a decent girl who had been interfered with, but now I see you're just another little hussy. Mr Ellis is a good man, a pillar of society, a regular churchgoer . . . and you've cast doubt on his good name, and in front of his equals, too. When that kind Mrs Ellis hears what you've done, she'll be very angry indeed, and small wonder!'

'I'm norra hussy, honest to God I'm not,' Rose said, much distressed to find the woman she had thought her friend completely misunderstanding the situation. 'And Mr Ellis isn't a good man, wharrever you may think. He—oh, I can't talk about it, but—' She stopped short, for Miss Haverstock was changing. She became slender and her bun of grey hair fell to her shoulders in a pageboy bob and turned a shining light brown. Before poor Rose's horrified gaze, Miss Haverstock became Mrs Ellis, her blue eyes full of reproach . . . and suddenly Rose saw that she held Ricky in the crook of her arm! Rose started forward. 'Don't you dare try to take my baby!' she said fiercely. 'If you do it's kidnappin', and the law won't let you gerraway wi' it. Just you purr'im down!'

Mrs Ellis sat Ricky on the edge of the kitchen table and the baby struggled out of his shawl and jumped down on to the kitchen floor and ran nimbly out of the door, across the hall and on to the landing. They heard the sound of his retreating feet stumbling down the stairs, then a crash and a muffled yell. Mrs Ellis said reproachfully: 'Now look what you've done, you wicked girl!' and Rose screamed and screamed and screamed . . . and woke. She was bathed in sweat and trembling violently and when a hand came out of the darkness and clasped hers she gave a squeak of fright and then relaxed.

'Oh, Mart, I were havin' the most horrible nightmare,' she said in a whisper, for she did not want to wake poor little Ricky, let alone Millie and Scotty, on the other side of the thin wall. 'I dreamed I were back in the tower block and Mrs Ellis had found me and said the most awful things! But did I yell very loudly?' She gave a shaky laugh. 'It must have been loud to wake you!'

'You didn't yell at all, just gave a little moan, but I guessed somethin' of the sort might happen. Besides, I was still awake,' Martin said comfortingly. 'Just you cuddle down and go back to sleep, queen. It's natural that you should have a nightmare after meeting that wicked old feller, even if you did make him think you weren't Gertrude. I'll sit on the edge of the bed until you drop off.'

'Thank you, Mart,' Rose said drowsily. 'I shan't be afraid while you're holding my hand. Tell you what, you'll get awful cold sitting on the bed. Come inside, under the covers, then we'll both be lovely and warm; warmer than you'd be in the camp bed, I'm sure.'

'Thanks, queen, but I reckon I'm best where I am,' Martin said quietly. 'I'm not too cold, honest to God I'm not. And anyway, I'll get back into my own bed once you've fallen asleep. I'll pull it over so I can go on holding your hand if you like.'

'But why not get into bed with me?' Rose asked plaintively. 'It 'ud be all right, honest it would.'

She opened her eyes and glanced towards him, seeing his profile outlined against the faint grey of the window; saw him shaking his head. 'No, it wouldn't be all right,' he said quietly. 'I know what I'm talking about, Rosie, so just you go back to sleep, like a good girl, or you'll be no manner of use in the morning.'

Rose did not attempt to argue further, but she felt that she had been rejected, and this was not only hurtful but also surprising. Ever since they had arrived in Rhyl, she had suspected that Martin was growing sweet on her. Now, she had to acknowledge that this was not the case. She knew of course that he liked her very much, that they were bezzies and would probably always be so, but they would never be lovers. Mainly because of her own attitude, their relationship had become more like that of a brother and sister, and perhaps it was for the best. After all, she had told Martin, only half laughingly, that she meant to marry someone tall, dark and handsome, if she ever married at all, and no one, no matter how biased in his favour, could consider Martin dark or handsome, though he was certainly tall.

'Rosie?' Martin's voice came out of the darkness, with a hint of apology. 'Rosie, are you still awake? I didn't mean . . . you know how fond I am of you . . .'

But it was all too much. Rose feigned sleep so successfully that Martin stopped speaking and presently withdrew his hand from hers, and after five minutes or so returned to his own bed.

When he had gone, Rose gave a little sigh. She listened until she heard Martin's breathing deepen and grow even, then snuggled further down the bed. But it was a long time before she slept again.

*   *   *

October came with gales, and several tides so high that water swept over the promenade, making it impossible for Martin to take Don for walks along the beach before they left for work. However, work on the funfair was reduced to a couple of days a week, and though Martin applied for every job that came up, he had no luck. He soon realised that he ought to leave Don in their room, since potential employers blanched when they saw the big greyhound, but even so, jobs in seaside towns, out of season, were few and far between and it seemed to Martin that he would have to admit defeat and try further afield.

However, on a wild and windy day in mid-November he came bounding up the stairs, with Don close on his heels, and burst into their room, talking excitedly as he came. 'Hey, Rosie, I've done it! I've gorra job. It won't interfere with the maintenance work on the funfair either, 'cos it's night watchman at a building site. What d'you think of that, eh? It starts at six in the evening and finishes at eight next morning.'

'Oh, Mart, aren't you clever?' Rose exclaimed.

Martin felt the blood rush to his cheeks and ducked his head deprecatingly. 'I don't know about clever, but it does just show that persistence pays off,' he said. 'And . . . well, you'll never guess what the bonus is!'

267

'More money? Do they give you your dinner?' Rose said.

'No, it ain't either of those things,' Martin said. He saw that she was about to take Ricky down for his bath, for she had a nightgown over one arm and the baby was wrapped in a towel. 'Can I bath him tonight? Only what wi' havin' two jobs I might not be able to do it again until next summer!'

'Tell me about the bonus first,' Rose said, but handed Ricky over. Martin cuddled the small body warmly against his chest. 'I've run the bath and Alex is probably already sloshing around in it, so you go down and I'll follow when I've put his dinner into a pan of hot water. Go on, what's this bonus?'

'They want Don as well as me, because he's such a big dog and will put folk off coming to thieve,' Martin told her. 'And when I said—jokin' like— that they ought to pay him a wage too, the boss said he'd give him five bob a week and as many rats as he could eat. What d'you think of that, eh? Our Don's a wage-earner!'

'That's marvellous. Don, you're a clever boy! But Mart, now I come to think of it, you'll be working a fourteen-hour night, and you plan to continue at the funfair? You mustn't do both jobs or you'll be dead beat after a month,' Rose said, looking worried. 'Tell Mr Foster you're quitting, but will return next summer. I expect the construction site will be finished by then and they won't need you. What are they building, anyway? Factories?'

'It's a new estate—houses and bungalows, and half a dozen shops,' Martin told her. 'I have to do a tour of the whole place every four hours, and in between I can kip down on a sort of padded bench

268

thing. I'm to share the job with an old feller, Mr Naylor; I do five nights and he does two. The money's not wonderful . . .' he named the sum he would earn weekly, 'but with your salary from the pyjama factory, we'll be doing okay.'

By this time, Rose had finished her preparations and the two of them began to descend the stairs together, with Ricky crowing in Martin's arms; he dearly loved the bath. 'Dadada,' he chanted, patting Martin's cheek. 'Dadada!'

'I thought all babies were supposed to say Mama first,' Rose grumbled as they entered the bathroom. She addressed Millie, who was swishing her son up and down the length of the bath, causing a tidal wave which had Alex shrieking with excitement. 'Does Alex say dada, Millie?'

'You know very well he does,' Millie said, grinning over her shoulder at her friends. 'Scotty would take it as a personal insult if he did anything else. Come along, put Ricky in the water before it goes cold.'

She waited until Martin had lowered an excited Ricky into the bath, then turned towards him. 'I heard you flying up the stairs two at a time and gabbling away like a monkey at the zoo; what was all the excitement about?'

Martin told her and received congratulations, an enquiry as to when the new job started, and a promise to visit him at the first opportunity. 'We could take Mrs Walshaw at her word and let her babysit for us one evening,' she said. 'We could come armed with chip butties and a flask of hot tea and have a little picnic in your night watchman's hut, or whatever. How about that, eh?'

Mrs Walshaw, a widow, had one of the ground-floor flats. She was a cheerful woman, blonde and rosy-cheeked, who loved babies, having seen four of her own grow up. She often popped up to the attic to coo over Ricky and Alex, and to offer to shop or babysit. Martin looked hopefully at Rose. He was to start his new job the following Monday and thought how nice it would be to show his friends round the housing estate. He had enquired the price of the smallest bungalow, but as yet it was beyond their reach.

'Well?' Millie demanded. 'Wouldn't it be a bit of a lark? Oh, I know we've never left the children with anyone before—unless you count the crèche—but what do you say, Rosie?'

Martin liked the sound of a picnic but doubted whether Rose would consider leaving her precious Ricky, even with the friendly and obviously competent Mrs Walshaw. However, he need not have worried. Rose agreed at once to the scheme and presently the three of them took the babies back to Millie's room where Scotty, being useful for once, was frying sausages on the Primus and wincing as they burst and spat. He greeted the news of Martin's job with a lift of one eyebrow. 'I've heard the money's pretty poor, but I dare say with what you earn on the funfair you'll be doing okay,' he said. He turned to his wife. 'Am I supposed to share my sausages with those two gannets?' he enquired, with a trace of peevishness. 'I only bought a pound—that's four for me and two for you—but of course, if you've already offered our hospitality . . .'

Martin laughed. 'What a generous beggar you are!' he said with mock admiration. 'However, we shan't strain your hospitality—or your sausages—

270

tonight. We're having an oxtail casserole—it was our turn for the oven in the kitchen—so you'll be able to eat them all.'

'Let's go out later for a drink, to celebrate,' Scotty said at once. 'I suppose we could take the girls if they promise to behave themselves and not make eyes at any of the chaps.'

Rose began to demur, saying that Ricky and Alex would be disturbed by the noise in the bar, but Millie cut in with a suggestion of her own. 'We haven't had a chance to tell you, Scotty, but we're going to take a picnic over to Mart's little hut, once he's settled in his new job. We thought we'd let Mrs Walshaw babysit, since she's offered to do so, so if it's all right with everyone I'll dash downstairs and ask her to sit with the boys for an hour or so this evening. It'll be a test, in a way. What d'you think?'

Scotty, eyes brightening, said he thought it an excellent scheme, particularly if it meant that they might enjoy other nights out. 'It's not good for any of us, working all day and then being cooped up here all night,' he said. 'Off you go then, Millie, and tell Mrs W that we'll bring her back a bottle of something warming. Ask her what she likes, because we'll want to use her again.'

Fortunately, Mrs Walshaw was delighted to come up to the attic and babysit, though when the four of them returned it was to find her wrapped in her winter coat and scarf, and sitting practically on top of the tiny electric fire which was all Mrs Osborne provided. 'I thought my own room was pretty cold, but this perishing attic beats it into a cocked hat for draughts,' she observed. 'It was kind of you to leave a pile of shillings for the meter—I kept as

271

warm as I could, but I'm surprised you've not explained to the old bat that babies need warmth, as well as all the other things. I take it she's lowered your rent, now that the season's over?'

Scotty slapped his head and pulled a face. 'D'you know, I completely forgot that the rent was supposed to go down in winter! As for a bigger fire, I don't know that it would make much difference because it's the draughts that chill us to the bone. You folk on the ground floor have gas fires, don't you? They're cheaper to run and I think they give out more heat. But it's such a business getting her to consider any change that we've more or less given up.'

The girls had swooped on their offspring as soon as they entered the room. Each boy was sleeping contentedly in his own little cot, and now Martin and Rose began to push Ricky's, not without difficulty, over to the open door. Rose turned round as they reached it, to address Mrs Walshaw. '*I* remembered about the rent,' she said proudly. 'I caught Ozzie on the doorstep one evening, having an argument with the paper boy. I reminded her that autumn had come and the holidaymakers had gone, but we were still paying the higher rate. I could see the paper boy grinning behind his hand—he told me afterwards that she argues over the bill every week—and for a moment Ozzie just stared at me with those bulging little eyes. Then she said: "Prices goes up all the time, and so does me rent. Come next Whit—if you're still here, that is—it'll go up again. However, seein' as how you youngsters are right at the top of the house and have to lug the babies up all them stairs, I'll mebbe consider knockin' off a bob or two, come

272

Christmas."'

'Well, of all the cheek!' Millie remarked, then turned to Mrs Walshaw. 'I take it she's put your rent back to its winter rate?'

'She has in a way, but remember I didn't move in until early August, so I was paying summer rates. I came to Rhyl to be near my son, thinking I might move in with him when the season was over, and when Ozzie thought I might move out she told me that after September the first she would knock five bob off. Only very soon I could tell it wouldn't work out. My son and Jane are newly-weds, and the house isn't a large one, so I told Ozzie I'd be staying a bit longer and she said in that case she could only afford to knock off half a crown.'

'The mean old devil . . .' Millie began, but Rose shook her head.

'Mrs Walshaw has two rooms, not one,' she reminded her friend. 'And she's got a little electric oven and two rings; though you can rely on Ozzie to charge for just about everything.'

Mrs Walshaw laughed. 'All landladies are the same,' she said cheerfully. 'And what I pay for two rooms and an electric oven isn't bad, particularly when you remember that the electricity in my room isn't metered, so I can cook more or less for free. I think she had to give me that because you get your cooking free in that scruffy little kitchen, isn't that right?'

'Spot on,' Scotty agreed. He turned to Millie. 'Don't be upset, love. I'll have a go at the old bat, see if I can get a cheaper rate before Christmas. Prices haven't gone up that much and I'm not above threatening her with a tribunal if she won't admit that we were promised a reduction in rent in

273

the winter.'

Mrs Walshaw wished them luck, then got to her feet. 'Thanks for the bottle of Babycham and the packet of crisps,' she said. 'I'll enjoy them both. And don't forget, any time you fancy an evening out, I'll sit with the little ones.'

'Isn't she nice?' Rose said as she and Mart settled Ricky's cot in its usual place and then began to prepare for bed. They still hung an old sheet between them for modesty's sake but chattered away as though it did not exist. 'But of course, once you start working nights there won't be any point in me goin' out.'

'There's weekends, when I won't be working; well, not in the evenings, anyway,' Martin pointed out. 'We might go out then, just for a stroll and a look at the shops.' He heard Rose's bedsprings creak as she climbed between the sheets and lowered his voice. 'Rosie? You slept pretty good last night, didn't you? No nightmares?'

He knew his companion had suffered dreadfully ever since her meeting with Mr Ellis, but the previous night, though he had slept lightly and been on the alert for any movement from the other bed, he had not been woken. In fact, he realised it had been his first undisturbed night since Rose and her attacker had met, though the nightmares had only been sufficiently frightening for him to go to Rose two or three times.

'Do you know, Mart, you're absolutely right! I had quite a nice dream, though I couldn't tell you for the life of me what it was about,' Rose said. 'Oh, I do hope the nightmares are over, especially since you won't be here to wake me up and tell me it was just a dream. But it's weeks since—since that

274

day on the prom, so perhaps I'll be okay from now on.'

'I'm sure you will,' Martin said comfortably. 'But there's another four days before the new job begins, so if your nightmares start up again . . .'

'You mustn't turn the job down, Mart,' Rose said quickly. 'We need the money—and I promise you I'll be fine. Especially once I've seen this building site you'll be working on—it were a good idea of Millie's to come and see you and bring a picnic, weren't it?'

'Oh aye, a grand idea, now you've settled that Mrs Walshaw can be relied on to give an eye to the littl'uns,' Martin said. 'But you know, Rose, we'll have to do something about the draughts in this place. If we can't get the old bat to seal the windows and get us a better electric fire then we'll threaten to move out . . . we might even have to do it. I read somewhere that draughts are more dangerous for babies than the cold itself.'

He heard another creak as Rose shot up in bed. 'More dangerous?' she quavered. 'Oh, Mart, I'll go out at the weekend and buy some of those old blankets from the market and make them into sausages for the door and the windows. I won't put Ricky at risk just to save a few bob!'

Chapter Twelve

Rose had put on her coat and was preparing to carry Ricky round to the Scotts' room when the knock came on the door. Hastily she lifted the child, well wrapped in blankets, and shouted,

'Come in,' guessing that her visitor would be Mrs Walshaw, for this evening, at long last, they were to visit Martin's place of work and see for themselves the delightful dwellings which he guarded from vandals and thieves.

'Evening, love! I can see you're ready for the off, but I thought I'd better give you a knock 'cos I've got a little something for your hubby. I know he's fond of Cornish pasties, so when I was baking earlier in the day I made one extra.'

She handed over a small package and Rose beamed and put it into the capacious satchel already slung from one shoulder. 'Thanks, Mrs Walshaw,' she said gratefully. 'I expect the Scotts are ready too, so you might as well give them a knock.'

The older woman did so and the door immediately shot open to reveal Millie, already in her coat and holding out her arms to take Ricky. 'On time as usual,' Millie said joyfully. 'We've turned the television on because there's a good film on later.' Mrs Walshaw nodded enthusiastically. In another few days it would be Christmas and Scotty, who had received a handsome bonus from his firm, had gone out and bought a television set.

'It's an early present, so you can begin to learn how to use it right away and will have it off pat by the great day itself,' he had told Millie. 'Only don't go expecting anything else, will you? Paying for the set outright has gobbled up every spare penny I had.'

Rose had wondered if there had been an element of guilt in such a handsome gift, for she had not been able to help noticing that her friend had not been her usual self of late. Oh, Millie laughed, squabbled and teased as much as ever, but somehow the old gaiety had gone.

Now, Mrs Walshaw glanced approvingly around the room and Rose, following her gaze, realised how cosy it had become since Millie had decided that whilst they lived in Bath Street they might as well be comfortable. Accordingly, she had bought a number of gay rugs and invested in a large electric fire. Scotty complained sometimes that the fire gobbled their shillings as though money grew on trees, but since he agreed with his wife that the baby must be kept warm he continued to supply the cash needed. Rose and Martin had also invested in a slightly larger electric fire than the one provided by their landlady and Rose, as she had promised, had not only made draught excluders for the bottoms of their door and windows, but had also bought tape from Woolworth's to cover up the source of any draught she discovered.

Now, as Mrs Walshaw settled in the armchair, Millie tucked Ricky into the foot of her son's cot and Rose leaned over and kissed her sleeping baby's cheek. 'Be a good boy for Auntie Walshaw,' she murmured. She turned to the older woman. 'Have a nice evening, Mrs Walshaw. We'll be home before ten.'

'Have a good time, my dears,' Mrs Walshaw said, then surged to her feet and stood in the doorway to wave them off. 'And if you're a little late, don't worry yourselves because I'll be quite happy here until midnight if necessary. Give Martin my love, as well as the Cornish pasty.'

'I will,' Rose called back. She was excited

because she knew very well that though the ostensible reason for visiting the building site was so that Martin could show them round his place of work, Scotty and Millie were saving up for a deposit on one of the bungalows. She was eager to see what they were like, and wondered whether she and Martin might one day own such a home.

The building site was the other side of the town, so the three of them caught a bus and then walked along a winding country road until they saw the bulk of the new buildings outlined against the starry sky. It was a freezing night, the trees rimed with frost, and when they arrived they were all glad of the warmth of the brazier before which Don lay sprawled in abandoned sleep. He woke as soon as he heard their voices, greeting them with his usual lopsided grin, flattened ears and wildly wagging tail, and presently accompanied them on their tour.

'It's awful posh,' Rose said, 'and much larger than I'd imagined. How many houses are there here, Mart?'

'Around fifty, only of course they aren't all houses; almost half are bungalows,' Martin told her. He turned to Scotty. 'You're interested in the small ones, aren't you? Two beds, one recep?'

'Oh, very professional; you'll be sellin' 'em next as well as keepin' out the thieves and robbers,' Rose said, giggling. 'Take us to the two beds, one recep then, Mart!'

Martin did so, and when they had examined the bungalow, which was almost complete, they returned to his 'office' and had their picnic, with much teasing of the would-be home owners.

Back in Bath Street, they thanked Mrs Walshaw

278

sincerely for looking after the children, told her how much they had enjoyed their evening, and went their separate ways, Rose with Ricky fast asleep in her arms. He no longer had a ten o'clock feed, but slept right through until six am, which was nice at weekends since it enabled Martin to have an undisturbed night.

She undressed and got into bed. It had been interesting all right to visit the estate where Martin spent so much time now, but also somewhat alarming. The place was huge, and Martin's long and lonely tours of the site must take him at least an hour. He was accompanied by Don, of course, but even so he checked every nook and cranny of every building, for intruders came in all shapes and sizes: kids playing dangerous games on piles of bricks; older youths looking for a spare bit of planking, some sand or cement, or even the odd bathroom fitting. Then of course there were the genuine thieves who would drive on to the site in a lorry, load up and drive away, or might have done so had Martin not been constantly on the alert. At the first sight of his torch beam, they would make off hurriedly and not return.

Martin said he enjoyed his work, but Rose was convinced that had anything more congenial been offered he would have consigned night watching to the devil and taken a job which did not mean he was away from Bath Street—and awake—all night. And with Christmas so near, there would be even more reason for people to steal, Rose thought worriedly now.

She and Millie were highly regarded at the pyjama factory. They were doing piecework and because they were both neat, accurate and quick, it had been suggested that if they ever wanted to try their hand at more elaborate garments a transfer to the factory in mid-Wales could be arranged. Rose had not even considered this option—she was truly happy where they were—but she had teased Millie that the suggestion must have come from Mr McDonald. 'He was clearly very struck by you that first day in reception,' she had said. 'And I've noticed he pops in to have a word with you whenever he's in Rhyl. Good thing you aren't in the same factory as Scotty, or I guess sparks would fly.'

Millie agreed that this was so. 'Scotty considers that I'm his property, just like a slave,' she informed her friend. 'He used to be terribly jealous, though I've never given him cause, and he'd start imagining things, so don't you say a word about being offered better jobs at the mid-Wales place, and I won't either.' However, since Rose was sure there was no more question of Millie's moving than there was of her own, she thought there was little fear that the topic would ever arise.

On the other hand, having seen the building site, Rose decided that she would nag Martin to look for another job. In fact, she would start getting the *Rhyl Journal*, where there were usually a few jobs advertised. Once she had thought of Martin as timid, but this evening had made her realise that it was not only she who had changed. A timid person could not possibly have held down the job of night watchman. Chasing kids off piles of bricks was one thing; tackling thieves with lorries quite another. But Martin had never complained or admitted to being nervous, so she must watch her step. She would say the cold and the long hours were not good for him, and point out that if he applied for a day job at least they could have their evenings together.

Satisfied that this would do the trick, she pulled the covers up over her ears and was soon asleep.

*   *   *

After Christmas they settled down to what Rose had heard described as 'the hungry months'. Ricky and Alex, who had enjoyed the jollity of the festive season and the different, more luxurious food, had each cut four teeth and their smiles were glorious to behold. Scotty, who had been to rather a lot of office parties and had often come home the worse for wear, vowed that he would be sober as a judge until next Christmas. Millie said rather sharply that she hoped he meant it, since coping with a full-time job, a baby who could now crawl and a squiffy husband who blamed her if anything went even remotely wrong was beginning to get her down.

Rose, who now took it for granted that Martin would not only do his share of the chores but also cope with a grizzling baby, thought Millie ought to insist that Scotty did his part, but her friend was oddly reluctant to force Scotty's hand and Rose knew better than to interfere.

'No one bar the folk concerned know what goes on in a marriage,' Mrs Walshaw had said wisely, when Rose had hinted that all might not be well. 'You leave them to sort it out, love. Besides, if you ask me, the weather's got a lot to do with it. We've not seen the sun in weeks; the sky presses down on us like a great wet blanket. I reckon some really cold, crisp weather would be better than what we've been having. In my opinion, your pal will be her usual self as soon as there's a sign of spring.'

'Well, I hope you're right,' Rose had said rather dubiously. It was January now and another difficulty had reared its ugly head—getting the washing dry. It was no use hanging it on the line, and though she bought a clothes horse and arranged it round the electric fire, she felt guilty for doing so since she thought a damp atmosphere was the reason Ricky had caught a cold and been poorly for several days. It was not so bad for Millie, who carted all her washing down to the launderette, but even so she brought the garments back only marginally less wet than Rose's hand-wrung nappies, and still had to find some way of drying and airing them.

Though Rose had searched the paper every evening for some suitable work for Martin which would not mean working nights, she had not been successful, and Martin assured her that the longer he was in the job the more he enjoyed it. 'And Don feels the same,' he told her. 'We both like bein' useful, and we are, Rosie. And the money's handy, ain't that so?'

Rose admitted that it was, and the four of them continued to slog through 'the hungry months' with Mrs Walshaw's help, for she willingly babysat so that they could enjoy the odd evening out. Martin was home at weekends, for the weather had put a stop to most of the maintenance at the funfair, and it struck Rose that the rather worrying noises which occasionally came to her ears from the room next door never occurred when Martin was around. In fact, when she had been truly disturbed by a crash followed by a sharp cry of pain and had gone round to enquire what had happened, Millie, with Alex in her arms, had said soothingly that she had tripped when carrying her empty dishes back to the kitchen, and had broken the lot, besides wrenching her ankle. 'So poor Scotty has volunteered to do the washing and wiping up, of the unbroken stuff that is,' she had said sweetly. 'Dear me, another visit to Woollies' crockery shelf in the morning, I fear.'

Scotty, all smiles, had agreed with Millie's version of events and had come down to the kitchen and washed up Rose's dishes as well as his own, but Rose had begun to wonder whether there was more to Millie's frequent accidents than met the eye. Her friend never made mistakes when she was using her big industrial sewing machine, or finishing off each garment by hand. Why should she be so constantly clumsy at home?

But when Rose had voiced her suspicions to Martin, he had scoffed at the very idea that Scotty might occasionally be violent to his wife. 'He worships her,' he had assured Rose. 'Can't do enough for her. Why, look at that lovely television set, and the silver horse brooch. No, no, you've got the wrong end of the stick there, queen.'

Martin was older and wiser than she, Rose told herself. And men no doubt talk amongst themselves, as women do. Martin would know if Scotty was the sort of man who liked hitting women . . . no, she was mad to even consider it.

Now, it was early on Wednesday afternoon and Martin had only just got into his camp bed. Rose had had a dentist's appointment and Martin had accompanied her to the surgery. Rose had decided to take the rest of the day off to get some shopping done and now she watched as Martin pulled the blankets up round his ears. He grinned at her, then held out an arm. 'Want to leave Ricky wi' me? I don't mind, honest I don't, Rosie. In fact if you leave him I'll mek a real effort and not go straight off to sleep.'

Rose shook her head. 'As if I'd be so cruel, when you and Don have been workin' all night, and come out with me this morning,' she protested. 'And now that Ricky can crawl you'd get no peace. No, you stay there and I'll take Don down for a gallop along the beach. Then he can guard the pram while I get some grub.'

'What about Millie and Alex? Are they shoppin'?' Martin asked.

'Millie gave me a list, so I'm going to get her stuff as well,' Rose told him. 'It was raining earlier, so we thought there was no sense in the pair of us getting wet. In fact she offered to have Ricky for me, but I think some fresh air will do him good. Besides, the rain has almost stopped, so we'll shop together, won't we, darling?' She bent over the old playpen she had bought and plucked her son, already dressed in his little blue coat and hat, out and on to her hip. 'Here, Don!'

The big dog, who had slumped down next to the camp bed, got to his feet and slapped a red tongue round Martin's face, then ran to the door. Rose grinned and went over to open it. 'He may have been up all night, but at the mere mention of a walk he's ready for the off,' she said. 'Bye, Mart. See you later!'

They walked down to the promenade and Don raced back and forth along the beach, and then they went to the shops, ending up in Woolworth's. Rose was examining a blue cardigan in the window of a small shop nearby when someone spoke from behind her. 'Gertrude?' the voice said. 'It is you, isn't it? Little Gertrude Pleavin, looking so grown up—and so pretty, my dear. Now don't rush away until you've heard me out. I want to explain . . .'

The speaker was Mrs Ellis! Rose took one startled, horrified look at her, turned on her heel and ran. She simply pelted away from the older woman, whilst Ricky crowed with pleasure in his sling and bounced up and down.

Rose did not run towards home but in the opposite direction, feeling instinctively that she must not let Mrs Ellis know they were living in Bath Street. She darted in and out of any little side alley that presented itself, and very soon she knew that the pursuit, if it had ever existed, was no longer on her heels. The pavements were almost empty now and darkness was complete, but even so Rose hesitated a long while before turning for home. Ricky was getting restless, beginning to mutter and wriggle. Very soon he would realise he was hungry and would start to wail—he might give her away, bring her enemy back! It was time to return to Bath Street, bright lights and sanity.

Rose could have kicked herself. I should have heard Mrs Ellis out, she thought; I've been told often enough that there's nothing she can do to harm either me or Ricky. But the conviction that Mrs Ellis would try to take her baby away, would say that Mr Ellis, as the father, had rights of which Rose knew nothing, would not be dismissed.

So even now she could not bring herself to go straight home. Suppose Mrs Ellis was still prowling

285

the streets, searching? She went by a roundabout route, not reaching the house until well past eight o'clock and then entering like a thief in the night. Shoulders hunched, knees bent, head turning this way and that, she finally slipped into the house and scuttled up the stairs, meaning to go straight to her own room, to feed Ricky and have a snack, and then to call on the Scotts.

However, as she reached the upper landing, it occurred to her that Millie might be worrying over her non-appearance, so instead of going straight to her own door she tapped lightly on the Scotts', waited a moment, and then opened it cautiously. She peered into the room and saw Millie bending over the cot. Her friend turned as she entered and gave Rose a travesty of a smile. She looked absolutely dreadful. Her face was swollen, one eye puffy and almost closed, and her lower lip was split and hanging open. All thoughts of the Ellises forgotten, Rose crossed the room and took Millie's hands in both of hers. 'Wharrever's happened, queen?' she asked, her voice high with shock. 'And don't tell me you fell down the stairs 'cos I shan't believe you.' She glanced around the room, seeing that it was more than usually chaotic. Clothes were piled on the bed and on the floor, and though Alex lay in his cot he was not in his nightgown, but fully dressed. 'Millie, what's been goin' on? Surely you can tell me.'

Millie gave a stifled sob. Tears ran down her cheeks, but were impatiently dashed away. She spoke stiffly, every word, Rose saw, causing her pain. 'It was Scotty,' she said. 'I was late getting in because I stopped off to buy a bag of spuds. When he got home, his dinner wasn't ready. I can tell you

286

my heart sank into my boots when he asked why it wasn't on the table. He—he punched me in the face. I guess you must realise it's happened before. Usually, I get out of his way, run out of the flat and go down to the kitchen, but . . . but . . .'

There was a pause, during which Rose took Ricky out of his sling and popped him into the cot beside Alex, where he immediately started to grizzle. 'He's hungry,' Rose said briefly. She pushed Millie into a chair, then took a bottle of prepared rose hip syrup out of her shopping bag and handed it to her son, who leaned back on the pillow, seized the bottle in both hands, and began to suck. Rose turned to her friend. 'Go on,' she said. 'We didn't know Scotty was violent, honest to God we didn't. I've sometimes wondered . . . but Martin likes him a lot—I don't think he's ever had a friend like Scotty before—so he won't believe ill of him.'

Millie laughed bitterly. 'I was the same myself, when we were first married,' she said. 'I couldn't— or wouldn't—believe that a bloke would hit his wife. God, I was a fool! He began knocking me about almost as soon as we moved in together, but then I got pregnant and he was all right for quite a long time. When you came here to live it was great, because the wall between our rooms is thin and he was worried that Martin might hear something and come calling . . .'

'If only we'd known! You should have told me,' Rose mourned. 'Between us we should have been able to show Scotty the error of his ways. Mart isn't terribly strong but he'd had given your feller something to think about if he'd known how things were. So go on. Scotty punched you in the face . . .'

'That's right, not just once, several times. And he broke one of my front teeth. One of my eyes doesn't seem to be working properly, and my lip is agony—I bit my tongue and there was blood everywhere. Usually he hits me where it won't show, but I reckon something must have gone wrong at work today and it made Scotty reckless. Oh, Rosie, I saw red! I jumped up—no, lurched up—and picked up that big heavy saucepan, and brought it cracking down on his head.' She chuckled faintly, then sniffed and began to weep once more. 'He went out like a light and I thought that was the end of it, for today at any rate. Alex was screaming fit to burst—he always does when Scotty hits me—so I went to the cot and picked him up. I collapsed into the armchair, with him on my lap, trying to soothe him. After a few minutes, I gave him his night-time bottle and he was sucking away quite happily when Scotty began to come round. He reached over and grabbed Alex out of my arms. He said that I could be put in prison for hitting him with an offensive weapon, and if I ever hit him again, he'd take Alex and go where I'd never find either of them.'

Rose hissed in her breath. 'No one seeing your face would side with him for a moment,' she said decidedly. She looked round the room. 'Where's Scotty now? It's past eight o'clock. Didn't Martin come round to ask where I was? I can't believe he could have looked at your face and not realised that something was badly wrong.'

Millie wiped a dribble of blood from her chin. 'Scotty's down at the pub, of course, drowning his sorrows, as they say. As for Martin, he left for work a bit later than usual, so he just called

288

through the door on his way out to say you weren't home yet instead of coming in.'

'And now I trust that you'll come down to the police station with me so that they can haul Scotty off to prison,' Rose said. 'One look at your face will be enough to convince them that Scotty's a danger to anyone who crosses him.'

Millie got stumblingly to her feet, shaking her head as she did so. 'No way! I'm leaving; getting away while the going's good. Oh, I know the police might question him if we report it, but he's clever is Scotty. He'd find a way to wriggle out of it, and come back here . . . he might chuck me down the stairs next time and break my neck, then say it was an accident. Or he might promise good behaviour, but I know better than to believe that one. No, I'm getting out. I told him not to come back here tonight or I'd have the law on him, but in fact I shall be away by nine o'clock. I'll leave him a note saying I've gone back to my parents. He's scared of my father, so he won't follow me.'

Rose looked at the chaos all around and realised that it was not, in fact, as bad as it appeared. Her friend had got a couple of bags and had been filling one with her own warm clothing and the other with Alex's. Now Millie turned and gave Rose an impulsive hug. 'I'm not *really* going back to Mother and Father,' she said, 'and not just because they'll say they told me so. I'd be scared to leave their house in case Scotty was hovering somewhere, waiting to catch me alone. He'd snatch Alex, I'm sure he would, and I couldn't bear that.'

Rose's hand flew to her mouth. 'Oh, Millie, the state of you put it right out of my head, but the reason I'm late . . .'

She told the story of her meeting with Mrs Ellis, and subsequent flight, and was surprised when her friend, at first aghast, began to look hopeful. 'We're in the same boat then,' Millie said joyfully, when she had finished. 'I'm taking off, but to tell you the truth I was dreading leaving you and Mart. Now I shan't have to, because all three of us, and the two babies, and Don of course, can run away together.'

Rose gasped. She understood completely how Millie felt, but could not believe that running away was the solution. Where would they run to, for a start? And how would they keep body and soul together? They could scarcely hope to hide from Scotty and Mrs Ellis whilst continuing to work at the pyjama factory.

She said as much and Millie gave a tiny crow of triumph. 'Of course we can't possibly continue to make pyjamas,' she said. 'But don't you remember? Management told us ages ago that if we ever wanted better paid and more intricate work the factory in mid-Wales would be delighted to employ us. Oh, Rose, don't shake your head at me! It's the obvious solution! I've never mentioned the mid-Wales factory to Scotty, and I remember you saying you wouldn't tell Martin, because there was no point, since neither of us wanted to move. I reckon it's the safest place for all of us. Martin will find work; you know how persistent he is. Please, please say you'll come with me! The very thought of travelling all those miles alone scares me stiff, but I've got to do it, for Alex's sake as much as my own. I'm serious when I say one day Scotty will kill me, and I don't fancy leaving my little son to his tender mercies. Say you and Martin will come, Rose!'

'Oh, but I can't speak for Mart,' Rose said wildly. 'I'm not saying he won't agree that we'd best leave Rhyl, but he hates doing anything in a hurry. He'll say we must give in our notice, arrange with management to start work in mid-Wales on a certain day, pay the rent of the flat until the end of the month . . . and he's sensible, is Mart. When we left Liverpool—'

'Yes, but that was different; no one was chasing you to beat you up,' Millie said through her stiff and swollen lips. 'Please, Rose, come with me! Martin can come on later. Scotty won't touch him, but if he decides that you know where I've gone, I wouldn't answer for your safety.'

'I'm not worried; Martin would be the one doing the killing if your husband set about me,' Rose said stoutly, but inwardly she quailed. Martin might not be around when Scotty decided to make her tell all . . . and suppose he grabbed Ricky . . . suppose Mrs Ellis discovered where they were living . . .

'Well? Will you come? Now, not at some time in the future, I mean.'

Rose stared miserably at her friend. 'Right now?' she quavered. 'But I can't speak for Mart . . . oh, Millie, I don't think I can leave that quick, norreven if you was to say tomorrer!'

'I've got to be out of here before they call time at the nearest pub, or I'm a dead duck. We'll leave Martin a letter . . . he can meet us somewhere away from Rhyl . . . please, Rosie! You've always been a good friend to me . . .'

'We-ell, I hate the thought of you goin' off alone . . .' Rose began, and Millie gave her another

291

hug and began hurling clothes into her zip-up bags.

'Go and start packing,' she instructed. 'And write that letter to your beloved! Oh, Rosie, I'll never forget your kindness . . .'

In trembling haste, Rose returned to her own room. She thrust a change of clothes for herself into the biggest bag she possessed, then began to sort out Ricky's things. She had left the child, now sleeping soundly, in Alex's cot, and when Millie came knocking on her door, a bare half-hour later, her packing was complete and she had written a letter to Martin, though she could not say too much in case Scotty, returning home and finding both his own and his friend's wives missing, might barge into their room, find the letter, and start out at once to follow them. It had to be carefully worded.

Dear Mart (she had written),
Millie and me have left, taking Ricky and Alex, of course. Poor Millie is in an awful state. Scotty beat her up, Mart, and so she's going home and I'm going with her. I shan't stay with her parents even if they ask me to, but will write to you, care of Mr Carruthers at the building site, letting you know exactly where to find me. And Mart, please stay away from Scotty because he's dangerous. He punched her and broke one of her front teeth and split her lip. Her eye is fat and oozing so she can't see out of it, and she's his own wife! Oh, Mart, I'm leaving you in the lurch but I know you'll understand. I couldn't let her go all that way alone.
Love from Rose and Millie.

292

PS It doesn't seem important now, but Mrs Ellis walked up to me in town this afternoon, and said we must talk. I know she will want to take Ricky and make him her own little boy. So of course I ran away. Another reason for leaving, you see.

Rose.

Rose showed the letter to her friend and laid it in Ricky's cot. Then she and Millie set off to walk to the station. They hurried, because Millie had already pointed out that if they did not get a move on they would miss the last train which would take them on the first step of their journey to mid-Wales.

'But what will we do when we get there?' Rose asked her friend. 'Mart and me have got a Post Office savings book, but we can't take any money out of that at this time of night, and it's far too cold for any of us to sleep under a hedge, or in a haystack, like they do in stories.'

'Oh, that's all right,' Millie said airily. 'I've always kept some of my salary from the pyjama factory in an old sock, stowed away in the bottom of the pram, just in case something like this happened. I checked it earlier and it was still all there, so I popped it into my handbag and we can bed and breakfast our way to our new life. Aren't I clever, Rosie? It will pay for train fares or however we want to travel. I've got a great deal of money in that sock.'

'That's grand, because I've left our Post Office book in our room, for Martin,' Rose said thankfully. 'Tell you what, queen, what's to stop us going out to Mart's building site, telling him what's happened, and finding a bed and breakfast place nearby?'

She looked hopefully at her friend, but Millie shook her head. 'It's January, you goose; most of the bed and breakfast signs have been taken down, 'cos folk who let to holidaymakers don't open during the winter months. Anyway, when Scotty realises we've both gone, my bet is he'll make straight for Martin's building site. I dare say you were about to suggest that we should kip down in one of the new houses, but it isn't on. Ricky or Alex might cry and give us away, or Don might start wagging his tail at the wrong moment. I'm telling you, Rosie, we've got to get that train! I've told you, I want to get right away from Rhyl. I didn't show you what I've written to Scotty, but I'll tell you now. I just said: "I'm leaving you, you bastard, going home. If you turn up there, my parents will have the police on you. Goodbye for ever, Millie."'

'That sounds a grand letter, so it does,' Rose said. 'Why don't you really go home, Millie? Then I could go back to Mart and we could face Mrs Ellis together.'

Millie shot her friend a curious look, but said firmly: 'I *won't* go home; it would be admitting defeat, particularly since one glance at my face will prove how right they were to distrust Scotty. I don't suppose you can understand this, Rosie, but when I do go home, I want to go as a success. I want to return as an independent woman, who has succeeded against the odds, with no help from anyone, and that includes my parents. Can you understand?'

'Not really,' Rose admitted. 'To tell the truth, I'd

be happy to get some help occasionally. And I rely heavily on Martin, so you can't say I'm very independent, can you?'

Millie started to speak, but at that moment they reached the station and she grabbed her friend's arm. 'That's our train . . . oh, oh, we really mustn't miss it!'

Chapter Thirteen

When the barman at the Grosvenor Hotel called time, Scotty had almost forgotten his throbbing head and injured pride, and was seeing life through a pleasant alcoholic haze. However, he had always known he would have to go home some time and have it out with Millie. So he got to his feet, pushed his empty glass across the bar, bade the staff and several of his cronies goodnight and headed for Bath Street, scarcely stumbling at all until he reached the foot of the stairs. Then he fell up the first three, cracking his knee painfully and catching one hand in the banister rails. Feeling almost inclined to burst into tears of self-pity—the fall had started his head throbbing again—he sat down on the fourth step to recover and to remind himself that whatever he did, it must be done quietly since most of the tenants would be home by now.

Accordingly, he sat where he was, steadying himself for the rest of the climb. He did not want to tumble down the whole flight; he might do himself a real mischief. What if he broke a leg or an arm, or even cracked his already painful head against some obstacle? He had switched on the light by the front door as he came in and reminded himself that he must turn it off when he reached the landing, otherwise old Ozzie would charge him extra, as she was always threatening. Slowly, he crawled up the stairs, switched off the light at the top, grabbed the banister rail of the flight to the attic and set off. There was a light at the head of the stairs but he did not turn it on, fearing that slight though the illumination was (was there such a thing as a ten watt bulb?) it might wake one of the babies. He crept up the second flight and stood outside his own door for five minutes, swaying from the effort of the climb but no longer feeling sick; the effect of the blow on the head was passing. By morning, he told himself, he would be fit as a fiddle. Better to steal into the room, take off his clothes and climb into bed. Tomorrow would be soon enough to sort things out with Millie.

With the utmost caution he opened the door, thankful that he had oiled the hinges so that it swung silently wide. He had expected to find the room in darkness, but instead it was full of starlight and he realised that Millie must have forgotten to draw the curtains before she got into bed. Stupid woman! How could she expect her man to sleep with the room so light? But of course it would help him to undress, which might have been difficult in the pitch dark. He went over to the window and began to unbutton his overcoat, suit jacket, shirt and trousers. He eased off his shoes as quietly as possible without undoing the laces. He left his clothes in a pile on the floor, the shoes with their knotted laces nearby. Let Millie hang everything up, iron the crumples out of his shirt, untie the laces and clean the mud off his shoes, he thought spitefully. Serve her bloody well right for hitting him.

He still could not work out what had made the worm turn, for he had frequently felt obliged to punish Millie when she did not provide his meals on time, forgot to iron his shirts, or did something else which inconvenienced and annoyed him. On those other occasions she had sometimes threatened to tell, but had never done so. What had changed? He must find out, though not right now; he was too tired. Tomorrow would be time enough.

He glanced over towards the bed and saw Millie's humped shape facing away from him. For a moment, he felt a rush of fondness for her. She wasn't a bad girl, not really, and in his heart of hearts he knew he had started the fight that evening. With a sudden flash of memory, he saw again his fist travelling towards her face with enough force to knock her flat on her back and cause her to drop the pan she was holding. There was blood, and when she began to cry, and to struggle to her knees, he had seen a broken piece of tooth dribbling down her chin amongst the red and for a moment he had actually been appalled by what he had done.

It must have been the broken tooth that had spurred her on to grab the saucepan. He had bent down to start picking up the potatoes the pan had contained when Millie had lurched to her feet, raised the saucepan and brought it crashing down on his head. The blow must have knocked him out, for he remembered nothing until he had opened his eyes to see one of the new rugs not an inch from his face, and heard Millie, still armed with the saucepan, telling him in a trembling voice that if he did not get out of the house that instant she would hit him again.

So he had gone; not because he was afraid of her, he told himself defiantly now, but because he needed a drink and a bit of friendly companionship and both, he knew, awaited him at the Grosvenor Hotel.

Now, however, he was back and longing for his bed. Millie looked so warm and comfortable curled up under the covers. He would climb in beside her, envelop her in a loving hug and tell her he forgave her for hitting him. Surely that would soften her hard heart? In the past, of course, he was the one who would have had to apologise, though always aware that it was all her fault. All she had to do was get his meals on time, wash and iron his clothing, and keep the place clean; it was little enough to ask. He never even made her hand over her wage packet. She was welcome to keep whatever she earned, and not all women could make that boast.

He was standing by the bed now, and he drew back the covers very gently and slid in beside her. He put an arm about where her waist should be and his heart gave a sickening lurch. She was all soft and squashy, not at all like the Millie he had come to know so well. Had he done more damage than he'd realised? Good God, now that he thought about it, she had not moved, even when he'd taken off his shoes, and he could hear no sound of breathing. He sat up like a jack-in-the-box, heart thundering. Then it slowed as he realised his mistake. This was not Millie! The wicked little bitch had pushed her pillow down the bed to fool him. Where could she be? But of course he knew the answer; she would have gone next door to claim a share of Rose's bed, thinking herself safe in there.

For a moment he contemplated going to Rose's room, full of righteous indignation, then dismissed the idea. He was dimly aware that he was still a trifle, just a trifle, the worse for wear and might be in no condition to explain to Rose—who would naturally take Millie's side—how the fight had all been Millie's fault. And he was not certain that any tale he told, even when sober, would be enough to explain the broken tooth . . . and he recalled a split lip, too, and an eye swollen up like a balloon.

In any case, it must be past eleven o'clock at night; no time to go bursting into someone else's bedroom. He would leave it until morning and hope that during the small hours something would occur to him which would make the state of Millie's face less . . . less . . .

Oh, but the bed was warm and comfortable! He had heaved the pillow out from under the sheets and put it back where it belonged, and now all he truly wanted was sleep. Sleep that knits up the what's-it sleeve of whichever, he told himself drowsily. Sleep that would bring a solution to all his problems. Sleep which . . . what . . . why . . . He slept.

*   *   *

Despite the things he had thought about Millie for leaving the curtains open, Scotty had not drawn

299

them across either and a good thing too, he told himself groggily, for he seemed to have slept through the alarm. Already, grey morning light was coming through the window.

He looked at the alarm clock which stood on the little bedside table and saw that the wretched thing had actually stopped. With a grunt of annoyance he swung his feet out of bed. Usually Millie got up first, switched on the electric fire, lit the Primus stove, and had a cup of tea waiting for him by the time he was ready to move. Not today. Today she had not even bothered to wind the alarm—she must positively want him to be late! Well, if he lost his job she would be smiling on the other side of her face.

He got out of bed and glanced at his wristwatch, which he had failed to take off the night before, though he had wound it. He wasn't late yet. In fact he would go downstairs to the bathroom, have a wash, clean his teeth and comb his hair.

Washed and dressed once more, he returned to his own room. He was as dry as a desert and longed for a cup of tea, and even as he pulled the kettle over the Primus stove an absolutely brilliant idea occurred to him. He would take the girls tea and toast! He would apologise humbly, explaining that the ding on the head which Millie had handed out must have caused him to go a trifle mad. In other words, the blow from the saucepan had started the fight, so could Millie please forgive him for his behaviour. He would beg her to let bygones be bygones, blame the drink, say he would sign the pledge and never touch another drop if only she would forget the hurt he had inflicted the previous evening.

When the kettle boiled, he suddenly remembered the baby, but was not at all surprised when he looked into the cot to find Alex missing. She would have taken him with her, of course. He turned away from the cot and his eye was caught by a folded sheet of paper from an exercise book, sitting in the middle of their drop-leaf table and weighted down with the salt cellar. He went across and picked it up, a frown creasing his brow. This was something new! But he supposed it was merely a note telling him she had gone to Rose. He unfolded the paper, and read the message written thereon.

Scotty's eyebrows shot up into his hair, then descended into a scowl. How dare she call him a bastard! His fingers gingerly felt the lump on his head; yes, it was still there, and still jolly painful. Yet she, who had caused the lump, actually meant to leave him. Ah, but had she already left, or was she still next door with Rose? He looked around the room properly for the first time. It was chaotic, with piles of clothing scattered about, though both Millie's warm winter coat and Alex's thickest jacket were missing. Now that he came to think of it, the room bore all the appearance of hurried packing, and the two holdalls which were usually stowed away under Alex's cot were there no longer.

Abandoning all thoughts of tea and toast, he rushed out of the room, tapped on the Thompsons' door, and barged in. One swift glance showed him that it was empty. Scotty frowned, puzzled. He acknowledged that Millie was untidy and that Rose was extremely neat, but the state in which Millie had left their room had gone far beyond mere untidiness. Carefully, Scotty looked round again, peeping under Rose's bed as though he suspected that he might find the girls, and their sons, hiding from him there. Instead, all he saw was Martin's camp bed. Straightening, he was about to leave the room when he saw another sheet of paper—by the look of it torn from the same exercise book and folded twice—lying in Ricky's cot.

Scotty did not hesitate for a moment, but grabbed the note and read it with mounting anger. He felt he might explode with wrath. This was a deliberate attempt to turn his friend against him. How could Martin go on liking him once he had read this note? And who the hell was Mrs Ellis? Why should she want to take Ricky? But an idea was forming. He looked at the clock on the shelf; it would be a full hour before Martin returned, and in that hour all sorts of things could happen. Scotty glanced around the room again; saw the notebook from which the page had been torn, and the biro which had written such false and terrible words. He sat down at the table and contemplated Rose's round, unformed hand. Then, with great care, he began to write. Five minutes later he gave a grunt of satisfaction and read over what he had written.

Dear Mart,

Millie and Scotty have had a quarrel; I think it was because she's been flirting with a fellow at work, but anyway she has decided to go home to her parents. I said I would go with her since this very afternoon Mrs Ellis came slap bang up to me in town and said we must talk. I ran away becos I know she will want to take Ricky and make him

*her own little boy. Please forgive me and be very
kind to Scotty. I will come back when Millie does.
    With love from Rose.*

He nodded to himself. Surely when Martin read
the note, he would accompany him to Millie's
parents' home and help him to persuade both girls
to return to Rhyl.

Well satisfied, Scotty returned to his own room,
made himself a pot of tea and a pile of toast and
marmalade, and settled down to wait for Martin.

*   *   *

Martin and Don walked briskly along Vale Road
and over the bridge, turned right along Kinmel
Street and then left into Bath Street. By now it was
half-past eight and the household was stirring. Mrs
Walshaw came out of her room with a paper
carrier containing her rubbish. She beamed at
Martin but refused his offer of help, saying that
her trip to the dustbin was likely to be the only
fresh air she would get until she walked round to
see her friend Doris at teatime. Martin smiled and
would have continued on his way, but Mrs
Walshaw put a detaining hand on the sleeve of his
duffel coat. 'Hang on a minute, Martin. What was
all that fuss last evening? People hurrying up and
down the stairs, opening and closing doors,
shouting? I would have gone to have a shufti—I'm
ever so curious, you know—but I was in bed with a
lovely hot water bottle, having decided I'd have an
early night, so I stayed where I was and thought I'd
find out in the morning.'

Martin chuckled. 'I expect it was the Bristows,'

he said. 'Ozzie has said, right from the start, that it would never surprise her if they did a moonlight. Not that I think they will, not so near the end of the month. I mean, why should they? Sally Bristow told Rose ages ago that Ozzie made them pay a month in advance, so if they did leave now it would be the old bat who owed them money and not vice versa.'

'Oh aye, I know all about the Bristows,' Mrs Walshaw said, nodding her head so vigorously that a lock of blonde hair fell across her face and had to be pushed behind her ear. 'No, it wasn't the Bristows. Whoever was doing the running about came down two flights of stairs, not one. Not that I want to alarm you, dear, because I don't think for one moment it was your Rose.' She lowered her voice conspiratorially. 'Your good lady had sort of hinted that she believed there might be trouble between the Scotts. I pooh-poohed the idea, but last night . . . still, you'd best go up and find out for yourself.'

Martin sighed, and when Mrs Walshaw had continued on her way to the dustbins he turned to Don. 'I'm sure it's nothing,' he said as they began to mount the stairs. 'If Rose has gone out with Millie and left me porridge I'll heat it up on the Primus with a bit of extra milk, and then I'll have the biggest pile of toast you've ever seen, 'cos this weather gives a man an appetite like a hungry wolf. How about you, old feller? I bet you could murder some toast and Marmite! Well, as soon as we get in—'

By now, he and Don were standing outside their own door, but before he could finish the sentence the Scotts' door shot open. Scotty stood there, hair

304

on end, eyes wild. He grabbed Martin's arm and shook it slightly. 'Have you been in yet? Did she leave you a note, tell you where she's gone? I would have come to meet you but I don't know which way you come home.' He stepped past Martin and threw open the other man's door. 'They've gone, honest to God! Millie left me a few lines scrawled on a page out of an exercise book, but she only said she was fed up with being married and having to do everything, and meant to return to her parents.'

Martin pushed past him, but a single glance round the room told him that Scotty was telling the truth. It was painfully tidy and there was a note propped up on Rose's pillow, where he could not fail to see it. Furthermore, their bags, which usually hung on two hooks by the door, were missing. Martin's heart began to thump unevenly. Whatever could have happened to send his Rose careering after Millie? He snatched up the note, unfolded it, read it once, then a second time.

Scotty, who had followed him into the room, made an impatient noise and held out a hand. 'What does she say? The same as Millie, I suppose. Martin, I can't understand it; they've got good jobs, nice homes—well, not nice, but they seem to like it here well enough—and husbands who care about them. I admit we had a bit of a tiff, Millie and I, and this one . . . oh, hang it, Mart, it turned rather nasty. She grabbed a saucepan and cracked me over the head with it, and I gave her a good slap and she fell over and banged her face on a chair . . .'

'You'd better read the note,' Martin said. He could not believe what was happening to him.

305

Rose might not want him the way he wanted her, but he knew she needed him. He watched, uneasily, whilst Scotty read Rose's note. He felt there was something not quite right about it, but could not put his finger on what was wrong. He realised, of course, that despite his reassurances Rose still believed that Mrs Ellis might try to take Ricky away from them, but he was positive that the woman could not legally do so. In fact, from what Rose had told him about the Ellises, he thought them too intelligent to make a move that could only end in their humiliation.

He took the note back from Scotty in order to read it yet again, and then turned to his friend, his hand held out. 'Let's have a look at Millie's note, Scotty. There may be some clue in that.'

Scotty hesitated for a moment, patting his pockets and looking puzzled. 'What the devil did I do with it? I was pretty angry, so my first reaction was to scrumple it up and shove it in one of my pockets.' He delved deeper, then seized the linings and pulled them out to show Martin that both his trouser pockets were empty. 'Dammit, I reckon it must have fallen out. Let's have another look in my room.'

They went next door and began to sift through the clothing and possessions that still littered floor and furniture, but without success. Suddenly Scotty smote his forehead. 'I know what's happened,' he said. 'I went down to the corner shop to buy a pint of milk—we'd run out and I was desperate for a cuppa—and it must have dropped out there. But honest, Mart, Millie's note said even less than Rose's. Just that she was fed up with being expected to work and manage the house and that she was sick of quarrelling . . . something like that. Anyway, it was only a couple of lines. I suppose I could go back to the corner shop, see if they've found it, but you won't be any the wiser once you've read it, I promise you.'

Martin shrugged. 'Never mind. But I shall need directions on how to reach Millie's parents' house, since I must go after them. I expect you think Rose can cope, but you don't know her as well as I do. She'll stand by Millie, but she won't expect to stay in the Sandersons' house and I don't suppose she's got a lot of money on her. Oh, God, and come to think of it she didn't even take our Post Office book because I remember seeing it lying on the dresser when you and I first went into our room. Does Millie have money on her?'

'Oh, she's bound to have. And if she hasn't, her parents would give her whatever she needs,' Scotty said blithely. 'But you're right, we must get after them as soon as we can. Only—only I'd rather we went together, if it's all the same to you, Mart. Tell me, who is this Mrs Ellis, and what does she want with Ricky?'

Martin, on his way to the door, stopped with his hand actually stretched out towards it. 'Oh, when Rose was first pregnant she offered to adopt the baby when it was born—she has no kids of her own—and she wasn't happy when Rose said she wanted to keep it. Rose thinks she probably signed adoption papers, thinking they were applications for housing or something. That's why we left Liverpool.'

He would have left the room at this point, but Scotty seized his arm. 'Hang on a minute, Mart. Why did you have to run away? Surely all you had

307

to do was to tell the authorities you had changed your minds?'

Martin heaved a sigh. He would have to tell Scotty at least some of the truth. 'Rose was only fifteen when the baby was conceived and of course we couldn't get married before she was sixteen. So Mrs Ellis was offering to adopt the child of an unmarried mother, which isn't at all unusual, you know.'

He tried to jerk himself free from Scotty's grip, but the other man hung on. 'Right, I understand that part of it,' he said, and Martin saw to his annoyance that he was grinning slightly, raising an eyebrow, as though he thought Rose—and Martin himself—were idiots. 'But why is she still afraid? You're a sensible chap, Mart. You must know that this Mrs Ellis has no possible claim on Ricky, not even if you and Rose had signed a dozen adoption papers.'

'Maybe not, but Rose can't see it that way,' Martin assured him. 'And now let me go and put a few things together. Not that I'm expecting to be away for days and days, just for long enough to talk Rosie into coming home, with or without Millie.'

Back in his own room, Martin made a pile of very untidy sandwiches, put a tin of Chappie and some dog biscuits into a paper carrier, and then began to search the room. He had not said so to Scotty, but he thought it likely that his friend, having read the note Millie had left for him, would have come straight round to consult Rose. He might easily have dropped Millie's note here, and then not liked to admit that he had been trespassing, if you could call it that.

How fortunate it is that Rose and I are both

308

quite tidy, Martin thought, sifting through a couple of magazines and some newspapers which lay on the chest of drawers. It won't take me anywhere near as long to search this room as it took for the two of us to hunt through Millie's muddle. Even as he was thinking this, he glanced towards the raffia wastepaper basket that Rose had bought at a jumble sale, and his heart gave a leap. He saw a piece of lined paper, similar to the one upon which Rose had written her own note to him. As he picked it up, it occurred to him to wonder why Scotty should have thrown Millie's note into the wastepaper basket, but then he unfolded it and smoothed the creases, and his heart sank into his boots. It was not a note, but a shopping list which he had actually watched Rose laboriously writing when he had got back from work the previous day. Sighing, he began to crumple the paper up, then changed his mind. He laid it carefully upon the Formica-topped table, smoothing it out yet again. Then he produced the note which Rose had left for him, and compared the two. After some moments of staring from one sheet to the other, he became convinced that the writing was not the same. Oh, it was very similar, but in the note Rose had left him there were perfect little circles, whereas on her shopping list, in at least one or two places, the o was carelessly made, so it looked more like an e. Furthermore, on the shopping list the s was smaller at the top and larger at the bottom, whereas in Rose's note to him the curves were uniform.

Martin sat down at the table, rested his chin on his hands, and stared ahead of him without seeing anything. Had she, for some reason, got someone else to write the note? She might have dictated it to Millie whilst she was doing the packing ... no, that was not right. He had often seen Millie's writing on lists or notes, and it was very distinctive, spiky and upright; quite different from Rose's. He knew of course that it could have nothing to do with Mrs Walshaw, nor for that matter any other member of the household. He and Rose were friendly and polite to other tenants, but apart from Mrs Walshaw they had neither received visitors in their attic room nor visited them in turn. And that leaves Scotty, Martin thought grimly. He had admitted that he and Millie had had a fight, but he had most definitely blamed it on his wife. If Rose had been right, and Scotty was responsible for Millie's 'accidents', Martin realised that Scotty might have written the note himself in order to fool him into helping persuade the girls to come back.

Martin half rose from his chair, then sank back into it again. This could not be right! He knew very well that though Millie had been told about the Ellises, Rose had sworn her to secrecy, begged her not to tell even Scotty about the older woman. And Scotty had had to ask him who Mrs Ellis was and what claim she had on Ricky, after he had read Rose's note. No, he was maligning his friend, thinking him the worst sort of cheat. There was simply no way he could have known about Mrs Ellis ...

Martin was actually beginning to relax when a little voice inside his head spoke in his inner ear. Unless Rose *did* leave you a note, the little voice suggested. And Scotty read it, didn't like what it said, and decided to substitute his own version. Of course, that must be it! He knew very well that Rose would never have left without telling him where she was going—and why on earth, now he came to think of it, should she say *be very kind to Scotty*? It wasn't the sort of thing one said to a fellow; and anyway, she had told him a couple of times of late that she was uneasy in Scotty's company, did not altogether trust him.

Martin got to his feet and went next door. Scotty was standing by the cupboard in which they kept their clothing, his hand in the pocket of his best suit, the one he saved for board meetings, interviews and other such events. He gave a gasp as Martin burst into the room, and turned away from the rack of clothing. 'Don't you ever knock before coming into someone else's room?' he enquired plaintively. 'I was just wondering if I should wear my best suit—Millie's parents are sticklers for convention.'

'What have you done with Rose's letter?' Martin said baldly. 'Don't lie, because I've worked it all out. You copied her handwriting pretty well, but not well enough.' He took a step towards Scotty, who moved hastily back. 'Give me the real letter or I'll break your bloody neck.'

He was watching Scotty's face as he spoke and read the expressions flickering across it. He saw fear, indecision and then a shame-faced acknowledgement before Scotty finally spoke. 'I can't show it to you, old fellow, because I burned it. She—she said some horrible things, which weren't true.'

Martin gave a growl of anger and loomed threateningly over Scotty, who had sat down on the nearest chair. 'My Rosie doesn't tell lies,' Martin

311

said through gritted teeth. 'Whatever she said must be true.'

Scotty shrank back in the chair, an abject figure, sweat running down his face. 'No, no, I'm sure you're right, but Millie had told her things . . . oh, I wish I hadn't burned the letter because I'm sure you'd see at once . . .'

But Martin was watching Don, who had followed him into the room and was now sniffing at Scotty's left hand, which was curled into a fist. 'What've you got there?' Martin demanded wrathfully. 'Even the perishin' dog knows you're hiding something. Hand it over, or it'll be the worse for you.'

Scotty's mouth opened and shut several times, though not a sound came out. He reminded Martin of a goldfish that had accidentally jumped out of its bowl and was lying gasping on the tabletop, but he felt no pity for the other man. 'C'mon, Scotty, give,' he said, then snatched the piece of paper which Scotty had been trying to conceal and read it at a glance: *I'm leaving you, you bastard, going home. If you turn up there, my parents will have the police on you. Goodbye for ever, Millie.*

Martin stepped back and jerked his head at his companion. 'Get your coat,' he snapped. 'I take it that I now know as much as you do yourself? Apart of course from the violence, which must be why Millie decided to give you up as a bad job and return to her parents.'

'She hit me with a saucepan; I can show you the huge lump she raised,' Scotty said sulkily, but he got to his feet, unhooked his coat and cap from the stand, and looked at Martin through his lashes. 'Where are we going? Not to the police station!'

'No, but the police may come later,' Martin said ominously.

Scotty paled. 'Honestly, Martin, you've always been a good friend to me; don't let me down now! Help me persuade the girls to come back to us. I'm sure Millie has told Rose, and Rose has told you, that Mr and Mrs Sanderson won't let Millie into the house whilst she and I are together. That tells you what sort of people they are, to try to separate a man from his wife. But it means I dare not go there myself and ask to see Millie. I'd have to hang around outside until the girls come out. But you can walk straight up to the front door and ask to see your wife and her friend. As I said, they're very conventional. They'll invite you in, probably offer you a cup of tea and a bun . . . I'll write a letter to Millie if you like, begging her to come home, and you can deliver it. Yes, that's a grand idea, because it gives you a reason for calling.'

Martin ignored him. He returned to his own room, put on his coat and picked up the bag of food he had prepared earlier. Then he and Scotty clattered down the stairs and out through the front door, closely followed by Don.

Scotty tried to talk to Martin several times, but Martin, preoccupied by his own thoughts and disgusted by Scotty's behaviour, did not answer. Now, however, he spoke. 'This way,' he said brusquely.

*   *   *

When Rose awoke, the morning after their flight from Rhyl, it was to a strange lodging house, for she and Millie had been tired out by the events of

313

the day and had barely noticed their surroundings before tumbling into bed.

The train from Rhyl had arrived in Chester at twenty minutes past ten, but Millie had assured her friend that there was a small lodging house about a hundred yards from the station, which would be open until midnight. She had heard it described as cheap but cheerful, and so it appeared, for the landlady had expressed neither surprise at the lateness of the hour, nor curiosity about the fact that each girl was carrying a sleeping baby in her arms. 'You'll be off the train from Wales,' she had said, ushering them into a small room dominated by a very large bed. 'We often get folk comin' in for a night's bed and breakfast, when their connections mean five or six hours hangin' about on a cold platform. I hopes as you and the kids can manage wi' the one bed, but I'm sure you're that tired you could probably sleep on a clothes line. I serve breakfast from seven o'clock until nine, if that suits.'

The girls had assured her that it would suit very well and had bundled the babies into the big bed before following them in their underwear, not bothering with nightgowns but simply collapsing between the clean, crisp sheets. Rose had not really expected to sleep because her mind had kept revolving around the events of the day, but in fact sleep had claimed her as soon as her head touched the pillow. And now, awakening, she was astounded to hear a clock somewhere chime seven, and reached over to shake her friend awake.

'Millie, do wake up! It's seven o'clock and the boys will be wanting a bottle and some groats. I was so tired last night I forgot to ask Mrs What's-

314

her-name if it would be all right to go down to her kitchen and prepare the boys' breakfasts in there.'

Millie sat up, and with the movement the babies, who had been sleeping between their mothers, awoke. They were flushed from their sleep, but to the girls' relief showed no signs of starting to bewail their lot. 'You go down and get their grub and I'll change their nappies,' Millie said. 'Oh, lor', what'll we do with the dirty ones?' She began to unbutton her son to reveal a very dirty nappy indeed. 'Oh, God, the pong! Can you bring some water back when you come, Rosie? You know, I thought this journey was going to be quite simple, but babies complicate everything, don't they?'

*   *   *

Because their departure had been so hurried, it had not occurred to Rose until they had left Chester and were on the train heading for Shrewsbury to ask her friend some pertinent questions. Rose had been surprised when several people had looked into their carriage and then turned away. Then she glanced across at Millie and knew why they were still alone in the compartment. Millie's face had stiffened and the bruising had come out in rainbow hues. They had left their temporary lodgings rather hurriedly and Millie's usually soft and shining black hair was rumpled, for she had given up the unequal task of combing out the tangles when the two of them, having enjoyed a cooked breakfast, had paid the bill and sprinted for the station, their babies gurgling in their arms.

Now, Rose leaned forward and tapped her

friend's knee. 'Millie, I know you've had a horrid time and I don't blame you at all for leaving Scotty; in fact if you ask me you should have done it weeks ago. But one thing bothers me, queen. You know too much! You knew the time of the last train from Rhyl to Chester, you knew where we could get a night's lodging, even though we turned up so late, and you seem to have no doubt that we'll be welcomed at Pollyanna Modes when we reach Dinas Newydd. It looks to me as though you've been planning this for some time.'

She watched as colour blotched her friend's face and neck, but when Millie spoke, it was defiantly. 'Well, naturally, I looked into things when we were offered jobs at Pollyanna. I suppose you could say that I needed an escape route. But I never thought things would get to a point when running away was the only answer. You see, Mr McDonald guessed things weren't right a while back. I think that was why he offered us the jobs in mid-Wales, but at the time I was still hoping that Scotty would see sense, grow up a bit, stop behaving like a spoilt kid . . .'

'Millie, he couldn't possibly have guessed, because though I must admit that I had my doubts about Scotty, I thought I was simply being over-imaginative,' Rose said indignantly. 'You *told* him Scotty knocked you about; you must have!'

'I did not,' Millie said. 'D'you remember when I said I'd fallen downstairs and caught my foot in the banister rail? Well, I was sent to the nurse. She asked me how I got my foot so mangled, so I told her the same story I told you, but apparently Nurse sees a lot of similar injuries and she guessed that someone had deliberately stamped on my foot. Anyway, I was limping out of her office when Mr

316

McDonald came along and asked what I'd done. Later, when I went over to the crèche in my lunch hour, he and I had a talk and I admitted that Scotty could be violent. He suggested that we see a marriage guidance counsellor, but when I mentioned it to Scotty he got so nasty that I simply grabbed the baby and rushed down to the kitchen. I stayed there until I heard him go down to the pub, then I went back to our room and got Alex ready for bed. When Scotty came back, I told him it had just been an idea and I wouldn't mention it again. And I didn't, because I could see that if I did so, I'd probably end up strangled.'

She gave a small, rather watery laugh and Rose was dismayed to see tears running down her friend's face. 'You guessed right, of course; from that moment on I began to make enquiries as to how one would get from Rhyl to Dinas Newydd. I told Mr McDonald that if things got worse, I would accept his offer of a job at Pollyanna Modes, or at least go down that way and have a look at Pollyanna Modes—see what all the fuss was about. I mean, everyone who works at Pollyanna Pyjamas has the perfection of the Dinas Newydd factory shoved down their throats. He was very kind, Rose, but the truth is I never really thought I'd make the move. I told myself that if we bought one of the new bungalows, the ones on Martin's estate, things would improve. Then it occurred to me that if we did buy a bungalow, we wouldn't have you next door, or the other tenants close at hand. We wouldn't even have lovely Mrs Walshaw to babysit. That was when I found out how one got from Rhyl to Dinas Newydd.'

'I see, more or less,' Rose said thoughtfully. 'So

317

you're telling me that Mr McDonald had nothing to do with any of this? I know I've teased you about him, but I was half serious, because you've only got to look at the feller to see he likes you. So if it was his idea that you should run away from Scotty—run to Mr McDonald, in fact—I don't see why you can't come straight out with it and say so.'

'Because it wouldn't be true,' Millie said, but again a betraying flush darkened her face and neck. 'He was sorry for me, but that's all there is to it. Well, you can scarcely pretend he knows me any better than he knows his other workers. And now, dear Rose, would you kindly drop it? Remember, we're hoping to get jobs at Pollyanna Modes, where I gather he's a power to be reckoned with.'

'All right, I won't mention it again,' Rose promised. She giggled. 'Besides, when he sees your poor face, I should think luring you to his love nest will be the last thing on his mind.'

Millie smiled reluctantly, then put her hands carefully to her mouth. 'Don't make me laugh; it hurts,' she mumbled. 'I hope there's a good dentist in Dinas Newydd, someone who can stick that piece of tooth back in.'

'Oh, I'm sure they'll do something,' Rose said comfortingly. 'There are things called crowns, which film stars have. They look just like real teeth and they're cemented into place. I expect they'll give you one of them.'

Chapter Fourteen

Scotty trailed unhappily after Martin. 'Where are we going?' he asked. 'This isn't the way to the station.'

Martin regarded him grimly. 'We're going to the building site. I care about my job even if you don't, so I need to tell them I won't be coming to work tonight, and find Mr Naylor to ask if he'll stand in for me.'

Unfortunately, when they finally ran the elderly night watchman to earth, he said he was unable to take over Martin's shift that evening. 'But don't worry,' he added. 'My son will do it—he's a reliable chap.' Martin was forced to accept, although he wished he had time to clear the new arrangement with the boss. But Mr Carruthers was not on site that morning, so he just had to hope everything would go well.

They were unlucky with the trains, and by the time they reached Formby Scotty announced that it was too late to call on Millie's parents that evening. Reluctantly, Martin agreed to find lodgings for the night and visit the Sandersons first thing the following morning. He spent an uncomfortable night, tossing and turning, worrying about Rose, wondering how young Naylor was getting on, and infuriated by the fact that Scotty, the cause of all his problems, seemed to have no trouble at all in dropping off to sleep as if he hadn't a care in the world. By the time Martin felt it would be reasonable to go down to breakfast he was anxious, exhausted and angry in equal measure, and could hardly bring himself to speak to his unwelcome travelling companion.

They arrived at their destination soon after nine o'clock. Despite the fury that still gripped him, Martin was impressed by his surroundings, for the drive that led up to the Sandersons' house wound between thick evergreens and was imposing enough to frighten anyone. Scotty declined to go further than halfway up the drive, handing Martin the note he had penned for Millie, with all its promises of good behaviour in the future. Privately, Martin thought the letter would be taken in and he would be dismissed, but in fact he spent almost half an hour with Millie's parents. When he re-joined Scotty, he almost couldn't bear to look at the other man. 'They aren't there,' he said, keeping his voice level with an effort. 'They never have been there, not either of them.'

He began to walk away. 'Who says they aren't there?' Scotty said belligerently, following him. 'Oh, how typical! They're lying, of course. I take it you saw Mr and Mrs Sanderson, and weren't fobbed off with a servant?'

'I wasn't fobbed off with anyone, and I saw Mr and Mrs Sanderson,' Martin said. 'They told me they'd not seen Millie since she left the shelter of their roof, and had never seen Rose. I believed them, of course. Why should they lie?'

'They'd lie to keep Millie and me apart,' Scotty said doggedly. 'You should have asked to search the house. You should have . . .'

Martin turned on him. His fists itched to hit the other man, but he did not want to start a brawl. 'Scotty, listen to what I'm saying. They are two very nice people, whose daughter has hurt them badly. They feel that they're the ones who have been cast off, but I'm sure that if Millie disowned you completely—divorced you, in fact—they would willingly accept her back; it's only you who prevent them from doing so. And they told me why they disapproved of Millie's having anything to do with you. How Mr Sanderson caught you beating up one of the village kids who was collecting windfalls in the orchard; the boy told you he'd had the Sandersons' permission, but you went on . . . well, you know what happened better than meself.'

By now they had reached the road and Scotty gave a bark of laughter. 'They've fooled you nicely, I can see,' he said derisively. 'They'd say anything to keep Millie and me apart.'

'Shut up,' Martin said brusquely. 'You've told me a grosh o' lies . . . just shut your mouth, d'you hear me?'

The journey back to Rhyl was largely conducted in silence, but when they were in the train once more Martin spoke, though coldly. 'When we get home, you can find yourself different lodgings because there's no point in even pretending that I want to be in your company, or have anything more to do with you,' he said with brutal frankness. 'You can go on searching for Millie if you like, but I'm telling you to your head that she won't want you. If you're determined to stay in Bath Street, then I reckon Rose and I will move out, because she'll think just as I do.' Scotty began to protest but Martin scowled at him. 'Don't bother arguin' 'cos me mind's made up. And now I'm goin' to have forty winks, or I'll be fit for nothing when I go to work tonight.'

Scotty began to plead, to suggest various places

where the girls might have gone, but Martin ignored him and presently Scotty's voice, and the rhythm of the train, took on the soothing cadence of waves on a sandy shore and Martin did indeed sleep.

*　　　*　　　*

Rose and Millie, clutching two by now rather fractious little boys, reached their destination in mid-afternoon. They stepped out on to a cold platform, and to Rose's horror snowflakes began to descend as they handed over their tickets to the collector. He was a small, skinny man, whose huge walrus moustache was stained yellow with nicotine. 'Nasty weather, girls,' he said conversationally, looking up at the tiny flakes whirling past. 'Where's you bound on such a day? If it weren't for them babbies, I'd say you was off to Pollyanna's, though come to think they've got a nursery—like for mams wi' little children—so you might be bound there?' He raised a grizzled eyebrow, turning what might have been a statement into a question. Millie smiled at him and Rose, much amused, saw the poor man do a double take as the hood which her friend had pulled well forward slid back to reveal her injured face. 'Oh, whatever happened, cariad? You poor thing!'

'I fell getting off a train in Shrewsbury,' Millie said untruthfully. 'We had to change there. Fortunately, my friend here was holding both babies, so my little boy wasn't hurt.'

'Lucky that was,' the man said. 'So you're not bound for the factory, then? Best place in the area for a girl to get work it is, though. Consider it you might, if you're stayin' here long.'

'We will,' Millie assured him. 'But for now we're looking for Ty Isa, which is a farm, I think. A—a friend said the people there would put us up for a couple of nights, just while we get work and find somewhere more permanent to stay.'

'Oh, yes, it's a farm,' the man said. 'But a mile or three outside the town, it is. And them babbies aren't lightweights from the looks. You'd best nip out and stop Huw Williams from lightin' out for home, 'cos he'll be thinkin' there's no one got off the three twenty.'

'Who's he?' Rose asked. 'Does he drive that old black taxi-cab? Because if so . . .'

But the ticket collector, following the direction of her gaze, gave a gasp and shot across the platform and into the road, holding up a hand, and presently the two girls, the babies and their baggage were safely stowed away in the cab. The driver, a young man with curly hair and an impudent grin, said he knew Ty Isa well, and very soon they were unloading their possessions in a warm farm kitchen and explaining to the farmer's wife that they had been recommended by Gwyneth Prydderch, a supervisor at the pyjama factory, to come to Ty Isa on their arrival. Rose knew that it had been Mr McDonald's idea to approach Gwyneth, but made no comment, and presently they were settled at the kitchen table, sipping hot tea, whilst the boys crawled around the floor and were cooed over by their hostess.

Explanations of course were called for, though the name Gwyneth Prydderch seemed to be the best introduction possible. 'A fine girl, Gwyneth is,'

Mrs Evans, the farmer's wife, assured them. 'Second cousin to my man's brother's wife,' she added, as though it explained everything. 'Worked at the factory, she did, but they moved her up to Rhyl. I dare say that's where you've come across her?'

'That's right,' Millie said easily. 'She sent a letter of recommendation to one of the directors, advising him that we're good workers and asking him to take us on. We're to go down to the factory tomorrow morning, to fill in application forms and take some sort of test. If we're successful, the firm have promised that the children can go into the nursery and they'll do their best to find us lodgings.

'Very organised, you are,' Mrs Evans said admiringly. 'Well, I wish you luck, and you're welcome to stay here until you find something more suitable. The difficulty is that we're a good two miles from the factory and no bus. Of course you could get Huw Williams to pick you up and bring you home, but a pretty penny that would cost!'

'We're good walkers, even when carrying the babies,' Rose said, rather timidly. She had borne up pretty well throughout the complications of the journey, but now she was tired and beginning to be worried. She was sure that Millie had been fibbing when she claimed that Gwyneth had written a letter of introduction, but she had no intention of letting her friend down by querying what she had said. Oh, if only Martin were here! But of course he had no idea where they had gone, so she could scarcely expect him to arrive, a knight in shining armour on a white horse, to rescue her from the

324

dragon. The Welsh dragon, she thought, with a little snort of amusement.

By now she had realised that Millie was almost certainly expected at Pollyanna Modes, thanks to Mr McDonald, but of her own reception she was far less confident. Millie had had no idea when she had discussed her situation with Mr McDonald that it would be two young women with two babies who needed work, a roof over their heads and places in the nursery wing of the factory. If Martin had been here, she told herself, he would know just what to do. However, by the time she had eaten a delicious stew, which Mrs Evans described as 'a bit of a scratch meal', she had begun to feel better.

When the boys had eaten mashed potato and gravy and had had their night-time bottles, they were quite happy to be carried upstairs and placed head to toe in the old cot that Mrs Evans had produced. 'In summer I take in families who don't mind that Ty Isa is a bit remote,' she had explained. 'They want their children to enjoy the countryside and life on the farm, so I got the cot from my daughter Megan when she said she'd finished with it, and very useful it has been.'

As soon as they were alone in the old-fashioned bedroom, with its low window and sloping ceiling, Millie said quietly: 'Mrs Evans is awfully nice, isn't she, Rose? It's not everyone who would be willing to put up a couple of young girls and their babies at a moment's notice. To tell you the truth, I'd love to get into that bed right now, but it isn't even seven o'clock yet, so we'd better go down and help with the washing up.'

They descended the narrow twisting stair, but

though they offered to help clear away the meal Mrs Evans, after a shrewd look at them, said that it would not be necessary. 'Mr Evans and my sons Arfon and Dewi will be in presently for supper,' she explained. 'No point in clearing up until they've had their meal. If you want to go off to bed, so's you're well rested for tomorrow, then that's what you should do.' She had been sitting at the table, but now she got to her feet and took Millie's hands. 'A right mess he's made of your face, me love,' she said gently. 'And don't go inventin' stories, because I've been around a long time and I was married before to a man who . . . but the less said of that the better. Now off to bed, the pair of you!'

*　　　*　　　*

Martin and Scotty arrived back in Rhyl at five o'clock and headed straight for Bath Street. Martin had bought a loaf and some cheese at the nearest shop and made some sandwiches and a flask, and then set off for the building site. When he reached it, however, a nasty shock awaited him. When he walked into the night watchman's hut, Jimmy Carruthers, the boss's son, was sitting at the small table, with a pile of papers in front of him. He looked up as Martin entered, but did not smile. 'So you're back, Thompson,' he said coldly. 'I don't suppose you know it, but a fine mess you got us into by going off the way you did.'

'But I arranged with Mr Naylor for his son to stand in for me,' Martin protested. 'His father's reliable, so I thought the son would be the same.'

'He may be reliable, but he's not experienced,'

326

Mr Jimmy said. 'Thanks to him we lost a load of wood and a quantity of bricks, probably to the same gypsies you chased off the other night. I'm not saying young Naylor isn't honest, but I am saying he wasn't up to the job, so this morning my father hired someone else; he starts work tonight.'

'I'm real sorry, Mr Jimmy,' Martin said contritely. 'But it won't happen again. If I have to go off on urgent business, like what I did on this occasion, I'll make sure—'

'It won't arise, Thompson. I said my father has hired someone else. He's a retired policeman and pretty tough. He'll be doing the job from now on.'

Martin stared. 'But Mr Jimmy, I've got to work,' he said wildly. 'There's me rent, money for grub . . . wharrabout Don here? Does the new chap have a dog?'

'Yes, he's got an Alsatian; not that it's any concern of yours any more,' the other man said frigidly. 'You can collect your papers, and any pay that's owing, tomorrow.'

Martin mumbled that he would see the boss in the morning and was halfway back to the door when something else occurred to him. 'Why are you here, Mr Jimmy?' he asked. 'It must be almost six o'clock.'

'Mr Naylor said you'd come back tonight, so I came over,' the other man said. 'Your replacement was told to come half an hour late this evening because I didn't fancy sacking you in front of him.'

Martin took a breath, then let it out in a long defeated sigh and left, a hand on Don's smooth, velvety head. Throughout the walk back to Bath Street he wrestled with the problem of how to pay the rent with only the income from the maintenance work on the fair. Unless Rose came back pretty quickly, he would be forced to go on the dole, and he knew very well that that would not cover all his expenses. He reflected, however, that the money he and Rose had saved in their Post Office account would come in useful until he got another full-time job.

On his return to his room, he shared the cheese sandwiches he had made earlier with Don, and racked his brain for a solution to his problem. Once, he would have gone next door and consulted Scotty, but not any more; never again, in fact. Instead, he planned a tour of every shop, office and building site in the town; decided to ask his ex-boss for a reference, even contemplated writing one himself. When at last he crawled into bed, he was feeling less hopeless; surely something would turn up? He would go to the funfair and ask Mr Foster if there was any chance of more work now that his weekdays would be free.

Satisfied that he had done all the planning possible, he got between the sheets, not on his camp bed, but in the big double which still smelled delightfully of Rose. He fell asleep at last, to dream of her clattering up the stairs to the attic and her warm breath on his cheek.

He awoke to find that Don had joined him on the bed and was breathing softly into his face, and this amused him so much that he got himself a breakfast of porridge and toast in an optimistic and cheerful frame of mind. He would find something. He was a good worker, and if only the boss would give him a decent reference . . .

His visit to the offices, however, produced only the wages owed and a grudging admission from the boss that, if asked, he would supply a reference. 'Of sorts,' he added, and Martin, sighing, realised that it might be wiser not to mention the building site when applying for other work.

*   *   *

As Rose had thought, Millie had been welcomed— and expected—at Pollyanna Modes, but Rose herself had come as a total surprise. At first, the lady in charge of the Personnel Department had simply said she would put Rose's name on the waiting list, but Millie, feeling that she had let her friend down, had insisted on an interview with Mr McDonald. After talking to Millie, he had said that Rose might work as a nursery assistant in the firm's crèche, and though the pay did not compare with that earned by the machinists and finishers in Pollyanna Modes, it would be sufficient if she were careful.

'I'm going to write to Martin tonight, telling him we're all right, but I won't suggest that he join us, because there's no work around here for a feller,' Rose said. 'It's odd, but I feel like somebody with only one arm because I'm not in touch with Martin.'

'Lucky you, to have a husband like him,' Millie said sincerely. 'But where will you send the letter? Oh, Rose, don't send it to Bath Street because I reckon Scotty will still be in the room next door and he's quite capable of sneaking in when Martin's at work and going through any papers lying about. I'm still afraid that he—Scotty, I mean—might have read the letter you left for Martin when we fled. Oh, I know you say there

329

were no clues to where we'd gone . . .'

'You read the perishin' letter,' Rose said indignantly, 'so you know very well what I said. If Scotty had guessed where we'd gone, he'd have been here by now. And I wouldn't dream of writing to Martin at Bath Street; I said I'd send it to his boss at the building site and ask him to hand it on.'

'I'm sorry, I'm sorry. Of course I read the letter and I know you'd not give me away, even by accident,' Millie said contritely. 'But you know I still can't sleep on my left side because my face is so sore, and whenever I laugh my mouth hurts like hell and it makes me remember . . . oh, all the worst things Scotty did to me.'

'Poor old Millie! But you look ever so much better now. However, I heard what Mr McDonald said when he first saw your face—that if Scotty tried to come near you he'd break his bloody neck. He didn't seem at all worried at the thought of coming between a man and his wife.' She looked shyly at her friend. 'He really does like you, Millie. Oh, how I wish you'd never married Scotty!'

They were sitting on their bed at Ty Isa and now Millie turned to her, a smile curving her swollen lips. 'That, dearest Rose, was the one folly I didn't commit. Scotty and I never did actually get married. Oddly enough, it was I who tried to persuade him to tie the knot, and he who kept drawing back. I always said he was immature. Part of that immaturity was his desire to remain unattached, a bachelor gay in fact, though he wanted to have a woman who would take care of him by cooking, cleaning and generally behaving more like a servant than a wife.'

330

'And he didn't want to marry you even when you told him you were expecting Alex?' Rose asked incredulously. 'What a fool Scotty is. But of course it's a blessing for you. He has no claim on you, or on Alex.' She grinned wickedly at her friend. 'You could say Alex was Peter McDonald's son, if push came to shove.'

Millie chuckled appreciatively. 'Peter wouldn't mind,' she said, and Rose realised it was the first time her friend had used Mr McDonald's Christian name, in her hearing at any rate. 'He really is nice, Rose; the opposite of Scotty, in fact. Oh, I know he's tall and very good-looking, but he's also gentle and kind. If he ever did ask me to—to go to a film or something, I'd know I'd be absolutely safe with him.'

'I don't see how you can know,' Rose said after some thought. 'I agree he's awfully popular in the factory, but Scotty was probably popular at his works; come to think of it, you said all the girls were after him. So don't you go trusting any feller until you know him real well.'

'I won't,' Millie promised, but the little smile still lurked. 'To tell you the truth, if you wouldn't mind babysitting Alex this evening, Peter *has* asked me out. He's told me quite a lot about himself. Apparently, he was engaged to be married once, only she ran off with someone else and it made him wary of all women.'

'Well, it would. Of course I'll babysit,' Rose said readily. 'But tell me, Millie, when did you learn all this about Mr McDonald? Oh, I know he used to talk to you whenever he came over to Rhyl, but I'm sure he never gave you the intimate details of his life. Or if he did, you never told me.'

Millie giggled again, looking self-conscious. 'Oh, I might as well tell you everything, I suppose. You know I went into the factory to be shown the ropes yesterday, while you were being taken round the crèche? Ever such a nice girl—her name's Anna—took me round and introduced me to everyone. She showed me how things worked, of course, but though the designs are far more complicated the machines are just the same as the ones at the pyjama factory. I did a sort of test on them and passed with flying colours. Then, before I came to find you, Mr McDonald called me into his office and we had a long talk. I told him everything he hadn't guessed about Scotty, including the fact that we weren't ever actually married, and I can tell you all the worry lines on his forehead smoothed out and he positively beamed. Then he went all serious and told me why he'd never married—he is thirty-eight after all.'

'Gosh!' Rose said inadequately. 'Go on.'

'Well, then he sort of mumbled that he had liked me from that time in the foyer, when he promised to put us on the waiting list for jobs. He said that after a few meetings he'd known I was the only girl for him, though he thought I was married and couldn't possibly feel the same. Only I told him I did—feel the same I mean—and then he smiled again and said he wouldn't rush me, but would I have dinner with him tonight, at a little riverside pub ten miles from here. He chose it because he didn't want people gossiping about me—tongues wag overtime in small communities—so of course I said I'd love to; I was sure you'd babysit if I asked.'

Rose chuckled. 'Considering we're two miles from town and I don't know a soul, it's pretty unlikely that I won't be here all evening,' she observed. 'So I'll babysit all right. And thanks for telling me how things stand, Millie. I've always liked Mr McDonald, but after your experience with Scotty I think you'd be wise to take things slowly, get to know one another properly.'

Millie agreed with this sage advice, though Rose thought it very unlikely that her friend would turn cautious overnight. She had always been impulsive, acting before she thought, and Rose feared that she would go on doing so, despite promises to the contrary.

As soon as Mr McDonald had called for her friend, parking his Ford Zephyr convertible with a flourish, Rose went to her room, checked that the babies were still sleeping, fetched her writing materials and went down to the kitchen. Being largely ignorant of cars, she merely remarked to Mrs Evans that the vehicle looked very expensive, and Arfon, eating at a great rate, informed her that indeed it was. 'It's the newest thing: a Ford Zephyr convertible with a 2,262 cc six cylinder engine,' he informed her. 'Grand it is to be the boss and take home a huge salary, because them cars simply drink petrol and prices haven't half risen since the Suez crisis.'

Rose agreed, though her personal recollection of the Suez crisis, which had taken place almost a year earlier, was confined to seeing a newspaper picture of a slogan which the Egyptians had painted on a railway bridge close to the Suez Canal. *Go home British, your king is a woman*, it had read, causing much amusement to the invading troops and the journalists who had accompanied them.

333

But before she could do more than agree that Millie was lucky to be riding in such a vehicle, Arfon and his brother had changed the subject and were discussing the latest film to be shown at the cinema in their small town. 'It's Bing Crosby and Frank Sinatra,' Arfon said through a mouthful of potato. 'We might see that and then go to the pub for a pint.'

His brother spread out the newspaper. 'It's *High Society*,' he read slowly. 'Yes, I'd like to see that.' He turned to Rose. 'Want to come with us, Mrs Thompson? You'd be welcome, though you'd have to ride in Da's old baby Austin.'

Rose, however, shook her head firmly. She liked both young men, but did not fancy being the bone between two dogs, and anyway she had other fish to fry tonight. Mrs Evans, producing a bread and butter pudding from the oven, offered to babysit but once more Rose shook her head. 'It's awfully kind of you, but the babies hardly know you really and they're nervous with strangers,' she said apologetically. 'Once they're used to you, it might be different. And anyway, we left so hurriedly that even our landlady doesn't have a forwarding address, so you see I must write some letters.' She glanced meaningfully at the farmer's sons. 'I'm hoping that my husband may join me if he can find work . . . oh, I realise he can't do that whilst we're staying with you, Mrs Evans, but once we've got a place of our own . . .'

'He could stay with us and welcome,' Mrs Evans said. 'However, Mrs Scott told me you'll be moving on because of the difficulties of getting to and from the factory.' She began to dish up the bread and butter pudding, glancing sideways at Rose as she did so. 'If you want to write letters, best go into the parlour, 'cos these two great lummocks are quite capable of spilling tea all over the page, or spraying it with bread and butter pudding.'

There was a great outcry at this from both young men, but Rose gathered up her writing materials and went into the small, stuffy room, which was filled with old-fashioned furniture. She sat down on a sofa upholstered in vivid green sateen, pulled an elaborate little side table towards her, spread out paper, ink and pen, and began to write. She told herself that she must not give too much away in case Scotty saw the letter, but she knew, really, that Martin would be careful to keep the information to himself. She had told him what Scotty had done to Millie, and though Millie had been convinced that Scotty would destroy the letter before Martin came back from his night's work, Rose was equally sure that Martin would discover the truth. At first she sat staring ahead of her, wondering how to begin, but once she had started the words flowed easily from her pen.

Dear Martin,

Sorry to have left in such a hurry, leaving you only a little scrap of a note, but Millie felt it wasn't safe to linger in case Scotty came back. I don't know how much you've guessed, but we're in a farmhouse in mid-Wales, a short distance from Dinas Newydd. It is a lovely spot and there is work for us both, though it is in a factory which only employs women, apart from the bosses of course, and some designers and engineers, and you, dear Mart, couldn't do that sort of work.

I left you our Post Office book so I know you'll

be okay for money for quite a while, though of course you do have your wages for the night work and also whatever you earn from maintaining the funfair, but I do think you ought to come here as soon as you can get leave from your various jobs so we can discuss our situation properly. Ty Isa isn't on the telephone and of course nor is Mrs Osborne, so we can't talk to one another; it has to be a visit. You will come, won't you, Mart? Drop me a line telling me when and I'll meet the train. We do miss you, all of us, and give Don a big hug and a kiss from me because we miss him, too.

Take care of yourself and don't wait too long before replying to this letter.

Your Rose.

Rose printed her new address at the bottom of the page, folded it, pushed it into an envelope and then considered what she should do next. She sealed the note, realising, however, that she could not send it since she had no stamps. At this point Mrs Evans came into the room to say that one of the boys was crying. 'I know they have a night-time bottle, so I put the kettle on as soon as I heard him begin to whimper,' she said.

Rose thanked her sincerely, but when she enquired about stamps, the farmer's wife shook her head. 'No, cariad, I'm not much of a letter writer, but of course you can buy some on Monday when the post office opens. Or are you starting work Monday, same as your pal?'

'Oh, Lord, of course I forgot tomorrow's Sunday; and yes, I do begin on Monday,' Rose admitted. 'I start at eight and don't finish until half-past six, because I'm working in the nursery, not in the factory itself. I suppose I could go in my dinner hour . . .'

Mrs Evans chuckled. 'Not unless you can run the four-minute mile!' she observed. 'The factory's a good way from the village. But I dare say someone in the office will sell you stamps.'

*   *   *

When Millie got back from her evening out she was flushed and smiling, full of how beautiful the riverside pub had been, how delicious the food and—after a shy glance at Rose—how delightful the company. But she was unable to provide her friend with any stamps and suggested that they might walk into the village the next day and see if they could find a vending machine.

When they woke on the Sunday morning, however, a curtain of rain had swept down on the countryside, causing Mrs Evans to advise them not to risk a chill by going out. The girls were determined, however, so their landlady lent them an old pram which had once belonged to her daughter and they donned their waterproofs, wrapped the boys up warmly and set off, needing fresh air and wanting to talk. Kind though Mrs Evans was, she was also curious, and both girls realised that they needed to discuss their situation without being overheard.

There was no stamp machine in the village, so the two of them turned aside into the gentle green hills and presently found an ancient barn where they could take shelter if the rain continued. They reached the barn just as the rain stopped—Sod's law, Millie said—and settled down on a pile of hay, for Rose had decided that, as Millie had confided in her, she should do the same. Accordingly, she admitted that she and Martin were not, in fact, married.

'Why ever not? I think the two of you really should marry. You're clearly very fond of one another, and there's Ricky . . .' Millie began.

But Rose shook her head obstinately. Having started, she realised she would have to tell her friend everything. 'Yes, but it's not love, it's just that we like each other very much. We're pals, you see,' she explained. 'To tell the truth, Millie, I don't think I really want to marry anyone, especially not Mart. He's—he's different, being so pink and white. And anyway, Martin isn't Ricky's father. I—I was interfered with by a much older man . . .'

'Mr Ellis!' Millie breathed. 'So *that* was why you got so scared that they'd take your baby away from you! Oh, Rose, you poor kid!'

Rose stared admiringly at her friend. 'Aren't you quick, Millie?' she said. 'Yes, it was horrible old Mr Ellis. We were at Guide camp . . .' The story took some time in the telling since Millie would keep interrupting, but it was done at last, and the girls set out once more into the beautiful, gentle hills which reared up around Ty Isa, and headed for home.

Millie was thoughtful for the last half-mile or so, but as they entered the farmyard she turned to Rose once more. 'It's a pity you say you don't want to marry Mart, because it's as plain as the nose on your face that he adores you. But you'll probably change your mind once Ricky begins to need two parents.'

Rose made some non-committal reply, but that night she lay awake for a long time, thinking over what Millie had said. Perhaps her friend was right and she would change her mind about wanting a husband. And if she did, could she .ever love anyone more than she loved Mart?

It was a long while before she slept.

Chapter Fifteen

Ever since Martin and Scotty had returned to Bath Street, Martin had listened for sounds from the room next door, wanting to hear none, hoping to learn that Scotty had left. But so far, though a fortnight had passed, this had not happened. The two men ignored one another completely, but Martin knew that Scotty went off to work at the usual time each morning and, when work finished, went straight to one of the many pubs that could provide him with a meal as well as a drink. He did not go to the Grosvenor, presumably because they might have asked questions, but then Martin did not go there either; he could not afford such luxuries. The barman at the Grosvenor had stopped Martin in the street one day and asked him what had gone wrong. 'I ain't sayin' you was particularly good customers,' he had said with a grin, 'but at least you was regular. We miss you, to tell you the truth. I guessed you'd lost your job 'cos I seen you going into the Labour Exchange a few days back.'

'You're right. There was a—an emergency, an'

me wife had to go back to her parents'. She may be gone awhile, so I took some time off an' when I got back the boss sacked me,' Martin had said. 'Nice of you to enquire, and if you hear of any job comin' up I'd be real obliged if you'd let me know.'

The two had parted and gone their separate ways, but Martin had felt warmed by the encounter and had begun his usual tour of possible employers more cheerfully as a result.

Unfortunately, jobs in seaside towns during the winter were few and far between, and Martin was beginning to realise that if Rose did not reappear soon he would have to sign on the dole, though he dreaded doing so; it seemed an admission of failure. He was still putting in odd hours at the funfair, but they scarcely kept him and Don in food. He knew he ought to look for cheaper lodgings, but he was still hoping to get a letter from Rose, giving him her new address.

*   *   *

Jimmy Carruthers hurried into the office, speaking as he entered his father's cosy little den. 'Morning, Pa! What a weekend, eh? I thought it would never stop raining, and it's still coming down as though we ought to be building an ark!' Mr Carruthers senior grunted irritably and Jimmy's heart sank. However, it would not do to show that his father's ill humour made him nervous, so he grinned at the older man and went back to the door, glancing upwards as he did so. 'But it won't last; there's blue sky over the sea,' he said encouragingly. 'What d'you want me to do today, Pa?'

'When the rain stops—if it ever does—you can

340

get on bricklaying at the big house on Plot 5,' Mr
Carruthers growled. 'One thing to be grateful for,
we only lost a few hours on Saturday morning. But
today . . . oh, well, we'll have to wait and see. Hand
me the post, would you?'

His son grabbed the pile of mail which the
postman had deposited on a rickety table near the
door and began to pass them to his father. Then
he stopped, staring at the envelope in his hand.
'There's one here that isn't for us, Pa,' he said. 'It's
for the feller that did night watchman for us a bit
back.'

'Who? Oh, Thomas, wasn't it? The weird one?
Chuck it in the bin, boy; he won't be coming round
here again. Not after I gave him his cards and what
little money was owing.'

'Can't do that, Pa,' Jimmy said righteously. 'It's
illegal to destroy mail addressed to someone
else . . . I'd best redirect it. Or shall I take it round
to his place? Not now,' he added hastily, seeing a
scowl descend on his father's brow, 'this evening,
after work.'

'Please yourself,' Mr Carruthers said, pulling the
rest of the mail towards him and beginning to slit
the envelopes with an ivory paper knife. He
pushed a large ledger towards his son. 'You'll find
the address in there.'

'27, Bath Street,' Jimmy said. 'Right, I'll drop it
off on my way home.'

He spent the day bricklaying and left a little
early, since he was to deliver the letter. He
wondered how Thompson was managing, if he had
a job yet, and whether he did in fact still live in
Bath Street. But he posted the small brown
envelope through the letter box of No. 27 and went

341

on his way, satisfied that his errand had been discharged. You never knew—the fellow might have applied for a job and the envelope might contain details of an interview. At any rate, Jimmy's conscience was now clear, and as he turned for home he began to whistle.

*　　　*　　　*

Scotty came home feeling downright cheerful for the first time since Millie had left him. He had been called into the boss's office that morning and had gone with some trepidation, fearing a dressing down because, though he had somehow managed to do his work, he was well aware that his usual cheerful demeanour had been lacking.

But the boss had been very understanding, said he had heard that Scotty's pretty young wife had left him . . . and had offered Scotty a six-month secondment to their Canadian works with an increase in pay, good lodgings and the use of a car. He had also hinted that if Scotty liked the work he might apply to take the job on permanently.

Scotty had pretended that he would have to think the offer over, but he knew he would accept it. It was the perfect escape from Rhyl, which had become loathsome in his eyes, and from Millie, against whom he still held an enormous grudge. But Alex . . . he missed Alex horribly and sometimes woke in the night, thinking he heard the baby crying. Then he would cry himself, saying through clenched teeth that he would make her sorry, one day, for ruining his life.

But if he made a home and a decent life for himself in Canada, who could say what might happen? He spent a pleasant ten minutes imagining that Millie would go down on her knees and beg to be taken along, and then another ten minutes plotting how he would take Alex away from her; first of course finding himself a wife who would look after the child whilst he worked.

Yes, that was the right attitude to take. If only he had managed to find out where the girls had gone it would be different. He could give Millie the lesson she richly deserved: take his son, and go off to Canada, possibly without anyone's knowing. He could give the kid a much better life than Millie could, so the authorities would let little Alex live with his father rather than his mother. But despite his most stringent efforts to find them, Rose, Millie and the two little boys had disappeared as completely as a couple of raindrops in a puddle. So he would go to Canada and have a damned good time and worry about Millie and the boy when it became necessary to do so.

He reached 27 Bath Street and slipped inside. Because of the offer of the job in Canada his boss had let him leave early, and he was about to climb the stairs to change his work suit for something more casually comfortable when he saw a letter lying on the hall linoleum. Odd! Mrs Osborne checked the post each morning and put her tenants' correspondence on the board, but perhaps this letter had come in the second post, or it could have been delivered by hand. Scotty turned the envelope over and his heart gave a gleeful leap. It was addressed to Martin, and he knew the writing well, for had he not studied it carefully before forging that note from Rose? He looked around him, then, still holding the letter, began to run up the stairs. It would undoubtedly contain their address, and though he did not have time to follow it up if he was to take the job in Canada, at least he would know where they could be found.

As soon as he reached his own room, Scotty shut the door and ripped open the envelope. He would destroy the letter once he had copied down the address. The girl would probably write again, but if she did not Scotty thought Martin would have been well served. He hated the other man and would positively enjoy injuring him in some way.

He wrote down the address, went to tear the letter across without reading it, then paused. A better revenge occurred to him. He would put on the envelope, in a good imitation of Martin's writing, *Not known at this address*, which, hopefully, would dissuade Rose from trying to get in touch again.

There was one snag, though. He could not remember seeing an example of Martin's hand. Then he remembered the exercise books in which, he assumed, Martin was scrawling down a kind of diary. He went next door, found one of them, copied Martin's small, neat script, and then returned to his own room. He would go down to the pub presently and tell his new cronies all about his amazing luck over the job in Canada. Then he would drop the letter from that nasty little gingery female back in the postbox. He would enjoy that, hugging to himself the knowledge that Rose was unlikely to write again after such a snub. And just to make things perfect, he meant to leave without paying Ozzie the rent he owed. She had criticised him, demanded her money, given that peculiar liquid sniff of hers when he promised to pay her at the end of the next week...the next...the next...

*   *   *

Martin set off earlier than usual, his plans for the day all mapped out. He would catch a bus to Prestatyn and ask each shop and office there whether they had work available.

He did as he had planned, but it was no use, and at the end of the day, tired and dispirited, he and Don returned to Bath Street with lagging steps. No one wanted staff and several times he had felt, rightly or wrongly, that it had been his appearance that had put prospective employers off. So he and Don toiled up the stairs feeling thoroughly disheartened. As soon as they reached the upper landing, however, Martin realised that something was going on. The door to Scotty's room was open and Mrs Osborne, with a duster tied round her greying hair and a number of paper carriers spread out before her, was impatiently filling them with what looked like garments of some description. Martin walked over to her, eyebrows rising. 'What's up,' Mrs Osborne? Can I take it Scotty's moving out?'

Mrs Osborne gave a loud and juicy sniff. 'Moving out? He's being thrown out, and not before time,' she announced. 'He's not paid me a penny of rent since his wife left him. I was sorry for the feller; he kept telling me his wife would be back soon, which weren't true, of course. But I'll say this for you, Mr Thompson, there's not a penny owing so far as you're concerned. I don't know what he told you, but he left me a note saying his firm were sending

345

him to Canada. He didn't expect to be coming back, but if he did it wouldn't be to here, and not a penny did he enclose of what he owes.'

Martin frowned. He knew Scotty earned a good salary and could easily have afforded to pay the rent. He looked questioningly across at Mrs Osborne.

'He's gone, Mr Thompson,' she said. 'Scarpered, cleared orf! Must have been this morning, when I'd nipped out to do me shoppin'. I've done everything I could. I rang his firm but they said he'd already left. The lady I spoke to told me to send in a bill and they would forward it on to him.' She sniffed again. 'A fat lot of good that will do! So I'm packing up everything he's left, such as it is, and taking it to the nearly new. He's took everything of any value. I reckon he's sold anything he could get a few bob for and then done a moonlight. I dare say, being a feller, you didn't notice that he was drinking heavily, which must have cost him a pretty penny.' She shovelled the last few garments into one of the carriers, then began to brush the floor vigorously, sending clouds of dust into the air. 'The mess and dirt is unbelievable!' she said. 'And I've got another tenant interested in these rooms, so if you're thinking of moving on at the end of the month, just let me know.'

Martin smiled but vouchsafed no reply. He was still hoping that Rose would get in touch; he was sure that a letter or at least a card would arrive in Bath Street soon. It was this hope alone, he knew, which kept him in his present room, though now that Scotty had moved out things would be a good deal pleasanter.

'Well, are you? Thinking of moving on, I mean. I know you're out of work at present, Mr Thompson . . .'

'If I mean to leave you, Mrs Osborne, I'll give you notice in the usual way,' Martin said, with an assumption of calm he did not feel. 'I'm truly sorry Mr Scott has behaved so badly, but he and I are very different. What do you mean to do with Mrs Scott's stuff, though? And little Alex's, of course?'

'I'm going to sell it to recoup me rent, and don't you go saying that it ain't honest, because I'm owed,' the landlady said crossly. 'My, the state of this room, though! I don't believe Mr Scott has lifted a finger since his wife left. He told me some story about a sick mother, but I didn't believe a word of it.' She lowered her voice. 'One or two of the other tenants reckon Mr Scott wasn't above giving his wife rough treatment for no real cause. What d'you say to that, eh?'

'I'm afraid it's true,' Martin admitted. 'Millie— Mrs Scott—went home to her parents because Mr Scott was violent, and Rose went with her. So don't regret losing a lodger, because Scotty was a real bad lot. And now if you'll excuse me, Don and I have got to get our supper ready.'

Martin went into his own room, closing the door behind him. He walked towards the food cupboard, then stopped short. He always left a small pile of shillings beside the meter, and he was sure he had done so that morning, but now not one coin remained. Perhaps he had put them on the mantelpiece, or on the table . . . he often put things down on the chest of drawers. He glanced in that direction, saw his rent book, and realised, with a stab of dismay, that the Post Office book was no

347

longer in its accustomed place.

At first, he simply refused to believe it and hunted wildly, going through every drawer, every cupboard, every possible hiding place. Don, sensing that something was wrong, followed him round, but after a fruitless search Martin was forced to descend to the basement to ask Mrs Osborne if there had been a Post Office book in the Scotts' room.

Mrs Osborne shook her head. 'Don't tell me he's stole your savings,' she said sadly. 'And I used to think the pair of you was thick as thieves, if you'll pardon the expression. If I was you, Mr Thompson, I'd go straight to the police station, though by now I reckon he'll have withdrawn every penny and made off.'

'Yes, I suppose you're right,' Martin said bleakly. 'You say he cleared off first thing this morning, whilst the house was empty? So by now he'll be long gone. I don't suppose he'll go back to his parents; he didn't seem to get on with them. I'll go to the scuffers—the police, I mean—but I expect it's useless.'

'You're probably right,' Mrs Osborne agreed. 'Still, you've got to try. Let me know how you get on.'

Martin went to the police station immediately, but, though sympathetic, the desk sergeant held out little hope of his getting his money back, so Martin returned to his room, black despair in his heart. He made himself and Don a hasty meal, then climbed into bed, cuddling up to Don's comforting warmth. Presently, to his shame, he began to cry, shaken by the situation in which he found himself, and was grateful when the big dog turned in his arms and began to lick the salt tears from his cheeks.

* * *

When her letter to Martin arrived back, with *Not known at this address* in Martin's neat, well-remembered handwriting, Rose did not even show the envelope to Millie, but took it to her own room and wept bitterly. It was all her fault! She had told him many times that she never meant to marry, but that if she did it would be to someone tall, dark and handsome. They had laughed over it, she remembered miserably, but Martin must have taken it seriously, and when he had come back to Bath Street and found her missing, without so much as a proper explanation, he must have decided that they would be best apart.

But after a couple of hours of abject misery and self-blame, Rose pulled herself together. Martin was her best pal, so she would find him one of these days and tell him . . . what? She still did not fancy marriage, not to anyone; she just wanted Martin, and their comfortable relationship, back. And anyway, it wasn't as if she was alone. She had Ricky, and she had Millie, though seeing the loving looks which Mr McDonald sent her friend when he thought no one was looking, she guessed that it would only be a matter of time before the two married . . . but by then I'll be truly independent, she told herself. The awful ache which losing Martin had left would have gone, and she would have made a new life for herself.

A couple of weeks passed, and then Millie came across to the crèche, where Rose was still working, agog with a new idea. 'We are a pair of idiots,' she said, pulling Rose into the corridor where they could talk in comparative seclusion. 'Haven't you remembered how clever Scotty is at forgery? Given time, he could copy almost anything. My bet is that when you sent the letter to the building site Martin shoved it in his pocket and took it back to Bath Street to read in his own room. And if Scotty saw it he'd have thought that a good way to get back at you for going off with me was to take the letter and send it back here. What d'you think?'

'I think you're clutching at straws, because Mart would have noticed the letter had gone. But you're right in one way: anything could have happened. The letter could have been returned by the local post office and someone with writing very like Mart's could have redirected it,' Rose said after a few minutes' thought. 'Look, I'm going to visit Rhyl again the moment I've saved enough for the fares. I'll go along to Bath Street and if Mart isn't there any longer I'll ask Ozzie to tell me what's been happening. I could write to her, of course, but I think a visit would be better. If Mart has moved on then I'll go to his building site and to the funfair—someone will know something, I'm sure. Will you give an eye to Ricky while I'm gone?'

'Course, love. I'm so happy that I want everyone else to be happy too,' Millie said. 'Oh, Rosie, I pray I'm right and you find your Mart safe and well and longing to see you again!'

*   *   *

When he awoke next morning, Martin did some sums in his head and decided that not even finding

350

cheaper lodgings would make up for the loss of both his job and their Post Office savings book. He would have to grit his teeth and sign on for the dole, and when he had done that he rather thought that his rent might be paid for him until he found himself a proper job. He would not declare the bit of work Mr Foster still gave him from time to time, because if he did so it would complicate matters, or so he understood from others searching the advertisements in the Labour Exchange.

He made himself a cup of tea and a pile of bread and margarine, then looked out of the window. It was still raining; just the sort of day when the Labour Exchange would be crammed full of wet and miserable people and jobs, needless to say, would be few. But he had made up his mind to have one more go at finding work, and if he was unsuccessful he would then sign on. He had paid Mrs Osborne up to the end of the month, that was one blessing, so he would have a roof over his head—and Don's, of course—for a little while yet.

Martin shared his bread and margarine with Don, then put on his trusty waterproof and set off into the downpour. If only Rose would write! He simply could not understand why she had not done so. He would have worried that harm might have befallen her or Ricky if he had not known she was with Millie; Millie was both brave and resourceful, as indeed was Rose. One of them would get in touch with him soon, he was sure. He would ask Mrs Osborne to forward any post addressed to him to his new lodgings, and as soon as he knew where the girls and their sons were he would set out, walking if necessary, to join them.

At the Labour Exchange he had what he

351

devoutly hoped might be a bit of luck. They wanted a porter at the railway station and the man behind the grille said that his previous experience of that work, though it had occurred a while ago, and had been of short duration, might give him a head start over other job seekers. Heartened by this idea, Martin set out at once. When he reached the station, however, the job had already been taken, and he was just leaving the forecourt when a voice hailed him.

'Martin? It *is* you, old feller, ain't it? Well, it must be because I ain't never met anyone else what looked like you does!'

Martin swung round, staring. Then a big beam spread across his face. 'Thomas! Well I never did! What the devil are you doin' in Rhyl on a rainy morning? Don't say you've biked here wi' a letter from the good old Cygnet. I can believe a lorra things, but that's a bit much for anyone to swallow.'

'Nah, course not,' Thomas said, coming to a halt beside Martin. 'I've got a couple of days off so I've come down to Rhyl to see me cousin what lives in Rhuddlan, an' I was just goin' to hop on a bus when I saw you. The Cygnet were all right, but somehow the fun went out of it when you buggered off. So after a bit I did the same: went as general dogsbody to Humphries & Renshaw, a smallish firm of printers, in case you've not heard of 'em.'

'Oh,' Martin said. 'Thomas, it's so good to see you! Tell me, were they very angry when I left the Cygnet the way I did? Only the truth is, we had no choice. We—we ran away from someone who—who wanted Rose to give up the baby when it were

352

born, and we couldn't have that.'

Thomas looked puzzled. 'If you say so, old feller, but it didn't go down too well wi' the bosses; I don't think they'd tek you on again. But if you *was* lookin' for a job in the 'Pool . . .' He paused, eyeing Martin doubtfully. 'I suppose you wouldn't consider applyin' for *my* job? It's nothin' grand—deliveries, post, that kind of thing—but the money's not bad.'

'I'd do anything,' Martin said eagerly. 'But you never said you were leaving the printers! Where are you off to?'

'I've gorra girl what works at Lewis's. She's got me a job in their despatch department,' Thomas said proudly, 'better money and shorter hours. What do you say, old feller? Are you on?' He grinned at his pal. 'One of the things I remember about you is your neat, clear writing, and that's something Mr Renshaw is keen on. Come to that, if you agree, I'll write you a reference meself!'

'I'd take just about anything,' Martin said at once. 'But wharrabout somewhere to live? The city's expensive, always was. And I don't have no money for the train fare.'

'YMCA until you find something better,' Thomas said promptly. 'As for gettin' from here to Liverpool, you can borrow some lolly from me; I'm pretty flush at the moment. What d'you say?'

'You're on,' Martin said promptly. He and Thomas rushed back to Bath Street, where Martin slung his few belongings into his old canvas bag and left a note for Mr Osborne, and by evening he was back in Liverpool, having booked himself into the YMCA, smuggled Don into his dormitory and spread out the dog's old blanket under his bed,

353

adjuring him to silence.

Next morning, Martin washed and dressed with care and walked to the printing works. An hour later he emerged, triumphant. He had got the job! He knew the work would suit him very well and the salary was sufficient to pay for a room when something cheap came up. He wrote another hasty note to Mrs Osborne telling her he had found work and giving her the address of the YMCA. Then he settled down to learning his new job.

*   *   *

It had not been easy to find decent lodgings because most landlords would not even consider taking Don, but when Mr Fisher, one of the compositors at Humphries & Renshaw, had been told of the problem he had recommended his brother-in-law, who was looking for what he called a steady young chap in regular employment, who would not disturb other lodgers by playing his wireless too loud, or by holding wild parties.

So within a couple of weeks of arriving in Liverpool Martin moved into a tall, old-fashioned house on Breck Road, off Heyworth Street, to a friendly welcome from Mr and Mrs Denby. He was led up a steep flight of stairs to a pleasant room on the first floor and both Denbys made a fuss of Don, telling him what a grand fellow he was and how nice it would be to have a dog in the house once more, since their own old spaniel had died the previous year.

The rent was reasonable and included breakfast, Mrs Denby having explained that she would provide an evening meal for an extra five bob a day. 'But of course if you'd prefer to cook for yourself, there's a Primus in your room, or you can use the kitchen after seven thirty,' she said. 'Does that suit, Mr Thompson?'

Martin said it suited him very well. With the warmer weather coming, he had been dreading going back to the long stuffy dormitory, redolent of unwashed socks, unwashed men and stale food, in the lodging house down by the docks to which he had been obliged to move when the YMCA had objected to Don. He had not even had to give notice that he was quitting, since he paid each night for his accommodation, but he had told the man in charge that he had found something permanent anyway. The man was old, and as dirty and smelly as most of his customers. He had merely grunted when Martin had said he had found a room and had made a nasty remark about Don, so that Martin had been doubly glad to leave.

It did not take him long to realise that he had fallen on his feet. The other two lodgers were middle-aged men who kept themselves to themselves, and Mrs Denby was an excellent cook. Martin treated himself to two or three of her meals each week, heating up soup, baked beans or boiled eggs in his own room when he was not enjoying his landlady's delicious fare. Weekends were different. There was a café further down the road and Martin had a midday dinner there on Saturdays. The proprietress was very attached to Don and one reason why Martin favoured her establishment was the large plate of scraps that she saved for the dog.

Now Martin lay in bed, with a shaft of sunlight playing across his face, rejoicing in the fact that it

355

was Saturday and he did not have to go to work. He knew he was lucky both in his job and in his lodgings, but he ached for Rose and thought about her and Ricky constantly. Why had she not written? He was sure she was not dead, but could not understand her silence; they had been good friends, if nothing more, and one did not lose touch with friends.

Martin sighed and got out of bed, clicking his fingers to Don, who jumped to his feet and grinned hopefully at his master. Martin began to dress, telling himself that he and Rose would meet up again soon. He would advertise . . . go back to Rhyl . . . but today he planned to revisit old haunts. He did not mean to return to the boys' home where he had been brought up until he was a success at something or other, but he did mean to stroll past and take a look at the place. Then he meant to visit the children's home where Rose had lived, so that he might see if she had contacted anyone there, though it seemed unlikely.

Last, but not least, he meant to go to the tower block in Everton Brow. He thought he would try to visit the old lady on the ninth floor, because he knew that Rose had been sorry for her and had popped in from time to time with small gifts such as a sausage roll or a meat and potato pie. She had known that the old lady appreciated home cooking and had been glad to be able to give pleasure, although of course when she could she had *sold* her baking so that she might have a little money of her own. Martin knew that Mrs Ellis had made his pal a generous allowance, but as time passed he had grown to understand that Rose wanted to be able to give the child she was expecting garments which she herself had paid for with money earned by her own efforts, not given to her from either guilt or charity.

Immediately after breakfast, Martin and Don set off. They checked out the children's homes—nothing seemed to have changed and Rose had not been in touch—and then made their way to the tower blocks. Martin felt a pang at the sight of them; he had been happy here, determined to do well so that one day he and Rose . . .

But she had scotched such hopes when she had told him they could be nothing but pals. Only of course hopes aren't quite so easily put to flight; they persist, sometimes by day, sometimes by night. As well as thinking of her constantly, he had begun to dream about her; dreams in which he saved her from some danger or other—a dragon, a sea-monster, or even just plain old Mr Ellis—and was rewarded by her undying love. Daydreams were almost as good. She came into the printing works, dress torn half off her back . . . she had been involved in a traffic accident, a fight with a jealous employer . . . she was trapped in a burning building from which only he, who knew a secret entrance, could rescue her . . .

But those were daydreams and this was reality. He entered the tower block confidently, glanced at the lift, which was out of order, naturally, and began to climb the stairs. One hand lay on Don's smooth head and in the other was a brown paper bag. It might not be Rose's cooking, but in Martin's opinion Sample's was the next best thing, so he had popped in there and bought two sausage rolls, a meat and potato pie and two sugary doughnuts. The old lady on the ninth floor—Mrs

Templeton—dearly loved a doughnut.

Panting slightly, Martin arrived. He cast a wistful glance up the next flight of concrete stairs which had led to the only real home he had ever known, but turned his eyes away resolutely. Rose's flat belonged to someone else now, and anyway, his errand was here. He banged on the door and waited. He could hear a wireless playing softly and smiled to himself; Mrs Templeton had been saving up to buy a wireless set, though she had confided to Rose that her son, who helped to build ships on the Clyde in Scotland, had hinted that she might receive a set sooner than she thought.

Martin was still smiling to himself at the thought of the old lady's pleasure when the sound of footsteps came to his ears. Mrs Templeton in her old carpet slippers had heard his knock. The door opened a slit and a beady eye was pressed to it. Martin hastily dragged the cap from his head, telling himself as he did so that she was more likely to recognise him by his white hair than anything else. 'It's me, Mrs Templeton; Rose's friend.'

'Who's you?' a cracked and elderly voice enquired. 'I don't know you, does I?'

'I think you met me once or twice, but it was Rose—her on the tenth floor—and old Don here that you knew best.' He waved the paper bag. 'I've brought you a little present. It's from Rose really.'

There was a rattling as the old lady took the chain off the door and swung it wide. 'Little present?' she said, peering hopefully at the brown paper bag. 'It ain't often as I get give a present! Wharris it?'

Martin stared. Whoever this lady might be, she was not Mrs Templeton. She was small and thin,

358

with draggly grey locks hanging half across her face and skin the colour of parchment. She was dressed in black, with a red woollen shawl about her shoulders and large carpet slippers, far too big for her, on her feet. She held out a claw-like hand towards Martin, saying as she did so: 'I doesn't reckernise you, but that don't mean much. You'd best come in.'

'I'm awful sorry, I thought you were Mrs Templeton,' Martin stammered. 'She—she and me wife were pals when we lived on the top floor. What's happened to her?'

'If you mean the old woman what had this flat till Michaelmas, she died. I'm Mrs Halloran,' the old woman said. 'I telled them, when they put me into this flat, that I shouldn't last much longer meself, climbing up an' down them bleedin' stairs. Still, there you are.' Her eyes, which had flickered over Martin from top to toe, came to rest on the paper bag. 'What'll you do with that there present? Only I doesn't get out to the shops much, bein' as the lift's always broke . . . well, thank you kindly!'

Martin thrust the bag into her hopefully extended hands. 'You're welcome,' he mumbled as she opened it and exclaimed joyfully over its contents. 'And I'm real sorry that Mrs Templeton has gone. I'll tell Rose. But now I must . . .'

He shook his head at her half-hearted invitation to share the contents of the brown paper bag and set off down the stairs once more, feeling chastened. He had so looked forward to calling on the old lady and reminiscing about Rose. Now all he had to tell Rose when they met up again was that her old friend had died some time after their departure.

He emerged from the tower block and set off down the slope of Everton Brow. Don, the most obedient and eager of companions as a rule, kept glancing back, and two or three times Martin had to call the dog to him. He was surprised when Don suddenly gave vent to a high, excited bark, for Martin had rarely heard the dog give tongue. He glanced ahead as the animal suddenly broke into a fast lope and saw, on the opposite pavement, a young woman pushing a large, old-fashioned pram. Light dawned. This was what Don would think of as 'Rose country', and he must have thought the young pram-pusher was Rose herself. Martin yelled the dog's name, shouted him to come to heel . . . but it was too late. Don had careered off the pavement and into the busy road; brakes shrieked, tyres squealed . . . and a bus came out of nowhere, or so it seemed to Martin.

One moment Don was all fast, fluid movement, the next he lay in the road whilst the bus driver tumbled out of his vehicle, exclaiming: 'It weren't my fault. The bloody animal just about ran under me wheels and committed suicide, so he did. It weren't my fault, I'm tellin' you.'

Martin had dived into the road, with no thought of apportioning blame in his mind. Don's hurt bad, he thought. Oh, God, why didn't I guess that he'd be lookin' for Rose the moment we got to Everton Brow? Why didn't I have my hand on his collar? If anyone caused the accident it were me . . . oh, God, lerr'im be all right, lerr'im not be suffering!

In a way, Martin's prayer was answered. When he fell to his knees beside the big dog, Don's eyes were already glazing in death and under his mouth the stream of blood was ceasing to flow as his pulse faltered and stopped. Martin pulled Don's beloved head on to his knee, and for one moment his heartbroken gaze met Don's and he thought he read understanding and forgiveness in those dark, liquid eyes; certainly there was love. Then recognition fled and what lay in the road was no longer his old pal but just an empty shell.

*   *   *

For weeks all Martin could do was reproach himself for Don's death. He missed him more than he would have thought possible, acknowledging now how much the dog had meant to him, not just as a companion but as a constant reminder of happier days with Rose and little Ricky. He could not think of the dog without tears coming to his eyes and an ache to his heart. Don's complete acceptance of Martin as someone fitting to receive his total trust and love, his pleasure in his master's company, even his obedience, haunted Martin with vain regrets. He was the best, yet I took him for granted, Martin told himself miserably. And in the end, I let him down.

But it was no use repining. The big dog had gone and, to make matters worse, for days and days Martin had to field enquiries as to Don's whereabouts and well-being. He had not realised how many people thought of himself and Don as a pair, or how popular the big dog had become, even at the printing works, where his sweetness of disposition, his obedience and his ability to blend into the background was now wistfully commented upon by many of the workers who had paid very little attention to him whilst he was alive.

Teddy, one of his fellow workers and a good friend, was once tactless enough to say that Martin's life must be easier without the dog. Martin grunted non-committally, but was grateful when one of the older printers was more understanding. 'When I were a kid I had a dirty little mongrel—a cross between a terrier and a rat, me dad used to say,' he told Martin. 'But I loved that perishin' dog as though he were me brother, and when he died it fair broke me heart. So you see I know what you're goin' through, and it's mighty hard. Time heals, though, old feller. In a few weeks that awful ache, the feelin' that your Don is just about to come through the doorway, will gradually ease, just you see if it don't.'

He was right. The pain of loss did ease and Martin was able to think of his old friend without tears. But what about Rose? Don had been as much her dog as his. He dared not think how she would feel when at last he was able to break the news of Don's death.

Chapter Sixteen

Rose had at last been given a job in the factory alongside Millie, and the extra money meant that by July she had saved up enough to visit Rhyl and find out what had happened to Martin. As promised, Millie looked after Ricky and Rose set off early in the morning, full of hope.

Returning, Rose felt very much happier and knew herself to be a good deal wiser, though she was still not in touch with Martin. She had gone straight to Bath Street, where Mrs Osborne had greeted her pleasantly enough, but had said that both Martin and Scotty had been gone for months. 'Mr Scott's gone to Canada, and your feller went to Liverpool, as I recall, though there's no sayin' he didn't jump on the next ship to Timbuctoo, 'cos we've not heard a word since. He paid every penny he owed, mind, which is more than I can say for Mr Scott.' She gave Rose a pathetic look. 'Weeks, it took, before his firm paid up, and then it weren't all that were owed, just the basic rent, like.'

'I'm so sorry; but it's Mr Thompson I'm enquiring about,' Rose said. 'I'm going to his building site next.'

'I shouldn't bother,' Mrs Osborne said. 'After you and that flighty young friend o' yourn disappeared the building site give him the elbow. Then Mr Scott stole his savings book . . .'

'What?' Rose said, thunderstruck. All along she had comforted herself with the thought that Martin had had some money; now she realised that this had not been so. 'Oh, poor Mart! Is that why he went back to the city?'

'Must ha' been,' Mrs Osborne said. 'So if the pair of you want to meet up—I never did believe you was married—you'll have to go to Liverpool.' She struck her forehead with a bony hand. 'I've just remembered! He told me to send any letters to the YMCA . . . can't remember which one, but he said there were quite a few. Acourse I kept the address for several weeks, but I don't have it no more. And no letters come, nor enquiries,' she finished. 'But I dare say you can find out where he were . . . 'cos if you'll excuse me sayin' so, your man ain't like other fellers, so if you asks for him you'll get him, if you see what I mean.'

Rose saw exactly what she meant. She returned home and immediately set about writing identical letters which she meant to despatch to every YMCA in the Liverpool telephone book. 'Now that I know more or less where he is, one of them is sure to find him,' she told Millie triumphantly. 'It may take a while if he really has moved on—if he's gone aboard ship for instance—but now I'm sure we'll meet up again one day!'

* * *

By the end of July Rose had received replies to all her letters to the various YMCAs in the city, and one of them caused her heart to give a hopeful leap. Yes, a Mr Martin Thompson had indeed registered with them the previous March, but had moved on after a couple of days because they had discovered that he was keeping a rather large dog in the dormitory and pets, she must realise, were not allowed. Unfortunately they could not give her Mr Thompson's present address because they did not know it, but they were fairly sure that her friend had not left the city since other residents, when asked, admitted to seeing him around from time to time.

Immensely heartened, Rose decided she would go to the city herself as soon as she was able. When she came back from the village late one afternoon to find Millie gleefully flaunting a large solitaire diamond ring on the third finger of her left hand, she wished her friend well and agreed to be bridesmaid without feeling one pang of jealousy, so sure was she that Martin and herself would be united by mid-October, which was when the wedding was to take place.

Later that week, however, a definite snag did arise. 'My Arfon's goin' to make an honest woman of young Gwenny come Christmas,' Mrs Evans said proudly. 'They've been walkin' out since May and Arfon's near on twenty-six, so it's high time he got married.' She paused, looking doubtfully at Rose. 'Of course, I know Millie will have gone by then, but . . .'

'Oh, Mrs Evans, I quite understand,' Rose said quickly, though her heart sank. They had been so happy here, she had hoped she and Ricky might continue to live at Ty Isa until she and Martin met up once more, but it was clearly not to be. 'They'll want our room of course. Well, don't worry. Ricky and meself will find somewhere nearer the factory well before then.'

Mrs Evans heaved a deep sigh. 'I'll miss you, and if you're still not settled when we've had the old barn converted to a little cottage for the young couple you can come back and welcome,' she said. 'I'll have a word in the village, see what we can find for you.'

*   *   *

It was early October and Rose and Millie had just put the little boys to bed. The children, now nearly eighteen months old, were tired after a visit to the seaside, for Mr McDonald, looking at the bright blue sky and golden sunlight when he had visited them earlier that morning, had said it might be their last chance to go to the beach before winter set in.

365

Generally, when he and Millie planned a day out Rose, though always invited, did not accompany them. She thought it unfair to 'horn in' on their time together, but on this occasion Millie had been pressing and Rose, knowing how Ricky loved the Rhyl beach, had allowed herself to be persuaded.

Now she was glad that she had gone with them, for they had had a perfect day. Mr McDonald had rolled up his trouser legs and played in the little pools as though he were a child himself. They had all made sandcastles, dug moats and collected shells, and at noon they had cleaned themselves up and Mr McDonald had taken them to a large hotel for lunch. The children had behaved beautifully, awed by their surroundings and hungry after their exertions on the beach, so that the meal had disappeared in a trice. After lunch, the boys had cuddled down on the back seat of Mr McDonald's Ford Zephyr and slept for almost two hours, waking eager to return to the beach where once more they dammed streams, chased tiny crabs and filled their little pockets with shells and stones of every description.

They had not been the only ones to sleep on the journey home, for Rose had nodded off, having thought as she did so that she should not fight it; it would give Mr McDonald and Millie a chance for some private conversation, for in three weeks' time they would become man and wife.

Already Mr McDonald and Alex were great pals, and no one seeing them together would have realised they were not father and son. They even looked rather alike, and Millie had long ago given up trying to stop her child from calling Mr McDonald 'Daddy'.

'Mid-October is an odd time for a wedding but it seemed downright daft to wait any longer when there was no need,' Millie had explained to their factory friends. 'Mr McDonald couldn't love Alex more if he had been his own son, and Alex thinks Mr McDonald *is* his father, so the sooner we make it official the better.'

But now, making their way down the stairs at Ty Isa, Rose brought up a subject which she had been meaning to raise with Millie since a shopping trip to Shrewsbury on the previous Saturday. 'Darlin' Millie, do you realise this is the first outing we've had for weeks where you haven't imagined seeing Scotty? Last week you reckoned you saw him at least three times, but it wasn't him at all, was it? Why, I got so fed up in the end that I tapped him on the shoulder and honest to God, Millie, when he turned to face us he was not a bit like your Scotty. C'mon now, admit it!'

Millie giggled. 'No, he was quite different. He had those awful puffin cheeks and a tight little mouth, like a woman's,' she said. 'And he's not "my Scotty", Rose Thompson! But it must have happened to you, because surely it happens to everyone? You see someone from the back and you're convinced it's an old friend, or maybe even an old enemy. Then you see them face on, and they're quite different. Why, I remember when we first went to Rhyl you kept "seeing" the Ellises!'

'Yes, you're right, I were pretty daft meself,' Rose said, 'but our cases are a bit different because I really did see the Ellises. But that was months ago, and since we've moved down here I've almost forgot their existence. But you know very well, because you took the trouble to find out, that

Scotty went to Canada quite soon after we ran away.'

Millie heaved a sigh. 'I know it's silly thinking I see Scotty when his boss said he'd gone to Canada and would most probably stay there,' she said. 'Even if he was still in England, there wouldn't be much point in him coming here because he and I were never married, but pretty soon now I shall be Mrs McDonald . . .' She gave a little skip, jumped the last three steps and turned to grin, wickedly, at her friend as they entered the small parlour which Mrs Evans had set aside for their use. 'But Rose, you never really knew Scotty, not the way I did. He was very, very possessive. He hated lending anything, and I told you he got terribly jealous if I so much as exchanged a friendly remark with another man.' She sat herself down on the small sofa and pulled Rose down to sit beside her. 'I know you won't be offended, love, but one reason why Scotty was happy to be friends with you and Martin was because he thought Martin posed no threat. He thought he was . . . well, I guess I don't have to put it into words.'

'No, you don't; you're trying to say Scotty thought Martin was some sort of freak, but if you ask me the freak was Scotty,' Rose said forcefully.

'Oh, let's forget beastly Robert Scott,' Millie said. 'And don't forget it was Scotty who thought Martin was a freak, not me. I think Mart is one of the nicest people one could hope to meet and you're an idiot not to grab him before someone else does.'

'I don't know whether he's up for grabs,' Rose said, rather gloomily. 'Sometimes I worry that when we meet up again we'll find we're strangers.'

Millie's eyebrows shot up. 'Nonsense,' she said robustly. 'I always thought you were the perfect couple. I remember at one time you said you thought of him as a brother, which is just plain daft. You've never had a brother, any more than I have, so how could you possibly know? I say, how about going for a walk to round off a perfect day? We can take a torch, but the moon is so bright that we shan't need it. I love moonlight.' She broke off. 'Mrs Evans will give an eye to the children, not that they're likely to stir. I believe the entire brass section of the local band could march through their room playing the Trumpet Voluntary, and neither of them would so much as blink an eyelid.' She broke into song. 'Moonlight becomes you . . .'

'I'm game,' Rose said, getting to her feet. 'We might offer to take Penny; she's on heat and shut up in the big barn, so I reckon she'd be glad of some exercise.'

Penny was a border collie bitch and a great favourite with the girls, and, as Millie had guessed, Mrs Evans agreed to listen out for the boys whilst handing them a length of rope to fasten to Penny's collar. 'Not that she'd run off, and I doubt there'll be visiting dogs around, but still,' she said, ushering them into the yard. 'Thanks, girls; I'll have a brew ready when you come back.'

The girls went straight to the barn and then set off along the tree-lined lane. They laughed and chatted, but had not gone far when Millie began to get the jitters. 'I could have sworn something moved in that big patch of shadow under the holly tree,' she said uneasily. She lowered her voice. 'Suppose—suppose someone was lurking there?'

Rose was inclined to laugh at such fears, but she

knew Millie was suffering from pre-wedding nerves, so suggested that they should only walk as far as the main road—if you could call it that—before turning back. 'It really isn't fair on Penny to get her all excited and then to cut her walk any shorter,' she said, tactfully. 'Besides, no tramp is likely to attack two healthy young women and an extremely large dog.'

Millie agreed that this seemed fair, but on their way back past the holly tree Rose noticed that the dog's hackles had risen and she was walking stiff-legged. Millie must have noticed at the same moment, for she grabbed Rose's arm and pointed to the dog. 'Penny doesn't like it either,' she whispered. 'Oh, Rose, let's hurry!'

They left Penny in the barn and burst into the kitchen, where Mrs Evans was setting out scones and a large pot of tea on the kitchen table. Breathlessly, Millie told her about the shadow under the holly tree and Penny's reaction, but their hostess merely chuckled. 'There's a badgers' sett under the roots of that holly and poor Penny don't care for badgers,' she observed. 'I reckon you reached the tree just as old Brock was starting out for a night's hunting. Now who wants jam on these scones and who will just have butter?'

*　　　*　　　*

Scotty stood as still as death in the shade of the big old holly tree, thinking back over the past few days. He had learned that Millie had moved to Dinas Newydd when he had read Rose's letter to Martin. At first he had felt tremendous elation: he knew where she was! Then the elation had been swamped by fury. Millie was *his*, his very own property; his possession, in fact. He had intended, upon his return from Canada, to demand that she come back to him, bringing their son with her. He had meant to explain that everything would be different, that he would respect her both as the mother of his child and as his wife, since he had seen the error of his ways and wanted to put their relationship on a proper footing. Once they were married, he was sure arguments and quarrels would be things of the past. His job in Canada was a good one; she would never need to work, a beautiful home was part of the deal, she would have a wonderful social life . . . everything would be just fine.

He did not mean to mention the fact that his new job was the managership of a factory in Quebec, where the first language was French. Millie, he knew, spoke the language like a native; her command of the language would be of inestimable value to him, and she might even teach him a few words.

Oddly, it had never occurred to him that she might have met someone else. His women never left him; the boot was always on the other foot. He grew tired of them, dumped them and moved on to the next. In fact, thinking back as he stood in the deep shade beneath the holly tree, he realised that Millie was the only girl who had reversed the trend. How dared she do such a thing! Every possessive instinct—and he had a good many of them—shrieked that this was not how things should be. She should be miserably lonely, searching for him in order to put things right between them. She should most certainly never consider that she had ended their relationship: that was his prerogative and it was his choice not to exercise it.

Beneath the tree he heard the girls approaching once more, on their way back to the farm. They were talking and laughing in low voices, and despite his resolve simply to observe for now the jealous rage which flowered within him made him long to reach out ice-cold fingers and clamp them round Millie's unfaithful throat. But he knew that would be madness. Though it might give him temporary satisfaction, dampen the flame of hate, now was not the moment. He needed Millie to be alone, so that he might explain, cajole . . . Damn Rose, damn the dog, damn the cold that was seeping into his very bones!

He must have moved slightly, or perhaps it was just the turning of his head, but suddenly he saw the dog's hackles rise, and then the three of them broke into a run and presently he saw the back door of the farm open, spilling golden light on to the cobbles. Their figures were outlined against the lamplight's glow for a moment, then the door slammed and Scotty was alone once more.

Filled with rage and bitterness, he took two steps towards the house, changed his mind, shrugged, and wound his scarf more securely round his mouth and chin. He must get Millie alone, must remind her that they had made Alex between them, that his claim on the boy was as strong as hers. He set off towards the car he had hired, plotting endlessly. He would get her alone and melt her hard heart, persuade her to return to him, to the new life in Canada. He knew himself to be attractive to women; Millie had been—would be—

no exception. Heartened by this thought, he slid behind the wheel of the car and started the engine. Tomorrow was another day. Tomorrow she would be his once more.

* * *

'Oh, Rose, I told you days ago that I was finishing early this afternoon to go for my last dress fitting! Don't say now that you can't come . . . and I'm picking Alex up from the nursery so I shan't have to come back here but can go straight home. *Why* can't you come?'

Rose looked reproachfully at her friend. 'You know very well that the dresses we're workin' on now are important and may mean a huge order for the factory,' she said. 'I'm not as quick as you yet— you finished your part of the work this morning, but I can't let Mr McDonald down by swanning off before mine are completed.'

The two girls were having their teatime break in the brand new canteen, and now Millie gave a reluctant nod. 'I suppose you're right and it wouldn't be fair,' she agreed. 'But it would have been so nice to have company. Miss Reynolds closes at five, and though she did offer to stay late I didn't feel I could ask it of her. She's been awfully good letting me create my own frock, because usually she only makes to her own design.'

'I wish I could come with you,' Rose said rather wistfully. 'But we can have a private dress show in our room on Friday, with me in my bridesmaid's finery and you in your wonderful creation. Look, why don't you leave Alex with me? He'll only be a nuisance in Miss Reynolds's little place—he'll get bored, and while she's sticking pins into your dress he'll be toddling round tugging at all the gowns and no doubt putting sticky fingerprints on everything.'

Millie laughed but shook her head. 'No, no; Miss Reynolds's niece, Sally, is going to take him to the ice cream parlour next door. She loves kids—well, she's not much more than a kid herself—which is why I promised I'd take him with me. Oh, Rosie, in another five days I'll be a married woman. I can't wait!'

'I'm longing to meet your parents,' Rose said. 'I bet they're really nice—as nice as old Mr and Mrs McDonald.'

'They are nice; you'll love them,' Millie admitted. 'Do you know, Rose, I can't imagine why I was so beastly to them, because I was, you know. But they've forgiven me and they do love Alex. And Peter too, of course.'

'Good,' Rose said absently as her friend got up to make for the door which led out of the factory. 'Well, cheerio for now. If you see Huw Williams, tell him not to forget to pick me up just because you're leaving early.'

'Okey dokey,' Millie called, and Rose reflected, as she hurried back to her work, that she was going to miss Millie dreadfully once she'd left the factory. But I dare say I'll grow accustomed, Rose told herself, bending over her bench and beginning to feed material into her machine once more. After all, she's not going far away. Her new house is only in the next village.

*　　　*　　　*

374

Millie settled Alex into his pushchair and turned, rather reluctantly, away from the brightly lit nursery towards the deepening gloom of the winding country road which led down the long hill into town. When a car drew to a halt beside her, her heart lifted. She had told Peter that she was quite capable of walking down into town, but he must have realised how cold and dark were the late afternoons and decided to give her a lift.

Hastily, she unbuckled Alex from the pushchair, folded it down and pushed it into the boot, then climbed into the front, stumbling a little as the courtesy light failed to come on. 'Oh, Peter, I told you I could—'

She stopped speaking as the man at the wheel revved the engine and the car shot forward with a squeal of tyres. The driver was not Peter McDonald, and though through the thick darkness it was difficult to make out his features, she knew instinctively by the way her flesh crept and the little hairs stood up on the back of her neck that it was Scotty. Scotty, who was supposed to be in Canada, had materialised in mid-Wales and was at the wheel of a car she had somehow mistaken for Peter's, and driving it far too fast for either comfort or safety.

Alex in her arms must have sensed her fear, for he began to cry and to lean towards the door. Millie had to think, and to act quickly. She remembered Scotty's possessiveness, his jealousy and his pointless rages, remembered too that any sort of opposition simply added fuel to the fire of his anger. She spoke slowly, therefore, and gently. 'Scotty? It is you, isn't it? It's so dark that I can't see you properly, but I'm sure it must be you, even though I was told you had emigrated to Canada. How did you find me? I never told you my address, that's for sure.'

Scotty laughed. 'I stole a letter from that little ginger bitch to the freak,' he said boastfully. 'I knew I'd need the address someday so I memorised it and sent the letter back.'

Millie sighed. So that was why Rose's letter had never reached Martin. But she said nothing on that score, merely remarking: 'I take it you want to talk? Then why don't we park the car and walk to the nearest café? It's impossible to discuss anything with the engine going and the wind so loud.'

The man beside her spoke again, his voice hoarse. 'I've been home from Canada for several days and I've learned the country round here quite well. There's a little lane no one seems to use much. It's overhung with trees and very dark, but I'll switch the interior light back on and we can talk.'

A dark and lonely little lane? Millie's heart missed a couple of beats, then began to thump unevenly. As he drew in and cut the engine, she clutched the child harder. 'What do you want to talk about?' she asked, and heard her voice tremble as she spoke. 'You know why I left and I suppose you went to Canada to try to start a new life. I expect you've met another girl—I hope you have—so if you want my blessing, you have it.'

'I want the boy. You as well, because I don't believe a child should be brought up by anyone but his own parents. However, the decision is yours. I've an excellent job and a beautiful house, and of course I've—I've changed. Millie, I didn't *know* I loved you until you left me. Then I realised. Being without you was hell, wondering if you were all right, how you were making out, whether you could possibly forgive me for the way I treated you. I must have been mad. If we'd married, I'm certain it would have been different. A man loves his wife, but when a woman agrees to live with a fellow, I think he loses respect for her—'

Millie could not contain herself. 'Scotty, that's complete balderdash,' she said crossly. 'What difference would it have made if we had got married? After all, when it comes right down to brass tacks, marriage is only a word. Would a word have stopped you smashing your fist into my mouth that last night? You say you love me, but I don't believe you know the meaning of the word.' She saw his quick angry movement, saw in the amber glow of the little light he had switched on his expression change from self-righteousness to hostility. Hastily, she remembered the loneliness of the spot he had chosen and the vulnerability of herself and Alex. 'I'm sorry, I shouldn't have said that and I didn't mean it,' she said quickly. 'You *will* learn to love one day, Scotty, when the right girl for you comes along. But that hasn't happened yet, and when it does you'll know the difference between whatever it was you felt for me and the real thing. You see, Scotty, when you truly love someone, you can't bear to hurt them, not even with a cross word, let alone with your fists.'

He had been staring at her, biting his lower lip, clenching and unclenching his hands, and suddenly Alex, who had stopped crying whilst his mother talked, began to wail again, louder this time. Scotty leaned over and tried to take the baby from her arms, but Alex resisted, shouting 'No, no, no' and clutching Millie's hair so hard that it hurt.

'Leave him alone, Scotty; he doesn't know you from Adam and kids his age are terrified of strangers,' Millie said, forgetting tact in her eagerness to keep Alex safe. 'Look, I'm awfully sorry, but this whole conversation is pointless. I'm getting married in five days and my fiancé loves Alex as though he were his own. You go back to Canada and we'll go back to the farm . . .'

She began to try to undo the door, but this meant slackening her hold on the baby, and in that moment Scotty snatched Alex from her arms and tossed him into the back seat as though he were just a rag doll. Then he caught hold of Millie by the hair with one hand and fastened the other round her throat. 'You'll marry me or no one!' he shouted, and for the first time it occurred to Millie that he might be truly mad. 'D'you hear me, false heart? You'll marry me or no one!'

Millie would have agreed to anything, just to get him to loosen his grip on her throat and to let go her hair before he pulled it out by the roots. On the back seat, Alex's screams had redoubled. Millie tried to tell Scotty that of course she would marry him, that the three of them would go to Canada just as soon as he could arrange a passage, but when she began to say so he screamed 'Liar, liar, liar!' and thrust her viciously away from him. She was lying on her back across the front seat, powerless to move, his weight pinning her down. The last thing she saw was his fist travelling towards her face, but it was not the last thing she felt. She was being torn apart. She felt the door handle smash into her skull, felt blood pour from her nose, felt her cheek split, felt herself being picked up and hurled down on hard ground.

Felt nothing.

* * *

Scotty jumped back into his hired car and pulled a flask of whisky from the glove compartment to take a long swig. He glanced at the little boy, huddled up on the back seat, and thought how furious Millie would be if she could see her son now. Safe, he told himself exultantly as he put the car into gear. Safe with his father and about to see Canada, because I'll not mess around here. I wanted Millie, or thought I did, but what use would she be to me with her face smashed in, and very likely bones broken as well? No, the boy and I will do better without her.

He swung out of the quiet, dark little lane on to the country road, not even glancing at the huddled figure of the woman he had pulled out of the car and dumped on the verge. There was no sound, no sign of other traffic, and in his exhilaration he put his foot down as he turned left, away from the town. On the back seat the little boy began to cry and Scotty turned to admonish him, to tell him that he was with his own daddy and would soon be on a big ship, heading for adventure and a new life!

He turned back, and saw a huge tree looming up, having apparently jumped out of the hedge to take up a position right in the middle of the roadway. He was actually giggling as the car hit the tree, travelling at such a speed that it was halfway up to the first spreading branches when he was catapulted out of his seat and his head met the trunk with shattering force. In the tiny moment between his first sight of the tree and the collision itself, Scotty had had his first—and last—unselfish thought. Alex! his mind had said. My God, no one knows I've got him—what will happen to Alex?

*　　*　　*

Huw Williams had been visiting his grandmother, Mrs Bethan Williams, as he tried to do at least twice a week, when their quiet, companionable chat was interrupted by a tremendous crash. Huw jumped and Mrs Williams squeaked; then Huw remarked that there must have been a traffic accident down on the main road and stood up, deserting his cup of tea to go and peer out of the window.

'Unless a war's broke out,' Mrs Williams suggested, getting out of her own chair somewhat reluctantly and joining her grandson at the window. 'A terrific explosion like that reminds me of the night the *Malakand* blew up.'

Mrs Williams had been a nurse until her marriage, stationed in Liverpool during the last war, and had often told her grandson about the May blitz and the suffering of the people of that city, but now Huw shook his head chidingly at her. 'Traffic accident,' he said briefly. 'Nearby, too. Better go and take a look.'

He got his coat and cap and ran out into the yard, but even as he reached his taxi his grandmother was getting into the passenger seat. 'There's no need for you to come along, Nan,' he said, knowing she would not take the slightest

380

notice. 'Maybe it was nothing, after all.'

'Well, if it's nothing, no harm in coming along,' his grandmother said placidly. 'But if you're right and it was a smash then a nurse, even an old one, might come in useful. I've not forgot my training, you know.'

Huw smiled at her and started the car. 'We'll mebbe have to look around us a bit,' he said as they bumped down the rutted lane and on to the country road which led to and from the town. 'Though it sounded close . . .'

*   *   *

Less than a minute later the taxi screeched to a halt, and Huw grabbed his flashlight, jumped out and ran to the mangled remains of what had once been a handsome vehicle. He could see that it had climbed the oak then crashed back to the ground again, leaving the driver . . . he shuddered. The man was slumped across the bonnet but there was no doubt he was dead. His entire head . . . Huw looked away, sickened, then seized the body beneath the armpits, dragged it out and laid it on the grass. He gave a cursory glance at the interior of the car and saw what he took to be a bundle of clothes in the well behind the front seats. Just as he was turning away there was a tiny movement and he dived back into the vehicle. The bundle of clothes was a baby—a baby he recognised as Alex Scott!

*   *   *

From the moment Scotty was identified, the search

for Millie began. Rose had already been worried by a telephone call from Miss Reynolds asking where Millie was, and when Huw Williams and his grandmother drove up to Ty Isa to tell Rose that Alex was in hospital, though he seemed to be totally unharmed, she blurted out the fear which had been growing in her: that Scotty had returned to Britain to reclaim the woman he thought of as his own property.

What she could not understand was why Millie had not been in the car as well, but the reason became clear when Millie was found later that evening, alive though badly injured, a mile from the scene of the crash. Rose was horrified to see the dreadful mess Scotty had made of her friend's once beautiful face, for she guessed it was his doing and not the result of any accident. Millie could not tell them because she was still deeply unconscious with what the nurses said was concussion.

'No one can forecast how long concussion will last,' a kindly grey-haired surgeon told Rose and Mr McDonald. 'But she's young and strong and has a good chance of recovery. In the meantime, since the little boy seems to have emerged from his ordeal with no physical injuries, and appears to have no recollection of anything which happened before he was found, I think you should take him back to Ty Isa. I'm sure you understand that he's best kept away from his mother until her injuries begin to heal and she regains consciousness.'

Rose was happy to obey and even happier when she realised that Alex truly remembered nothing of his recent ordeal. He missed Millie and asked for her often, but accepted, in the way a child will, that Mummy had had to go away but would return just as soon as she could. In the meantime he was with Ricky, herself and all his other friends, particularly Daddy Mac, and as soon as Mummy returned to them they would move into their lovely new house—just Mummy, Daddy and Alex of course, as Rose and Ricky had their own quarters at Ty Isa. Rose was sure that as soon as Millie regained consciousness the two would be reunited and the horrors of Scotty's treatment would be forgotten; time is a great healer.

*   *   *

Later, Rose could not remember any detail of those weeks after Scotty's attack on Millie and his subsequent death. It had been difficult, she thought ruefully, to remember her own name, so busy had she been. And the lies she and Mr McDonald had had to tell! They had held an emergency meeting at Ty Isa that first evening, and had settled that there was no point in disagreeing with the story which would be bruited abroad—that Scotty had come to see Millie, had snatched the baby and had knocked Millie down as he drove off, not realising what he had done. Huh! Rose had thought, even as she repeated the tale; his possessive jealousy had come to the fore and . . . well, the rest, as they say, was history. And it was a story his parents would find easier to accept than the horrible truth.

Ever since then, poor Rose had been rushed off her feet, so busy with the multitudinous tasks which the events of that day had made necessary that the hours ran into days whilst she struggled to do what was needed.

She threw herself wholeheartedly into solving all the various problems as they occurred. Mr McDonald spent every spare moment at Millie's bedside and Rose was there whenever she could manage it, but there was so much to do! She had to see to Ricky and Alex, and had gone back to her machine at the factory so that there was still money coming in, though Mr McDonald vowed that he would pay for everything, that money did not matter. What mattered was that Millie should recover. The boys had returned to the nursery, which they loved, because Rose knew that at their tender age familiar routine was important.

However, things were not as black as they might have been, for five days after the car crash Peter was sitting by his fiancée's bed when the slight hump beneath the blankets which was Millie stirred, and even as he jumped to his feet he saw her eyes slowly open. For a moment they looked blank; then, as Peter leaned closer, recognition dawned.

'Peter?' she said in a tiny thread of a voice. 'Oh, my God, Scotty came back! But where am I? And where's Scotty? Alex? I got into the car—I thought it was *you*, Peter—and . . .' She passed a hand fretfully across her forehead. 'I can't remember what happened next.'

'Scotty drove into a tree and killed himself,' Peter said, judging it best to ease her mind on that particular score. 'But Alex is fine. Rose is taking care of him until you can do so yourself—and though you've had a rotten time of it, my darling, you're going to get completely well. The doctors and nurses all say so, and they'll be delighted that you've regained consciousness so quickly.' He leaned across and rang the bell which hung beside the bed. 'I promised to let the staff know the moment you came back to us . . . oh, my dearest love, why are you crying?'

Millie sniffed dolefully and dabbed at her wet cheeks with the sheet. 'I know I'm being silly, but I loved Scotty once,' she mumbled. 'He was hateful towards the end, but at the beginning . . . oh, I can't explain.'

'You don't have to,' Peter said tenderly. 'And think, Millie! If he'd not been killed you'd have spent the rest of your life worrying that he'd turn up again and harm either you or Alex. Now dry your eyes and I'll get a nurse to bring you a nice cup of tea.'

Millie sank back on her pillows. 'You're right, of course,' she said, then gave a watery little giggle. 'A cup of tea is the cure for all ills.' She put a tentative hand to her face and ran her fingers along the dressings and the neat rows of stitches. 'Oh, darling Peter, I must be a God-awful mess, and we were getting married . . . heavens, what's the date? Don't say I've missed my own wedding!'

Peter laughed. 'We've postponed the ceremony, the reception and the honeymoon until you feel you can cope,' he said tactfully, just as the door opened to admit first Rose and then a nurse. Peter turned to beam at them. 'She's come round!' he said exultantly. 'She's better! And we're going to make new wedding plans!'

'Not until I've had that cup of tea,' Millie muttered as Rose bent over the bed and gave her a careful kiss 'Oh, Rosie, I can't wait to see Alex!'

Chapter Seventeen

A week before the wedding, Rose was packing and letting her mind go back over the hectic time since Millie had come round on the hospital ward. Her friend had made a miracle recovery, according to the medical staff, and within a couple of weeks of the car crash she was out of hospital, recuperating at Ty Isa and spending all her time planning her wedding. Actually, she didn't have to do all that much, Rose thought now, carefully folding Ricky's clothing and putting it into the smaller of her two holdalls, because there had been no difficulty in rearranging everything as November was not a popular time for weddings. The Grand Hotel had been happy to agree to have the reception later than originally planned, the rector at the local church saw no difficulty in marrying Peter and Millie at noon on the rescheduled day and the honeymoon hotel simply changed the dates and assured Peter that all would be well.

For her part, Rose would be moving out of Ty Isa the day before the wedding because, thanks she knew to Peter, she was to take over the tenancy of an empty cottage within half a mile of the factory. The place was badly neglected, not having been lived in for two or three years, so Peter had insisted on doing all sorts of repairs before he would let Rose move in. However, she had remained firm on one point, and when Peter had tried to override her Millie had intervened.

'It's kind of you, my darling, to want to redecorate and put in a few sticks of furniture, but if you do that you'll take away a good deal of Rose's pleasure in her new home,' she had explained to her crestfallen fiancé. Then she had turned to Rose. 'It's natural that you want to feel you've contributed, partly because of the low rent and partly because the more you do, the more you will make it your own,' she said, smiling understandingly at her friend. 'Peter would put expensive paper on the walls and he'd have all the floorboards stained and polished. He'd do away with that ancient kitchen range and install a modern Aga. He'd choose curtains which were far too grand for a cottage and carpets so thick you had to wade through the pile. He'd—'

'I wouldn't . . .' Peter had begun, then laughed and raised his hands in a gesture of defeat. 'Well, perhaps you're right. OK, Rosie-posie, but if you run out of money or need something we can provide . . .'

Everyone had been so kind, Rose thought now, folding nappies. Mrs Evans had assured her that there would be no need to leave Ty Isa before her son and his wife returned from their two-day honeymoon in Cardiff, but Rose was now very keen to move into her new home. She meant to start whitewashing the walls, cleaning up the floorboards and generally making the place fit for habitation and had the week off work, though she meant to take Ricky to the crèche each day, partly in order not to disturb his routine but mainly because at eighteen months Ricky needed a lot of attention and Rose knew he would hold up her work.

She had enough furniture, having been given an old double bed, two basket chairs and a kitchen table as well as the cot Ricky had used at Ty Isa and enough sheets and blankets to ensure that both she and Ricky were warm at night. She had also acquired an old and rusty bicycle with a carrier on the back, and though it was less than a mile to the factory she intended to ride there when winter was over.

But just now she was packing, going down to the kitchen every so often to make a pot of tea and have a brief chat with Mrs Evans, who was almost as excited over the old cottage as Rose was herself. They had settled that Mrs Evans would come to the cottage the day after Rose had moved in to show her how to cook on the old stove, and to make sure that Rose knew how to bring up water from the well without losing half of it, because the cottage, needless to say, had neither running water nor sanitation. Peter had insisted on installing a chemical toilet at the end of the garden and this, too, needed some demonstration, Rose thought now, putting Ricky's little blue pyjamas into the holdall and reaching for a pile of small Chilprufe vests. She glanced around the room, deciding she had done enough for now and would go downstairs and help Mrs Evans to get the midday meal. Millie was out shopping for her own big, brand-new house on the opposite side of the town, but had promised to be back in time for lunch. She and Peter would be going off for an extended honeymoon—a whole month—though their destination was a closely guarded secret. Rose suspected Italy or Greece, but when she hinted Millie just laughed. 'M.y.o.b.,' she had said tauntingly when Rose had suggested the two countries. 'You'll know where we are when you get

388

our first postcard . . . oh, Rosie, I can't wait!'

At first, when the wedding arrangements were completed, Millie had nagged Rose on and on about trying harder to get in touch with Martin. 'I want him at my wedding,' she had wailed. 'And brides should have what they want, it's one of the rules. Why don't you advertise? Or go back to Liverpool and search every nook and cranny? Oh, Rose, you know you want him here even more than I do!'

But Rose had merely tightened her lips. 'The story about you and Scotty was even in the national papers,' she had pointed out when Millie persisted. 'Martin must know what happened and where we are, and he's not attempted to get in touch. He's probably married to someone else by now, and serve me right. Besides, I did advertise in the *Liverpool Echo* and no one replied.' She had given a small, unamused laugh. 'Well, I said I didn't want to marry anyone, and now it looks as though I shan't have the opportunity, so that's all right.'

'You mean you've changed your mind and would marry Mart if he turned up?' Millie had said slyly. 'Oh, don't deny it. That's what you meant.'

Rose had turned and glared at her friend. They were in their bedroom at Ty Isa. 'It is *not* what I meant,' she had said hotly. 'Besides, Mart has never so much as hinted at marriage, far less actually proposed. So forget it, Millie.'

*   *   *

Millie had pretended to be chastened, had apologised, had said she would leave the subject

389

alone in future, and had seen—with some glee—
Rose's guilty reaction. But really she was
determined to do something, though at first she
could not imagine what. She did not know the city
of Liverpool at all, really, and had no friends there
to whom she could appeal. There were what she
called, in her head, the Authorities, which meant
police, council officials and similar persons, but
she was afraid she might get Martin into trouble by
bringing him to their attention. Suppose he was
sleeping rough again? She did not think it likely—
he was both intelligent and resourceful—but one
never knew . . .

Then she had a positive brainwave. Mrs Ellis!
She had been, at one time, very much Rose's
friend, and Millie had thought all along that Rose
had misinterpreted the older woman's attempts to
get in touch. She had tried to convince Rose that
any desire on Mrs Ellis's part to take Ricky would
have long disappeared, but Rose, though she
agreed, would not contact her one-time friend.
And Millie knew that Mrs Ellis worked for the
social services department, or had done only a
little more than a year ago. Such jobs were well
paid and secure, or so she believed. She could not
imagine that Mrs Ellis was not still in her post.

Of course she knew that the other woman did
not know Martin; had never, to the best of Millie's
knowledge, even met him. But Martin's height,
white dandelion-clock hair and strange
complexion, the eyes which were so pale a greyish-
pink that he needed strong spectacles for even the
simplest task . . . yes, if only she could contact Mrs
Ellis and the woman was agreeable, it would be . . .
well, if not simple, at least not impossible to trace

390

the young man.

Millie longed to confide in Peter, to see what he thought, only she had a shrewd suspicion that she would be told, though lovingly, to mind her own business. So she said nothing, but shut herself away in the parlour, pretending to be sorting through the names and addresses of various relatives who might—or might not—be invited to the wedding. But really she was composing a letter to Mrs Ellis, and that took some doing. She had tried telling the whole story, from the moment Rose and Martin had run away to the present, but even to herself it sounded too like rather bad fiction. Then she had begun with the baby's birth and Martin's fondness both for Rose and for her little son . . . but that had sounded too sentimental and might not persuade the older woman to search for Martin. Finally, she had written a very much shorter note.

Dear Mrs Ellis,
You don't know me, but I've heard about you from Gertrude Pleavin—she calls herself Rose Thompson now—who is a great friend. I know that once you were her friend too, and so I thought I'd get in touch because she's in trouble and you might be able to help . . .

The letter went on to outline the situation—how Rose had accompanied Millie when she had fled from Scotty's violence and had lost touch with Martin—then gave Martin's full name and description. Millie begged Mrs Ellis to try to find him, telling the other woman that the only thing they knew for certain was that he had returned to

Liverpool. She had said that she herself was about to get married, and was anxious to find Martin so that Rose would not find herself alone when she, Millie, left the lodgings they shared. She explained about the cottage, and gave its address as well as that of Ty Isa. And then there was nothing more she could do but hope and wait.

For days after the letter was despatched she flew to the post each morning and evening, but there had been no reply so far and she was beginning to despair. Rose would move out of Ty Isa next Friday, and on the following day Millie and Peter would marry. And Rose would be alone in that cottage with its sagging roof and unkempt garden.

Millie had not said a word to Peter about writing to Mrs Ellis, but now she felt she must confide in someone. She could not tell Rose, who might be either angry with her for interfering or miserable because her interference had not succeeded. So she told Peter, who was unexpectedly supportive and never even hinted that she should not have written—quite the opposite, in fact.

'You did the right thing,' he told her approvingly. 'Rose has been a very good friend to you and you were trying to do the one thing which would please her most—persuade Martin to get in touch. And don't forget, you sent the letter to a department rather than to a personal address. If this Mrs Ellis is working part time or has a few days off, she might not even have received it yet. Or she may be searching the city for either Martin himself or someone who knows where he is to be found.'

'Oh, darling Peter, *how* I love you,' Millie said rapturously, throwing her arms round her fiancé's neck and giving him a hard hug. 'I'll stop worrying from now on, and start dreaming about the wedding. Rose didn't want to wear pink because of her hair being ginger . . . sorry, red, I meant . . . but that very pale shade, candy pink they're calling it, looks wonderful on—' She clapped a hand to her mouth. 'Heavens, you aren't supposed to know what we're wearing and now I've given the game away.'

Peter picked her up and whirled her round, kissed her, and stood her down. 'That's my girl,' he said tenderly. 'And don't worry about it, because I'd marry you if you were wearing sackcloth and ashes. Or nothing at all,' he added, with a wicked grin. 'Oh, sweetheart, I can't wait for Saturday!'

*   *   *

Isobel Ellis was taking a week off work but had popped in this morning just to check that everything was running smoothly in her absence, and had been handed an envelope with the words *Personal and Private* printed above her name.

'Thank you, Miss Armstrong,' she had said politely, taking the envelope and slipping it into her handbag. 'I'll see you on Monday.'

She had walked back to her car and in the driver's seat she had opened the letter and read it, whilst her heart bounded about in her chest and a smile kept spreading across her face. She was in touch with Gertrude—with Rose, rather! Well, not in touch exactly, but she knew where the girl was and would go there today, explain, see if she could help in some way . . .

But she could help, she knew that! Rose—she must remember to call her that now—wanted to get in touch with a young man called Martin Thompson. It might take Isobel a day or two, possibly even longer, but she was sure she could trace him. Then she would give him Ger— Rose's address and the two could be reunited whilst she, who had brought them together, could explain why she had sought so desperately to get back in touch with her young friend.

She had been sitting behind the wheel of her car, staring into space and thinking, but now she started the engine, selected first gear, and headed for Bold Street. She had always had her hair done by Mr Mann at his salon above the modelling agency and this time she ran up the stairs, eager for once to get her appointment over so that she could start her search for Martin.

Mr Mann, however, was an old friend, and as soon as she was settled in the chair he must have sensed her excitement, because instead of automatically calling a girl to shampoo it he ran his fingers through her shoulder-length, light brown hair and asked her if she would not try something different this time.

'I believe the gamine style which Miss Hepburn has brought to popularity in that film about Rome would suit you,' he suggested. 'Several of my ladies have had their hair cut and shaped to their heads, but it does not look well on everyone. I think that it would look very good on you, Mrs Ellis. May I suggest that we go for a more—more adventurous cut on this occasion?'

Mrs Ellis agreed; she would have agreed to almost anything in her present mood of delighted anticipation, for suddenly she had the feeling that this time she would not fail, as she had failed when she and Rose had met face to face in Rhyl.

And presently, because it was so much on her mind, Isobel Ellis told Mr Mann that she had been asked to look for someone, a young man called Martin Thompson, and intended to start her search as soon as she left his salon.

'He's lost touch with an old friend who is desperate to find him. It won't be easy, because I've never actually set eyes on Mr Thompson,' she said blithely. 'But he's an albino, or so I'm informed. Apparently he's got white hair, odd blotched skin and pinkish eyes.'

Mr Mann met her eyes in the mirror, looking thoughtful. 'He's one of my clients,' he said. 'His hair is very fine, almost like a dandelion clock, and difficult to cut. I did it for him free—oh, it must be at least a year ago, probably more—but now he's a regular customer, comes in every four weeks and chats away about his job, his lodgings . . . I'm afraid I can't give you his address, but I can tell you where he works, if that would help.'

'Help?' Isobel almost shouted. 'Oh, Mr Mann, I'd be eternally grateful. You see . . .'

Then the story came tumbling out—how she had meant to help Rose by adopting her baby, how Rose had fled, how she, Isobel, had searched and searched, intending to tell Rose that she would not dream of trying to adopt the baby if that was not what Rose wanted . . . and Mr Mann listened quietly and clipped away and nodded and smiled his understanding, interpolating a question now and then when it seemed that his client had come to a halt.

When her story and his ministrations had both ceased, he picked up a thick, soft brush and began

395

to dust the stray hairs from her shoulders. 'Well? What do you think?' he enquired, and Isobel realised that the stranger who looked back at her from the big glass was herself, but looking so different, so much younger and . . . and livelier, somehow, that she had not, at first glance, recognised her reflection.

'It's—oh, it's really nice,' she breathed. 'Thank you so much, Mr Mann. And now, if you wouldn't mind telling me where the young man is employed . . .'

And presently, armed with her new knowledge, Isobel got back into her little car and drove to the address she had been given. There, she parked in the yard and went into the small and rather stuffy little reception area and asked, tentatively, if she could have a word with one of their employees, a Mr Martin Thompson.

*　　　*　　　*

Martin sighed when the girl came trotting through and told him he was wanted in the front office, but he went anyway. First thing that morning he had delivered a couple of thousand flyers, printed in red and black, to an awkward customer who almost always dreamed up some complaint about their work in the hope that the firm would reduce the price. Martin thought that this time they would be objecting to the fact that the flyers had been printed in a larger font than usual, and prepared for battle.

However, when he came into the front office and saw a tall, slender woman waiting for him, he smiled and looked enquiringly at her. 'Good morning, madam,' he said politely. 'Can I help you?'

'Yes, if you are Martin Thompson,' the woman said. 'I'm Isobel Ellis . . . I dare say you've heard Rose speak of me. I wonder . . . is there somewhere we could talk?'

Martin's heart began to thump unevenly. 'Do you know where Rose is?' he said, his voice husky with suppressed emotion. 'We've lost touch.'

Mrs Ellis nodded. 'I know exactly where she is,' she said quietly. 'Her friend Millie wrote to me. I'll let you read the letter. Millie is the girl whose child was snatched by the father, who drove into a tree and killed himself. Didn't you read all about it in the papers?'

'No. I have to do rather a lot of reading in my job and my eyes are weak so I tend to avoid newsprint,' Martin explained. 'My God, are you trying to tell me that Scotty kidnapped Alex and then drove into a tree and killed himself? Is Alex all right? And Millie? Scotty was very possessive. If he snatched Alex then he might easily have hurt Millie. And it was in the papers, you say, and I never saw, never knew . . .' He looked wildly round him, then headed for the door which led into the yard. 'We'd best go outside. I can't believe you're going to tell me where I can find my Rosie. It's what I've longed for more than anything these past dreadful months.'

'We'll sit in my car,' Isobel Ellis suggested. 'You can read the letter and copy out all the relevant details, but quite frankly, my dear boy, I'm going to drive down to Dinas Newydd just as soon as I leave you. I can give you a lift if it would help.'

They reached the car and slid into the two front

397

seats. Martin began to nod his head eagerly, then changed his mind. 'No, it wouldn't be fair on my employers,' he said. 'They've been awful good to me, and . . . well, there's something I have to do here before I can face Rosie, something I've—I've achieved. I want to make her proud of me, make her see . . . oh, hang it, I can't explain, but I'll see my boss, finish off here, and then come down to Dinas Newydd by train. I can't drive—never shall be able to because my eyesight is so poor—but I'm an old hand at reading timetables and getting to my destination as quickly as can be. And now may I read the letter, please?'

Mrs Ellis handed it over and Martin read and reread, his eyes shining. 'Oh, bless Millie, she's a real brick,' he said at last. 'If I didn't love Rose with all my heart I declare I'd love Millie! So she's getting married? Well, Scotty was a real bad lot; she's better off without him. I just hope the feller she's marrying on Saturday loves Alex the way I love Ricky, and will treat them both right.'

'I hope so too,' Mrs Ellis said. 'I hope you've guessed that I've been trying to find Rose to tell her that I never would have suggested adopting her child if I'd known she didn't like the idea. I saw her in Rhyl, you know, and tried to speak to her, but she simply turned and ran.' She smiled wryly at Martin. 'But if I beard the little lioness in her own den I'm sure she'll hear me out and understand that when I suggested adoption I meant it for the best.'

Martin laughed, and saw a smile lurking on his companion's lips. He said curiously, 'I never could understand Rose's fear of you, because you'd been so good to her. You got her the flat, bought baby clothes, took her little treats . . .' He hesitated, then blurted out what had been on his mind now for some time. 'Why did you help Rose, Mrs Ellis? Oh, I know your husband ra— well, Rose always said "interfered with" her, but I've a feeling it wasn't just that. Most women would have drawn away from someone who had . . . oh, dear. You know what I mean, though.'

'Yes, I know what you mean. In fact, it was a sort of fellow feeling which made me want to help Rose. I'd—I'd been in the same position, you see. Alone, frightened, and pregnant. But my baby was killed in the Blitz, and I don't think I ever quite got over it. I'd—I'd abandoned her, you see, left her on a doorstep and fled. So when the opportunity came to help someone in a similar position, I jumped at it.' She gave him a rather shaky smile. 'I've never told another living soul and I don't quite know why I told you. But please don't repeat what I've said.'

'Of course I won't,' Martin said readily. 'Rose would understand, mind, but if you'd rather I said nothing . . .'

'I might tell her one day, but not yet,' Mrs Ellis said quickly. 'I'm still ashamed of what I did. And now let's change the subject. Since I'll be driving down to mid-Wales at once, I'll arrive at the cottage well before you can. May I tell Rose that you'll be with her just as soon as you can manage it?'

'Yes, please,' Martin said. 'And—and thanks for tracking me down, Mrs Ellis. I reckon both Rose and myself will be eternally grateful to you, because now that I know she's been trying to get in touch, it's marriage or nothing, and so I'll tell her!'

Rose had spent all day at the cottage, whitewashing walls, scrubbing floors and generally tidying up. Millie had offered to pick Ricky up from the crèche, in order that her friend might continue to work on the cottage until she felt she had done enough for one day, so Rose scarcely glanced at the old alarm clock perched on the sloping wooden mantelpiece and only realised how much time had passed when the light began to fade.

Feeling very housewifely, she lit the oil lamp and then, because it was growing colder as day turned into evening, she considered putting a match to the logs in the parlour grate. It would certainly give the place a more homely feeling, but on the other hand she was growing tired and did not intend to work for very much longer. It had been agreed that she would walk as far as the main road and telephone Huw Williams from the box on the corner, and he would come and fetch her and take her back to Ty Isa in time for the evening meal. So lighting the parlour fire or the kitchen range would be foolish, and she had the Primus, after all.

Having made up her mind that she would leave in a few minutes, Rose was halfway up the stairs, going to check that the bedroom windows were closed, when someone knocked on the door. She smiled to herself and began to descend to the ground floor. She had told Millie that she would walk down to the main road and ring when she was ready to leave, but after her awful experience with Scotty Millie worried over even a suggestion that a

400

woman might go out unaccompanied once dusk had fallen. Doubtless she had persuaded either the young taxi driver or her fiancé to drive to the cottage and pick up her friend.

'Coming!' she called as she ran across the kitchen. She threw open the door without any caution whatsoever, for she was sure that a friend waited outside.

For a moment she did not recognise the tall, slender woman standing on the doorstep. Then Mrs Ellis smiled and held out her hands, and quite without meaning to do so Rose simply clutched the hands and then hugged their owner, saying brokenly: 'Oh, Mrs Ellis, I'm so sorry! Only I were young, and very alone . . . but you'd been so good to me I should have known you wouldn't take my baby once you knew I wanted to keep him!'

Mrs Ellis returned the hug. 'It was all my fault for not being frank,' she said remorsefully. 'I—I do think that perhaps, in my heart, I knew you wanted the baby, but I wanted him too, so I let myself think that you'd part with him willingly. But, dear Rose, I'll swear on the Holy Book that I'd never, never have stolen him from you.' She smiled crookedly, and Rose realised her guest was biting back tears. 'May I come in? Only I've been driving for what seems like days, and I would so like to sit down.'

'Oh, how rude I am!' Rose said remorsefully. 'Come in and sit down and I'll light the Primus and put the kettle on. I've no fresh milk 'cos I don't move in until Friday, but there's conny-onny. I wish I could introduce you to Ricky, but he's at Ty Isa with my friend Millie. Oh, I suppose you don't know about Millie, or Ty Isa for that matter. But

401

how did you find me? At first I hid because I was frightened, but then I thought you'd do best to forget me, so I never tried to get in touch.'

'Your friend Millie wrote to me,' Mrs Ellis said, sinking into a chair with a long sigh. 'Oh, but I'm tired! And we've so much to tell one another. You start.'

So over the tea, strong mugs of it, Rose gave a succinct account of all that had happened to her since she had run away from Liverpool, and then it was the turn of Mrs Ellis.

'I'll start by telling you that Mr Ellis and I have separated,' she said. 'I found he was having an affair with a seventeen-year-old girl in his office. It had happened before and I'd blamed myself—if I'd been more loving, more outgoing, if I'd given him the child for which he said he longed, if, if, if—but this was just one time too many. After the pain and misery he had caused you . . . well, I told him to go and then I sold the house, so there was nowhere for him to come back to. I accepted the offer of a better job with the same department, and then Alice and I—you've never met Alice, but she's been with my family since I was born— moved into a flat in Liverpool, and though I thought I'd miss having Mr Ellis about the place and be lonely and miserable I couldn't have been more wrong, because I've never been happier.' She smiled at Rose. 'And that just about wraps up what has happened to me over the past months.'

'I'm real glad for you, Mrs Ellis,' Rose said. 'That you've left Mr Ellis and found that you're happier without him, I mean. But it's different for me. I miss Martin all the time, and wish—oh, that I'd told him how I felt about him, how much he meant to me. But I didn't, and now the pain of missing him is rather like toothache. You may forget it for a bit whilst you're concentrating on something else, but the moment you're alone, back it comes, ache, ache, ache, until it nigh on drives you mad.'

Mrs Ellis got to her feet. She was smiling. 'Well, you're going to get the opportunity to tell him how you feel about him very soon,' she said. 'Your friend Millie didn't write to ask me to get in touch with you again so that I could explain. She asked me to find a Mr Martin Thompson, who was living somewhere in the city. It sounded like a pretty tall order, difficult if not impossible, but I had an enormous stroke of luck . . .'

She told the story simply and well and Rose felt her heartbeat quicken and the hot colour rise to her cheeks. 'So he's on his way?' she said breathlessly. 'You're trying to tell me that he might be here any moment? Oh, Mrs Ellis, if you're right I shall be the happiest person on earth—happier even than Millie, and she's getting married on Saturday!'

'I don't know whether he'll be able to make it today,' Mrs Ellis said rather doubtfully. She got to her feet and began to pull on her gloves, then perched her fashionable little hat on her smooth hair once more. 'I drove, you see, and your young man will be coming by train and bus . . . or perhaps a taxi, if there's one at the railway station. It may well be tomorrow, or even the day after, before he arrives.' She glanced at the window. 'I'm not too keen on driving in the dark, so I've booked myself into a bed and breakfast place.' Rose saw that she was flushing. 'I wonder . . . I would so much like to meet your little boy. I shall still be here tomorrow . . . would it be possible . . . ?'

'Of course it would,' Rose said heartily, and meant it. 'I'm awful proud of him, Mrs Ellis, and love showing him off to folk. He's at Ty Isa right now, and if I know you're coming I'll not take him to the nursery in the morning.' She hesitated, and then said shyly: 'Martin and I have got no relatives that we know of, so Ricky has no grandparents, not even step-ones. Would you like . . .'

'I'd *love* to be an honorary grandmother,' Mrs Ellis said eagerly. She went to the door and opened it, letting in a breath of very cold air. 'You are generous, Rose; you always were. Can I give you a lift back to your lodgings? I'd be happy to do so.'

Rose, however, shook her head. 'I'm getting a lift, thank you,' she said. 'And when I think of your generosity to me I feel ashamed that all I can offer is pretend grandmotherhood, if there is such a word. Goodnight, Mrs Ellis, and—and thank you for everything. See you in the morning!'

*   *   *

Rose waited until the older woman had driven off, then sat down with a fresh mug of tea and wondered why she had refused Mrs Ellis's offer of a lift. It would have made sense . . . yet despite the difficulties of getting from Liverpool to mid-Wales, she felt she could not leave the cottage if there was the tiniest chance of Martin turning up. On the other hand, Huw Williams would be waiting for her call, not putting his car away knowing that she would be ringing. And Millie, too, would be

404

expecting her. She had said she would not continue to work after eight o'clock, or nine at the latest, and it was already ten past eight.

She finished the tea in her mug and stood up, glancing towards the darkened window. She began tidying away—tomorrow was another day and she still had plenty to do—yet still she hesitated. Martin might come! How would he feel if he arrived to find the place cold and deserted? She glanced once more at the alarm clock on the mantelpiece. I'll give him another twenty minutes, and if he's not arrived by then I'll leave the door unlocked and a note on the table, telling him ... oh, telling him to go to the telephone box at the end of the lane and ring for a taxi ... only suppose he doesn't have enough money for a taxi? I could say I'll pay when he reached Ty Isa, but somehow ...

Rose began, desultorily, to sweep the already well-swept brick floor.

*   *   *

Martin turned into the narrow lane which led, he had been told, to the cottage. By now it was full dark, the cold beginning to bite and the stars overhead twinkling frostily whilst the moon, newly risen, was casting long shadows. She may not be there, Martin told himself, but he felt in his bones that he was going in the right direction. He was late, of course, later than he had intended, but he had had to wait for the packet in his pocket, the packet which would prove to his Rosie that there was more to her Martin than she had dreamed. More than I dreamed myself, Martin thought with

405

an inward grin. More than his boss had dreamed when at the interview he had asked Martin for a sample of his handwriting, since in his new job he would be addressing parcels and packages, envelopes too, and it was important that these should be clear and easily read.

He had produced his current diary and the boss had taken it, read a few pages, given Martin a long, hard look, and then handed it back, only commenting that the writing was certainly both clear and neat and that Martin might have the job on a month's trial.

At the end of that first month, however, he had asked Martin casually whether he had been keeping diaries for long. Martin had explained that he had kept notes even at the children's home and had expanded them into a proper diary as soon as he moved into Rose's tower block. The boss nodded and looked undecided, then asked Martin, almost shyly, if he might read one or two of the exercise books.

Martin knew and trusted—indeed, liked—Mr Renshaw by now and handed over the diaries willingly, but, as he told his fellow workers, you could have knocked him down with a feather a couple of days later, when Mr Renshaw had called him into his office. 'I'd like to tidy the first couple of books up a bit and publish them as a true story, which they undoubtedly are,' he had said. 'It would make you a bit of money, and if it sells well, which I think it will, I'd like to consider the later ones for publication too.'

Martin had stammered out that he would be delighted . . . honoured . . . and had scarcely believed his luck. To be a published author before he was twenty-one! He had longed and longed to tell Rosie, to make her proud of him, but he had begun to despair of getting in touch with her. Then, on the very day that the first completed book, *The Happy Orphan* by Martin Thompson, was due back from the binders, there was Mrs Ellis, asking for him, giving him Rose's address, saying that his poor Rose had been desperate to get in touch, had even advertised in the *Liverpool Echo*, though without result. She had offered him a lift to Dinas Newydd but he had known his book—HIS BOOK!—would be delivered later that day. When the books had arrived he had gone to Mr Renshaw and asked for time off, which had been willingly granted.

And now here he was, in the one place in the world where he most longed to be—approaching his Rosie at long last. After his conversation with Mrs Ellis all his doubts and fears had disappeared. Of course Rose loved him! She might not have known it when they had last been together, but she knew it now, must have known the same aching, gnawing hunger for him that he had felt for her. He was not looking forward to telling her that Don had been killed, but he knew that she would understand, would grieve for Don as he had grieved, but would not blame him for the accident.

He continued to walk up the lane, quickening his pace a little as the high banks on the left-hand side grew lower and lower, the winter hedges sparse enough, now, for him to see through them, though still far ahead, a glimmering light. Lamplight. Martin shoved a hand into his overcoat pocket, checking for the hundredth time that his book—HIS BOOK!—still nestled within. Then he lengthened his stride until he was almost running, until he was almost opposite the golden glow which lit the window of a small thatched cottage. Nearly there! Another few yards and he could see, in the moonlight, a small wicket gate set in a broken-down fence.

He fumbled briefly with the latch, opened the gate, stepped through it . . . and the light went out.

*   *   *

Rose sighed as she doused the lamp and put the note she had written to Martin in a prominent position, then turned to the door. She was already dressed in coat, hat and gloves, the pennies she would need for the telephone in her pocket. It would have been lovely if Martin and dear old Don had somehow managed to arrive in time, but she was sure that they would make it next day. She cast one last glance round the moonlit kitchen, then opened the door and stepped on to the path.

*   *   *

Martin saw her shape and never hesitated. He fairly flew up the path and held out his arms, knowing it was Rose though she was still half turned away from him, doing something to the door, he could not tell what. She gave a little squeak of surprise, then turned in his embrace and hugged him hard. Then she said: 'Don?' her voice trembling, and he knew she had guessed that, had Don been alive, he would never have left the dog behind.

He took a deep, shaking breath. 'He died in a

road accident. He didn't suffer.' He would never tell her how Don had been heading for the girl with the pram. 'Oh, Rose, I'd give anything . . .'

Rose nodded. He could tell by her uneven breathing that she was trying to stifle sobs, and smoothed a hand down her face so that he could tilt her chin and look into her wide, tear-drenched eyes.

Slowly, he lowered his mouth to hers, knowing instinctively that a kiss could say all the things that he could not, just yet, put into words: his grief over Don's death and his love for his Rose. Then he must have pressed Rose against the door, which could not have been properly shut, for the pair of them tumbled into the kitchen. Hastily, Rose disengaged herself and crossed to the table, picked up the matches, and relit the oil lamp. Only when it was burning evenly did she turn to him once more. 'Oh, Mart, I've missed you so!' she uttered, clutching his hands as though she would never let him go. 'Has anyone ever told you that you're tall, dark and handsome? Well, I'm bleedin' well tellin' you now! Will you marry me?'

Martin laughed shakily. 'I might, if you're real keen on it,' he said huskily. 'Did anyone ever tell you that you're beautiful?'

Secure in their illusions, they smiled at each other. 'Hang on a mo'. I've got something to show you,' Martin said, pulling the book out of his pocket.

Rose took it from him, and gazed first at the title page and then at his face. 'Oh, Mart,' she said faintly. 'Oh, Mart, you're so clever!'

In the warm lamplight, Martin took Rose in his arms and kissed her as lightly as a moth. Then, when she did not draw back, he kissed her again, a proper kiss this time.

'So this is what everyone talks about,' Rose said breathlessly, snuggling against him, when she could speak once more. 'Oh, Martin, how much time we've wasted, and it's all been my fault! But now I *know* I love you with all my heart.'